You Are My Sunshine

You Are My Sunshine

JUDITH SAXTON

ST. MARTIN'S PRESS ✿ NEW YORK

"You are my sunshine" (Davis/Mitchell) © 1940
Peer International Corp, USA.
Peermusic (UK) Ltd., 8-14 Verulam Street, London WC1.
Used by permission.

www.stmartins.com

ISBN 0-312-26700-2

First published in the United Kingdom by
William Heinemann, Random House UK Limited

First U.S. Edition: November 2000

10 9 8 7 6 5 4 3 2 1

For Bet Carter (née Douglas), whose memories of her wartime work with barrage balloons made this book possible – and whose evocative prose made me feel as if I, too, had been there.

Acknowledgements

A great many people, mostly WAAFs, have helped me with this book, in particular Bet Carter, whose article in a daily newspaper started me off on the idea, and Dorothy Pepper Williams, who patiently answered all my questions, drew me diagrams and told me what life had been like on her various sites.

Additionally, the Imperial War Museum did their usual brilliant job and got me a great deal of information, whilst my own branch library in Wrexham, North Wales, and the Central Library in Liverpool, worked extremely hard on my behalf.

And I would also like to thank Canon Richard Hanmer of Norwich for doing his best to answer my questions concerning Christ Church and Eaton Parish Church in the forties.

Since I did the research and began to write this book, I have been smitten with M.E., which is partly why it has taken so long to appear in print . . . and since M.E. fuzzes the brain, I do apologise if I have left anyone out of these acknowledgements.

September 1941

When Kay Duffield had walked, beside her father, into the little flint church it had been chilly, with an overcast sky and a sharp wind blowing, trying to drag the veil off her primrose-blonde hair, cheekily billowing up under her white silken skirt. Her father had held her arm very tightly and slapped at her skirt and laughed with her, but she had still been able to see a faint trace of apprehension at the back of his warm grey eyes. Yet when she came out again, on Philip Markham's arm, with a big smile from ear to ear and her happiness so great that it was almost tangible, the September sun was shining and the breeze was warm and smelled of chestnuts.

Coming down the aisle, Kay's fingers had rested lightly on her husband's arm and she was warmly aware of how comfortable and at ease she felt in Christ Church. It wasn't a particularly beautiful church but it was the one in which the Duffield family had worshipped for all of Kay's life. She glanced affectionately at the Sunday School corner as she passed it, remembering happy afternoons spent there listening to Bible stories, drawing and colouring, eating peppermints on the sly with her best friend, Tessa. The third pew from the front was the one her parents favoured, the stone font by the West door was the font in which she had been christened and, when she emerged into the sunshine and looked around her, it was at a scene which was as familiar to her as her own home.

The church had no graveyard, no lawns or flowerbeds, because it was surrounded on both sides by Church Avenue, which cut between Christchurch Road and Mile End Road, but the ancient trees with their heavy burden of autumn-tinted leaves had been there for as long as Kay, or her parents for that matter, could remember.

We could have got married in a big, fashionable church in the city, she reminded herself, but I didn't want to, and I'm glad. Christ Church knows me and I know Christ Church; it'll see me from cradle to grave if I'm lucky – and one day I'll have my children christened here, no matter where Phil and I may end up living.

'Look this way, Mrs Markham,' someone called and Kay looked round for Philip's mother and suddenly realised that she was Mrs Markham now. She turned, blushing and smiling, towards the speaker, her mother's brother George.

'That's it, smile, m'dear,' Uncle George said encouragingly, bending over his ancient box brownie and holding up a hand like a traffic bobby to make them keep the pose. 'Keep still, Philip; don't fidget, boy!'

Uncle George had been headmaster of a famous boys' school before his retirement in '38. Now, only three years later, he was back again, teaching in place of the younger men – men like Philip, who had left their jobs to fight for their country. But he had abandoned his school for the weekend and come down to Norwich for the wedding of his only niece. Several cameras clicked when Kay smiled for Uncle George and his daughter, Kay's cousin Betty, came bustling forward to arrange the lace train to its best advantage and to fiddle with the veil depending from the wreath of pearls in Kay's fine blonde hair.

'Let me straighten your veil, Kay,' she said in her

2

bossy, school-prefect's voice. 'The pearls look wonderful – if it's all right with you, I'm going to borrow them for my own wedding, when Ceddy gets home. They'll look most awfully good on dark hair, too.'

Kay had never been particularly fond of Betty, but now she squeezed the other girl's hand, feeling a spasm of pity for her. Cedric was with the Army in Malaya or Burma, she wasn't sure which; God alone knew when he would come home to marry Betty – God alone knew if he would come home.

'Of course you can borrow the pearls, you know Mummy would be delighted to lend them,' she said warmly. 'You could borrow the dress, too, I imagine. My wing officer gets it from Pinewood Studios whenever a WAAF gets married, so if you were to ring them up, or call in . . .'

'It's a dream dress, but I'm not a WAAF, remember,' Betty said wistfully. 'Wish I was! But there's Daddy, and the school, and the house . . .'

'They're your part of the war effort, Bet,' Philip said. 'How many more pictures is your father going to take, old girl? My brand-new mother-in-law has laid on a marvellous spread back at the house; the chaps and I are longing to dig in, feed our faces.'

Laughing with him, Kay looked around for another blue uniform, another young man with wings on his shoulders. Steve Minton had lived next door to the Duffields for as long as either could remember and the families had been friendly enough but she and Steve had been really close. In fact, the last time their leaves had coincided she had gone dancing with him to the Samson & Hercules, where they had swayed to the music of 'You are my Sunshine', and he had whispered in her ear that it must be their tune, written especially for them. He had lightly kissed the top of her hair and said that when she was around, the sun always seemed to be shining, but then the music had stopped and they had returned to the group of friends they were with. She had been wondering, last night, as she prepared for bed, how Steve would take her marriage. He had always assumed, she supposed, that he, being two years the older, would marry first, but it hadn't happened that way. So she wanted to gloat a bit – and to introduce him to Philip. Philip was the most important person in her life now, but once it had been Steve, so the two of them must meet, become friends. But not on this occasion, apparently, for though she had spotted Mr and Mrs Minton – Mr Minton was taking a photograph – Steve was not with them, nor, so far as she could see, was he with the various other uniforms scattered about the roadway. Oh, well. Probably he couldn't get even a forty-eight, Kay told herself philosophically; and smiled towards Mr Minton, who had just turned his camera on her, before relaxing and glancing around once more.

There was quite a batch of best blues directly in front of her, she saw. She guessed that the men were Philip's fellow fliers mingling already with the two families and their friends. One of them, a man with ginger hair and a great many freckles, was talking to her mother, a hand on her arm, his head bent earnestly. Sara Duffield was look-ing up at him and laughing at something the young man had said, calling Kay's father over to introduce the two of them, then glancing over at Kay, giving her a little wave and then pointing significantly to her small gold wrist-watch. The majority of the younger guests were in the services and had managed to get a forty-eight, but time

4

flew; if they didn't get moving soon some people would have to leave halfway through the reception.

'Kay? Come on, your mother agrees with me – she wants her guests to have something to eat before they have to rush off home.' Philip squeezed her arm and turned her towards the hired car which would take them back to the house on Unthank Road.

'You're right, Phil, but how like a man to think of food on a day like this,' Kay protested, half-laughing. 'It's a once-in-a-lifetime thing, a wedding! Anyway, the photographers must be finished now; film is so difficult to get and there will be other weddings.'

Philip squeezed her waist and then slid a warm hand round her chin, turning her to face him.

'Sweetheart, don't I know it? Shall we have a little kiss, just for the cameras? After all, that dress was probably worn by a dozen film stars and today you look like all of them rolled into one.'

'Do you mean I'm fat, because if so . . .' Kay began, then stopped speaking as his lips met hers. It was a kiss at once gentle and tender yet with a subtle promise of something else, something stronger, more satisfying. Kay's breathing speeded up and she guessed that the white satin bodice of the dream dress would be pulsing to her quickened heartbeat. She put her arms shyly round his neck to a subdued cheer from the wedding guests and let herself enjoy the closeness of him, the warmth.

'Oh, my darling,' Philip breathed as they drew apart. 'I can't wait to get you alone!'

Kay squeezed his hand. 'A whole four days,' she marvelled. 'Just you and me and a Devonshire cottage for four whole days! Oh Phil, it will be heaven!'

*

'You all right there, Bevan?'

ACW Emily Bevan had managed to get a seat on the crowded train, unlike ACW Josephine Stewart, who had just spoken to her. Jo was standing, swaying easily to the movements of the train, looking neat and competent in her best blues, her cap at a rakish angle on her pompadour of smooth, toffee-brown hair. But Emily, squeezed between a naval rating with a lot of badges on his jacket and a fat little man in a worn black overcoat, was alternately pushed this way and that both by the train's movement and by those of her travelling companions. But at least I'm sitting down, she reminded herself, smiling and nodding at Jo. At least I'm taking the weight off my feet for half an hour, whereas poor Stewart is still upright and likely to be so for a while, yet.

'Yes, I'm fine thanks, Jo,' Emily said, mouthing the words so that Jo could lip-read, for the train was noisy and crowded. 'But I'll willingly swap if you want a sit down for a bit.'

Jo leaned towards her and shook her head. 'It's all right, I'm fine. Besides, it won't be long now. And for a miracle, the train's only going to be about forty minutes late.'

Emily nodded and turned her attention to the sooty windowpane. She could just about make out the passing countryside and she could not help comparing the flat green fields and the huge black-faced sheep with those at home.

The Bevans had a sheep farm high up in the mountains of North Wales. Their ewes and rams, however, were skinny, agile creatures about half the size of the saddle-backed sheep which Emily had seen grazing in the meadows of Hampshire and Surrey. But mountain sheep couldn't afford to grow fat and placid; they had to graze

6

on almost vertical slopes, to survive on what grass they could find amongst the rocky screes. And they had to be able to jump the low stone walls, wend their way amongst the rocks, climb like mountain goats. And their meat was all the sweeter for it, Emily reminded herself stoutly, turning her eyes away from the window for a moment. Welsh lamb was highly regarded, so there was no need to feel defensive because the Bevan sheep were smaller than these fat lowland creatures.

ACW Stewart had fished a magazine out of her pocket and was reading it one-handed, frowning down at the newsprint as she moved and swayed with the train. Emily stared at the other girl. She was very pretty, but Emily scarcely knew her. They had not exchanged more than half a dozen words during their six weeks of basic training until today. Emily had been writing home, sitting on her bed in the hut when ACW Stewart had come bursting in. She saw Emily and waved something at her.

'Hey, would you credit it? Kay Duffield's getting married today, and one of the other girls and me were going up to London to give her a cheer when she and her husband change trains at Liverpool Street. We got permission from the wing officer, which was pretty decent of her, and now ACW Bachelor's trotting round the perimeter track with a pack on her back because she was a pair of stockings short at kit inspection! And I'd been down and bought our tickets and everything . . . I'm not so keen to go alone, I don't know London very well.'

'That's a shame,' Emily said, wondering why Stewart was so chatty all of a sudden. 'But surely there are other people who'd really love to go; have you asked anyone else, Stewart?'

'My name's Josephine; Jo to my friends,' ACW

Stewart said a trifle reproachfully. 'The trouble is, this is our first free afternoon, just about, and everyone's gone off, or most of them have. So I came in here feeling dreadfully miserable, and there you were, just sitting around, and I couldn't help wondering . . . you don't look awfully busy, and a trip to London – with a meal thrown in – might be more fun . . . and Kay is such a dear, I do want to surprise her. What do you say?'

'I don't know her very well,' Emily said doubtfully. She knew ACW Duffield by sight of course, the other girl's fragile blonde prettiness was memorable and besides, Duffield was a friendly person, even to a quiet little mouse like Emily.

'None of us know each other terribly well,' Jo pointed out. 'But you'd like to come to London, wouldn't you? Oh come on, Bevan, be a sport. I mean what will you do if you stay here?'

'Write home; darn my stockings,' Emily said. 'There's not much choice, really.'

'Well, there's a ticket to London going begging . . . and you've put down for balloons, haven't you?'

'That's right, balloon operative,' Emily agreed.

'There you are then!' Jo said triumphantly. 'You and I are both going down to Balloon Command to do our training, so we ought to get to know one another before we go. There are only four prospective balloon operatives from this intake, you know. So wouldn't you like to come and wish Kay all the best?'

'Kay?'

'Kay Duffield; you know! Only she'll be Kay Markham by the time we reach London. She's going in for balloons, too. We both passed the fitness test and the written papers, so on Monday week we'll all be off

8

together. In fact, oddly enough it's just you, me, Kay and Biddy Bachelor, the girl I told you about, who've been accepted for balloons. Well, you must remember Biddy – she's the one who had the awful nightmares when we first joined up. She's got a Liverpool accent you could cut with a knife what's more. Come to think of it, we ought to get to know one another, it'll be easier if the four of us are already pals.'

'I remember her – poor thing, those nightmares must have been dreadful,' Emily said. 'All right, I'll come with you, then.' As she spoke the words, Emily knew a great lightening of the heart. She had not enjoyed her basic training, or at least she had enjoyed the work but had felt like a fish out of water in the huts with all the girls jabbering away nineteen to the dozen in English, whilst she listened wistfully, for Welsh was her first language. 'When do we leave?'

Jo consulted her wristwatch. 'Now,' she said briskly. 'Well, in fifteen minutes, say. There's a lorry going down to the station so we can get a lift that far. How are you off for money, though? I can treat you to a cheap meal if you're stony-broke.'

'I've got a bob,' Emily said doubtfully. She sent as much money home as she could, but they were paid so little, and she sometimes had to keep a few bob for extras which the service did not provide, like soap, make-up – when you could get it – and a cuppa in the NAAFI from time to time. In fact that was why she had volunteered for balloons, because the officer who interviewed them told them that the balloon operatives were the highest paid of all WAAF trades.

'Oh, we'll manage. I'm quite well off at present,' Jo said cheerfully, going over to her bed and getting her washing things out of her locker. 'I'll just nip over to the ablutions, shan't be a tick, then we can get going.'

So now here was Emily, who had this very day written a lying letter to her mother telling her how happy she was and how nice the other girls in her billet were, sitting in the train with a popular, pretty fellow-WAAF going up to London to 'give a cheer' to another popular and pretty WAAF. And then she would be going out for a meal – in London, a city she had only set eyes on once in her entire life, if you can count getting off one train at Euston and hurrying on the underground to Charing Cross as seeing anywhere.

Jo shoved her magazine into her respirator case and looked around her. She was a friendly and talkative girl. Emily had often envied her her easy, outgoing nature and now she was clearly hoping for a chat.

'Shan't be long now, I shouldn't think,' Jo said, leaning down at a perilous angle and shouting almost into Emily's wincing ear. 'I adore London, it'll be wizard to be there with no reason to hurry straight through for once.'

There was a young Air Force corporal standing next to Jo. He turned at her words and grinned at her.

'Got a forty-eight?' he asked cheerfully. 'Wish they'd give us leave and not count journey time in it, don't you? It would be a lot fairer on those of us who have a good distance to travel. I live up north, it takes me most of my leave just to get there and back.'

Jo brightened; Emily, who felt she was beginning to know Jo quite well already, realised that Jo's ploy had been successful. She was about to start a chat with the corporal which would probably last until they reached Charing Cross and might well lead to a pleasant friendship. Jo plainly didn't know the meaning of the word shy, and had never suffered, as Emily did, from a horror that she might say the wrong thing or be thought a fool by her companions.

But Jo was talking again, so Emily listened with interest; perhaps she could learn how it was done!

'No, not a forty-eight, Corp,' Jo was saying cheerfully. 'It isn't leave, just a few hours off until twenty-three fifty-nine tonight, like Cinderella. It's so we can meet one of our pals for half an hour. She got married this morning and she'll be going through London on her way to her honeymoon, so we're going to meet her train, give her a cheer.'

'And they wouldn't let you go to the wedding? Shame,' the young man sympathised. 'Not been in long enough to get a proper leave, I suppose?'

Jo glanced down at her pristine uniform, at the buttons which gleamed with far too golden a hue, at her unscuffed lace-up shoes. Then Emily saw Jo's eyes flicker to the corporal – his uniform was clean and tidy but you could see it was enviably worn. Everyone wanted to look like an old hand, even Emily had secretly kicked her cap round the hut when no one was watching and tried to take the gold off her buttons by using Silvo instead of Brasso; the corporal, however, had not cheated, he had just been in for some considerable time.

'We've just finished our basic training,' Jo admitted. 'We're due a week's leave some time, but not yet. We're being posted on Monday week.'

'Oh aye? What are you doing? Typists? Telephone?'

"Balloon section,' Jo said nonchalantly. 'The WAAF are taking over from the chaps as you probably know, so we'll be off to the Training Centre and then to a site somewhere after that. We'll have our first leave from there, I suppose.'

11

'Balloons, eh? Well, if that isn't a coincidence – I was on balloons for four months. And didn't you say "we"?' The young man looked down at Emily. 'She's your oppo, then?'

'That's right,' Jo said, leaning forward and tweaking Emily's curly fawn-coloured hair. 'Some feller gave her his seat when he got off at the last station.' She grinned down at her friend. 'Not long now, Bev . . . I mean Emily . . . soon be at Charing Cross.'

Emily nodded to show she had heard and pulled a warning face at Jo. They had been told often enough to watch what they said about service matters in crowded places and this train could scarcely have been more crowded. Jo, however, cocked her head and raised her eyebrows, then decided to ignore whatever it was her companion was trying to communicate and turned back to the corporal.

'Balloons, eh?' the corporal repeated thoughtfully. 'I'd not have thought you'd got the strength, not a couple of bits of kids like you.'

Emily, who was barely over five foot tall and knew herself to be slightly built, could not have objected to this description. She was just past seventeen, Jo was probably around the same age, but it was clear that the other girl did not relish being referred to as 'a bit of a kid.' Jo drew herself up to her full height – she was around five foot seven inches – and frowned at the corporal.

'We've passed the written exams and the physical, and that was pretty tough let me tell you! You can't judge by appearances, you know, Emily and I are a lot stronger than we look at first glance.'

The corporal grinned ruefully.

'Sorry, sorry, tactlessly put,' he said. 'But remember,

I've worked with balloons and I know from personal experience how tough they are. We heard they were bringing in girls, but I thought they'd be . . . well, bigger, more muscular. Someone said they were calling them the young Amazons.'

'Some of the girls are probably heftier than us, but I doubt if they're a lot stronger,' Jo said with remarkable forbearance, Emily thought. 'If you were a balloon operator, Corp, you'll know that there's more than one way to kill a cat.'

'Ye-es . . . but sometimes it took all of us to bring our Bertha down to close-haul. You girls haven't got the weight, I can't see . . .'

Emily unwedged herself from between her two seated companions and staggered to her feet as the train began to slow for the station. 'Walls have ears,' she remarked reproachfully, addressing both Jo and the corporal now. 'You know we aren't supposed to talk about what we do, you never know who's listening.'

'We may not have the weight . . . well, they say they'll need twelve of us to replace a seven of you,' Jo said fiercely, continuing with the conversation as though Emily had not spoken. 'But I think you'll find, Corp, that we cope with the balloons even better than the blokes did. They told us at basic training that wherever WAAFs have replaced RAF they've ended up doing a better job, so put that in your pipe and smoke it!'

'Hey, less of that,' the corporal said, but Emily could see he was laughing. 'Wait till you get on a site, that's all! It's hard work, it's incredibly lonely out there without any station personnel to back you up, and the facilities are pretty basic. No nice hot showers or baths, just a kettle and cold water from a tap a hundred yards away. No station

13

dances, cinemas, other entertainments and precious little free time. Wait until you're hauling down in a force eight, or trying to unload the gas cylinders, or just patching whilst she's on close-haul!'

'Close-haul?' Emily said blankly. 'Hauling down?'

The corporal waved a hand. 'Bop talk, you'll soon pick it up,' he said airily. 'The blimp – that's the balloon – the blimp's just like a bag, see, filled with hydrogen gas. The gas makes her want to rise, only she's tethered down, see, so you untie her, gradually winch out the steel cable and up she goes. Now when you bring her down again she'd lash around something rotten if you didn't catch hold of the guys – they're the ropes which trail from the blimp – and heave until you can knot 'em to the big concrete blocks again. That's close-haul and it controls her, more or less, until you want to fly her again. I reckon it sounds easy, put into words, but it ain't. It's hard enough for us blokes . . .' he flexed an arm, '. . . with our steely muscles and that, but for girls . . .' he gave a low whistle. 'I dunno how you'll manage.'

'We knew all that,' Jo said quickly – and untruthfully, Emily was sure. 'But there were only seven of you to a team – there's going to be twelve of us. And what's this about patching? Surely they don't expect us to *darn* the thing?'

'Aye, they do. When she tears you put a canvas patch over the hole, or the gas would all come roaring out. And when you're dodging round underneath her, trying to get the patch in position . . .'

The train jerked and stopped. Outside the window people jostled and pushed, porters wheeled carts piled high with badly balanced luggage, children wailed, dogs barked. It looked as though half the population of London

14

had decided to spend the day on Charing Cross station. Jo grabbed Emily's arm.

'Come on, Emily, we've got to get across to Liverpool Street in less than twenty minutes, so let's hope Kay's train is late, too.' The corporal opened the door and jumped down, then turned to give them a hand. Emily was glad of it, but Jo studiously ignored him, jumping down whilst he was still steadying Emily and striding away up the platform.

'Wait, Jo,' Emily said, panting along in the rear. 'Oy, Stewart, do wait a mo, my legs are shorter than yours!'

'Hang on, Aircraftwoman,' the corporal called after Jo. 'Don't get on your high horse . . . What's your name? You might be going to the site I served on . . . hang on!'

Emily turned and looked back. The corporal was a long way behind them now, with his kitbag over one shoulder, looking wistful. She jerked Jo's arm, trying to slow the taller girl's determined stride.

'Jo, he was nice, really. Couldn't you . . . ?'

'Nope,' Jo said briefly, continuing to hurry across the station concourse towards the entrance to the underground. 'He wasn't nice, he was one of those superior, pat-you-on-the-head types. I can't stand men like that.'

'I don't think he meant . . .' Emily began, but Jo was having none of it.

'Don't you remember what we were saying in our hut a few nights ago? It's our war as much as the fellows', and we're going to do a good job so we deserve respect. Remember?'

'Oh yes, but what's that got to do with . . .'

'Everything, you goose,' Jo said triumphantly. They reached the top of the underground steps and she plunged downwards, towing Emily behind. 'That man, that

15

corporal, thinks women are inferior to men, regardless of the truth. We want nothing to do with men like that.'

Emily, who knew very well that she was inferior to men, sighed. If her da could hear Jo, whatever would he say? He would push his stained old cap to the back of his head, so that you could see how his face was weathered to a deep reddish brown to an inch above his eyebrows, whilst the rest of it was white as snow.

'Women better than men, is it?' he would say in his heavily accented voice. 'A women can give birth, but it takes a man to plant the seed. I think that says it all, don't you agree, Siriol-fach?'

And Emily's mother, who was forty-four and looked sixty, would smile timidly up at the man she loved devotedly but never expected to understand and say meekly, 'If you say so, Eifion.'

'Here we are; the ticket office,' Jo said now, leaning down to speak through the little glass partition. 'Two to Liverpool Street, please. Oh . . . do you sell returns?'

It had been a wonderful wedding, with the sort of reception which few couples married in wartime enjoy. Mummy and Daddy worked terribly hard to make it a memorable day for both of us, Kay thought gratefully now, leaning her head against the worn upholstery of the third-class carriage and feeling, with an anticipatory thrill, Philip's thigh pressed warmly against her own. I just hope they liked Phil as much as I told them they would, that they understood why I'd been and gone and done it!

She had met Philip Markham a mere twelve weeks before, when they were both playing tennis at the Lime Tree Road Club. Philip was stationed at Horsham St Faiths and had been on leave, so perhaps that was why he had approached her at once. He had also known, too, that he was to be posted abroad, another reason for not wasting any time once he had decided she was the girl for him. But at first, of course, it had just been dating, fun.

'Come dancing,' he had urged her. 'Come swimming . . . let's take a picnic to that park with the river running through it that you were telling me about . . . there's a play at the Maddermarket, a concert in St Andrews Hall, let's get a boat and go on the broads . . .'

She had agreed with all his suggestions – dancing, swimming, listening to music, laughing at the theatre. When, at the end of his leave, he asked her to write she had complied willingly. She had joined the WAAF in a way just for his sake; it was their war, they should both be involved.

He had not been pleased when she told him, though.

'I wanted us to marry soon, sweetheart,' he had said disconsolately over the telephone, with the static buzzing between them. 'You'll probably be posted to the Outer Hebrides and I'll be down in Land's End – we won't meet until the war is over!'

'We can marry whether I'm a WAAF or a civilian,' Kay had said, greatly daring. 'If you really want to, that is.'

He had wanted to, very much. He was going abroad for special training, probably to Africa, and wanted to marry before he went.

'I'm not being a dog in the manger,' he told her earnestly, the night he had come round to her house to meet her parents. 'But I want you all to myself for always, I don't want to leave the country wondering . . . believing . . .'

'I'm not that sort of girl,' Kay had said softly, loving him for his jealousy, his need of her. 'I'll be true to you,

17

Phil, whether we marry or not. The first time I saw you, I knew that . . .well, that . . .'

It was not easy to say the words; she hadn't known him long enough to be completely at ease with him. But he had smiled and held her close.

'I, Philip Markham, love thee, Kay Duffield. Will you marry me, my darling girl?'

He knew the answer, of course, knew the ardent 'yes' which trembled on her lips, but when she said that she would, that life held no pleasure for her greater than marrying him, he hugged her convulsively, unable to speak for a moment, actually having to search for the right words.

'Sweetheart! God, I'm so happy! But you won't want to get married in uniform – could we get a special licence do you suppose, marry in a few days?'

But this her parents had totally refused to countenance. They had only one daughter and she was going to have a proper wedding, even if it did mean an awful lot of work, a lot of desperate beggings and borrowings. And when she explained, Philip had been good about it, though he had not wanted a big wedding.

'Never mind, my darling, it's your right, it's every woman's right,' he had said tenderly, when she told him about her parents' plans. 'If only you didn't have to join the wretched WAAF! But you've signed, you say?'

He knew she had signed; knew, too, that she wanted to be a WAAF. She wanted to do her bit for her country and thought she would enjoy being in uniform, doing important and valuable work. And he was going abroad, it was not as if they could have been together.

'I'll be doing my bit,' she had reminded him when they said goodbye before she went off to do her basic training.

'It's not a huge sacrifice, Phil – and we'll be married very soon. Then we can be together until you have to leave.'

She was wildly excited by the thought of marriage, because already Philip's kisses and caresses had made her aware of her body and its needs. She wanted fulfilment very badly, though she had utterly refused to allow him any intimacies other than kissing and cuddling until after the wedding.

'I'm not being silly, or prudish,' she had explained carefully, two evenings before their wedding day when her parents had gone up to bed and left them alone downstairs. 'It's not all that pure young girl in white thing, either. It would seem like cheating on Mummy and Daddy, if you really want to know, and I won't do that. After all, what's two days?'

'What indeed?' Phil had echoed rather glumly. 'Oh Kay, I adore you!'

So the following evening she had not objected when he and his friends went off for a stag night, though he came home with a dreadful headache and woke the family up by falling down the attic stairs – he was sleeping in the attic because his parents were in the spare room. The Markhams were from Rutland, not local at all, but they seemed nice people, and were friendly towards their daughter-in-law-to-be. Even Kay's parents had said, without reserve, that Mr and Mrs Markham were pleasant.

And now their marriage was a fact, she was Mrs Kay Markham and Philip was her rightful husband. The train was entering Liverpool Street Station and very soon now they would cross the city in a taxi to Waterloo and get on another train which would take them to the very village

19

where their honeymoon cottage was situated. What, Kay thought dreamily, could be better?

'There she is!' Jo's shriek was enough to turn heads other than Kay's. 'Kay, we're over here!' She shook Emily's shoulder gently. 'Have you got that rice, Bev . . . I mean Emily?'

Emily fished in her tunic pocket and handed over one of the packets of rice which a cookhouse WAAF had given them before they left the station, then tipped the contents of the second packet into her own small palm. Kay came down the platform towards them, hanging on the arm of a tall and very handsome young RAF officer who must be her new husband. Kay was radiant in a cream linen dress and jacket which was almost the same colour as her long, shining hair, and her face was wreathed in smiles. She even smiled through the showers of rice, which showed, Emily thought, that she had a nice nature because rice can sting and Jo threw hard.

'Jo, how marvellous to see you! Oh, you are good to come all this way! And you, too, Bevan, of course. Phil, this is my friend Jo Stewart and this is ACW Bevan . . . I'm afraid . . . I don't know . . .'

'I'm Emily,' Emily said shyly. 'You look wonderful, Kay – well, you both look wonderful.'

'Sorry, yes of course, Emily. And this is Philip, girls.'

Her pride shone in every glance, and no wonder, Emily thought enviously. Philip was so tall, so golden-haired, so undoubtedly gorgeous – he and Kay made a perfect couple.

'Hello, girls, nice to meet you,' Philip said. He held out his hand, first to Jo, then to Emily. 'I've heard all about you, of course and Kay tells me you've been accepted to

20

fly balloons, of all things. I just hope you don't do yourselves an injury, I'm told it's heavy work.'

'Oh, we can tackle it,' Jo said at once, giving Philip the benefit of her warm and friendly smile. 'We like a challenge, Kay and me – and Emily here. Actually, Biddy Bachelor would have come as well, only she's doing punishment drill. She's a balloon op, too.'

'You're all very brave,' Philip said. He turned politely to Emily, who was hovering on the edge of the little group. 'Why did you volunteer for balloons, Emily? You aren't very big, are you?'

'The money's good,' Emily said thoughtlessly, then could have kicked herself. What a horrible, mercenary sort of thing to say, even if it were true. But Jo was nodding at her as though she thought Emily had said something rather clever.

'Yes, the money is good, and WAAFs are always short of money. What's more, they say the balloon operatives get more rations than other trades, and we're more independent. I know we'll miss out on the social life of a station, but there are bound to be compensations. And they really do need us, you know, now that they're taking the men for other jobs.'

'There, you see! I told you I shan't be dancing or flirting with other men, because there won't be anyone to flirt with on a balloon site,' Kay said bracingly to her husband. 'And that means I'll be able to save my money for when you come back to Blighty, darling. As for social life, mine will be spent writing letters to you and pestering the post office for replies.'

'Oh, I'll reply by return, though how long it will take before you get the letters is anyone's guess,' Philip said. 'Look, darling, I don't want to hurry you but we've a train to catch and this one was twenty minutes late so we really should . . .'

'Of course, we must dash,' Kay said. She kissed Jo's cheek, then bent and kissed Emily, too. 'Thank you both for coming, you are good, it was a marvellous surprise. See you in four days, then.'

'Yes, see you in four days,' Emily echoed, whilst Jo stood and waved wistfully after the two departing backs. 'Don't they make a perfect couple? Isn't he wonderfully good looking? And Duff . . . I mean Kay is awfully pretty.'

'Yes, they seem just right for each other,' Jo agreed. 'Look, our train back to the camp doesn't go for another hour, shall we try to get a meal somewhere like I said? I can afford it, honest, and I'm grateful that you agreed to come with me. It wouldn't have been much fun alone.'

'I've enjoyed it,' Emily said, and discovered rather to her surprise that she meant every word. 'If you're sure you can afford it, it would be fun. Do we need coupons, though?'

'Honestly, Emily, haven't you been out for a meal since the war started? All we need do is to find some small restaurant or café which won't cost the earth. We'll go out of the station, turn left and walk till we find somewhere. Right?'

'Or we could ask,' Emily said, greatly daring. She did not altogether fancy tramping the streets of London in the gathering dusk. 'Daft it seems, to walk miles when someone could advise us.'

Jo began to say she wasn't going to ask anyone, anyone at all, then stopped and gave Emily a sheepish grin.

'You're right, of course, and I'm just being silly. I'm still seething from the things that nasty little corporal on the train said about us to tell you the truth. Let's ask that news vendor over there. Those fellows know everything worth knowing, I reckon.'

Jo was right. The news vendor advised them to try a small café not far down the road and they soon found themselves settled at a window table with a hot meal – mutton stew, cabbage and potatoes – steaming before them.

'Bit different from what Kay's probably having,' Jo remarked cheerfully, speaking through a generous mouthful of potato and gravy. 'I expect it's a big dinner in a posh hotel, don't you?'

'I don't know much about honeymoons, but I thought they'd have wanted to be alone,' Emily ventured. 'I thought that was what it was all about, to be just the two of you. Didn't you say they'd taken a cottage in Devon?'

Jo shrugged. 'That's true, they do have a cottage, only I don't think Kay's much of a cook. She's never lived away from home until she joined the WAAF and I don't know if you've noticed but she isn't exactly handy, is she?'

Emily giggled. Everyone in the hut had noticed Kay because she really didn't have a clue and her plaintive voice had been heard, in the early days, requesting that someone show her how to fasten her collar stud . . . sew on a button . . . fold and unfold her blankets. Indeed, Kay had freely confessed that at home she had never lifted a finger, far less cooked a meal or darned a stocking. But she would have to start doing all sorts, now. They had been told that on balloon sites the WAAFs would take it in turns to cook and clean.

'Yes, I forgot that. I wonder if Philip knows? Not that he'll care – she's so pretty, isn't she, Jo?'

23

It was warm in the little café and the food was good. Jo ate another forkful of meat and gravy, then stopped to consider the question. 'He knows about her not being able to cook, you mean? Well, I suspect you're right, it's not for her cooking that he's married Kay, so he won't mind about the food – not yet, anyway. And she'll learn once we're on site, the same as she learned to fasten her collar stud and darn her stockings. Oh, look at that clock, we'd better get a move on. Have we time for a pud, do you suppose?'

'I should think so; the train's bound to be late,' Emily said placidly, wiping the last remnants of stew off her plate with a slice of grey-looking National loaf. 'It's steamed jam roll and custard, isn't it? I know it'll be dried milk and probably rhubarb jam but it looks delicious. I'll eat fast, honest I will.'

'Right.' Jo stood up and made her way over to the counter, then turned back. 'Shall we have another cup of tea too, Em? It's such good tea, lovely and strong.'

Em! Most of the other WAAFs and all the officers called her Bevan. Only her father called her Em, but she loved the sound of it. She felt accepted, warmed by the familiarity of it. But she could not possibly let Jo see how pleased she was.

'You're right, the spoon could stand upright in that tea,' Emily agreed. 'Yes, I'd like another cup, please.'

The girls were eating pudding at a great rate and sipping their hot tea when a familiar wail brought their heads round.

'Oh damn, it's a raid,' Jo muttered. 'Gobble up, Em, and we'll leave. I think they close the underground during raids, don't they?'

At the next table a middle-aged taxi driver was sitting,

24

doing the crossword with a stump of pencil in a creased copy of *The Times*. At Jo's words he pushed the paper away, looked across at them and grinned.

'Nah, they don't close the subways, they're the only safe place to be, but fings get disrupted, like,' he said cheerfully. 'Tell you what, I've finished for the day; where are you bound?'

'Charing Cross,' Jo said at once. 'We've got about twenty minutes, I reckon.'

'Trains is always delayed these days, I reckon yours'll be late in and late out again,' the man remarked. 'Well, whadda you fink? Wanna chanst the underground or will you ride in my motor? I don't mind goin' that way; it's on my road 'ome, more or less.'

'Gosh, thanks,' Jo said. 'That would be wizard, wouldn't it, Em?' She started to get to her feet but the driver waved her down again.

'Finish your tea, gel; I'm finishin' mine,' he said. 'There won't be much traffic on the streets, not once the siren's sounded, so we'll make good time to Charing Cross.'

Kay and Philip arrived in the sleepy little Devonshire town at six o'clock, both very tired and rather dirty. Philip ordered a taxi and when they reached the cottage, he found the key under the flowerpot, where their landlady had said she would put it, and then turned to Kay and kissed the tip of her chilly nose.

'Welcome to our love nest, sweetheart! I'd carry you over the threshhold if I didn't have to lug the cases, and anyway, we'll probably have to turn right round and go out again because I wouldn't expect you to cook us a meal after such a hectic day,' he said tenderly, fitting the key in

25

the lock and turning it. 'We'll have a wash and brush up and then go down to the local pub for a pie and a pint.'

'I'd just as soon have a cup of tea and some bread and cheese,' Kay said faintly. She was terribly tired and did not even want to have to consider going out again tonight. And though she had leaned back in the taxi and told herself she was the most fortunate of girls, she was beginning to feel nervous and a long way from home.

But as soon as they got inside the cottage, all that changed. There was something welcoming about it, though the hall which they entered when Philip unlocked the door seemed dark and chilly at first. But then Philip clicked the light switch and a pleasant, gold-shaded light flooded the room. Kay could see some nice watercolours on the walls whilst an umbrella stand, a china pot with an aspidistra growing in it and a jumble of magazines and newspapers on the hallstand reminded her that this was a lived-in cottage, that the owner was just down the road and would come in each day to help out if they wanted her.

'Look, Phil, Mrs Whatsit's even left us wet-weather gear,' Kay exclaimed as she glanced at the pegs behind the door. Two bright yellow sou'westers with matching oilskins hung there and beneath them stood a row of wellington boots in various sizes. 'Wasn't that kind of her?'

'Very thoughtful,' Philip said with a chuckle. 'Devon, Devon, glorious Devon, always rains six days out of seven. Not that I care if it rains seven days out of seven, all I need is right under this roof.'

Kay smiled but felt rather silly, like one of those awful old honeymoon jokes she had sniggered over as a schoolgirl. But she followed Philip into the living room and as soon as they entered she realised their luck was in. There was a fire lit in the hearth with a big basket of logs standing nearby for replenishing, and a note pinned to one of the low beams informed them laconically: 'Hot meal in Aga, second oven. Make yourselves at home. M. Cottingham.'

'Isn't that grand?' Philip demanded, picking up the poker and prodding the fire into a fresh and lively blaze and then throwing another log on with the prodigal hand of one who didn't saw, fetch indoors or even pay for the wood. 'That puts an end to walking down to the pub tonight and I can't say I'm sorry, we're both pretty whacked. Want to take a look in the Aga, pet, see what Mrs Cottingham has left us?'

Kay looked, and saw a big, old-fashioned casserole dish from which wonderful smells were emanating, and another dish covered with pastry which was probably a fruit pie of some description. She found an oven cloth and gingerly took the brown casserole out of the oven, removing the lid when it was standing squarely on the kitchen table. A rich and wonderful stew seemed to smile at her, bubbling beneath a layer of thinly sliced, golden-brown potatoes.

'Gosh,' Kay said reverently. She had warned Philip that she knew nothing about cooking and he had said they would eat out, except for breakfasts, which he imagined she could make. Kay, who knew all too well her own deficiencies in the cookery department, had decided, on the spur of the moment, that she would suggest tea and toast as being better for them and put the thought of cooking so much as a boiled egg firmly out of her mind. Who wanted to cook on their honeymoon, anyway? She was sure they would find better things to do!

27

'What is it?' Philip said, coming into the kitchen behind her. He looped an arm round her waist and pulled her close to him, peering over her shoulder into the casserole. 'It smells divine – it smells pre-war!'

'I think it's probably rabbit,' Kay said cautiously. 'With all the vegetables you can think of, Phil, so it's a meal in itself. And there's a pie, I think it's a plum one. Gosh, I didn't think I could ever be hungry again after that wedding breakfast, but I am now!'

'Can't eat until we've cleaned up a bit,' Philip said, as Kay pulled away from him and picked up a serving spoon. 'Come on, the Aga's lit so there will be hot water. We'll share the bath, shall we?'

'Don't be silly, there wouldn't be room,' Kay said. She felt her cheeks begin to glow with embarrassment. 'Can't we eat first? I – I'm starving, really I am.'

Philip turned her in his arms and examined her bright cheeks curiously. Then he smiled and kissed her lightly on the nose.

'Little goose,' he murmured. 'All right, just wash your face and hands, you can do that at the sink if you like, then we'll eat, and then we'll . . .'

Kay hurried over to the sink and turned on the big brass tap. Cold water gushed out, splashing her cream linen jacket, but she ingnored it and reached for the big bar of red scrubbing soap. It smelt like latrines but she washed her hands, dunked her face in the water, dried herself on a tea towel and then went back to the table so that Philip could take her place. Whilst he washed she dished up, then they sat down on opposite sides of the table and began to eat.

'Our first meal together,' Kay said presently, when her initial pangs of hunger had been satisfied. 'Isn't it romantic, Phil, just the two of us in this beautiful old cottage?'

'Very romantic. Oh, I put your suitcase on the right hand side of the bed and mine on the left. Is that all right?'

'Er . . . yes, th-that's fine,' Kay stammered. You are longing for Phil to take you to bed you little ninny, she scolded herself. Do stop going scarlet with embarrassment over what is a perfectly normal, delightful act. Isn't it? Well, if you don't relax you won't find out!

When they had finished the meal Kay washed the dishes and Philip dried them. The sheer domesticity of it all made Kay practically purr with contentment. Then they went and sat by the fire for a little while, but Kay was in danger of simply falling asleep and Philip was restless; he even suggested a visit to the pub, though he didn't seem disappointed when Kay said she was sorry but she was just too tired. He's as embarrassed as I am, Kay told herself. It would be sensible to put us both out of our misery and go to bed, then we could get it over with.

This was so different to the way she had felt for the past few weeks that she blinked with astonishment at her own craven thoughts. But you want to experience real love, she reminded herself, you can't wait to go all the way, as the girls say, and find out what it's really like. You've been telling anyone who would listen how keen you were to get married for the past six weeks – more!

'Shall we go up, then? If you want a bath you can go first.'

Philip had lounged to his feet; he looked taller, blonder . . . different, all of a sudden. He's a stranger to me really, Kay told herself wildly. We don't know each other a bit, I don't know if he likes animals, or cage-birds, or whether he absolutely hates small children or old ladies. He might want curry for every meal, or wear frilly underwear or – or have a spotty chest! The man's a total stranger yet we're about to share a bed, we're legally able to do embarrassing things to each other – oh, I wish I hadn't come!

'Kay, darling? Do you want a bath?'

'Is – is there a bathroom? Upstairs, I mean?'

'Yes, but the WC's just outside the back door, so if you want to go there you'd better go now, before bed. And take the torch, because it's pretty dark in there.'

Kay stared. 'An outside lavatory? And no electricity? My God, it's as bad as the basic training centre.'

Philip grinned. 'You're a spoilt little lady,' he murmured. 'Indoor lavatories are still a luxury to half the population, believe me. Want to go before I do?'

'Umm . . . yes, I'd better. Well, if Mrs Whatsit could afford a bathroom upstairs, why on earth didn't she put a toilet in at the same time? She could have put it in the bathroom, lots of small houses have a lavatory in the bathroom.' Kay got up and walked past Phil, across the kitchen and out of the back door. Seconds later she was in again, whitefaced, gripping the torch like a truncheon.

'Phil, there's the most enormous spider . . . can you make it go away? It's right above the lavatory seat, I'm sure it will fall on me if I go in there.'

'It's probably been there years, it won't fall tonight,' Philip assured her. 'I don't think spiders do fall, anyway. And if I try to dislodge it now, sweetie, the chances are it will just scuttle away and reappear where you least expect it. Just shut your eyes and pretend you're peeing for Britain.'

A small, watery giggle escaped Kay. 'Oh, but suppose . . . I know! You go first, I'll go next.'

Shrugging, Philip disappeared out of the back door and

Kay rushed to the row of cloakroom pegs in the hall. When Philip returned to the kitchen a few minutes later his love stood demurely by the table, clad in the sou'wester which she had noticed when they first entered the cottage. Philip gave a shout of laughter. 'Your anti-spider device, I see! Oh Kay, you're priceless! Get going, then.'

Kay went doubtfully into the dark little lavatory, keeping her eyes averted from the spider's lofty perch. When she sat down she was slightly heartened to see that there was a heart-shaped hole in the door so that she could watch the stars as she worked, so to speak. With the sou'wester guarding her hair, she was not as afraid of the spider as she might have been, and anyway, she supposed that Philip was right; the spider was scarcely likely to descend from its perch simply to scare her stiff. It had its own reasons for being up there – ugh ugh – and hers not to reason why, hers but to pee and fly! But she still thought a cottage which Mrs Whatsername had fitted out so beautifully for paying guests might at least have had an inside lavatory.

When she finished she shone the torch all round but could not find the lavatory paper, so had to make do with some sheets of newspaper which hung from a loop of string near at hand. This was not a good substitute, but she used it anyway and then ran indoors, threw her sou'wester at Phil because he was laughing at her, and washed her hands under the gushing brass tap.

'I bet you don't like spiders either, that's why you wouldn't chase it away,' she told him as she dried her hands on the roller towel behind the door. 'I'm not having a bath, I'm too tired, so if you want one, go ahead. Oh, and another time if you use the last of the bog-paper, you might at least warn me.'

31

'There was plenty of paper,' Philip assured her. 'Miles, I should think. Couldn't you find it in the dark? Oh, Christopher, you weren't looking for San Izal, were you?'

'You don't mean that bundle of old newspaper was their idea of a toilet roll, do you?' Kay asked, revolted. 'My God, I'm glad I don't live in the country if that's how they treat their . . . their . . .'

'Bums?' Philip asked sweetly, making her splutter on a reluctant laugh. 'First it's spiders, then it's bog-paper . . . poor old Kay, you've got a lot to learn, sweetie.'

Kay laughed again, and found that somehow, what with the spider, the bog-paper and their laughter, she was no longer regarding Phil as a frightening stranger. Perhaps it will be all right, she thought hopefully. Perhaps I didn't make the worst mistake in the world after all. Perhaps I'm actually going to enjoy . . .

'Ready to climb the wooden stair to Bedfordshire?' Phil asked facetiously, when he had made them two mugs of cocoa. 'I'm extraordinarily tired.'

'Might as well, I suppose,' Kay quavered with what she hoped was cool insouciance but feared was probably more like squeaky bravado. 'I'm tired, too.'

They climbed the stairs together, hand in hand, like two children, leaving the fire-warmed living room and going up into the dark of the upper storey.

'No electricity upstairs,' Phil said, striking a match and lighting the lamp which stood ready on the mantel. 'But lamplight's awfully soft and pretty. Much more romantic, don't you think?'

'Much,' Kay said breathlessly. 'This cottage is thatched, isn't it? I do hope there aren't spiders in the bedrooms, Phil.'

Phil turned and smiled at her. 'If there are, I'll guard

you from them,' he said. 'Just jump into bed, darling, and we'll pull the covers up over our head and cuddle down together.'

'I wonder if Kay and Phil are doing it now, or if they've finished,' Jo mused that night as she and Emily trudged over to the ablutions for a wash before bed. They had caught the train and had actually arrived back in reasonably good time, so there would be no black marks against their names when they started at the Balloon Centre in just over a week's time. 'Come to that, they might have decided to give it a miss tonight, after all that journeying and everything. Especially if Kay's cooked him a meal,' she added with a chuckle.

'We shouldn't talk about it though, should we?' Emily said uneasily. 'It's a private thing, isn't it? There used to be bundling in Wales, but when I asked my mam about it once she got all red-faced with me, said I was talking dirty. Since then, I keep my thoughts to myself.'

'Well, I don't,' Jo said. 'I'm intrigued by the whole business to tell you the truth, Emily. The trouble is, we're so very ignorant. No one tells you much, they just tell you you shouldn't do it. And if there's one thing I do know, it's that the things you shouldn't do are always much more fun than the things you should do. Don't you agree?'

Emily considered the question seriously, whilst stripping off her outer clothing and wrapping herself in her overcoat.

'Well, some things everyone advises you against are fun,' she admitted as they went quietly out of the hut and began to cross the short stretch of open ground between their sleeping quarters and the ablutions. 'But others aren't. They tell you not to go out and stare up at the sky

33

during raids, and if you did it and got killed that wouldn't be much fun, would it?'

'Don't be so literal,' Jo said crossly. She pushed the door of the ablutions open cautiously and the two girls made their way past the blackout curtain which hung behind the door and then Jo reached for the light switch. The tiny, faint bulb illuminated the rows of basins and taps, the two shower cubicles and the long stretch of linoleumed floor. 'I'm fascinated by the sex business, actually, I love listening when the bad girls are talking about their boyfriends. But it's just an academic fascination, I suppose, because I can't imagine wanting to do it myself. I like boys all right, don't get me wrong, but I'd be so scared of not knowing how to do it and making a fool of myself. How about you, Em? You're a farmer's daughter, aren't you? They're supposed to know what goes on because of the animals. So do you want to marry and do all those odd things?'

'Not if it's what rams and ewes do,' Emily said thoughtlessly, then felt her cheeks go hot. What a thing to have said – and anyway, people were different, they couldn't possibly . . . why, her own parents . . . her thoughts broke down in confusion and she pushed the plug into the handbasin and began to run water. She had turned the hot tap, but it was cold at this time of night, naturally. 'Don't talk daft anyway, Jo. Everyone wants to get married, don't they?'

Another girl had entered the ablutions soon after they did and now she stripped off her overcoat and began to run water as well. Emily smiled at her; it was ACW Biddy Bachelor, the fourth balloon operative; she still felt grateful to Biddy for being on punishment drill so that Jo had been forced to suggest that Emily should accompany her to London. Biddy returned the smile with a broad grin, then addressed them.

'Wharron earth are you two goin' on about?' she asked affably in a strong Liverpool accent. 'There's nothing wrong wi' marriage, you cloth-'eads, it's the most natural thing in the world. We'd none of us be here without it, would we?'

'You've got a point, Biddy,' Jo said grudgingly, splashing water. 'But I don't think I fancy it, much. What was it Queen Victoria is supposed to have said? "I close my eyes and think of England," wasn't it?'

'It 'ud be close my eyes and think of Wales for me, of course,' Emily said with a giggle. 'Oh, let's talk about something different, I keep going all hot.'

'Yes, I can just see them; shoals and shoals of whales, swimming in a huge blue sea and making fountains come out of the tops of their shiny black heads,' Jo said dreamily. 'It 'ud be better than counting sheep, you'd drop off in no time.'

'You two are quite mad,' Biddy Bachelor said when she'd stopped giggling. 'Sex, whales, sheep . . . I never know what you're goin' to come up with next! Oh, by the way, what did the bride look like? I paid for me sins by trampin' round the perimeter track, but I thought about you. Bet Kay looked lovely, eh?'

'You're right, she looked gorgeous.' Jo lathered her hands until the soapsuds were grey and turned to stare at Biddy. 'Emily came with me instead of you, and do you know, she's going to be a balloon operative too? So there'll be four of us starting there, Monday.'

'We done the right thing,' Biddy said, sloshing water. 'I thought about cook 'cos me granda' were a chef, but they didn't want more cooks and the money's awful good in balloons. The food's prime, too, so I were told, and I passed the physical all right. So I signed up, didn't I? I jost 'ope I don't live to regret it!'

Emily eyed Biddy covertly whilst they washed. She was a tall girl, but skinny, with pale, acne-scarred skin and bright, hungry eyes. The other WAAFs teased her about the amount she ate, but now it occurred to Emily that before she joined the WAAF Biddy had probably needed more food than she had been accustomed to receive; even in six short weeks she had put on weight and looked both healthier and happier than she had done when they started at the training camp.

'You won't regret it, not with us to hold your hand,' Jo said exuberantly. 'Things are always easier if there are a few of you in it together. Oh damn, that was the last of my soap, and I was going to clean my teeth with it, only I went and forgot and used it all. I suppose neither of you could spare a squeeze of toothpaste?'

'You can have a squeeze of mine,' Emily said quickly, splashing cold water up into her soapy face and groaning as it ran down and wetted her pink issue brassiere. 'Duw, I've even wet my hair . . . can you reach my towel, Jo?'

'Hair's supposed to get wet when you wash properly,' Jo pointed out righteously. She took Emily's towel off the hook and chucked it over, then dunked her own head, hair and all, into the basin of cold water, blowing out vigorously at the same time and making a great deal of noise and even more splashes. 'My, isn't this just the healthiest way to end the day?' she spluttered, coming up for air.

'Jo Stewart, you are a slob,' Biddy said reproachfully. 'There's soapsuds all over me shirt and water splashes on me shoes. Do you have to do everything so violently, chuck?'

'Yes,' Jo said, smiling sweetly as, in her own turn, she groped for her towel. Water was channelling down her neck and her eyes were still screwed tightly shut. 'And if you were a clean person like me, Biddy, you wouldn't be wearing a shirt whilst you're washing.'

'She's a goody-goody an' all,' Biddy mumbled, ostentatiously wiping soapsuds off her shirtsleeve. 'And reverting to our previous topic, girls, I pity the poor devil what gets landed with ACW Stewart here, because she's gorra thing against sex and that can ruin the best marriage.'

'I'm not at all sure I want to marry,' Jo reminded her. She rubbed her face until it glowed and then began to wash her legs, covering the floor with water. 'But if I met the right feller and decided to go ahead then I'd probably enjoy the sex side of it. So put that in your pipe and smoke it, Biddy me old mavoureen! And if you're from Liverpool, why do you have an Irish name?'

''Cos half the scousers I know came from Ireland, way back,' Biddy said. She got a brush out of her sponge bag and attacked her hair half-heartedly. 'Are you coming back to the billets, girls? Only I don't like walkin' back on me own through the dark.'

'I wonder what the girls are doing?' Kay said drowsily, her mouth resting on the bare skin of Philip's chest. 'I wonder if they wonder what we're doing, Phil?'

'Let them wonder; we aren't doing anything now, anyway,' Phil pointed out. He stroked her hair, his hand teasing its way round the back of her neck. 'Did you enjoy that, pussy-cat?'

'Mm hmm. Well, I enjoyed it in the end,' Kay said truthfully. 'I didn't like it much at the beginning, but it was lovely in the end.'

Phil chuckled and rubbed a lazy finger round Kay's soft pink nipple. She felt it harden into a response and gave a mutter of complaint.

'Don't, Phil! I'm still all of a dither, you know.'

'Yes, I do know, or I think I do. Well, that spider saved the day, didn't it?'

'I don't know what you mean,' Kay said suspiciously. 'It's not in here, is it?'

Philip laughed again. 'Even your terror at the thought of your eight-legged friend is all soft and cuddly,' he said, stroking along the line of her naked back. 'But pre-spider you were awfully prickly, Kay-baby. I think you were considering running off, not being married after all.'

'I was,' Kay admitted after a short pause. 'I can't explain, but all of a sudden I realised I – I hardly knew you. Daft, wasn't it?'

There was another pause. Philip's hand stroked and smoothed before he spoke, but when he did speak it was reflectively.

'No, I don't think it was daft at all, really. We haven't known each other long though it was long enough to fall in love. But we'll remedy that, pet – and it will be great fun.'

'Kay, could you be a dear and help me with my recognition? If I fail the course it will be because I can't tell a Spitfire from a Hurricane, or a Heinkel from a JU 88, and we wouldn't want that, would we? I've got the cards and I've had a go at them this afternoon, so if you could just test me perhaps I may pass the exam after all.'

Kay, who had come quietly into their hut hoping to write a letter or two, groaned, but knew better than to refuse. They all helped each other, particularly the four of them who had come up from the same basic training centre, and besides, you never knew when you might need help yourself.

'Yes, all right,' she said now, going over to Jo's bed and sitting beside her friend, who was poring over a collection of aircraft silhouettes, each one depicted from several angles on its own small white card. 'I don't really understand why you find it so hard to recognise them, though . . . it isn't as if there were thousands, and they're all quite different.'

'They all have two wings and a tail, and that means they all look alike to me,' Jo said heavily. 'I don't see the point in knowing them, that's the truth of it. Why should it matter? If it drops bombs on you or fires guns it's the enemy, if it waggles its wing and goes right on by, it's one of ours. Besides, an intelligent person like me isn't going to stand there gazing at the sky, an intelligent person will pelt for cover the moment a suspicious looking aircraft goes over. And another thing, a balloon isn't something you can throw at a plane, or fire at one, is it? You see, my intelligence doesn't see the point, so it won't take it in. Now someone like Biddy can reel them off whichever angle the card shows because she just does as she's told and never wonders why. Still, if I've got to learn them isn't there some little wrinkle you could teach me, so I could get it right?'

'Divide them into fighter or bomber, friend and enemy for a start,' Kay said, reaching for the cards. 'When you're learning, try to find one particular feature on each silhouette which is totally different from all the others. Don't look now, I'll shuffle them and hold them up one at a time. And since it's raining and we're free for the evening, after I've written my letters you can test me on the procedures which follow a gas attack.'

'All this theory,' Jo muttered, whilst Kay was shuffling the cards. 'Why can't we just get out there and fly the balloons? I'm sure to be awfully good at that – bound to be. Why, we've been here over a month and what have we done so far?'

'Drilled, marched, learned the most complex knots, spliced rope, played tug o'war, done some weight-lifting – and we lost Kitty Brown at that stage since she wrenched her back and had to go – and of course we've tackled a lot of written exams,' Kay said patiently. 'But we've got through a third of the training, look at it that way, kid. By Christmas we'll be home and dry – unless we muck up.'

'Christmas is a million years away, and we waste our time playing stupid games,' Jo said, but she lay back on her bed, hands behind her head, and sighed. 'Go on then, start.'

Kay began to hold the cards up. She knew the aircraft

silhouettes so well, herself, that she did not once have to glance at the back of the card to find out which was what, but poor Jo peered, cursed, guessed . . . then thumped her brow with a closed fist to try, she said, to get her head to open up to a bit of information for a change.

'But you do awfully well with everything else,' Kay reminded her. 'I wish I could splice rope like you can, and you know all the knots, even the most obscure ones. Now Emily and I have a terrible job remembering them, far less tying them.' She held up a card as she spoke. 'What's that? And take it slowly, Jo.'

'Well, I can see the point of splicing rope because we shall be using it when we move onto a site. But we're not going to get near to any planes, so what does it matter whether we recognise them or not? And . . . let me see . . . that one's a bomber, and it's got two engines,' Jo said, staring at the small card. 'It's one of ours . . . God, what a waste of time and intelligence this is! Oh, don't frown, I'm getting there . . . it's the one called a shoe or a boot or something, isn't it?'

'Oh Jo, honestly! It's a Wellington bomber; is that what you meant?'

'Naturally,' Jo said with dignity. 'What other bombers sound like boots or shoes?'

'Perhaps if you just learned the names . . .' Kay was beginning, when the door of the hut opened and closed and the curtain was swished aside for a moment so that two girls could enter. 'Ah, Emily, I'm testing Jo on air-craft recognition; want to play? What about you, Biddy?'

'No need, I'm silhouette-perfect,' Biddy said with more than a trace of satisfaction in her voice. 'Listen, Mandy Richards says when she was the age what I am she used a face scrub. What's one o'them?'

41

'I think she means she used a very soft sort of brush, and something like a skin milk,' Emily said in her soft Welsh voice. 'Magazines sometimes suggest trying it.'

'Wharron earth's skin milk?' Biddy said incredulously. 'Like cow's milk, is it?'

'No, of course not. Well, it looks like ordinary milk but you spread it on your skin to get your make-up off,' Kay said. 'But you won't be able to get any, you know how short things like that are.'

'Nor I don't have no make-up, neither,' Biddy said quite cheerfully. 'Oh well, I'll give me face a goin' over wi' me nailbrush, that oughter do something.'

'Take the skin off, probably,' Jo said briskly. 'Go away, you two, me and Kay are trying to work.'

'Can't. We're on earlies tomorrow, remember, so we thought we'd steal a march on the others and go to bed now,' Emily said placidly. 'It's tear-gas practice, so make sure your respirator's in its case and not stuffed under the bed or in your locker somewhere, in case they spray us with the stuff, just for a lark, you know.'

'A lark? I'll give anyone lark if they try to spray gas over me,' Jo said indignantly. 'But they won't do it any more than they did with that poisoned gas, so why should they do it with tear gas? It'll just be another try-on to make us look small, you mark my words.'

The sergeant was a large man with a large moustache, a cruel haircut and a very large voice. He stood in the middle of the parade ground and pointed to an ordinary looking Nissen hut which stood there, its double doors open invitingly wide.

'Now, gels, you are ha-goin' to happroach that 'ut in pairs . . . get me? Pairs means two of you at a time, marchin' togevver, not 'oldin' 'ands nor clutchin' nor squealin', just togevver. Get it?'

'Flatulant old bore,' Jo muttered from behind a fixed smile. She told herself that she was sick of being bossed about by a man old enough to be her father but not nearly intelligent enough. 'Why does he keep making awful, unfunny jokes? What does he think this is, a kindergarten?'

'Shut up,' Kay hissed back. 'This could be important, Jo. Just listen for once and try to take it in.'

'I'm listening, I'm listening! But I can think and listen at the same time, unlike some, and I think . . .'

'Are you ready, gels? Line up in pairs, then. And put them respirator cases on the grahnd, because you won't be needin' 'em. Because, you loverly bunch o'coconuts, you're goin' to run through that 'ut, in pairs an' at the double, wivvout no respirators, get me? You takes a deep breaf when you goes in, an' you bloody 'olds it, see? If you does it right, everyfing'll be 'unky-dory. If you does it wrong . . .' the sergeant gave a bloodthirsty chuckle, '. . . if you does it wrong you needn't come cryin' to me for sympathy, 'cos you 'ave been warned!'

'I'm not running straight into a hut full of gas,' Jo said rebelliously. 'Not that it'll be gas, mind you – he wouldn't dare. He's just trying to make fools of us . . . again.'

The poison gas he had sworn was being hissed into a covered trench through which they had to crawl had proved to be one small, grinning AC plonk with a short length of garden hosepipe, through which he blew at intervals.

'Just do as you're told,' Kay muttered out of the corner of her mouth. 'In pairs, at the double . . . we'll be out the other end in no time.'

'No need to do anything, because this'll be another trick, just like last time,' Jo said confidently, as the first pair set off under the sergeant's bellowed instructions. 'Mind, that AC plonk's breath was probably bad enough to make you think it was poison gas, if you'd got near him and his wretched garden hose. No, this will be another of the sarge's little . . .'

'Next! Come on, let's be 'avin' you, Stewart an' Markham,' the sergeant shouted as the girls jogged past him.

I bet his wife bullies him, Jo thought to herself, pretending to goosestep just to annoy Kay. Bossing us about is probably the only fun he gets and he intends to make the most of it, never mind our feelings.

'No lurkin' at the back, 'opin' to be let orf, hin you goes! Come along, Bevan an' Bachelor, hat the double, one-two-one-two . . . that's right, 'old your breff like I tell you!'

No more than a yard or so into the hut, Jo turned to Kay. 'Told you there was . . . aaargh!'

Tear gas is unpleasant, if not deadly. In a couple of seconds Jo was coughing and wheezing, with tears pouring down her face. She wanted to vent her feelings on the sergeant, to call him every name in the book, but it was all she could do to breathe, speech was definitely beyond her. She tried to turn and run out of the hut again, but Kay grabbed her arm and shook her head, pointing back. Through tear-filled eyes, Jo could just about make out first the stream of WAAFs following on their heels and then the sergeant's huge figure, all but blocking out the light.

The man was a sadist, Jo thought bitterly, shambling along with Kay's grip like a tourniquet round the top of her arm. But surely even a sadistic sergeant would not throw a WAAF back into a hut filled with tear gas, if she tried to escape?

But she knew he would, of course. The Air Force was singularly lacking in the softer emotions and this whole experience was doubtless designed to teach would-be balloon operatives to obey commands, to take the advice handed out by NCOs, and to listen when they were told to do so.

I'll show the old bully, Jo vowed, as Kay hauled her out into the fresh air and let go of her arm. I'll show him I'm made of sterner stuff than he thought. Unfortunately however, as Kay let go of her Jo swayed and dropped to her knees, then simply collapsed onto her stomach, taking enormous gulps of the sweet, fresh air of late October. Her lungs felt as if they were on fire and so did her eyes . . . oh, oh, if only she had simply obeyed instructions, if only she hadn't decided it was just a trick! It was the sergeant's fault, though. He must have known that the more intelligent amongst them would remember the gas-filled trench, assume they were being fooled again.

'Serve you right, Jo.' Kay, who was always sym-pathetic, gave her a nudge in the ribs with one stout lace-up, then bent over her. 'That'll teach you to be such a flipping know-all . . . of course it won't be gas, it'll be another trick, like last time,' she mimicked. 'Honest, old love, you've got to stop kicking against the pricks or you aren't going to pass at the end of the course.'

Not pass? Jo gazed up at the faces surrounding her, horrified that Kay could voice such a sentiment. Kay was supposed to be her friend!

'Course I shall pass,' she said indignantly, rubbing at the still free-running tears with the palms of her dirty hands. 'I don't mean to be left behind when you lot go off

45

to have fun with balloons – I'm coming too. Why, Kay, you know I'm more capable than most of our lot – much more.'

'You don't like authority much, Jo,' Emily said mildly. 'And if you aren't careful, you'll find that authority won't like you. They can punish you just by separating us, can't they? Only it would be punishing us all, of course.'

Jo stared up at Emily's pale, rather timid face with watery-eyed indignation. These girls were her friends, could they not see . . . ?

Biddy joined the small group, her chest heaving but without a tear to be seen. Biddy had obeyed instructions; they were just like sheep, they didn't have any initiative, they . . .

'You're a fool to yourself, our Jo,' Biddy said loudly. 'We don't wanna lose you – why can't you act like the rest of us? You can think wharrever you want to think, but you keeps it under your hat, see? And you oughter learn them silhouettes, because you could; you just don't see the point so you've stopped trying.'

Out of the mouths of babes and sucklings, Jo thought, awed. That was it, of course. She could easily have learned the silhouettes if she had wanted to do so – look how quickly she had mastered even the most intricate of knots – but because she couldn't see the point of aircraft recognition she had not really tried to master it.

'Nah what 'ave we 'ere? Oo thought they knew best, eh?' The sergeant loomed up beside her, leaned down and hauled her to her feet. He did not look like an ogre now but like a normal, almost fatherly man whose children were occasionally extremely silly. 'Oh well, young Stewart, you aren't the first an' you won't be the last. What'll you never do again, eh?'

'I won't ever breathe in tear gas, not if I can help it,' Jo said with the beginnings of a grin. 'Cor, Sarge, my lungs feel like torn paper.'

'An' the sad fing is you 'ave to go through again in 'alf an hour,' the sergeant told her. 'Cos we don't wanna find out 'oo's a bolshie little WAAF and 'oo hain't, we wanna find out whevver your lungs can take in a good breff an' 'old it for free minutes. See? Lung capacity's important in the sorta work you've volunteered to do.'

'I see,' Jo said meekly. 'It wasn't just a trick then, Sarge?'

'There's a purpose in most o' what we does,' the sergeant told her. D'you feel awright now, gel? If so, 'ow habout goin' through agin – wiv your breff 'eld, this time? Then we can all go 'ome!'

That night, Kay lay in her bed and considered her day. Classes, rope splicing with the most gorgeous young instructor – Jo had actually made eyes at him, not that he'd taken the slightest notice – then the tear-gas test followed by a huge high tea in the cookhouse.

I think we all learned a thing or two today, not just Jo, Kay mused, as the corporal walked softly down the hut, a ghostly figure in her blue and white striped pyjamas, drawing back the blackout curtains and opening each window a crack. We learned that there is often a point to even the most apparently pointless of Air Force tests. The main trouble is no one bothers to explain so often you're working in the dark, and Jo isn't the sort of girl to like that. She's highly intelligent, manually dexterous as the Air Force says, or good with her hands as the rest of us put it, fond of her own way, and . . . well, a good person to have by you when things go wrong.

47

Kay had been almost dozing when the last thought popped into her mind and now she lay back and considered it carefully. A good person to have by you when things went wrong? Now why on earth should she have thought that? So far, Jo had been a bit of a bind, always arguing, making fun of the officers, whispering in class, deliberately out of step, you might say. It was strange because Jo was attractive, with her pompadour of rich brown hair, rosy cheeks and bright blue eyes, and attractive people usually expected folk to like them and were consequently friendly and easy. Jo was prickly and difficult, she didn't seem particularly interested in the chaps, which was convenient for Kay, who was only interested in Philip now, but it seemed strange, too.

Yet I like Jo better than anyone else in our intake, Kay told herself now. She's going to be a first-rate WAAF, I'm sure she is, and a good friend, too. We've just got to see her over the rough patch she seems to be going through, then we'll reap our reward, I'm sure of it. Why, even today I could see she was improving. She went through the tear-gas hut a second time like a veteran, came out laughing and hugged all the girls who had stood around and cheered her on. Oh yes, Jo's going to do all right, once she gets herself sorted out.

And I like Emily a lot as well, Kay's thoughts continued as she gazed out at the stars twinkling in the dark night sky. Emily was an odd little thing, small, shy and mousy, with a tendency to weep silently and privately when things went wrong. Or she had been; already life in the WAAF had given her self-confidence and as she grew easier with her fellows a quick sense of humour had surfaced, and an equally quick wit.

Then there was Biddy, tall and gangling, with that

dreadful accent in which she said so many sensible, practical things! Biddy was plain as a pikestaff and she wasn't yet sixteen, she had lied about her age to get into the WAAF. She'd let it slip once, but only to Kay and Jo and they weren't going to blow the whistle on her. Fifteen's a difficult age, Kay mused now, so probably Biddy's skin, which was awful, would improve as she got older. But that still left a blunt, rather large nose and a pair of small eyes. But if Biddy wasn't pretty, she more than made up for it by being such a character and by her rich and robust sense of humour.

I wonder what Mummy and Daddy would make of Biddy, though, Kay thought sleepily. They aren't snobs exactly, but I don't believe they would understand her. They would think her rather a common little girl from the slums of a big city and wonder why we seemed to get on so well. But the truth is, there's a lot of Biddy that isn't immediately apparent. She's three years younger than the rest of us, but she's much more knowing about some things and she's got patience and plenty of guts and she's never at a loss, she's got an answer for everything.

Someone further up the hut coughed and someone else followed suit. Kay groaned beneath her breath. She usually slept like a log but she knew from experience that a cough in a hutful of girls was catching. One person coughed, then another, then another, and it became difficult to do anything but lie awake, tense as a violin string, waiting for the next cough. To distract herself, she thought about her last letter to Phil . . . then her mind slid joyfully back to their honeymoon, to the golden Devonshire beaches, the wild moors, the gently rolling hills. She was almost asleep when the figure in the next bed sat up on one elbow, leaned across the gap and tugged at her blanket.

49

'Kay, are you asleep?'

'I was, Jo, but you've put paid to all that,' Kay hissed crossly. 'What do you want now?'

'I just want to tell you that I – I'm sorry for mucking about in the tear-gas hut. I shan't do it again because I'm determined to pass the course. G'night.'

'Night, Jo . . . and I never doubted you'd pass, in the end,' Kay said honestly. 'I knew you'd realise and pull yourself together before it was too late.'

'Thanks, Kay. It's an aircraft recognition test first thing; I bet I get full marks!'

Kay muttered something and snuggled under the covers once more to hide her grin. Full marks indeed, for someone who thought a Wellington was a boot! But that was Jo Stewart for you; some things never changed.

'Heave, girls . . . heave the reds! Come on, give it a bit of beef there . . . Angela, lean back my dear, they need your weight . . . come along, greens, give it all you've got, the flag's almost over the line . . . almost . . . almost . . . one more long pull . . .'

Biddy heaved with all her strength and tried to keep her feet on the slippery grass but the handkerchief which marked the middle of the rope gradually inched its way over the winning line and the red team let go of the rope to cheer their victory. Naturally, when the rope suddenly went slack the greens tumbled ignominiously over onto the grass, cheeks scarlet, chests heaving, Emily and Biddy amongst them.

'Well done, everyone,' Sergeant Anne Simpson said, mopping her own brow as though she had been on the winning end of the tug o'war rope, though in fact all she had done was shout rather a lot, run up and down and encourage first one team and then the other. 'There's cocoa and wads in the cookhouse . . . off you go! See you back here in fifteen minutes for some speed marching.'

There was a groan, of course, but Biddy didn't add her voice to those of the other WAAFs. She enjoyed playing tug o'war even when she ended up on the grass with green stains on her knees and burnt palms to her hands and she enjoyed cocoa and bread and cheese too – doorsteps were either bread and cheese or bread and jam and Biddy liked either.

Biddy had never eaten so well in all of her fifteen years as she had since joining the WAAF. The meals were bliss, the clothes were wonderful, the facilities exceeded her highest expectations. At home she had lived in a four-roomed terrace house with her parents, five brothers and three sisters. After the raids of December last year an aunt and two cousins who had been bombed out had moved in. None of the houses had running water or indoor sanitation – the first time Biddy heard a girl grumble because she had to leave her hut and walk across a few yards of concrete to reach the ablutions she had been shocked; how could anyone make a fuss over such a thing? At least when you got there the lavatory flushed, the water did not have to be fetched from a communal tap, and was quite often hot.

They don't know they're born, she had thought, not contemptuously nor enviously, but just matter of factly. They all came from richer backgrounds than she could imagine, the lucky blighters, but people were just people underneath, and it seemed she was in with a nice crowd who took the good things of life for granted and grumbled when everything wasn't just so.

I'll have to learn to think the way they does, Biddy concluded, having watched and listened almost without a word for a fortnight. This was hell, for she was by nature garrulous and friendly, but she had soon realised she had a lot to learn and with every day that passed she saw more clearly how she must behave in order to win friends. All she needed to do to became acceptable, she concluded after that fortnight had passed, was to fit in. Not to agree if she disagreed, not to become a yes-woman, but so far as in her lay, to do as they did. Because of the uniform everyone looked alike, but the girls she most wanted as her friends – at first Jo and Kay, now Emily, too – were always that bit smarter than the rest. So Biddy began to care about her personal appearance not just because they did but because, increasingly, she was proud of what she had become. She was a WAAF and a WAAF did not slouch or look slyly at people from beneath lowered brows. She faced the world straight on, eye to eye, and Biddy soon knew that a frank approach paid off. The NCOs, who had not appeared to like her much at the basic training camp, got on well with her at the Balloon Centre and she got on well with them.

And Biddy was discovering other things about herself: that she had a capacity for learning her work which would have astonished her old school teachers. She downright enjoyed taking her books and sitting in the hut with the others girls of an evening, studying. She had slacked and messed around at school, but that was because she could see no future for herself. Now she could see a future and it was a bright one, too. I'll stay in the WAAF, even when the war's over, she decided. It's lovely . . . it's much better than working my socks off looking after kids and trying to put food on the table, like me mam. I was always hungry before I joined the WAAF but not any more, not now. Yes, this is the life all right, and anyone who thinks different – well, they didn't live in our street!

But she still loved her mam and her brothers and sisters, though her feelings for her idle, beer-swilling father had solidified from a sort of nervous contempt into a lively dislike. He was working on the docks now that they weren't so fussy who they took, but Biddy would have put money on the fact that the job wouldn't last long. Dad's jobs never did.

She had been delighted to find that quiet and countrified Emily was a good sort, very like herself in some ways. Emily sent money home too, unlike Kay and Jo, who kept their wages to themselves and expected their parents to send them money rather than the other way about. At first, so determined had she been to win Kay's and Jo's friendship, Biddy had tended to ignore Emily, but now the two of them were good friends, and small though Emily was she could certainly pull, Biddy acknowledged. Scrambling to their feet to go over to the cookhouse for their cocoa, she said as much.

'You're only little, Emily, but you're worth havin' on a tug o' war team . . . you must be stronger than you look.'

'It's humping sacks of feed and carryin' lambs,' Emily said. 'Potatoes, too. We grow them down by the river; they all have to be brought up to the house, come harvest.'

'Aye, that'll make you strong,' Biddy said thoughtfully. 'I daresay the grub's good on a farm, too?'

Emily laughed.

'Lots of potatoes and roast mutton, too, when Da kills an old ewe,' she confirmed. 'We grows greens, of course, we've got the best part of three acres down to turnips, cabbage, kale and parsnips. And there's two hives for honey. Pretty self-sufficient we like to be, up in the hills.'

'Cor,' Biddy said, wide-eyed. 'Do you have a cow? I

seen cows in the fields from the train; they're pretty.'

'Pretty? Yes, I suppose . . . but we don't keep a cow, be a bit too high for her. Our fields are all steep and rocky, too. We have goats, though, goats don't mind climbing. Mam milks 'em – or I do.'

'Cor,' Biddy repeated. They had been walking across the hard standing between the huts and now they went into the steamy warmth of the cookhouse and queued for the big mugs of cocoa and the hefty slices of bread and jam. 'Wish I could milk. Wish I could touch a cow, come to that. Just on the nose, like,' she added hastily. 'I wouldn't like to touch them dangly things.'

'Cows won't hurt you,' Emily said. 'I've milked 'em when I've been staying over with my Uncle Arwen. Oh . . . I'll have cheese, please.' She took her food and the mug of cocoa and headed outside again, for despite a high wind which took the leaves off the trees and whirled them across the open grassland of the Balloon Training Centre, it was pleasant in the pale autumn sunshine. 'What's next on the agenda, anyway?'

'Splicing wire,' Biddy said, examining her scribbled timetable. 'That's why they've divided us into groups, because wire's a right bugger to splice. Shall we walk over to the hut, ask Kay and Jo how they got on as they come out?'

The two girls walked across together with a mug in one hand and their collosal sandwiches in the other and sat on the concrete waiting for Kay and Jo to emerge. 'How was it?' they chorussed as soon as the others appeared. 'We're next – got any tips?'

Kay held up her hands. The beautifully shaped, narrow filbert nails which were her pride and joy looked as though they had been nibbled by steel-toothed rats.

'It's murder,' she said bitterly. 'It ruins your nails. I wish I'd never joined, I'll never be able to splice wire, not without reducing my fingers to little, bleeding stumps.'

Jo, coming out of the hut with her hands jammed into the pockets of her jacket, winked at them.

'Poor Lady Muck,' she murmured. 'She'll survive – Sarge says tomorrow he'll teach us a trick or two to get round our weak womanly hands – his words, not mine. So don't try too hard or he may think we can all do it the tough way.'

'I just tell myself that every day that passes without me being slung out is a day nearer getting a site of our own,' Kay said, gazing sadly at her ruined nails. 'Can you believe it, in another month we'll be doing our practical!'

Biddy nodded and spoke through a mouthful of bread and cheese. 'Aye, I can believe it. Most days, when I've a moment free, I go down to the big field to watch the senior crews havin' a go with the real balloons, and with every lecture we're gerrin' nearer that stage. It's exciting . . . it looks easy, but I don't suppose it is. Gee, I'll be made up when I'm a real balloon operator!'

'Won't we all? And Corpy was saying there's a real chance of us staying together, going to the same site, because they want whole crews now that girls are taking over completely from the blokes. That really would be a turn-up for the books, wouldn't you say?' Biddy, who had not even considered the possibility of being separated until this moment, nodded vigorously.'

'Aye . . . it 'ud be grand to work together.'

They marched out to the practice field when they were almost at the end of their course, heads up, spines straight, arms swinging in perfect unison. It was a cold day in

December and a few days before they had heard on the wireless that the Japs had attacked the United States Pacific fleet as it lay at anchor in Pearl Harbour. The news had electrified everyone; now there could be no doubt, America would no longer hang back, they would be honour bound to come in.

'The Japs sank five battleships and killed over two thousand Yankees,' their flight sergeant told them as they drank cocoa by the NAAFI van and blew steaming breath into the icy air. 'They won't stand back and shake their heads now – they dare not. And with an extra Gawd knows how many men and ships and tanks, we'll mop 'em up in half the time.' He shook his head slowly to and fro. 'I pity them Japs an' Jerries, they won't know what hit 'em once the Yanks come in.'

So now Kay and Jo strode out, shoulders all but touching, excited by the thought of the Yanks doing their bit, proving that Britain no longer stood alone. Kay could see, out of the corner of her eye, first Biddy's swinging arm and then, when they wheeled, the peak of Emily's hat as they followed close behind. Emily and Biddy marched side by side, though the drill sergeant preferred them to pair up more or less to height and there was a good eight inches difference between ACW Bevan and ACW Bachelor.

But not even the news that Japan had declared war on Britain and the United States and that the United States had roared its own declaration of war after a hasty meeting of congress was sufficient to take the girls' minds off their own small part in the conflict.

'Don't forget, keep together,' Jo had hissed at them as they formed a line. 'Remember what Cocky said.'

Cocky Cochrane was their drill sergeant and he had

told the girls that they would be working on the balloons in groups and that, if a group worked well together, they would almost certainly be posted together.

'You could go anywhere, London, Liverpool, Cardiff, anywhere,' he informed them. 'But a good crew of balloon operatives are worth having; the Air Force will keep you together if they can.'

Naturally, this had given rise to an urgent wish to go around like Siamese twins and in the hut the previous night the girls had picked their own crews, partly in fun but, in Jo's case at least, mostly in earnest.

'We all know we get along fine with most people, but there's always someone you'd hate to find yourself stranded on a desert island with,' she said with all her usual bluntness. 'From what we've been told, balloon sites are pretty isolated from the rest of the Air Force, so we owe it to ourselves to get into compatible groups as far as possible.'

It sounded good, even easy, but Kay, marching along with her chin up and bottom tucked in, the way the drill sergeant recommended, could not help thinking that it was unlikely to be as simple as it appeared. The Air Force had a way of letting you believe you were winning and then leaping on you from a great height.

'Flight . . . Halt! Now, gels, for some genu-whine practice,' roared the flight sergeant. 'After all the thee-ory, let's see how you can handle the pigs. Smith, Burroughes, Bevan, Andrade, Markham, Green, Samuels, Bachelor, Hopkins, Matthews, with Corporal Beman . . . Dismiss! Frewin, Briggs, Stewart, Coleman . . .'

Oh damn, damn, damn, Kay thought, so much for getting into compatible groupings! That just means you, you and you. But she marched off with the other girls in the direction Corporal Beman had indicated. It was rotten luck that Jo wasn't with them, or perhaps it was fairer to say it was lucky that she, Emily and Biddy were together. And since they were being told off in tens, and a balloon crew should number a dozen, it probably didn't mean a thing. It would sort itself out over the next ten days or so.

As the corporal gave the order to stand easy Kay glanced back. Jo, with her team, was no more than fifty or sixty yards away and didn't look rebellious or sulky; indeed, she appeared to be listening intently, with a serious face, to what the NCO was saying. Perhaps she really is learning, Kay thought hopefully. Perhaps she's realised, as the rest of us have, that a bit of guile can do more for you in the service than all the rage and fury in the world. But soon she was too busy, too involved, to give much thought to Jo's behaviour. Their first close encounter with a balloon was about to begin, after ten weeks of classwork and preparation. And although, like the rest of the flight, she had occasionally watched the more advanced balloon operatives handling the great rubber monsters, she had never been this close to one before.

It was huge! A great, rotund silver elephant, it lay on the grass as though deeply asleep, tethered by ropes and sandbags to its bed until such time as the commands to 'Switch on winch . . . untie rip cord . . . untie guys . . . pay out spider . . .' were given.

'Very soon now you're goin' to put 'er up, girls,' the corporal said pleasantly. 'But she won't go up as she is . . . anyone know why?'

'She's not been topped up with gas, Corp,' someone said. 'That's why she's lying sort of floppy, like.'

'Well done, Matthews. But before we top 'er up, we do

an inspection and that gets done daily, so don't you never forget it. Now who's going to start? You, Bevan, Gawd knows you're small enough.'

Emily grinned and went forward to the nearest inspection port. She bent down and wriggled inside, the corporal getting his head and shoulders inside too. It was odd, Kay reflected, that constant familiarity with every part of a balloon in the textbooks did not prepare you for the sheer size of them, the toughness of the material from which they were made, the strangeness of these air monsters. The instructors called them pigs, but Kay thought her early nickname of rubber elephants was more accurate. And though there was nothing evil about them, though they looked thoroughly benign, seeing Emily simply swallowed up by this one had been a chastening experience.

And we're going to fly them, control them, Kay was telling herself, when the corporal beckoned her forward.

'You next, Markham. You're tall, but you'll still get inside. Once in, you check for . . . what?'

'Holes, tears, gas leakages, foreign bodies,' Kay said rapidly. 'Can I go in now, Corp?'

'Aye, get in. You won't be in such a hurry tomorrer!'

Kay bent and squeezed into the balloon's interior. It smelt odd, of the dope that small boys put on model aeroplanes and of the gas which was used to inflate it. It also smelt of wet tents – Kay had been a Guide in her youth – and was very much warmer inside than out, which gave her a moment's panic before she realised that of course it was warmer, it was out of the wind.

'Well, Markham? See anything?'

Kay's eyes had been scanning ever since she got inside. Now she shook her head and turned towards the corporal's head and shoulders, sticking up through the inspection port.

'No sign of trouble, Corp,' she said cheerfully. 'Can I come out, now?'

'Aye . . . come along, Andrade, you're next!'

'Topping up next, girls. How many weak little WAAFs does it take to lift a cylinder, then, eh?'

'Five . . . but we'll try it with four if you like, Corp,' Biddy said demurely. The corporal, who had been grinning tauntingly – why do men have to ram their physical superiority down our throats all the while? Kay wondered – wiped the smirk off his face and scowled, instead.

'Ho no you don't, Airwoman, that's against the rules and disobeyin' rules means . . . what does it mean, Airwoman?'

'A couple o' ruptures an' a broken back, Corp?' Biddy said. 'Or was you thinkin' more on the lines of me thunderin' round the parade ground with a thirty-pound pack on me back?'

The corporal didn't want to grin, but the girls could see he was having a job to keep a straight face. Good for Biddy, Kay thought exultantly. But I do hope the corporal doesn't get a down on her for answering back.

'Either or both, Airwoman,' the corporal said promptly, however, having gained control of his grin. 'Five of you . . . you, you, you, you and you . . . get over to the cylinders and fetch half-a-dozen over, one at a time. You, Markham and you, whatsername, connect up the hose.'

Kay and Emily ran to connect the hose. They knew how, in theory, and it did show that learning things from

60

textbooks wasn't entirely wasted because they had it in position in no time and very soon the big, heavy hose was connected to the topping-up trunk and the hydrogen was hissing into the balloon.

'It's grand, ain't it?' Biddy murmured as she and Kay stood watching the balloon gradually puffing out its cheeks. 'How high will they let us send it this time, d'you reckon?'

'Not far; just to close-haul I imagine,' Kay told her. 'If you and I and Em move round and stand about halfway down it, Corpy might tell us to free off one of the guys.'

'I'd rather be on the winch,' Biddy said longingly. 'I've always wanted to drive a lorry; this is the next best thing!'

Ten days later they got their postings and rushed to their hut to discuss who was going where. Biddy, running with the rest, told herself it would not have mattered, that she would have survived . . . but she felt as though she could have flown, she was so happy and relieved.

'We're together, the four of us,' Jo said, blowing out her cheeks with relief. 'Phew, it was touch and go, you know. But the thought of being incarcerated on a balloon site with Mildred Rawlings and Esther Pickles was so awful that I actually asked, politely, if I could be with you lot, because we worked well together, and though the wing officer only said, "We'll see," I tell myself she understood.'

'Doesn't matter whether she did or not,' Biddy observed. She would never have admitted it to anyone, but she had prayed nightly for the past month that God would be kind enough to keep her with the other three. Now, they were all sprawling on Kay's bed, whilst around them WAAFs discussed their postings or wrote letters to parents, giving their new addresses. 'What matters, queen, is that we're off to London tomorrer, all of us, to work at the same site. Ain't that just wonderful?'

'London, though,' Kay said rather gloomily. 'It'll be pretty grim, I shouldn't wonder. They have more raids than anywhere . . . still, that's why we joined, to whack the jerries, and whack them we will.'

'London's still got more going on in it than anywhere else, though.' Jo pointed out. 'More dances, more theatres, more cinemas . . . and lots of lovely men on leave, I expect . . . Yanks, too. They say Rainbow Corner's alive with 'em.'

'Oh, doughboys; I can take 'em or leave 'em,' Biddy said with grand disdain. 'I can't gerrover us being together, though.' As she spoke she was unbuttoning her battledress top and flinging it on the bed. 'Do you realise by Christmas we'll be snugged down on our brand-new site, with our own pig to fly? Eh, it'll be good to get away from that bloody old drill sergeant, made me life a misery he has.'

'We're going to be the best balloon ops the Air Force has ever seen,' Jo said with all her usual conviction. She got to her feet and grabbed Kay, and together they polkad between the beds whilst Biddy ran alongside them doing a sort of old-tyme waltz and Emily watched and smiled.

'I'm going to write to Mam and Da, tell them the good news,' Emily said at last, when the others had finished gloating and flung themselves onto their beds. 'They knew I was worried in case we got separated. They'll be pleased for us.'

'We all ought to write,' Kay said at once. 'I'll tell Phil, though heaven knows when he'll get my letter. Or if, I suppose. Africa's a long way away.'

'Walls have ears,' Biddy and Emily chorused. 'Or so you're always telling us, Kay,' Emily added.

Kay shrugged.

'I know . . . well, let's get writing, because we'll have to pack tonight if we're leaving first thing tomorrow and I can't see both my uniforms fitting into my kitbag, let alone all the bits and bobs I've somehow managed to acquire. Oh, I'm out of airmail paper; anyone got some I can scrounge?'

Another girl, also in their flight, tossed a pad across and Kay thanked her, got out her pen and bottle of Quink, and started to write. After some skirmishing the others joined her. Jo was the first to finish and Biddy thought, not for the first time, that Jo's letters were always short and quite rare, too. Thinking about it, she realised that Jo never talked about her home or her people, either, unlike everyone else. Now that is odd, Biddy told herself, because I know all about Emily's parents and her farm and her sheepdog, Skittle, and almost more than I want to know about Phil Markham – you could scarcely get a remark out of Kay at first without her inserting Phil's name in it somewhere – and about Kay's father who works for the Min. of Ag., and her mother who is something important in the Women's Voluntary Service. And they know all about me mam and dad and the kids, Biddy thought now, making an ink blot and hastily rubbing it up with the edge of her handkerchief. I told 'em about the time our Maria got a good conduct mark in school though it was her what climbed up an' stuck some school knickers on the weathervane. And about our Bobby getting hauled before the beak for nickin' a cabbage. Now Jo comes from a nice place, Chester's a lovely city, I remember me mam saying so, she's got no brothers or sisters, but she almost never mentions her home or her mam and dad. Now that I do call odd.

Still. Everyone was different and no doubt Jo had her reasons. We'll find out what they are, in time, Biddy told herself comfortably, continuing with her letter. Presently she looked up, frowning across at Emily.

'Em . . . how d'you spell "velocity"?'

3

The day was cold with a sharp wind blowing and grey clouds scudding overhead. As the girls walked rather uncertainly onto the site there was a sharp flurry of snow. Kay had been put in temporary charge of the party whilst on board the train and in the gharry which had brought them first to their new HQ to draw their bedding and then here, but suddenly she felt very inadequate. She looked around her. The balloon site was a girl's school – or rather, it had been. The school buildings had been taken over as living accommodation for an ack-ack battery and were now separated from the games field by six-foot chain link fencing, and the site itself, on a freezing December day with snow falling, looked horribly unwelcoming. In the middle distance she could see what looked like a cricket pavilion and that was flanked by a long, low hut, but apart from the barrage balloon, bedded down and swaying gently in its rope cradle, there was nothing else to see.

'And where the 'ell do we go from 'ere?' someone muttered and Kay thought wretchedly that she felt just the same, only as she had been put in charge, she could scarcely give voice her own feelings. 'Where's the red carpet, eh, girls? Where's the bloody reception committee?'

'They'll be down there, in the hut . . . or the pavilion or whatever,' Kay said. She straightened her shoulders and hefted her kitbag once more, picked up her suitcase which she had stood down at her feet whilst the girls disembarked from the gharry, and headed determinedly out across the frosted grass. 'Remember we're taking over from blokes, so you can't expect much of a welcome – they're going off to be trained as fitters and mechanics and things, that'll be all they're thinking about.'

'Different from most other blokes, then,' someone whispered in the ranks. Kay frowned and turned round sharply; fifteen bland little faces beneath shiny peaked caps looked back at her.

'All right? Then we'd best get over there.'

She strode off and Jo caught up with her, giving her a lopsided, excited grin.

'What a turn-up for the books, eh? D'you think they've already left? They could have done, perhaps it's an empty hut, like the *Marie Celeste*, sailing onwards forever across the school playing fields.'

'Oh shut up, Jo,' Kay muttered, narrowing her eyes against the whirling flakes. 'Besides, there'll be a corporal and a sergeant to meet us, and an officer of some description – a WAAF officer, I think, not a feller. They won't all have gone off, someone will be around just you see.'

They reached the pavilion. Kay stared at the dark windows, then swung round to her companions.

'Right, let's go in. Someone probably hasn't heard us, they must be crouching over a stove or . . . or something. I thought every site had two guards on duty, day and night. These are odd sorts of guards . . . but it is a vile day.'

She marched up the three wooden steps, banged on the door and after a moment opened it. A largish, dark room met her eyes, with a stove, all too plainly out and cold, a pile of what looked like folding chairs and tables gathering dust against one wall and a couple of sagging easy chairs. Nothing else, neither carpet nor curtains, though there were the inevitable blackout blinds half pulled down already.

'I told you,' Jo muttered gleefully in her ear. 'It's the *Marie Celeste*; it's been abandoned.'

'But we were told they'd wait until we arrived, hand over properly,' Kay said, bewildered. 'And where are the NCOs?'

'Yes, where the blazes are they?' Jo echoed. 'Oh well, you're the boss, Kay. What do we do next?'

There was just a trace of malice in her tone and Kay, who had been feeling very lost and lonely, suddenly felt good, old-fashioned anger warm her. This was the sort of situation where it would be easy to flounder, lose control, which was what Jo obviously expected, but Kay intended to do no such thing. If she was in charge then she would be in charge – no, she would bloody well be in charge, she told herself . . . and turned to the girls now crowding uncertainly around the doorway.

'Very well, the fellers have left but we're not helpless, so we'll make ourselves at home. Is that a kitchen out the back, through that door? Bevan, go and take a look, would you? Go with her, Matthews, and put a kettle on, try to get some tea on the go. We've been travelling all day, we could all do with a wad and some char.'

Emily and ACW Matthews dumped their belongings and hurried across the room and into the back. Emily popped her head round the door after a few seconds.

'Yes, it's a kitchen, Kay,' she said joyfully. 'There's a kettle and a tap and a cooker but no matches. Anyone got any?'

The smokers all fumbled in their pockets and a box of matches sailed through the air. Emily fielded it neatly and disappeared once more.

'Thanks,' she said, her voice slightly muffled. 'Tea in ten minutes – if we can find the tea, that is.'

'Now, anyone any good at lighting fires?' Kay asked briskly. 'That stove's the sort we had at the training centre, it shouldn't be too hard to light. Jo, can you? Thanks. The rest of us will go over to the hut, find our sleeping accommodation and see what's what.'

'Could someone take my bedding?' Jo asked hopefully. 'That stove hasn't been lit for some time and I'll have to find kindling, paper and so on. It is going to take me a while to get it going and I don't want to be stuck with a bed right by the door in the draught, or under a broken window or something.'

'Self, self,' Biddy said mockingly, bending down and taking Jo's bedding from the floor where she had dropped it. 'We don't none of us fancy that, queen. Still, I'll bag you a decent pit if you like.'

'Thanks, Biddy,' Jo said, sounding genuinely grateful. 'What about grub, Kay? I'm starving.'

'We all are,' Kay said shortly. 'There'll be food in the kitchen no doubt and when we get our bedding sorted out we'll try to get a meal of some description together. Anyway, the NCOs are bound to turn up soon.'

'Not if there's been a mistake and they've all be posted,' Betty Meadowes said mournfully. 'I've got a bad feel about this place, Kay. I bet there's ghosts.'

'Oh Betty, try not to be a bigger fool than you really are,' Betty's friend Edna said despairingly. 'You get ghosts in old halls and manors and that, not in day schools! Kay's right, we ought to go and look in the hut.'

Kay led the way out of the pavilion and over to the Nissen hut. Jo had been right when she said there would be draughts and a broken window; was it first-rate guesswork or had she spotted the pane of glass which lay broken beside the hut, Kay wondered, approaching the long wooden building. She pushed uncertainly at the door and it swung inwards with a loud creak which, despite herself, make her jump and step back, a hand flying to her throat. Good job Jo was still in the pavilion with the stove, she thought thankfully; she would not have let Kay's moment of fright go unremarked.

Kay pushed the blackout curtain hanging in front of the door aside and walked into the hut. There were a great many beds, much closer than in normal WAAF billets, stacked at present with the pillows neatly on top of the three sections of 'biscuit' which made up into a mattress, but obviously awaiting the new arrivals. The windows were criss-crossed with sticky tape against bomb blast, and there were the usual blackout curtains, all pulled back now, though dusk was rapidly falling. Kay cleared her throat.

'Grab a bed, everyone, and make it up. I suppose we'd better light the stove . . . Andy, you've got a sensible head on your shoulders, can you go and see how Jo and the teamakers are getting along? We'll double up to get your bed and the others' made up by the time you get back.'

'Is the electric light working?' someone said uncertainly. Before Kay could answer the girl who had spoken had pressed the switch; pale light flooded the room, turning the windows from grey to black and causing at least a dozen people to say sharply, 'Put that bloody light out!' before Kay had leapt for the switch and flicked it up once more.

'Sorry, Kay,' the girl said, reddening. 'But it's not really dark out, yet, I just wanted to see . . .'

'You should have pulled the curtains first,' Kay

advised her. 'Better safe than sorry, Pauline. Now girls, let's pull all the curtains across and then we can have the light on without worrying. I think for speed's sake we should get into pairs to make the beds.'

She wondered whether the girls would continue to obey her instructions now that they were actually on site; after all, they had been told she was in charge until they arrived at their destination, when it was expected by everyone, including the girls themselves, that NCOs, if not their officer, would be there to greet them. But it was soon clear that the Air Force had done its work well. The girls simply knuckled down to getting the beds made up as quickly as possible and then, at Kay's suggestion, swiftly unpacked and began to hang up uniforms and fill lockers with their miscellaneous possessions. Photographs of loved ones were produced, and some posters. Very soon the hut began to look almost like a home, Kay thought.

By the time this was finished, Andrews, carefully bearing a shovel with a few live coals on it, came back into the hut accompanied by Jo, who had a bucket swinging from one hand which contained a crumpled newspaper, a handful of kindling wood and a quantity of coke.

'Oh, well done, you two,' Kay said spontaneously and saw the pair smile proudly.

'Better done than you know, Kay,' Jo said. 'There was no wood or newspaper and precious little fuel, so I nipped round to the gunners from the ack-ack battery and asked if we could borrow some, just for tonight. They were really nice and gave me enough for both stoves and then they told me there's a fish and chip van comes round in an hour, if we can't find any food here.'

'Oh, there's bound to be food, isn't there?' Kay said

uneasily. 'They wouldn't leave us here without any grub, surely? Besides, fish and chips aren't cheap . . . the Air Force is supposed to feed us, not abandon us!'

'And there's a phone in the pavilion place,' Andy volunteered. 'Can't we ring HQ or the nearest Balloon Centre, explain what's happened?'

'Yes, of course, and that's what we'll do if no one's turned up by the time we've drunk our tea,' Kay said, greatly relieved to realise that there was a way out of this apparent mess. 'All the beds are done, so if you just light the stove, you two, then we can all go over to the pavilion and get ourselves a drink. Did the girls find any bread or anything in the kitchen, do you know?'

'Emily was really cheesed off,' Jo said, crumpling the newsprint into balls and dropping it in through the round hole at the top, then leaning in and endeavouring to get the kindling to stand upright. 'She says there's nothing . . . but perhaps she'll have found the grubbery by this time.'

'If there is one,' someone else said ruefully. 'If the RAF haven't taken it all with them.'

'They left the blimp,' another girl put in. 'It's getting dark, Kay; should we check her before it's too dark to see?'

'Oh, crumpets, I suppose we ought . . . no, perhaps not, we don't even know where the cylinders are stored . . . suppose there's a raid?' Kay said rapidly, clutching her head. 'Honestly girls, I don't think we should start peering into the blimp's guts in the dusk, and as for putting her up . . . well, it's a dreadful night, we'd probably lose her. If we have a phone call from the centre we'll explain what's happened and they'll send someone down. Now we'll go back to the pavilion and see how the cooks are getting on and decide what to do about a meal.'

71

'I'll have to stay here,' Jo said disgustedly. 'The bloody thing won't light! It ignored the live coals completely and I've dropped six matches in and they just go out without a word!'

'Have you cleared the ash?' Andy said. 'If not . . .'

'Oh! Bugger bugger bugger,' Jo said rapidly. 'I don't think the ash has been emptied for a million years, now you come to mention it. It's pressing up against the bars . . . I'll just . . .'

She lifted the door-flap in the bottom of the stove and pulled; ash, fine and pinkish grey, billowed out, covering everything within a radius of ten feet, including WAAFs. Choice language issued from more than one mouth and Jo swore colourfully as she scraped her knuckles on the descending door.

'Damn and blast and hell and worse!' she exclaimed furiously. 'Oh, empty it someone, I can't do everything!'

'You're doing very well,' Kay said, tactfully if untruthfully. 'See you in a moment, Jo. If you aren't over in five minutes I'll send someone back here with a cuppa.'

Jo did her best with that stove. She cursed it, pleaded with it, made it extravagant promises and used a whole box of matches on it. She tried dropping matches in through the hole at the top and lighting it more conventionally through the flap at the bottom. The stove just stood there, smirking at her, and refused, totally refused, to light.

After ten minutes of trying Emily came in carrying two cups of tea.

'Hey, Jo, I've bought your char and mine,' she said, sinking onto the end of the nearest bed. 'Is that the famous stove? I should think it's a relic from the Boer War, wouldn't you? How on earth did you manage to light it?'

'Ha bloody ha,' Jo said sulkily. 'I haven't lit it, you blithering bonehead, it's dead as a dodo – deader, probably. It's a beastly stove and I hate it and I'm giving up. You can have a go if you've got any matches, I've used all mine.'

'How about boot polish? Or Brasso?' Emily said.

Jo stared, wide-eyed at such low cunning. 'You couldn't light it with Brasso, could you? Or boot polish?'

'Dunno; we could give it a whirl, though. Hang on here and drink your tea whilst I fetch some more matches.'

Emily came back with the matches and the news that Kay had found some food but was doubtful whether they ought to use it. 'It's all packed in a big old chest, and it's labelled Emergency Rations – use only if ordered to do so,' she explained. 'Kay's standing on one foot with her forefinger in her mouth, staring at it as though it might explode at any moment. Oh Jo, aren't you glad you're not her?'

'In a way I am,' Jo said guardedly. She took the matches and bent over the stove once more. 'Light, you bastard!' she commanded it. 'Light or it's the dreaded Brasso down your beastly gullet next!'

Half an hour later two weary, sooty WAAFs made their way across to the pavilion. The stove had beaten them. It had devoured the second box of matches, the best part of a tin of Brasso and kindling cunningly smeared with Cherry Blossom Boot Polish, and it had refused to delight their hearts with even the slightest smudge of smoke.

'Who would believe the stove existed that just wouldn't light?' Jo moaned as she and Emily climbed the three steps and pushed open the curtain-shrouded door. 'How did the fellers go on, d'you suppose? Ah, God, I could murder a stew, even that awful stuff that cooky used to produce at the training centre. I say, what's that wonderful smell?' They entered the room to find WAAFs squatting on the floor, on the chairs, even perched on the long table. Kay looked up and waved greasy fingers at them.

'Yours is in the oven,' she said thickly. 'Fish and chips, because there really isn't anything else, only dried milk and a bit of tea. Did you get it going?'

'No,' Jo admitted crossly. She had wanted so badly to show Kay that she, Jo, could be just as efficient, given the opportunity. 'There's something wrong with it, but I don't know what. Em and I tried and tried, we used two whole boxes of matches and it never even sparked. We're going to have to sleep in an icy hut, I'm afraid.'

'Well, we're all so tired we could probably sleep on the parade ground,' Kay said quite cheerfully. 'Sit down, both of you. I'll fetch your grub.'

'On what?' growled poor Jo, looking round her. 'All the chairs are taken and I'm fed up with floors.'

'Yes, fair's fair. Simmonds and Peck, you've finished your grub, can you sit on the floor for a bit, whilst these two eat?'

Two girls got up and Jo and Emily collapsed onto their seats whilst Kay bustled out into the kitchen and came back presently with two newspaper wrapped parcels. 'Cod and chips twice,' she said grandly. 'I just hope the Air Force will pay us back – we had a whip-round because no one had enough money to buy thirty-two lots of fish and chips, but it isn't fair to make us pay for our own meals.'

'There isn't even any cocoa,' Biddy said in an outraged tone, shuffling over to sit by Jo. 'Not even a loaf! And that

74

stove's not throwing out much heat, I can tell you that. When our officer comes round tomorrer I'm goin' to tell her a thing or three.'

'Let Kay do a proper report,' Jo advised, rapidly eating chips. 'Was there any salt? My top chips are lovely and salty, but the underneath ones are rather bland.'

'Don't be so fussy, we did our best,' Kay called, hearing the complaint. 'They've been in the oven a while, that's the snag. And I've tried the phone, incidentally, but the wretched thing only makes buzzing noises at me. It doesn't seem to be properly connected.'

'Well it's very dark and overcast, I don't suppose there will be a raid, which is one comfort . . .' Jo was beginning, when the telephone bell rang sharply.

Kay had snatched it off its cradle and put it to her ear before she had thought. 'Yes? ACW Markham speaking,' she said briskly. 'May I ask . . . oh!'

'What was it?' Jo asked curiously. Kay's eyes had rounded and the colour had drained from her cheeks. 'What happened?'

'It's an alert,' Kay said hollowly. 'I – I didn't get a chance to explain or anything, I'm not even sure if the fellow the other end heard me. He just barked "Raiders crossing the south coast; Site 12 balloon to five thousand feet," and then his receiver crashed down.'

'Dear God! We can't . . . we don't know anything about this balloon . . . she'll need topping up . . . we shan't have time . . .' The chorus of voices battered at Kay's ears but at least it gave her time to think. When she had thought she held up a hand.

'Hush! We've got time, if we start at once. We've done it a hundred times, in practice, now we can do it for real. Can't we?'

75

'Not without someone to give the orders . . . what about the inspection, suppose she's bedded down because she's torn . . . shot at.' The chorus sounded as appalled as Kay realised she felt, but she shook her head at them.

'Inspection's carried out every day, regardless. Right? She'll have been inspected this morning, she'll be fit to fly. Come on, only you'd best put your greatcoats on, it's dreadfully cold out there.'

It was cold. Frightening, too, Emily considered, as they surrounded the balloon. A crew should have consisted of twelve WAAFs, but both crews were out here, which would be a real help because of their inexperience.

They had started by topping up with gas and this had gone extraordinarily well. Kay had praised everyone concerned lavishly, and now she was sending people to different positions, and Jo was climbing aboard the winch lorry. Biddy was on the cradle which paid the cable in and out, looking calm and unworried, Emily was on the port guy and Kay was standing close to the winch, saying something to Jo, perched in the cab above her. Those two are downright comical, Emily thought, they're so different, Kay's cool and determined to do things right, and Jo is simply determined to have her own way at all cost. But when trouble comes they'll work as a team and a darned good one, too.

And they did. Standing behind the winch, Kay began to shout the orders and Jo repeated them in stentorian tones which were all too necessary since, though the snow had stopped, it was windy and dark.

'Everyone in their places? Right. We'll have her up to close-haul first, then higher. We won't arm her – we can't, we haven't got the time, but we'll do everything else right.

76

I'm relying on you, girls! All set? Then switch on the winch . . . untie the ripcord . . .'

Thinking about it later that night, when she was curled up on a chair in the pavilion, with the telephone close by her and her blanket and various garments spread over her, Kay decided they had not done badly. After all, it was the first time they had flown a balloon at night, the first time they'd had neither corporal nor sergeant to give the orders, the first time they had been forced to hurry.

And it had gone off extraordinarily well. From the moment when she had shouted, 'Stop winch,' and had seen Jo obey, she had known in her heart that they had cracked it; above their heads, in the windy dark with the snow gusting fitfully around her, the blimp which the girls had already christened Bessie Bunter floated, yawing to port and starboard but in her rightful place, now. They could not see her because the cloud cover was low, but they could see the cable which tethered her to the earth when all the guy ropes had been released, and it curved away into the blackness in the way that Kay thought it should.

The girls were standing back, gazing up at the grey clouds above as though they expected them to part and allow the balloon to make an appearance, presumably bowing to right and left, the way a star should. Jo had climbed down from the winch lorry and was massaging her upper arms and several of the girls were doing the loosening exercises which one of the PT instructors had told them to use after hard physical effort. Kay cleared her throat and spoke.

'Right, everyone. We'll have four on watch out here, plus me, four in the pavilion, and we'd better have two on guard duty, only it won't be normal guard duty, because we've not been issued with truncheons and anyway we've not done guard duty when we practised our work. We'll just walk around the perimeter of the site, in pairs, keeping an eye open for – well, for anything unusual. And the rest of you had better go to bed. Only when the raiders start coming over you'd best get under your beds and when the call comes from HQ to bring her down you'll have to get up, so don't undress, just lie on top of the covers and – and snooze.'

I could have said it more succinctly, Kay told herself rather despairingly as she handed out jobs, but I'm thinking on my feet; I don't believe I'm doing badly either, all things considered.

Kay had seen everyone deployed – she had picked Jo and Emily to do guard duty, which was taking friendship rather far, perhaps, but she knew she could trust them. They had both worked like dogs ever since they had arrived at the site, and it must have gone against the grain for Jo to take orders from me, Kay told herself. Jo would probably have managed the whole thing much better had she been the one in charge, but it just happened that the officer's eye had lighted on Kay first . . .

The girls were beginning to disperse and Kay was about to go into the kitchen when the telephone had rung again. Kay turned away from the kitchen and raced to the instrument, grabbing it off its hook so sharply that she nearly dropped it and had to fumble it to her ear, heart racing.

'ACW Mark . . .' she began, but was interrupted.

'Raiders turned back after attacking coastal towns,' the voice said laconically. 'No further alert.'

Kay tried to stop a big smile from spreading over her

face as the receiver the other end went down, but she couldn't help it. Thank God! She had been absolutely dreading the appearance of aircraft, the necessity of finding some sort of air raid shelter for the girls under her command if enemy action started, having to calm fears, perhaps persuade them to go out into a barrage of bombs and gunfire to bring the balloon down to close-haul or something similar. And now she would be all right. She would get the girls together again, tell everyone to get to bed, and sit quietly in the pavilion by the telephone until morning.

But there had to be guards, she knew that very well. Balloon sites were vulnerable not only to enemy attack but also to petty theft; they had been warned at the training centre that they must keep an eye open all the time for unauthorised personnel poking around on their sites. Jo and Emily could do the first half of the night, she would tell someone else to relieve them at . . . she glanced at her watch. Goodness, it was already eleven o'clock, so if she got Gillian Price and Laura Atkins to do the four a.m. to eight a.m. watch, that would mean Jo and Emily got some sleep, if not a great deal.

Accordingly, she had instructed the girls to go to bed and had told Gillian and Laura to set their alarm for 3.45 a.m. She also warned them that if they didn't wake, someone would have to wake them, using any means at their disposal, such as cold water and shouts. Laura nodded, but a deep frown appeared on Gillian's brow.

'You was only in charge on the train an' that, Kay Markham,' she said aggressively. 'I don't see you've any right to order me an' Laura around like that. I'm going to bed and I'm goin' to stay there. I've had a hard day, I need my rest an' I intend to get it.'

They were in the pavilion, with a dozen or more girls listening. Kay felt the hot blood rush up under her pale skin and wanted to die of embarrassment. She was only doing her best, that Gillian was a horrible girl! But she drew herself up to her full height and looked coldly down at Gillian Price, who had greasy hair and a vindictive little weasel-face. This was only another form of school bullying and if she let Gillian get away with it everyone would think she was a walkover and treat her accordingly.

'If I have any nonsense of that sort, ACW Price, you'll find yourself on a charge tomorrow,' she said quite pleasantly. 'The only reason I'm not doing anything now is that I appreciate you really are tired, as we all are. But that doesn't excuse insubordination, does it?'

Gillian turned away, mumbling something under her breath, something which Kay deemed it politic not to hear. She looked across at the other WAAFs, waiting to be dismissed, and could tell from the way they looked back at her that they, at least, thought she had won the encounter.

'Now any questions, anyone?' she had asked briskly. 'Jo, Emily? Have you got good strong torches?'

'Yes thanks, Kay,' Jo said, answering for them both since Emily had only nodded. She was grinning; Jo thinks I've done all right and doesn't mind me knowing it, Kay thought, very relieved. She's all right herself, is Jo. 'Can we have a hot drink before we start?'

'Good idea,' Kay had said at once. She was longing for a drink too, now that Jo had mentioned it. 'I'll go and boil a kettle, then I'll do guard duty whilst you have your drink – well, I'll keep an eye on Bessie and the perimeter fence whilst you have your drink, anyway – then I'll sit by the

80

telephone until morning, just in case a call comes through.'

Biddy was glad to settle down in her bed, though like most of the other girls she did not undress. The cold was too severe for that. Instead, she simply took off her greatcoat and jacket, slid off her skirt and shoes and put on the trousers they had been issued with, and sat down on the edge of her bed. She would have liked to have a chat to Emily, but Emily was on guard duty, so she turned to Joan Rogers, in the next bed.

'Well, wharra turn-up, eh, Joanie? It's perishin' cold in this bleedin' hut, but warmer than marchin' round outside – poor old Em, eh?'

'Rather her than me,' Joan agreed. 'Reckon we'll sleep like tops tonight though, Biddy, after the sort of day we've had.'

'Hope you're right,' Biddy said absently. 'Wonder if I could get my pyjamas over this lot. Or does it make you cold if your clothes is too tight?'

'I wouldn't risk it,' Joan advised. She climbed briskly between the blankets and lay her head cautiously on the pillow. 'Night then, Biddy. Sweet dreams.'

'Yes, don't choose tonight to 'ave one o' them screamin' fits,' Gillian Price said aggressively from her own bed. 'If you keep me awake you can bleedin' well do guard duty instead o' me, I'm tellin' ya.'

Biddy climbed into her own bed and pulled the blankets up as far as they would go. 'I don't 'ave them nightmares no more,' she said with dignity. 'Anyroad, if you'd been in the 'Pool when it were bombed I daresay you'd 'ave nightmares.'

ACW Price sniffed but said no more and the girl on the

other side of Joan, who was only just prepared for bed, looked around her. 'Can I turn the light out an' pull the blackouts back?' she asked. 'I'm last tonight.'

It was already traditional amongst them that the last into bed should turn the light out and pull back the curtains if there was no corporal to do it for them.

'Yes but don't open the windows,' a voice answered. 'If you do, the others will come in tomorrow and find a couple of dozen frozen corpses.'

'Aye, you're right there,' Joan said, her voice muffled by blankets. 'Not that we'll wake when it gets light, not after today.'

Biddy lay and watched as Sylvia turned off the light and padded up the hut, pulling the curtains back to let in the dim grey light. Wish I could thump that Price gal, she found herself thinking. Always making trouble for someone – as if I enjoyed having nightmares! But with luck they wouldn't happen any more, now she was used to her new life.

Biddy curled into a ball to conserve what warmth she had and within seconds was deeply sleep. She did not dream.

'All right, Em, Jo? Off you go, then, but come back for a warm every now and then and I'll go out for a turn or two. It'll be fairer.'

Emily smiled at Kay. The white-gold hair, caught back from her face with a rubber band, looked as impeccable as ever, but Kay's face was pale, her blue eyes dark shadowed, her skin smudged with fatigue. But Emily thought Kay had worked miracles – Gillian Price was a frightening and difficult person for an NCO to deal with, let alone a fellow Aircraftwoman – and was devoutly

82

grateful that the officer's eye had not fallen on ACW Bevan when she was handing out duties earlier that day. I'd never even have got them to London, Emily thought as she put her empty mug down on the nearest table. I don't have a way with folk, like Kay does. Why, Jo resented Kay telling us what to do at first, but I think she realised that it wasn't all that easy, to give orders to girls who have only known you as one of themselves before, and she ended up admiring Kay. And Jo's generous, her thoughts continued. What's more, she's the only other person in the whole flight who could have done what Kay did – you have to give her credit.

'Come along, Emily,' Jo said now, having finished her tea and put her own cup down. 'Let's get out into all that cold and dark. At least the snow's stopped.' She turned to Kay. 'Try to sleep, hon,' she said, and her voice was gentler than Emily had ever heard it before. 'We've all had a tough day, but yours beggars description.'

Kay nodded. 'I'll try,' she said. 'Don't forget, come back every hour and I'll give you each a fifteen minute break.'

Jo picked up her torch and headed for the door, Emily following close on her heels. They made sure the blackout curtain had fallen into place behind them before they pushed open the door and slipped out into the night.

'Round to the left first, I think,' Jo murmured, when they had got their night-eyes. 'We won't shine our torches unless we see something suspicious. And we'll keep our eyes peeled for a shelter, because sometimes they're underground – we don't want to find it the hard way.'

'The hard way?'

'Oh Em, by falling down the steps,' Jo said impatiently. 'Mind where you walk in other words. Isn't it odd how the dark gradually becomes light when you've been out in it for a bit?'

'Yes. It's just the contrast which makes it seem so dark,' Emily said. 'Doesn't the school look huge against the sky? I can't see Bessie, can you?'

Jo stared upwards.

'No. But it hasn't snowed much apart from those few flurries when we first arrived and the wind's not strong. In fact it's scarcely more than a breeze, so she'll be keeping her position quite well I imagine. And that's her job – to stop the jerries from flying low and strafing the streets. They say the aircraft can get cut clean in two if they hit the cable, so I hope they leave her up until it's light – then we'll be able to see what's happening as we bed her down.'

'True. Mind you, Kay may let us sleep over a bit, having done our stint until four a.m. D'you think she's done well, Jo?'

'Very well,' Jo said. 'I think I could take command, but I wouldn't have been so cool with Gilly Price, I'd have batted her silly head and got the cops to chuck her into the cooler, that's what I'd have done.'

'There isn't a cooler,' Emily said with a chuckle. 'Nor any cops for that matter. This isn't Balloon Centre, you know.'

'No. That's what I mean. Kay was thrown very much on her own resources, and they didn't let her down. But I'm going to learn from today, because I don't want to spend the whole war as an aircraftwoman. My father would be very disappointed if I did. He thinks I'm officer material and I'd love to prove him right. He'd be most awfully pleased, Em, and I do want to please him.'

They were walking at a good pace round the perimeter

fence and were just about opposite the school at this point. Emily had never heard Jo talk about her family and was intrigued to find that Jo, like herself, regarded her father highly. Emily loved her mother very much, but Da was something different again.

'My dad didn't really want me to join the WAAF at first, because I was useful, like, on the farm,' she said shyly. 'But he come round to it, in the end. Said it wasn't right that none of the Bevans had gone, said it was the least he and Mam could do, to let me help in the fight. But I'm not officer material, and Da would be the first to admit it. A good follower, yes, I hope so, but never a leader.'

Jo laughed. 'You mustn't be so timid, Em, I bet you've got qualities which the WAAF can bring out, you could probably lead just as well as Kay or myself. I say, what are those little hut things round the back of the pavilion?'

'Lavvies,' Emily said, after a good look. 'Earth closets. We've got one on the farm, it's a twin-seater.'

'A twin-seater? Good God! Does that mean . . . well, it seems rather strange . . . who . . . how?'

Emily gave Jo a shove. 'Honestly, Jo! You don't share it – well, I suppose you could, but we don't. It – it takes twice as long to fill, that's all.'

'Oh. And that's one of them?'

'It's three, I think,' Emily said after another long look. 'Shall we walk round that way this time? After all, someone could be lurking back there, I suppose.'

'In that case don't let's,' Jo said, nevertheless walking towards the small huts. 'I don't want to be a dead hero, I just want to be a live WAAF!'

'I don't suppose lurkers want to kill WAAFs, they probably just want to nick our grub, unless they're spies, of course, and then they'll want to listen to our

85

conversation and hear how many guns and things we've got,' Emily said rather doubtfully. 'Not that I'd choose to eavesdrop on privy talk, I don't think.'

'Rather not,' Jo agreed, entering into the spirit of the thing. 'Especially if you had to get really close and stick your ear against the door . . . pooh!'

'Better than your nose . . .' Emily was beginning, when a very odd noise indeed came from the last of the small huts. She clutched Jo's arm. 'My God, what was that?'

'Someone's having a sitting,' Jo said brightly after a moment. 'Whoever it is is having problems . . . what an upset stomach!'

A low, gurgling moan came from the last of the huts. Emily shook her head at Jo and pulled her to a halt. 'It's not that at all, someone's in trouble, by the sound of it. What'll we do, Jo?'

'Knock on the door? Ask if whoever's in there needs help?' Jo suggested. 'Only we might get a dusty answer . . . tell you what, let's move away and then come back noisily. If someone really is in trouble, perhaps he or she will hear our voices and call out.'

Accordingly, they retraced their steps and approached the row of earth-closets once more, this time talking quite audibly instead of in the hushed tones natural to wakeful people amongst assorted sleepers.

'So I went over to the ack-ack battery and asked them if they knew where everyone was, and the chap in charge said they'd left earlier in the day and a few girls had turned up and then gone again and they didn't know what was going on either. Then I asked where our lot had kept their coke and kindling and he didn't know but he offered to lend us some of theirs, and told me about the fish and chip van . . . what was that?'

86

The gurgling moan broke out again but this time, or so it seemed to Emily, it was full of menace, laced liberally with warning. Now just where had she heard a sound like that before? She knew it, only it was just on the outer edge of her memory, as elusive as one tune when another is being played.

'I don't know . . . is it coming from the hut, Jo, or behind it?'

Jo shrugged; even in the darkness Emily could see how uneasy her friend had become. 'Can't tell. It's a damned funny noise . . .' She moved nearer the hut and suddenly raised her voice. 'Hello you in there – are you all right?'

'Jo, it's coming from the end hut – and the door's swinging open!'

Before their horrified eyes the door did indeed swing partly open, but no one emerged and Jo's composure suddenly broke.

'It's a ghost!' she yelped. 'Run, Em!' She grabbed Emily's arm and tried to pull her away but Emily stood her ground.

'I don't believe in ghosts and nor do you, Jo,' she said severely. 'Let's get a bit closer.'

'A bit closer?' Jo squeaked with the air of one who doubts the other's sanity. 'A bit closer, when you saw the door swing open and no one come out?'

'No one came out, so someone's still in there,' Emily said soothingly. 'Come on, be sensible. You aren't really scared of a creaking privy door, are you?'

'Scared? Me?' Jo was drawing herself up and starting to glare when the gurgling moan broke out again and Jo, abandoning principles – and Emily – hurled herself backwards trying to get her torch out of her pocket as she did so and dropping it heavily onto the cold ground. 'Em

. . . do be careful, there could be anything in there!'

Emily walked – admittedly on tiptoe – nearer to the end hut. It was true enough, the door was now half open and she could see no one, the place appeared to be completely empty. But there had been that odd noise, they had both heard it, and the door could scarcely have opened of its own accord. She got out her torch and flashed it cautiously into the dark aperture behind the door and . . . oh my God!

In a brief flash of the torchlight she could see eyes. Flashing one moment green, the next red, they were phantom eyes all right, and furious eyes too, narrowed and vindictive. Despite her resolve, Emily gave a squeak and, in moving back, collided with Jo, cautiously moving forward. The torch jerked . . . pointed ears, a long, pointed snout . . .

'It's a bloody wolf!' Jo exclaimed, grabbing Emily's arm and shaking it excitedly. 'It'll have us for two pins . . . let's get out of here!'

'It's a dog,' Emily said dampingly. She had, in the second flash of the torch, seen the apprehensive look in the animal's eyes. 'Poor thing, it's far more frightened of us than we are of him. He's probably hidden away in there to keep out of the cold . . . he's probably a stray from the bombing.'

Jo, letting go Emily's arm, moved forward herself. The dog immediately gave a low, threatening growl once more, just as it had been doing on and off for the last ten minutes. Once you knew it was a dog, you recognised the growl at once, Emily thought, it was only when it might have been a werewolf or a ghost that you were doubtful.

'It's an Alsatian,' Jo said suddenly. 'They're guard dogs, police dogs, all sorts. I say . . . it's rather big, isn't it?'

'If they live out of doors they grow a sort of double

coat,' Emily told her. 'Our farm dogs do, anyway, and I suppose all dogs are the same. But why's it in a privy, d'you suppose?'

'I thought you said it had sneaked in to get out of the cold?' Jo said. 'Even I wouldn't suggest it had gone in there to spend a penny!'

'I said that before I realised . . . oh Jo, use your eyes,' Emily said impatiently. 'We aren't supposed to keep flashing our torches, but . . .'

She flashed her torch again, letting it wander slowly all over the dog and the small wooden hut.

'It isn't an earth-closet any more; they've taken the toilet seat away and put in a bale of straw,' Jo said triumphantly. 'It's a kennel!'

'Yes. And he's a guard dog, I suppose. He's awfully big, though, even for an Alsatian – I wonder if he'll take to us, once he realises the RAF have abandoned him? I mean, we're strangers in every sense of the word . . . here boy, what's your name, eh?'

The dog, finding itself addressed in a friendly tone, stared across at them but, not surprisingly, vouchsafed no reply.

'He wants food!' Jo exclaimed with the air of one making a profound and fascinating discovery. 'The Air Force bods couldn't have fed him before they lit out this morning and now he's really hungry. In fact, he's looking at you, Em, like the wolf in the fairy story looked at the three little pigs. Shall we go back to the pavilion and bring him a bribe?'

'A nice cup of tea?' Emily said sarcastically. 'Because that was all we could find if you remember. Apart from the emergency rations and Kay said we shouldn't touch those.'

'But we weren't searching for dog food,' Jo pointed out. 'There must be something . . . poor fellow, just you wait here whilst we go and forage.'

They returned to the pavilion hot-foot, to find Kay, very white-faced, making them tea in the kitchen.

'I'm scared I'll fall asleep and miss the phone ringing,' she explained when Jo took her to task for not sleeping. 'But I've made the tea – had a nice, uneventful night so far, have you?'

'Ye-es . . . but we've found a dog, a big one, in a – a kennel out there,' Jo said, rooting around under the sink. 'We think it's hungry, it probably hasn't been fed since last night. We thought . . . ah!'

'What's that?' Kay asked suspiciously. 'Don't give it anything you find under the sink, it could be rat-poison.'

'No, it's a stone bowl with Dog written on it,' Jo said triumphantly. 'Didn't anyone leave any fish and chips, Kay? That would do, I don't suppose an Alsatian the size of that one can afford to be fussy.'

'There are some bits,' Kay admitted. 'What a good job I didn't throw them out – well, I didn't know where the bin was, to tell you the truth. Here, let me scrape them into that bowl.'

'I'll make up some dried milk so it has a drink,' Emily said as the other two filled the stone bowl with scraps. 'I wonder where they fed it? You don't feed dogs in their kennels, you know. I wonder if it's chained?'

'Well, you two take it the food and then come back and have a sit down; I'll walk round with the torch for a bit,' Kay said. 'With two of you in here, it won't matter if you both drop off; one is bound to wake if the phone rings.'

'Right,' Jo said. 'Come on, Em, let's go and do our good deed for the day – or night, rather.'

'Doesn't he have a short memory?' Jo marvelled as they returned to the kennel-hut once more, to be greeted with a volley of unpleasant growls. 'We're your friends, stupid – we've brought you some loverly grub, isn't that kind of us?'

The dog whined, a remarkably shrill whistling sound, and peered out at them but made no attempt to come forward when they put the food and the milk mixture on the ground.

'He must be chained,' Emily said. She was not afraid of dogs but felt that approaching a very large Alsatian in the dead of night, especially a very large Alsatian which keeps growling warningly, was not the most sensible thing one could do. 'Oh dear, I suppose I'd better see. You hold the torch up so I can see what's happening.'

'So you can see his teeth sink into living flesh, you mean,' Jo said apprehensively yet with relish. 'You wouldn't catch me going within grabbing distance of those excellent fangs.'

'No, but someone's got to,' Emily pointed out, edging closer with the bowl of scraps held placatingly before her. 'Come on, old feller, come and see what Emily's got for you.'

The dog made a sharp rush at her and Emily backed equally quickly. A piece of battered cod leapt from the bowl and nose-dived towards the ground. It never made it; the dog leapt, snapped . . . and the fish was not even a memory.

'There, I said he was hungry,' Jo said from a safe distance. 'He won't hurt us, Em, he just wants feeding, that's all. Why not put the bowl down and let him eat in peace?'

'I might as well; he certainly isn't chained,' Emily

agreed. She put the scraps down, retreated for the milk, put that down too, and stood back. The dog came out slowly this time, and even in the darkness she could see the ridge of hair along its back rising with each step. Emily, who had been brought up with dogs, could read the message in its gait well, even if her friend could not. 'Jo, the poor thing's still scared stiff. Look, I'm going to move backwards very slowly, and then sit down. When he sees I'm not going to pounce or take the food back, perhaps he'll relax a bit.'

'Oh Em, just leave him,' Jo begged. 'It's cold and we're both tired . . . don't let's stay here playing silly buggers with a damned great dog when we could be sitting down and drinking hot tea! He'll probably enjoy the grub more if we're not here watching him.'

'But we'll need to be able to approach him,' Emily pointed out. Her father's lean, intelligent border collies were friends, trusting and trustworthy. If this dog was to be of any use as a camp guard then it should realise right from the start who had provided the food it was about to devour. 'You go in, Jo. I'm quite all right out here.'

'No indeed. I'll stay,' Jo said with decision. 'But I'm not coming any nearer, and it's not because I'm scared, honest. If I move again he'll probably shoot back into the kennel-thing and it'll just prolong the agony. Tell him to eat up, then we can all get some shuteye.'

The dog, however, seemed to have made up its mind that they were, if not friends, at least relatively harmless. It came out and began to eat with considerable enthusiasm, gulping the food down in large mouthfuls.

'You can tell it's never met my grandmother,' Jo said after a moment. 'Chew your food a hundred times and it will do you good,' she imitated, speaking in a quavering falsetto voice very different from her usual almost gruff tones. 'Gulping gives one indigestion and indigestion causes piles.'

'Piles! My God!' Emily exclaimed. 'Well, he's finished the fish and chips; will he go for the milk next, I wonder?'

'Wonder no more,' Jo muttered presently, as the dog's long tongue slid regretfully round the now empty pudding bowl. 'You liked that, didn't you, old chap?'

The old chap, however, didn't so much as glance at her but returned to the hut, where they could hear it rustling in the straw as it made itself comfortable once more.

'I wonder if we should push the door to?' Emily said doubtfully, picking up the well-polished bowls. 'But I don't think it's necessary, that straw's deep and the dog's got a wonderful coat. No, let's leave it. We'll come out and see him again in the morning.'

'I,' Jo said decidedly as they walked round to the front of the pavilion and climbed the three wooden steps once more, 'am going to sleep until noon tomorrow, dog or no dog. And I'm sure Kay will say it's all right,' she added, forestalling Emily's objection. 'If our NCOs haven't arrived by then, of course. And if they have, and try to stop me sleeping . . .'

'It'll be the worse for them,' Emily finished, chuckling. 'I wonder what time it is, Jo? It can't be far off four o'clock!'

It was strange not to wake to reveille, stranger to know that unless you got up, breakfast simply would not exist. Jo struggled up out of the deep well of exhaustion in which she had wallowed for six hours and lay for a moment staring at the wooden ceiling above her head and trying to remember why she felt so very weary.

She remembered arriving on site – the sharp spat of snow, the cold, unwelcoming buildings, the lack of food, the fires that would not light. She remembered her own remarks about the *Marie Celeste*, everyone's dismay upon realising that she was not so very far out – the situation was almost as strange as that to which she had referred. No one to tell them what to do, the weird telephone call which Kay had taken telling them that the balloon must go up but not giving Kay time to explain that they were a rooky crew, that they had no NCOs or officers with them, that they had never flown a balloon at night before.

The dog came next; crouched in its straw, hating them, growling, wanted to refuse the food but too hungry to do so . . . Emily being so brave and practical – Emily, who would not say boo to a goose, who never contradicted, always agreed, had proved that with something she understood she could be both brave, sensitive and sensible.

The night had flown, though. Cups of tea, Kay desperately fighting sleep, nearly falling over as she slogged round the perimeter fence because she was so exhausted. Then four o'clock and a bog-eyed Laura Atkins and a resentful Gillian Price appeared, took the torches, disappeared down the steps and out into the night.

'You two are to go to bed,' Kay said, her face almost transparent with tiredness. 'Don't worry about me, I'll just stay by the telephone, snooze, make tea for Laura and Gillian. I'll be fine.'

'You will be fine,' Emily had said gently, smiling up into Kay's face. 'Because the others will be woken at seven and then you can come back into the hut and sleep. No one will expect you to stay awake for thirty-six hours, Kay. You'll make yourself ill.'

Kay had grinned at Emily.

'Oh, I'm tougher than I seem; it's this wretched yellow hair, people think I'm a bleeding daffodil when really I'm a nettle; just about unkillable,' she said. 'See you in the morning, girls.'

And now it was morning. Jo, who had done all her thinking with her eyes fixed on the ceiling, lowered her gaze and looked muzzily around her. Empty beds met her eyes. They had been stripped and the biscuits were stacked, with the pillows on top of them, blankets folded, striped service pyjamas out of sight in lockers. How on earth did the girls do all this without waking me? Jo thought, slowly sitting up on one elbow and glancing around the rest of the room. They must have crept round like mice and that isn't like them – I wonder whether Kay's in bed yet? Emily was in her bed, though all Jo could see of her was the top of her rumpled, fawn-coloured hair. But Kay, whose bed was on the far side of Emily's, had either got up earlier or not gone to bed at all yet.

Well, whichever, I'd better get up myself, Jo thought reluctantly, pushing back the blanket and the greatcoat, the seaman's jersey and the assorted scarves and jumpers which she had piled on top of her bedding to help to keep her warm. I wonder if they brought Bessie down or if she's still up there, floating in the blue above the clouds?

She looked out of the window. She would have been able to see the balloon had it been up – or if not the balloon itself, at least the cable – but she could see nothing until she moved to the right and then there was Bessie, on close-haul, with small figures clustered round her. Inspection, then topping up, Jo thought contentedly, going back to her bed and picking up her clothes. She would just wash . . .

She was halfway to the door when she realised they had not seen an ablutions hut at all the previous day. Funny! Where was she supposed to wash? The unit had several ablutions huts, some showers, some baths. She had not envisaged arriving on a site without any such facilities but it seemed clear she had done so. She looked around her; under each bed was a round tin bowl, was she supposed to fill that and then wash?

But it was cold and anyway the question was purely academic since Jo had no intention of wandering round a balloon site in her pyjamas looking for hot water. Washing would be given a miss this morning; she would make up for it tomorrow, get herself a real hot bath. For now she would just dress and go and report to – well, to whoever had turned up to take charge of them.

By the time Jo was dressed Emily was stirring so Jo went and sat on the edge of her bed and told her what the score was.

'The balloon's on close-haul and they'll bed her down as soon as they've done all the necessary,' she said. 'Then it'll be ordinary maintenance, I expect. I'm really looking forward to going out there, getting down to it. And to having breakfast, too. I'm bloody starving – how about you, Em?'

'Where do we wash? Yes, I am hungry,' Emily admitted, getting out of bed and promptly starting to shiver. 'My God, I'm cold, too. I suppose the stove's gone out?'

'It never got lit, don't you remember,' Jo said sadly. And there's no water here for washing, so we'll have to leave it until later. But breakfast . . . well, there must be breakfast, mustn't there? Surely someone will have brought us some grub by now?'

'Yes, bound to have done,' Emily said, struggling into her clothes. Jo finished off her own toilet as Emily dressed. She brushed her crisp brown hair and rubbed a dry toothbrush over her teeth which made her mouth feel livelier, then she shoved the toothbrush into the pocket of her battledress and yawned hugely, stretching as she did so.

'Oh Lor', what a day yesterday was! Today has to be an improvement wouldn't you say, Em? Has it occurred to you to wonder why we weren't woken by the din when the others got up, incidentally? Or to wonder where Kay is for that matter?'

'I was dead tired; I don't ever remember being so worn out before,' Emily said flatly. 'I could have slept through the last trump, I should think. As for Kay . . . well, let's go and find out!'

'Bread and marge and tea for breakfast? But that isn't breakfast, it's just a snack,' Jo said forcefully as she and Emily stood in the kitchen, looking at each other across a large National loaf and a small packet of margarine. 'Everyone said how well the bops ate – it was one of the things which made me choose ballooning as a trade. Well, of all the cheek, bread and marge!'

'Kay said it was emergency rations, sent down from HQ when she finally managed to phone through to them earlier and let them know we were here,' Emily told her. 'Kay said HQ are awfully sorry and they're sorting something out. She said they'd taken a bashing in a raid the day before we arrived and hadn't got themselves together yet. I'm sure we'll get proper food as soon as they can manage it.'

Jo snorted. She had gone with Emily to find Kay and

97

had been sent back to the kitchen to prepare some breakfast for the two of them whilst Kay told Emily where things stood. And so far as Jo could see, they did not really stand at all but sagged, with HQ not really trying to right the wrongs of the previous day.

'That's a poor excuse, but all they could think of, I suppose,' Jo said, hacking two large slices off the loaf and beginning to spread them with margarine. 'You can't mean there's no jam or marmalade or anything? Not even a scraping of Marmite?'

'Only what's there; did you put the kettle on?' Emily said hopefully. 'Jo, I'm so thirsty I could drink a river. I can manage without food – well, so long as I have some bread and marge, anyway – but I can't go on without a hot drink.'

'The tea's made, it's just brewing,' Jo said gruffly. 'What about the NCOs and the officer? When are they going to put in an appearance?'

'Later. Apparently they're being brought in from other sites. Well, not the officer, she'll come from HQ, but the others. And Kay said HQ have absolutely promised proper food by noon, so that's something to be thankful for.'

'What about washing?'

'Oh, we're supposed to dip water out of a metal drum which stands by the door of the hut – we didn't notice it last night, it was too dark and we were too tired – and use that. There are tin basins under our beds, apparently.'

'I know, I saw them. But . . . cold water, Emily? They want us to wash in cold water?'

'We have to at home, except once a week,' Emily said mildly. 'We manage all right, Jo.'

'Yes, but . . . you can't get as mucky at home as we

98

shall here! It's awfully dirty work, hauling ropes and scrambling about patching Bessie and oiling the drum and keeping the grass cut . . . we'll need hot baths!'

'Sheep farming's dirty work,' Emily said. 'We'll manage, same as we do at home. They'll see we get baths once a week, I'm sure. T'wouldn't be decent, else.'

'Hey, what about that dog?' Jo said presently, when they had drunk a cup of tea each and dulled their hunger with huge doorsteps of bread and marge. 'Has anyone been out to it this morning, do you know? We didn't leave it water . . . I know you should leave dogs water, I once had an uncle who kept hounds.'

'We'll take it some bread and milk, poor thing,' Emily said at once. 'Kay said not to rush, there are plenty of them out there for now. Have you eaten enough bread? You'll burst out of your trousers if you have any more.'

'All right, I've finished,' Jo said. 'You crumble the bread, I'll make up some dried milk.'

Armed with the two bowls once again, they went round to the row of wooden huts and approached the end one. The door was fully open now and though it was still overcast and cold, the morning light illumined the hut a good deal better than the torches had done during the night.

'Here we are, old feller,' Jo said in ringing tones. The Alsatian promptly appeared, looking very nearly as big in daylight as he had looked by the light of the torch. 'Nice bread and milk today . . . what about that, eh?'

The dog came out, using all the caution it had shown the previous day, ate the bread and milk and returned to its nest in the straw. But this time, despite a very nasty look and a couple of warning growls, Emily went after it and hunkered down just outside the hut.

'What's the matter, old boy? We aren't going to hurt you; didn't you like that nice bread and milk?' she asked gently. 'Come on out and take a good look at us – we won't bite!'

'Even if you do,' said cautious Jo, from a safe distance. 'And you better hadn't or it'll be the last meal you get from these fair hands.'

But Emily, putting out a hand towards the Alsatian, had made a discovery. She turned round, a wide smile spreading across her face.

'Jo, you'll never guess! We've been calling the dog "old boy" and "old feller", when we ought to have said "old lady". She's a bitch!'

'How do you know? It's lying down, isn't it?' Jo said, refusing to be drawn. 'Or does it have a collar with its name on?'

'No, it's something much more indicative,' Emily said. 'Come and look at this, Jo!'

'I don't want to get too close in case he – or she – takes it wrong,' Jo explained, coming cautiously closer. 'Oh, my God, what is it? Has the dog killed a rat?'

'No indeed, that isn't a rat, it's her family. She's got puppies, Jo, no wonder she was so shy last night!'

4

'When I look back on the day we arrived, I wonder how on earth we kept our sanity,' Kay said, standing before the small piece of mirror which was all they had managed to acquire for the hut, and checking, somewhat doubtfully, the set of her knitted woolly cap on her smooth blonde hair. She knows it doesn't matter how she looks here, Biddy thought, amused, but she's so used to being well-turned-out that she can't stop just because she's doing hard manual work on a balloon site and not swanning around some office or other, being the beautiful Miss Markham – no, it would have been Miss Duffield of course, pre-war.

'No NCOs, since they'd been sent to the wrong site, no food, no instructions . . . and mad Mollie crouching in her kennel and threatening to eat anyone who went within six feet of her,' Kay continued, turning back to her bed to pick up her thick woolly gloves. 'Why we didn't all just chuck in the towel I don't know.'

'Well, once the sarge arrived, with Corporal Withers to back him up, things sort of fell into place,' Jo reminded her. 'Besides, we hadn't realised how dangerous it is putting a balloon up in the dark, on a site you don't know. But we've survived, thank God.'

'Who's mekkin' brekker?' Angela's voice cut in plaintively. 'Someone who can cook, I hope.'

'It's Laura and Andy,' Kay said. 'They're awfully good – they're going to feed Mollie and the pups, too.'

'Good,' Angela said. 'Are there any eggs, d'you know?'

'Don't change the subject, Angie; Jackie Rooster could have drowned the pups and taken Mollie with him,' Biddy pointed out, deciding to put her oar in. 'The truth is, it were more trouble than just leavin' the lot of 'em. I'll give that Jackie what for if he ever shows up here again,' she added grimly. 'Everyone knows if you drown puppies at birth they don't feel nothin'. You don't just abandon 'em, like Jackie Rooster did.'

'Oh come on, Bid, he knew WAAFs were coming, and wouldn't let the animals starve,' Emily said reasonably. She was sitting on her bed putting on a pair of extra-thick socks since she was on morning guard duty which meant plodding around the perimeter getting cold rather than hauling Bessie down from the heights which would, at least, keep the haulers warm. 'Besides, you're as fond of the pups as we all are.'

'Oh aye, they're all right from a distance,' Biddy agreed. 'But if you slip in their mess, like I did, you wouldn't feel all that pleased.'

There was a crow of laughter from several throats; Biddy's fall, and her subsequent shunning by the whole crew, still had the power to amuse.

'You did smell a bit ripe,' Jo said mildly. 'Anyone ready? We might as well get some brekker inside us before we bring her down.'

'Biddy and I are ready, and Kay's been prinking quite long enough,' Emily said, tying her last bootlace and standing up. 'There'll be plenty of work to do once she's bedded so the sooner we eat the better.'

Emily's come out of her shell no end, Biddy thought as the four of them made their way across to the pavilion where breakfast would be served presently. They were well-wrapped against the weather, for winter seemed to be dragging on and on with very little let up in the icy temperatures. If she goes on like this her parents won't know their shy little girl. In six short weeks she's begun to realise her worth – and she's a very good bop, one of the best, despite not being very big.

'We're off tonight, aren't we?' Kay said as they climbed the pavilion steps. 'Anyone want to come up West, see a flick or something? There's a dance at the Palais on Saturday, but we might not be able to get away. I could ask Corpy, but rotas keep changing.'

'We'll all come,' Biddy said. 'I smell fried eggs – where did they get the fat to fry 'em, eh? D'you suppose there might be bacon?'

There was, and despite the earliness of the hour – it was only just seven o'clock and the winter morning was still dark – the girls all fished their irons out of their battledress pockets and queued up hopefully for a share. Laura, coming in bearing the big black frying pan full of eggs, grinned at them.

'Trust you four to get in first,' she said. 'Come on then, grub's up! Anyone want a round or two of fried bread?'

'All of us, please. And where did you get the fat?' Jo asked the question for all of them. 'Last time we put in for some we were just told it wasn't possible. I say, it smells wizard!'

'They sent us a chunk of bacon fat, so we put that in the pan first and the rest came natural, you might say. Bacon would have been nicer, perhaps, but this is all right and we've got a can of catering beans, too, only we thought we'd save them until elevenses. Then we can have beans on toast and cocoa, which will set us up until dinner.'

'All bops do is eat,' Biddy said, holding out her plate for anything going and only removing it when Laura

103

showed no desire to add anything else. 'Well, eat and work bloody hard, that is. And the work means we deserve our grub so let's get this lot inside us; it'll help to keep out the cold.'

When Corporal Withers entered the steamy warmth of the pavilion and shouted, 'Let's be havin' you, Airwomen!' everyone was pleasantly full of food and tea and though there was a certain reluctance at the thought of facing up to the icy air outside, they followed the corporal willingly enough.

'Close-haul first,' Corporal Withers said briskly. 'Then we'll bed her down for inspection and so on. Who's on the winch this week?'

'Me, Corp,' one of the girls said, climbing onto the lorry. 'What does the meter read?'

'Two thousand feet,' the corporal said. 'Ready, every-one? Right. Switch on winch!'

The balloon was soon down and bedded, the inspection revealed only a very small hole in the outer canvas, and the ordinary day-to-day jobs started. Girls greased the cradles, checked the wire, spliced a guy rope which was unravel-ling from the strain. A sandbag needed repair so it was heaved to one side and Biddy, swearing, began to patch it with a square of sailmaker's canvas and a big, curved needle. Whilst she painfully stitched, Kay and Jo took the winch engine to pieces to find out why it had coughed and spluttered when it had started up the previous night and Emily, who was both conveniently small and neat-fingered, crawled in through Bessie's inspection hatch with more canvas and patched the hole.

'My finger-ends are ginger from that bloody sand,' Biddy grumbled as they went into the pavilion for dinner.

'And the rest of my hand's blue from the cold. I dunno why we does it, do you? What's on at the flicks, anyhow?'

'Dunno. Does it matter? We'll be sitting down, in the warm, and watching beautiful people,' Kay said. 'The only trouble is we'll probably fall asleep as soon as the lights go out. We so often do!'

'Never mind; it's an evening out,' Biddy said comfortably. 'But if we're off Sat'day, I'm going to the Palais. I want to meet some fellers, never mind how you lot feel.' She held out her plate and grinned at today's cook. 'Ta, luv, there's nothin' like a nice stew for keeping out the cold.'

'Not too many spuds,' Emily warned as Laura spooned mash on to her plate. 'Yes, apart from the sarge we don't meet many blokes. Which sort do you have in mind, Biddy? Civilians or service?'

Biddy, carrying her plate back to their table, shrugged. She was beginning to feel that if she didn't meet up with a feller soon she'd have nothing at all to write home about in her weekly letters. Other girls in the services seemed to spend all their time chasing flight lieutenants or ground crew; apart from the flight sergeant, the bops seldom saw a man.

'Does it matter, girls? Provided he can afford me, anyone will do.'

'Yanks,' Jo said with relish. She sat down and began to tuck into her food, then spoke through a full mouth. 'They're arriving in droves, thanks to the little yellow Japs. They've got chewing gum and silk stockings and big boxes of chocolates – I want to bag me a Yank.'

'I'm not coming dancing,' Kay said quickly. 'Phil might not like it – besides, it wouldn't be fair. I don't think they have much of a social life in Africa.'

'I don't want no truck with Yanks,' Emily said nervously. 'They're awful fast, you know, have your knickers off soon as look at you, Sue said.'

'Sue? How would she know? And anyway, a feller's only as fast as you let him be,' Jo said with all her usual decisiveness. 'Besides, there's a war on. It's our duty to make a bloke happy . . . by which I don't mean we ought to go all the way, but just . . . well, just some of it, I guess.'

'You're an odd girl, Jo,' Emily said reflectively. 'You say lots of things you don't mean . . . you wouldn't behave like that just because there's a war on, would you?'

Jo shrugged, but Biddy saw that her cheeks had flushed slightly and rushed into speech.

'Why not? I reckon Jo only said what we're all thinkin'. We're all good pals on site, but it would be a real treat to talk to a bloke for a change. Oh our Em, you're so bleedin' serious, sometimes.'

'Oh!' Emily said doubtfully. 'Oh, I didn't . . . I'm sorry, Jo, I just thought . . .'

'No you didn't, that's the bloomin' trouble,' Biddy grumbled. 'You just spoke, you never thought or you'd norra said it; right?'

'That's right,' Emily said meekly. 'So we'll all go to the flicks this evening and I'll come to the Palais with you when you go. It'll be a bit of fun, eh, Jo?'

'Isn't it grand to see someone else waiting to fly Bessie for a change?' Kay said as she and Jo, with Emily and Biddy close behind, left the pavilion and set off for the bus stop. It was very dark but they were used to that and had decided to catch a bus into the West End. Their nearest underground station was a good walk away, and anyway they preferred the bus.

106

'There's a queue,' Emily said as they walked along the darkened pavement. 'Is that a good sign or a bad one? I'm never sure. If there are a lot of people waiting it usually means a bus is due, but it may also mean you won't be able to get aboard.'

'Oh tag on the end, Em, and don't worry,' Jo said blithely. She gave a little skip. This was going to be fun, even if the film was a rotten one. Just to be away from Bessie Bunter for a whole evening, she told herself, was pleasure enough. And they would undoubtedly get fish and chips somewhere before they came back to their site. 'We're off on a jaunt, remember . . . it seems weeks since we had a night off.'

'It is,' Kay said, as they joined the end of the queue. 'Still, at least it's not actually freezing.'

'It will be, by the time we come out of the flicks,' Biddy said. 'Still, we can go and boil a kettle in the kitchen, no one else will be in there I don't suppose. There's nothing quite like a nice hotwater bottle to cuddle, is there? Unless it's a fe . . .'

Jo had been standing idly in the queue, glancing about her, and she had suddenly realised that she was not the only one. A group of young men ahead of them had grinned at them as they came up and now one of them was looking at her as though he were puzzling over where he had seen her before. Jo stared back, trying to pierce the darkness, but all she could make out was the pale oval of his face and a uniform which looked like Army, though because of the absence of light, it could be almost any service, including a bus inspector! But if she did know the bloke, she didn't want him to hear Biddy's artless comment about the similar comforting abilities of men and hotwater bottles in one's bed.

107

Accordingly, Jo drove her elbow hard into Biddy's side, hearing her gasp with a fair amount of satisfaction. Serve her right for behaving as though they were alone in the queue – just because it was dark . . .

'Hello there! Long time no see – did you manage to light the fire that night?'

Jo stared. It was the young man in the queue ahead of them. 'Sorry? I don't think I know you, do I? Only it's so damned dark . . .'

The young man shook his head sorrowfully. 'Now I knew it was you as soon as you hove into view, and when you spoke I was certain. Did you think I was trying to pick you up? I could do better than that if I was, but in fact we have met. You came and borrowed some coke and kindling from my platoon the night you took over the balloon site; remember me now?'

'Yes, of course! I'm so sorry, I don't even know your name . . . and the darned fire didn't light, it's still dread-fully temperamental. The chimney has to be absolutely clear . . . oh, I'm ACW Jo Stewart, by the way.'

The young man stuck out a hand and grasped Jo's.

'Nice to meet properly, at last. I'm Alec Culdrain. Sergeant, if you want my title.'

Jo sighed. 'Ought we salute?' she said, her voice so resigned that several people chuckled. 'Only it's awfully dark and we can't see your stripes or whatever, if you hadn't spoken . . .'

'No need at all,' the sergeant said. 'Oh, I should have introduced you to my friends . . . this is Bill Cooke and the tall one is Johnny Kerfoot.'

'Nice to meet you,' Jo said at once. She could not have said whether the young men were dark or fair, handsome or ugly, but they were young men. Jo, who enjoyed the company of her own sex had begun, like Biddy, to long for a leavening of male company, if only now and then. It was all right for Kay, madly in love with her Philip, and some of the other girls were deeply committed to some fellow, somewhere, but for the rest of them the female-dominated life they led was beginning to be resented. 'Are you all sergeants? We're all ACWs. The blonde one is Kay Markham, this is Biddy Bachelor and the little one's Emily Bevan. She's Welsh.'

There was a chorus of murmured greetings but they had not had the chance to exchange another word before the queue stirred and began to shuffle forward; the bus was in sight.

'Where are you girls off to?' Alec Culdrain said as the queue began to get aboard the blue-lit bus. 'We thought we'd try the dance at the Majestic, on Anstruther Street. The chaps say it's all right, the floor's well-sprung and they have famous dance-bands sometimes. A lot of service people go there.'

'We're going to the flicks. We don't know what's on, but it's a change from flying Bessie,' Jo said frankly. 'We need a break now and then.'

'Why don't you come to the dance instead?' Sergeant Kerfoot said, standing back to let them get aboard the bus first. 'We'll show you the way there . . . we'll even see you home.'

'Oh, I don't know . . .' Jo was beginning when Biddy dug her in the ribs. It was a hard dig, a get-back for the way I biffed my elbow into her earlier, Jo thought with a grin. Out loud she said, 'What, Biddy? Do you know what film's showing, then?'

'I expect she'd rather come dancing,' Sergeant Kerfoot said. In the blue-lit bus his hair looked black and his eyes dark pits, but Jo could see that he was young and rather nice looking. 'Come on, give it a go why don't you?'

'Don't over-persuade the lady; her friends have opinions too, you know,' Sergeant Culdrain said. He had a slight Scottish lilt to his voice which Jo decided, on the spur of the moment, was rather attractive. 'Why not put it to the vote? To dance or not to dance?'

They were standing, strap hanging, because the bus was full. Jo looked carefully at all three men. They were all, she judged, in their mid-twenties, all strong, capable-looking young blokes in neatly pressed uniforms. She sighed.

'All right, we'll vote and be truly democratic. Kay, you're first. What do you say?' Jo had asked Kay first out of a sense of fair play, because Kay had already said she wouldn't go dancing with them because of Phil and she knew the others, especially Emily, often went along with what Kay said because they thought the other girl sensible and kindly. Which, Jo reminded herself honestly, Kay most definitely was. Only . . . that didn't mean she was a better leader than Jo herself, of course!

'Dancing sounds fun,' Kay said unexpectedly. 'What do you think, Jo?'

'Oh, I'd like it all right, if the vote goes that way,' Jo said casually, but the glance she gave Biddy was tense. 'Bid? Dance or flicks?'

'Dance,' Biddy said baldly. 'Em?'

'How much do it cost?' Emily said with equal frankness. 'I send money home, I do. A bit mean I may seem, but my mam can do with the extra. Snowed up they've been all through January.'

'It's ten bob to civilians and two bob for the armed forces, which is why we go,' Sergeant Culdrain said.

'Drinks aren't cheap but you won't be buying your own and anyway they serve coffee and sandwiches at eleven-thirty – they're free.'

'Gee whizz,' Jo said reverently. 'Free grub, girls . . . and it's no more expensive than the flicks, Em. So what do you say?'

Emily smiled her small, secret Welsh smile; Jo always thought of her friend's sweet, three-cornered smile as being particularly Welsh. 'I say let's dance,' Emily answered. 'We're supposed to be in by ten-thirty, but it's an open camp and no one tells on anyone else.'

'Same here,' Sergeant Culdrain said. 'Right then, girls. To the dance!'

Kay sat on one of the small chairs which surrounded the tiny dance floor and revelled in the warmth, the scent of perfume, the beautiful dresses of the few women present. She, Jo, Emily and Biddy were the only representatives of the women's services and the proprietor had been delighted to see them.

'The lads have talked about you girls,' he said, indicating the three sergeants who were buying drinks at the bar. 'They were telling me and the wife, one evening, about the strength needed to fly a balloon and get it down again in poor weather conditions. I take my hat off to all of you; I wouldn't like to tackle a job like that. In fact I'm honoured that you've come to our little dance when you must be whacked and long for nothing more than a good sleep.'

'Unfortunately we do fall asleep rather often,' Jo had admitted ruefully. 'Especially in the flicks. But somehow I don't think we shall fall asleep tonight!'

There was an Air Force band playing, and playing

extremely well, Kay thought. The four of them were sitting round a table, with their caps in the middle of it, watching the dancers. A tall, slender woman was moving sinuously to a tango rhythm, whilst her partner, even taller and if anything thinner, guided her round the small floor.

'Bill's awfully quiet,' Biddy said at last. 'He's the tall feller, isn't he? I wonder if he's a dancer, or if he just likes to watch?'

'I expect they'll all dance,' Kay said. 'They're awfully kind – fancy paying for us to get in! I don't suppose they're any better off than us, either. We do all right, even in the ranks.'

'We earn every penny,' Jo said shortly. 'Oh Christopher Columbus, look what's coming over!'

A middle-aged man with thinning hair, a self-confident and cocky grin and a loud striped shirt was homing in on them, one hand held out as though about to introduce himself, as indeed he was.

'Albert Necke – and ain't I well-named?' he announced in a strong cockney accent. 'You 'ave to admit I've got a neck, walkin' up to a buncher beautifal gels wivout bein' interdooced! Still, we're all friends here, eh? Nah which of you loverly ladies is gonna 'ave the honour of the next quickstep?'

Kay laughed but remained seated, Jo went bright red and Emily shrank back in her seat. Only Biddy grinned straight back at him and got to her feet.

'Are you rich an' lonely?' she asked. 'If so, I don't mind havin' a quickstep with you. You can buy me a drink too, if you like.'

'Well, ain't you the bees knees? What's your name, sugar-plum? Albert Necke likes a gel wot ain't afraid to give 'im a bit o' lip . . . let's quickstep, babe!'

112

Biddy was taller than Mr Necke but as soon as they got on the floor their respective heights, accents and frank phraseology were forgotten. Biddy, unlikely as it seemed, danced like a dream and Mr Necke was pretty good, whisking long Biddy into a number of Astaire-like positions all of which she seemed to take completely in her stride.

'Well I'm blowed,' Jo said slowly. 'I thought we'd have a laugh, but she's good – they're both good. Who'd have thought it?'

The men, returning with a couple of drinks each, whistled at Biddy as she whisked past, then turned laughing faces to the girls still seated at the table.

'Well, what about that, then? Who's your friend's friend?'

'He's a total stranger to us all, including Biddy, but he asked one of us to dance – any one – and she said she would,' Kay said, unable to stop her eyes from twinkling, though she would not let herself smile. 'We're flabbergasted, we had no idea she could dance like that, let alone him!'

'They'll make the rest of us look pretty ordinary,' Jo said resignedly. 'I'm a clodhopper, myself. Still, it's good exercise. Sarge would smile with glee if he knew how we were spending our free evening!'

'Our sergeant makes us do drill if things are quiet, to keep us fit for hauling,' Kay explained since the young men looked rather puzzled. 'He's always on at us to take up cycling or cross-country running, he seems to be afraid that if we let up for a moment we'll go soft on him.'

'Young Amazons someone said you were,' Sergeant Culdrain said, sitting down between Kay and Jo. 'Well, which one of you is going to take to the floor with me when your friend's stopped her exhibition tango?'

113

'Not me – that's a quickstep they're doing,' Kay said, smirking. 'I don't fancy making a fool of myself by tangoing round the floor whilst everyone else, including the band, quicksteps.'

'Sorry . . . you've rumbled me,' the sergeant admitted. 'I'm a lousy dancer, but I love the cuddly bits; will you cuddle round the floor with me, either of you?'

'Kay's sitting this one out,' Jo said, getting to her feet. 'But I'll have a go, if you're sure you want to take a chance.'

They moved off and presently were seen to be quick-stepping quite neatly round the floor whilst Jo laughed at something the sergeant said.

'May I have the pleasure?' Sergeant Bill Cooke said formally to Kay. 'I wouldn't dare ask Emily because Johnny would probably kill me. He's from the border counties himself – a little place called Knighton, in mid-Wales, he's been longing to find someone else who can speak Welsh from time to time.'

Emily, who had been listening, turned an incredulous glance on the remaining man. He was dark and rather sharp-featured but he grinned at her and said something in a language which Kay did not recognise. Blushing and smiling, Emily got to her feet and held out her hand. The two shook, then Johnny Kerfoot said something else and Emily laughed. 'I don't mind having a go,' she said in English. 'Come on Kay, before the music ends.'

Kay had meant to refuse, but it would have been difficult, and besides, she adored dancing. Of course she didn't want to dance with anyone but Phil . . . but Phil was thousands of miles away, though his letters were anxiously awaited, and Sergeant Cooke was right here,

114

and besides, dancing was only dancing, it wasn't a commitment of any sort.

Bill Cooke was about the same height as Phil, too, and he danced with a sort of looselimbed ease which Kay found oddly soothing. Dear Phil, she remembered, had not been a good dancer in the accepted sense of the words, he was too self-conscious, too aware of his steps. Bill, on the other hand, held her so loosely that she did not feel she was being led; they were dancing together, two people who enjoyed this simple form of exercise. And presently, because he neither clutched her close nor tried to mould her body to his, she found herself dancing closer anyway, because that was what the music wanted, and she leaned back and smiled up into his face, seeing her enjoyment mirrored there.

'You like dancing, don't you, Bill? Do you come here often?'

He smiled down at her. He had a homely, pleasant sort of face and a gap between his front teeth. He was not handsome, thank goodness, Kay told herself, but he did seem nice.

'Yes, I love dancing. We come here a couple of times a week when we're not on duty and I usually enjoy myself but it isn't often I get to dance with the prettiest girl in the room. Good old Alec, trust him to find us the pick of the WAAF! You like dancing too, don't you?'

'I do.' Kay paused, then said deliberately. 'So does my husband. But he's abroad at present.'

He looked sympathetic but not at all surprised, far less shocked.

'Is that so? Air Force I suppose?'

Kay nodded. 'That's right. He's a flight lieutenant. Did – did you guess I was married?'

For a moment she found herself dreading that he would say yes, he had guessed because she looked married, as though by spending four nights in Phil's bed some awful matronliness had crept over her, marking her as boringly wed as certainly as though the words had been stamped on her forehead. Not that it mattered, she wasn't in the market for an admirer, far less a lover, but even so . . . She glanced up at him; he was nodding.

'Yes, I knew you were married . . . saw the ring when we got on the bus. And since I'm married as well, it seemed right that we should be partners, just on the dance floor at any rate. It's so stupid, but girls seem to assume that if a bloke's married then he shouldn't want to dance, or buy them a drink, or even sit in a corner and talk for a bit. My wife's in the WRNS, stationed in Scotland. We've been married six months and I miss her hellishly, but life's too short to turn away from every form of enjoyment just because we can't share it. Don't you agree?'

'I think I do,' Kay said cautiously as Bill gripped her waist in order to spin her round like a top as they found a tiny space near the band. 'Only I wouldn't like to hurt Phil, or let people think that being married didn't matter to me. Because it does, it's the most important thing in my life.'

'Same for me,' Bill assured her. 'Noreen – that's my wife's name, Noreen – is a New Zealander. She came over here with her brother when the war started and joined up then. We didn't meet until early '41 but we knew at once that we were right for each other. The pity of it is that we're both in services which keep us apart. If I have enough leave I rush up to Scotland and we meet for a couple of days, if she has leave she comes down here. But it's not the same as a normal, stable relationship. Even letters don't make up for not seeing each other over the breakfast table each morning, kissing goodnight each evening.'

'We only had four days before Phil was posted,' Kay said. 'I'm afraid of forgetting him, to tell you the truth. Oh, not how he looks, I'll never forget how he looks if I live to be a hundred. But all the other things; how he sounds, feels . . .'

'Tastes, even,' Bill finished for her, without any self-consciousness. 'Noreen's skin has a lovely sort of smell, and . . . oh hell, let's dance!'

By the time they reached the balloon site once more they were all on first-name terms, and Biddy was taking a lot of teasing over Albert Necke.

'He wasn't a bad old bugger,' she said tolerantly, when they laughed at her. 'Couldn't he just dance up a storm, though? But that Charlie Prince was a bit of awright, I wouldn't mind him walkin' me home.'

'Did he offer?' Bill asked curiously. 'He seemed very keen, Biddy.'

'Couldn't. He's on a balloon site the other side of the city. Odd that, wasn't it – he's the flight sergeant in charge of some WAAFs, and I'm a bop meself . . . quite a coincidence, really.'

'Gave you something to talk about, I dare say,' Alec commented. He had a very casual arm around Jo's shoulders; Kay could see that Jo was made tense by it and wondered a little about her friend. Jo had said she wanted a feller, yet when it looked as though she might have got one, she wasn't at all relaxed, she did not even seem particularly pleased.

'Huh!' Biddy said. 'We had better things to talk about

than bleedin' balloons. Still, I know what you mean.'

'I wonder why he's still on site,' Emily said idly. 'He's a bit younger than our sergeant. I thought the younger men were all being moved from balloons back into the RAF proper.'

'He'll be off as soon as they train someone else up to take his place,' Biddy said gloomily. 'It's always the way, you meet someone and they're nice and you get along, then they're moved on.'

'Biddy, how can you say such a thing in that resigned voice?' Jo said, sounding scandalised. 'We've not met a soul apart from the chaps we've met tonight since we joined the WAAFs.'

The men laughed incredulously and Biddy laughed too, though she answered swiftly enough.

'It's true, you don't meet fellers on balloon sites, but everyone knows that if you do meet someone, they get moved away after a few dates,' she said defensively. 'It isn't only in the cinema, it happens over and over in real life. Not to us yet, I know . . . well, not to me . . . but it does happen, honest.'

'All right, we take your point,' Alec said. They reached the low wicket gate which led into the playing fields and he opened it for them, then stood back. 'It's been grand meeting you, girls. Any chance of a repeat?'

'We'll pop over the next time we get an evening off, see if you're free as well,' Kay said, when none of the others answered. At least marriage means you can say things like that without being thought fast, or forward, she thought. These three men all know I'm spoken for, and it makes relationships ever so much easier. Look at Jo, tense as a guy rope in a high wind, and Emily, frightened they'll think she's easy if she so much as smiles at a man. Biddy's all right, she's got brothers, cousins, she's been chaffing fellers for the last five years, probably, she really doesn't think of men as superior beings, as Em does, or a race apart, like Jo. Considering she's only a kid she does well for herself all round, but the other two need a bit more experience of life, though Jo would be furious if I told her so.

'Right. We'll hope to see you quite soon, then,' Alec said. 'Goodnight, girls. Pleasant dreams.'

The girls said goodnight and set off across the windy playing fields.

'It's nice that the snow really seems to have gone at last,' Jo said as they approached the hut. 'But it could be weeks before we get an evening off again; bet we've seen the last of those fellers for a bit!'

Kay was on parade with the rest of the crew when Section Officer Monica Canning told her that she would like a word with her that afternoon.

'You're taking a group of your WAAFs to the public baths your sergeant tells me,' she said briskly. 'When they've had their baths send them home alone and come up to the Balloon Centre and ask for me. I won't keep you more than thirty or forty minutes, I don't suppose. Oh, and I'll see ACW Stewart this afternoon as well, so if she's one of your party you can come up together.'

Bath parties were, Kay thought as she arranged to see Section Officer Canning at fifteen hundred hours, a nuisance, a real bind. There were no public baths near at hand so the girls had to go by bus, which meant changing vehicles at least once and marching quite a long way at the end of the journey. Being clever, she and Jo decided, one afternoon, to investigate other possibilities, but it had not got them far. There was a Turkish bath only a few streets away to be sure, but it was for men, not women, and the only other public baths they found and examined proved to be totally unsuitable.

'There are quite big gaps in the walls; you can see into the next door cubicle,' Jo said, outraged, as they met afterwards on the pavement to compare notes. 'I'm used to being seen naked by a couple of dozen other WAAFs, but I don't fancy half North London eyeing me up . . . especially the male half!'

'I agree. The Air Force has its faults – well, it has millions of faults – but they know decent public baths when they see them. We'll just have to put up with a route march once a week, then.'

'A route march and two bus journeys,' Jo said gloomily. 'But it is worth it, isn't it, Kay? It's the only time I feel truly warm all over.'

And now Kay, getting herself ready for the bath party whilst idly wondering what Section Officer Canning wanted to say to her, could only agree with the sentiments Jo had so succinctly expressed.

They were all cold most of the time. It had been a bitter winter so far and they had so few places where they could warm up! It wasn't bad when you were working, particularly when you were bringing Bessie up or down. Then the sheer physical effort involved kept you in a glow. But off-duty or at mealtimes the pavilion was draughty, their sleeping billet was worse, so though you wore your woolly under-drawers which came down to your knees, though you donned your thickest socks and the scarves and gloves your loving relatives had knitted, you spent an awful lot of time simply shuddering with cold and dreaming of the summer to come. And that wretched tortoise stove! Kay gave it a glare as she slid her button stick into position and attacked her first button. They sometimes managed to light it but it burnt slow and sulkily, as though well aware of its power over them.

'It hates us,' Jo had stormed on one occasion, raising a sooty and despairing face to Kay's after they had spent the best part of an hour coaxing it to light. 'It's a bloody Nazi stove and it's part of Herr Hitler's war effort, not ours! One of these days I'll tear it up by the roots and hurl it out into the snow, see if I don't!'

Kay hadn't even laughed; nothing much amused you when you were freezing cold and the fire simply wouldn't light.

'And I'd dance on its grave,' she had said viciously. 'We all would.'

But soon enough now they would be warm. Of course they first had a journey through desolate London streets, but at the end of it, that delicious little cubicle with its piping hot water waited. Oh, the joy of stepping slowly down into all that warmth and softness, the comfort of hot water on limbs which hadn't been warm for at least a week! It gave your chilblains gyp at first, but the MO had come up with some really good stuff which took the fire out of them, and Kay still had a few precious bath salts left so she would be able to lean back in the water and simply relax.

'Kay, are you going to clean those buttons or stare at the stove with a silly grin on your silly face?' Jo said wrathfully. 'Because I want to borrow your button stick when you've done. Don't forget, SO Canning wants to see both of us.'

'Yes, all right, you can have it,' Kay said, handing over the button stick. 'Where's yours?'

'Gone AWOL,' Jo said briefly. 'If I ever had one, that is. I wonder what we've done?'

'Nothing good, you may be sure,' Emily chipped in. She grinned at them. Lately, because of a shortage of kirby grips, she had persuaded one of the girls who had been a hairdresser in civvy street to cut her hair into a neat bob which was shaped round her ears and came to a point on the back of her neck. There had been some unkind comments about trying to look like a feller just because she hadn't got one, but Kay thought the new style suited her friend. Emily had a small, pointy face and neat ears – like Ratty in *The Wind in the Willows* – and the soft, fawn-coloured hair which framed her face suited her very much better than the rather stiff and unnatural pompadour had done.

'Aw, c'mon, they're never bad, not our Kay or our Jo,' Biddy protested. 'I'm gonna wash me hair in the bath, or I will if someone can lend me a teeny blob of shampoo.'

'Shampoo? Use soap, like the rest of us,' Jo said. 'I always wash my hair in the bath anyhow; doesn't everyone?'

'Soap would do; who can spare me a little bit o' soap?' Biddy said coaxingly. 'I dunno where mine goes, honest to God!'

'You send it home to your mam,' Emily said, but quietly. 'You can have a bit of mine. We're due another issue soon, aren't we?'

Soap was handed out with abnormal stinginess by the Powers That Be, considering how frequently they preached to the WAAFs about the pleasures of cleanliness.

'Right. I'm ready.' Kay reached for her greatcoat and struggled into it, then went to the piece of mirror to check on her cap. They always wore their best blues to appear in

122

public, though it seemed rather a waste of time when you thought their clothing would be hung all anyhow in a steamy bath cubicle for the best part of half an hour. 'Everyone else ready?'

'I've been ready for ages,' Jo said waspishly. 'Come on, or we'll miss the bus.'

'The bus is always late,' Kay observed as they left the hut. It would have been fun to amble across the site as they pleased but it was decreed that they should march in pairs, so march they must. Usually one person headed the double file but today, because SO Canning had added Jo to the bath party, there were eight of them – the four girls themselves and four more – ACWs Price, Prothero, Elkins and Shaw. So they set off with Kay and Jo in the lead, arms swinging, feet in their clumsy issue lace-ups – so less comfortable than their working boots – tapping sharply on the concrete apron which led onto the pavement.

'Lucky buggers,' ACW Andrews, who was on guard duty, said as they swung past her. 'Still, our turn tomorrow.'

Kay grinned at her. 'In an hour we'll be submerging ourselves in hot – and I mean hot – water, Andy. On the other hand, when you're having your bath tomorrow, we'll have another week to wait!'

They left the site behind and made for the bus stop. As they passed the school playground where the ack-ack battery was situated someone wolf-whistled and when they continued to march, cheeks ablaze, called out.

'Hey, Kay . . . Jo! Do you always ignore your friends?'

It was Alec, with another bloke. They were both in shirt sleeves despite the cold and were doing something to their beloved gun – dirty rags and bits and pieces of machinery were much in evidence and there was a smear of oil across Alec's forehead.

123

'Flight . . . halt!' Kay said. The girls stopped and she smiled at Alec. 'We're on bath parade – don't you think it's ridiculous to make us march when we're carrying towels and soap and stuff? But that's the Air Force for you.'

'We've got our own bath,' Alec said smugly. 'It's in the caretaker's flat, it's quite a decent one. If you ever want to make a loan of it you've only got to ask. We won't even hang about the building if it makes you shy.'

'I wish we could, but there are too many of us,' Kay said wistfully. 'We'd get into awful trouble, too. They'd never believe we were just having a bath!'

Alec grinned. 'Probably not. Well, it was a nice thought, wasn't it? Got any nights off coming up?'

Kay was shaking her head and Jo was saying that they did not get any regular time off when a voice spoke from the ranks behind them.

'Me and Angie's off tomorrer night if you fellers is short of a date. Looks like you must be if you're anglin' for a married woman and ACW Steward . . . Gawd, you must be bleedin' desperate.'

Alec laughed but Kay and Jo turned simultaneously and shot a murderous look at Gillian Price who looked blandly back at them as though butter would not melt in her mouth.

'That girl!' Jo hissed between her teeth. 'I'll bloody hang for her one of these days.'

'We'll shove her in the tortoise stove and ship them both off to Germany,' Kay agreed, then said aloud, 'Kind of you, Aircraftwoman, to offer, but I don't think the brown jobs are that desperate. Flight . . . march!'

The baths, when they reached them, lived up to all expectations and Kay sprinkled her bath salts, climbed into the steaming hot water and lay back to dream a little. And with Kay, dreams always led in the same direction. Philip. Smiling lazily down at her, telling her she was beautiful, that he loved her. Proving he loved her, holding her, kissing her.

The trouble was, of course, that the scenario never varied. It was always their honeymoon cottage, or the little church where they had married, or the wedding reception. Not for the first time, Kay found herself regretting that she and Phil had no past together. If she went back even a year, there were her parents, her relatives, Steve Minton who had lived next door to Kay all his life, his older brother, Gerald, who had once knocked the small Kay into the river and jolly nearly drowned her. There, in her head, was the house with its two turret rooms, the herbaceous borders rich with old-fashioned flowers, and the stabling which had been converted into a games room. There too was Chrissie who cleaned for her mother, brought little Kay homemade fudge when she was ill with measles, told on her when she hung out of the window in mid-winter clad only in a nightdress, to whisper secrets down to young Steve in the yard below.

She could see their faces clear as clear, every last pimple, but if she tried too hard to bring Philip into her mind he began to blur at the edges. A four-day honeymoon, no matter how romantic or ecstatic, is no substitute for the crowded years of childhood, the rich emotional memories of adolescence. There were his letters of course, lovingly read and re-read, then tied with pink ribbon and hidden in her kitbag. But they were so short, so school-boyish, so – so similar. She needed more detail, more gossip more – more intimate details of his life.

But such fruitless longing for a shared past was pointless because what she and Phil would share, once the war was over, was a future. So what's wrong with you, girl? she scolded herself now, sitting up and beginning, at last, to wash. Use the imagination God gave you, bring Phil here, make him kneel by the bath, look hungrily down at your lovely clean, wet body, all pink and warm and inviting. And then you can look up into his eyes, imagine his hands, soapy and warm, running caressingly . . .

'Sod it!' she said the words out loud, slamming both fists into the water so that it arced up, soaking her hair. 'Sod it, sod it!'

'What's up, Kay?' That was Jo, in the cubicle next door. 'Water gone cold on you?'

It had indeed, Kay thought grimly, whilst explaining, mendaciously, that she had slipped on the soap. She had already learned the painful uselessness of arousing in herself the demons of desire and longing. Better to stick to remembering the walks in the autumn woods with Philip's hand in hers, the cosy suppers eaten by firelight in the cottage, the warm and wonderful love which he tried to put into words when he wrote to her.

But Jo was gabbling on; better listen.

'We should have asked the sergeant why the SO wanted to speak to us; bet he knows, the old devil. Sergeants know everything; he's always telling us that, so we should put it to the test. Still, it won't be long before we're finding out for ourselves. Oh Lor', my hair's wet, it'll still be wet when we reach the Balloon Centre. Damn, damn, damn, why don't I ever think?'

'Because you ain't got nothin' to think with,' a well-remembered, spiteful voice announced. 'No wonder them brahn jobs are lookin' for a different gal to date if you're what they fished out o' the puddin' last time.'

126

'Shut your gob,' Biddy called sharply. 'It's girls like you, Price, what give all women a bad name. What's more, no one in his senses 'ud want to get within arm's length of a slut like you.'

'Don't you talk to me like that, you Scouse git,' ACW Price shrieked. 'Common as muck, that's you . . . wiv a gob on you big enough to git a gran' pianner in, sideways. You mind your bleedin' business.'

Kay, listening, began to heave herself out of the water. Thank God I'm only in charge so far as getting them here's concerned, she told herself devoutly, reaching for her towel. I'll have a quiet word with Biddy, but I hope it will make a difference. Those two are oil and water, they're spoiling for a fight. Let's hope they have it when I'm well clear!

'Well, Markham, I expect you've guessed why I want to see you.' The Section Officer paused expectantly.

'No, ma'am, I can't imagine,' Kay said truthfully. 'It wouldn't be about the tortoise stove in our billet, I suppose? There's something badly wrong with it, ma'am, and some nights we've nearly frozen in our beds but still can't get it to light.'

Section Officer Canning was a handsome young woman, with very fair hair, very blue eyes, and perfect skin. Now, her pale brows rose slightly.

'A tortoise stove? Why on earth would I be interested in a tortoise stove, Markham?' Kay longed to suggest that, since Monica Canning was in charge of the WAAFs on the site, she might be interested in the welfare of her crew, but she realised that it would not only be tactless in the extreme but also unfair. The girl was only two years older than herself. How would I bear up under such a weight of responsibility if I was an officer? Kay asked herself, and knew that the answer was problematical. Not that it was likely to happen, since she had no urge for promotion.

'Well, Markham?'

School prefect, Kay reminded herself. You had to answer them when they asked a question, no matter how rhetorical.

'Sorry ma'am. I just thought . . . it's the only problem we have, so I just thought . . .'

'I'll send one of the chaps round to look at it for you,' Monica Canning said, suddenly relenting. 'And now to why I wanted to see you . . .'

An hour later, Kay was hanging round outside the Balloon Centre when Jo came out. Jo looked exceedingly pleased with herself. Her cheeks were pink and she fairly bounced across to her friend.

'Hi, Kay! Ever since they made us up to ACW first class I've wondered whether . . . but this is it! I'm to go for an NCO's course! What about you?'

'The same,' Kay said. She did not add that the Section Officer had made it clear that she expected Kay to make sergeant quite quickly, and to go on to officer training in the fullness of time. She knew Jo had not been offered the same carrot, so had decided not to mention it. And for her own part she didn't know whether she felt glad or sorry that she was being offered promotion, but she suspected that sorrow predominated. More exams and training and bookwork which would end in her being despatched to some other, strange balloon site, where she would take on the responsibilities which she had not the slightest desire to do. It was more fun being one of the crowd, doing as you were told, having no real responsibility save for

128

yourself. But she wanted to do her bit, and Corporal Withers and others like him were needed now for their various skills and abilities. If they were freed from the admittedly essential work of flying balloons they could do other, much more valuable work, which WAAFs could not tackle. Therefore if a WAAF could take the place of a NCO . . .

'So you'll do it! Good for you, Kay!' Jo fell into step beside her as they walked back along the pavement to their first bus stop. 'I must say I wondered – your first taste of command wasn't too fortunate, was it?'

'It wasn't bad, actually,' Kay said rather stiffly. She knew the reason that she had been put forward for officer training had been largely because of those first awful forty-eight hours, but she did not intend to tell Jo, feeling instinctively that Jo would resent it and probably make snide remarks. And life is hard enough without adding a resentful Jo to my list of troubles, she told herself. But the truth was, Monica Canning had been quite frank.

'You did yourself a good turn, Markham, when you coped so well with that hiccup at the start of your posting, and it isn't only me who thinks you're cut out for something better than Balloon Operative,' the section officer had said. She had smiled at Kay, and suddenly her face lit up and lost its seriousness; she looked no older than Kay herself and full of life and mischief. 'Best of luck, anyway, I'm absolutely certain you'll make a go of it.'

'You were marvellous that day,' Jo said now, with sudden generosity. 'I don't think I could have done it. But at least we'll be in it together, Kay. I must admit I feel better about it, knowing there'll be two of us. I say, this will be one in the eye for some of the crew!'

'Who? Bid and Emily, or the dreaded ACW Price?'

Jo chuckled. 'Price and her ilk, of course. But now that you've mentioned it, it'll be hard on Biddy and Emily.'

'Yes, I know what you mean. We've been a close little quartet, it's a shame to lose all that.'

'Who says we will?' Jo said comfortably. 'Besides, we can't go on an NCO course until there is one. We might have to wait weeks and weeks.'

'But we won't come back here,' Kay said sadly. 'You must have noticed, no one ever gets posted to a flight that knows them; discipline's probably difficult, I suppose.'

'You can see their point,' Jo agreed. 'Can you see Price obeying a command given by you or me? Like fun she would!'

'And there will be Prices all over Britain, there's at least one and probably more in every crew,' Kay said. 'Oh well, we'll face that when we come to it. But until then, let's enjoy just being together.'

'Mollie? Come on, old girl, it's time you went walkies.'

Emily clicked her fingers and the big Alsatian came slowly out of her shed, then saw the lead and began to prance. She loved her walks and counted being taken round on guard duty as fun, though the girls did not share her pleasure in that particular exercise.

Biddy and Emily were on guard duty from midnight until four next morning, but since it was a clear night with a strong March wind they had decided to take Mollie for a walk before they went on duty. Bessie had been bedded for a couple of days but a clear sky could mean raids, and a strong wind meant tussling to fly her, so they knew that, having got her aloft, they would need a couple of hours rest before they started their trick of guard duty, hence Mollie being walked rather earlier than usual.

130

'Good old girl,' Emily said as she put Mollie on the lead. 'Isn't it nice and quiet in your kennel without your puppies, then? You're not a natural mother, old girl – you saw your littl'uns off without so much as a tear in your eye.'

'Mams can be like that an' all,' Biddy said with a grin. 'Me mam heaved a sigh of relief when I joined up. Well, she never split on me, and she could've.'

'She wanted you to be happy, Bid,' Emily said gently. She assumed that Biddy, whilst loudly praising her mother for not 'splitting' on her daughter's true age, secretly thought it a sign of deep parental disinterest. 'You wouldn't have liked it much if she had split, would you?'

'No, course not,' Biddy muttered. 'Are we goin' to walk round to the school?'

Ever since Kay and Jo had gone off on the NCO course Biddy and Emily had spent a good deal of time with the men of the ack-ack battery. Not, Emily reminded herself hastily, because any of them were interested in each other but because they had become friends. We all like dancing, and that Alec's a nice bloke, she told herself. Jo likes him and he likes talking about Jo, so it's a kindness to go round there.

'Yes, why not?' she said now. 'They usually save some bits for Mollie, what's more. And she might like to visit her son.'

One of the male puppies, the pick of the litter, had gone to the ack-ack battery. 'He might put a stop to the petty theft,' Alec had said. 'When he's bigger, anyway.' Like everyone else, they suffered from kids sneaking round the buildings whenever they could and stealing anything that wasn't nailed down.

It was mid-March and the evenings were getting progressively lighter, so the girls did not need a torch as they walked across the site and along the pavement.

'We'll walk first and then say hello to the fellers,' Emily decided. 'We might get some chips when the shop opens, the fellers never say no to a few chips.'

Accordingly the two of them and Mollie walked for a couple of miles, bought chips from a small chip van parked on a bomb-site and then returned to their area as the light was fading from the sky and a deep blue dusk was creeping over the land. Stars were pricking the sky above as they turned into the school gate and called out to the men, who were playing an impromptu game of football with a bundle of rags wrapped into a ball-shape with a great deal of string. Several of the men waved, but only Alec and Bill, standing on the sidelines watching, came over to the gate.

'Hello, you two – want to see Sunny Jim? He's had so much to eat he's nearly circular . . . Sunny old boy, your mum's come visiting!'

Sunny, as fat a puppy as you could wish to see, came rolling out from the school porch, his tiny, inadequate tail wagging violently, small squeaks of delight greeting his mother as soon as he set eyes on her. Mollie, less vocal but equally keen on the reunion, promptly rolled her son on his back and began to clean him up and Sunny, after suffering this for a moment, bit her playfully on the nose.

'They're not fighting, they're just playing,' Emily shouted above the din when Alec seemed inclined to take a bass broom to them. 'They'll stop in a minute, they always do.'

'We thought . . .' Biddy was beginning when the telephone rang inside the building. Alec sprinted in and

132

answered it; they heard the ringing stop, the deep burr of his voice, then his hasty footsteps hurrying back again.

'Raiders over the coast,' he announced, bringing the football game to an abrupt end. 'Everyone up to the guns! You'd better get back, girls. Your call will be through any minute.'

'Right – good shooting, get a jerry for us,' Emily said. 'Come on, Bid, we'd better run.'

Balloon operatives worked so hard and so constantly that their corporal and sergeant allowed them as much freedom as possible, but both girls knew that they should have been back on site half an hour ago, and hurried accordingly. When they got back they were glad they had hurried. It was almost completely dark now but as they neared the site they saw it was buzzing with WAAFs. Sergeant Potter spotted them out of the corner of his eye and hailed them at once.

'Ah, Bevan, get on the tail guy and Bachelor, stand by the spider. We're almost set.'

They had all but finished topping up, Emily saw guiltily. But no one had actually said they might not leave the site. And they were back in time, so there was no harm done. She slipped Mollie's lead off and gave the big dog a gentle push. 'Go on, back to your kennel,' she commanded. 'I'll come and see you later, old girl.'

Mollie slid away like a shadow and Emily knuckled down to her task – and very soon, with the wind freshening by the minute, she was far too busy to worry about anything but the work in hand. Prothero and Shaw were on the winch and the sergeant was fixing the armaments. He beckoned Emily over, then grinned at her.

'Best get this right,' he said. 'I'll clamp the bombs on if you'll keep an eye on the meter, let me know when she

133

reaches the appropriate height. There's a big wind building up, I wouldn't be surprised if we have trouble with her later, so I want to get this spot on.'

'Aye aye, Sarge,' Emily said at once. 'What's it to be? What's the height?'

'We're flying at six thousand feet tonight,' Sergeant Potter said. 'So we'll clamp the armaments at two thousand and three thousand feet. Watch the meter, girl.'

Emily could scarcely see the meter in the darkness, but she put her nose almost on it and managed to make out the figures, which were clicking round as the balloon steadily gained height.

'Hold it at two,' she shouted, and the girl on the winch obediently killed her engine.

Sergeant Potter clicked his fingers at her and she handed him the bomb and watched him clamp it securely in position. 'Right, Aud, switch on winch!'

Presently she could see that the meter was close on three thousand feet. 'Hold it at three,' she called, and once more the sergeant clicked his fingers and she moved away from the meter to hand him the armament and watch him clamp it securely to the cable before ordering Audrey to 'Switch on winch!' once more.

At six thousand feet the command to stop the winch was obeyed and the spider was clamped. High above them, dark against the stars, Bessie Bunter swayed and curved the thin line of the cable which tethered her to earth. The March wind was carrying the balloon well over to starboard, but there was nothing they could do about that and perhaps the wind would have eased off before they had to bring Bessie down again.

'Right; get back to your huts and fetch your steel helmets. Withers, get the girls out of it . . . see they've got

134

their lids . . . then straight to the shelter till we're needed out here. Those aircraft are bloody close.'

Emily just stood and stared, unable to believe what she was hearing – and seeing – until Biddy grabbed her arm. Dark shapes against the stars, the steady roar of engines . . . shapes which she recognised, with a stab of pure dismay, from those training silhouettes. This was their first real raid of any magnitude and it had to happen on a windy night so that Bessie might not give of her best.

'Em, don't just stand there, you heard what the sarge said! Get back to the hut and grab your helmet, then we'll run for the shelter, then if there's flak and shell-cases and things . . . Come on!'

There was no panic, Emily was glad to see, despite the suddenness of the raid. The girls swooped into the hut, grabbed their helmets from various resting places and swooped out again, a flock of bluebirds in their denims and battledress. Outside, the night was noisy already. Emily lingered a moment, looking up, and saw the shapes more clearly now, bulking huge and ominous against the night sky. And even as she watched an object detached itself from the aircraft in the lead and fell to earth. The resultant explosion seemed to rock the night, to suck the air from her lungs and then to fling her sideways, though as she and Biddy reeled she realised they had only staggered a couple of steps.

'Em, for God's sake! Hangin' around like that, you could've killed the pair of us!' Biddy seized Emily's arm. 'Run, you cloth-'ead, they won't stop at one, y'know.'

Emily ran and as she and Biddy clattered down the short flight of concrete steps, Emily remembered to be glad that the shelter was actually here – but for the grace of God, she was thinking, as she heard the next stick of bombs hurtle to earth, we should have been in a far less safe place. A week ago the shelter had been dug and roofed; before that they had been told to go into the pavilion and get under the tables. No one seemed bothered that since the tables were flimsy folding ones they were unlikely to make much difference, and though they had all examined the shelter with distaste and complained about the narrow wooden benches and the horrid smell of damp and concrete, it had its charms when, outside, bombs were dropping and the sky was full of strange lights and evil-looking aircraft.

There wasn't much spare space in the shelter, not with two crews jammed in like sardines in a tin. 'You're last,' Corporal Withers said as they almost fell into the dark, damp little box. 'About time too, girls. Move in a bit, though, the sarge an' me wants to be nearest the doorway.'

'First out, eh, Corp?' A voice from the darkness said sceptically. 'Cor, what a pong dahn 'ere! Reckon you'll be trampled to death in the rush when the all clear goes.'

A smelly sacking curtain could be dropped if necessary, but the shelter still lacked a door so the curtain was looped back. There was an orange glow to one side of it and Emily was just about to remark that something seemed to be on fire when she remembered Mollie. She jumped to her feet. The dog would be scared out of her mind!

'Sarge, I've got to go out for a sec; it's the dog, she's in the shed with the door open . . . she may not even have gone back there, she could be . . .'

'Siddown, Bevan,' Sergeant Potter said. 'No one leave 'ere till I say; understand?'

'Understood, Sarge,' Emily said ruefully. She sat down. 'I just hope this isn't going to last till morning, because when we ran for the hut to get our helmets I really wanted to go . . .'

'Hold it, don't talk about it, cross your bleedin' legs,' the sergeant ordered. 'Or, halternatively, pass the hat round! Now let's have a sing-song shall we? We'll start off with "Roll Out the Barrel". One, two . . .'

'Wish we had a cuppa char,' Biddy murmured into Emily's ear after some considerable time had elapsed. They were all crammed into the small space, scarcely able to move at all, yet their mutual closeness in the damp darkness was surprisingly comforting. 'Cor, I'm spittin' bricks here.'

'Yeah; I'd even make do with a drink o' water,' another voice said yearningly. 'It were sudden, this raid – why didn't we get more warning?'

'Warning enough,' the sergeant's voice rumbled comfortingly. 'We got Bessie up in good time and ourselves down here. Now we'll just have to sit it out.'

'Oh . . . but Em and I are on guard duty,' Biddy said after a few moment's quiet, during which they could once more hear the rumble of aero-engines overhead. 'Shouldn't we be out there? It sounds like the planes are goin' home now, to me. I couldn't half do with a breath of air.'

'No point,' Sergeant Potter said. 'Only get yourself killed, give us more trouble.'

Emily shifted uncomfortably on the hard wooden shelf which the authorities called a bench. The sergeant put out a large hand and patted her knee comfortingly.

'Forget about the dog, lass. If she takes a direct hit there ain't nothing anyone can do. Leave it. It can't last for ever, you know.'

But it felt like forever. It had been bad enough when bombs were falling every few minutes – the whine of their descent, the thud, the boom which rocked the shelter, the

137

after-shock when the sounds seemed to peak and swell ear-burstingly close. Throughout all that Emily had sat quietly, waiting for it to finish. Poor Mollie, she kept thinking, poor old girl – what'll she do, what'll she think? She's only an animal, she'll never understand! And somehow, her fears for the dog made her own fear lessen – at least she understood why the bombs were falling, the sirens shrieking.

At first she had asked the sergeant more than once if she might just pop up for a moment but, though understanding, he was firm.

'Leave it, m'dear,' he said. 'We don't want to lose you, we can't afford to. You're a damned good op, we'll need you until this bleedin' war is over. So sit tight and don't fret, 'cos it won't help none.'

But now, with the enemy aircraft passing overhead once more, surely with their bomb bays empty, it seemed almost more than Emily could bear to stay down here whilst up above Mollie could be hurt, in need of help . . . even dead. And anyway, if we don't go up soon I'll have to use the hat like the sarge said, she thought despairingly. My bladder's bursting – why didn't I go as soon as we got back instead of putting it off?

'Sarge? Can we go now? I've not heard an aero-engine for ages.'

An hour passed, and then another. Finally the sergeant stood up, creakingly. Poor man, Emily thought, he was in his mid-fifties and had a limp caused, he had once told her, by arthritis in a wound from the Great War. It couldn't have helped being stuck down here for so long.

'Yes, I think the worst's over,' he said now, having peered long and hard out of the doorway. 'Come on then, let's be 'aving you!'

*

138

It was still dark when the last of the raiders had disappeared from the sky and the girls began straggling up from their retreat. Several of them had slept despite the noise, the discomfort and the cold, which, as the night wore on, seemed to enter Emily's very bones. Neither she nor Biddy slept, Emily because she was too strung up, Biddy because she had gone through this before and, she had told Emily in an undertone earlier in the night, she had suddenly found herself reliving those terrible raids in Liverpool, when she and her family had thought themselves doomed a thousand times.

'We was all right, though. Us Bachelors lived through the May blitz, which was the worst, believe me, so I pray to God I'll live through this,' she had murmured to Emily as they clung together in the friendly dark. 'But that don't mean I like it, or that it's not so scary the second time around, because it's worse if anything. Is Bessie all right, d'you reckon?'

'The sergeant's keeping an eye on her, he'd have said if she'd gone down in flames,' Emily had whispered. 'I wonder how the fellers are on the ack-ack battery?'

'They don't have a shelter because they have to keep firin' that bleedin' gun,' Biddy said mournfully. 'And they're on a rooftop, Alec said. I do like them fellers, Em. I do hope they're goin' to be all right.'

'Sure they'll be all right,' Emily said with a cheerfulness she was far from feeling. 'It is definitely quietening down, Bid. Any time now the sarge will let us go above ground.'

And of course, once it was quiet, he told them to go back to their hut and get what sleep they could.

'I'll just check around, see there's no damage,' he said vaguely. 'But you girls get some kip.'

'I'm going to take a look around as well,' Emily said doggedly. 'I'd feel happier, Sarge.'

'Me too,' Biddy said, her voice small. 'I can't sleep until I know what's happened.'

The sergeant sighed and shook his head, but made no objection when they tagged on behind him.

Despite the darkness it was possible to take a good look at everything because of the fires burning up on the main street. The site itself didn't seem too badly affected, though an incendiary had landed on one of the earth closets and it was still smouldering. There was flak everywhere, though, and fragments of buildings, brick and the like.

'I do hope Mollie's all right,' Emily said rather grimly.

Mollie, however, was not in her kennel. They searched the site, called and shouted, but there was no sign of the dog.

'She ain't killed, dear,' the sergeant said comfortingly. 'She's just run off – scared by the din, likely. She'll come back.'

But Emily, going sadly off to bed, doubted it. Why should the dog return to the place where she had been scared out of her wits? And if she'd run off in a complete panic, anything could have happened to her.

Knowing what sort of a night his crew had had, the sergeant did not ring their reveille bell until eleven and when she stumbled out of bed, dressed and made for the pavilion, Emily was greeted at once by Alec, who was grinning all over his face.

'We had a visitor whilst we were out last night,' he said cheerfully. 'She came over to check on junior, I think. Sam was on guard duty at our billet so he shut the pair of 'em into the broom cupboard, with a marrow bone and a couple of blankets. He looked in when the worst was over and Mollie was curled round Sunny and they were both fast asleep. So if you were worried . . .'

'I was out of my mind,' Emily said. 'Where is she?'

'Still at the school. I thought you might like to fetch her, later, but for now she's probably better where she is.' He paused, scanning Emily's pale and weary face. 'She's had a bit of a bang, to tell you the truth. Flying glass, probably. Anyway, the MO came round this morning and he put a couple of stitches in it. She was good as gold, he said.'

'Stitches? What . . .?'

'A cut on her flank. The MO shaved the area and stitched it and gave me some ointment to give you so you could apply it morning and evening. She's well and cheerful, so don't worry, Emily.'

'Thanks, Alec, you're so good,' Emily said faintly. 'We worried about you, too, really we did. Up on that roof in the middle of the warehouse area – you can't go to a shelter, Biddy said. Is that true?'

'Yes, it's true all right. A fat lot of good we'd be if we ran and hid when the action started! It's take aim and fire all night, until the buggers . . . sorry, lass, I meant blighters . . . hightail it for home. We think we could have got one, too – Max swears it staggered.'

'Max would! Is everyone else all right? Bill? The rest of your platoon?'

'They're all fine, though poor Freddy's gone deaf; got too near the barrel when it was almost red-hot and making an infernal din, of course. But we're all back now, so come over and see us later, when you've sorted yourselves out.'

'We'll be getting Bessie down any minute; Sarge and the corporal brought her down to close-haul in the early hours, but we'll have to bed her down now to do the inspection,' Emily said. 'I'll come over after that, and thanks again, Alec. Awful, wasn't it?'

For some reason she needed his confirmation, as though to assure herself that her own reaction had not been exaggerated.

'Yes, it was pretty bad,' Alec said. 'We're going to see what we can do to help later, though most of the damage, so far as we can make out, is a couple of miles from us. But there's a crater as big as a bus in the main street and there's half a warehouse leaning over it.'

Emily shuddered. 'And to think we walked down there yesterday! Oh, well, that's the war for you. See you later then, Alec. And thanks again.'

5

'Well, we've got our stripes and now we're going to have our first proper leave. And when I come off leave I'm being sent to a site not two miles away from our old one,' Jo said happily as she and Kay left the breakfast table and headed for their quarters. She looked proudly down at the flashes which denoted her rank. 'I never thought I'd make it, in my heart, Kay. I thought I'd lose my temper and balls it all up.'

'Yes, I wondered if you might,' Kay admitted. 'I'm most awfully glad you didn't though, Jo. Have you rung home yet, about your leave?'

'No. I'm going to surprise them,' Jo said. 'Have you had your posting yet, Kay?'

'Yes. I'm not on the outer ring this time, I'm on the inner, which means we'll be billeted in one of the houses the RAF has taken over. It will be nicer in lots of ways than a hut on a balloon site. They want women NCOs on the inner ring, because they can all muck in together, I imagine. But we'll be able to meet up when we're off-duty, if we can find some way to get in touch.'

'Oh, we'll find a way,' Jo said confidently. 'First time I get off I'm going over to No 12 site to see Em and Biddy. They'll be chuffed that we've got our stripes – I wonder if they'll move on and up too, given time?'

'Dunno,' Kay said. 'They've both got the ability, but they need ops on the ground, they can't go making all of us up to NCO. It'll be odd to be back in dungarees and battledress, won't it, after ten days of number ones?'

'Odd but nice,' Jo said. 'Aren't stockings and skirts chilly when you've been used to long under-drawers and thick serge trousers? Once or twice I've felt really self-conscious over showing my legs!'

'Oh, you! Well, at least it's the end of exams for a bit. How I hate the hush of an examination room and the scratching of heads! To be honest, I'd sooner haul Bessie Bunter any day.'

Kay had managed to get a corner seat in the train going home and now she sat with her nose close to the glass, seeing the burgeoning spring countryside chug past and half-hearing the tickety-boosh of wheels on rails whilst her mind soared and danced, sometimes exploring the happenings of the past six months, at others letting her imagination roam ahead, to home.

She had not been back since her wedding day, largely because she had taken her leave in order to get married but partly, it must be admitted, because she dreaded the slight but definite aura of disapproval which had hung over both her parents ever since she had – defiantly – announced her forthcoming marriage to Philip.

'Darling, you hardly know him . . . he's very handsome, but you've nothing in common, nothing at all! It's just like a holiday romance and those seldom last. Get engaged if that's what you want, but give yourselves time to get to know each other. A year, perhaps two . . . Oh Kay, darling. Marriage can mean babies, you know, and you're scarcely more than a child,' Sara Markham had said, her big greeny-grey eyes pleading for Kay's understanding, agreement. 'Take your time, enjoy being a beautiful, intelligent young woman with the world at your feet, and when he comes back from wherever he's off to, see how you feel then.'

144

'But the world at my feet doesn't matter, Mummy, he's being posted abroad and we might not see each other for years! And we love each other, really we do. We can neither of us bear the thought of being separated, having no claim . . .'

Her father had said nothing at first. He had listened to the arguments going back and forth and he had puffed at his pipe and stared into the fire, for despite the fact that it was August the evenings had already begun to grow chilly. When he did speak, however, he talked sense; even Kay could see that.

'You're rushing, darling,' he said slowly, taking his pipe out of his mouth and holding it in one hand whilst he spoke. 'This is the most important decision of your life and you're simply closing both your eyes and jumping into the water without even considering whether you can swim or not. Look, I'm sure Philip's everything that you want and need, so forget all the conventional ideas about what you've got in common, where you were brought up. I agree that to a couple of young people who are convinced they are in love that's irrelevant, and rightly so. But being in love is no reason for burning your boats, committing yourselves. No one, thank God, can see into the future, but when you've been apart for two years, perhaps more, living different lives, fighting different wars, even, you may find that you are no longer the girl Philip admires – and he most certainly won't be the young man you first met. You'll mature at a much faster rate, people always do in wartime, and whilst that's not a bad thing, it's a fact of life which you should be taking into consideration. Will the new Kay like the new Philip the way she liked the old one, and vice versa? Kay darling, you know how dear you are to me and to

Mummy. Get engaged, you'll have our blessing, but don't rush into marriage.'

It had made a miserable sort of sense, so she had put it to Philip, dreading that he might agree and end her hopes for a speedy marriage, but he had pulled a face.

'An engagement, what good's that? Darling Kay, I want you and I want you to be mine. I don't want to sit in some foreign field, wondering who you're dating whilst I'm far away. It's a cruel fact of life that a little gold ring on the third finger of a girl's left hand is a bigger deterrent than warts or a flat chest to some would-be romeos.'

'So you want me in a dog-in-the-manger way?' Kay had said, giggling. 'Phil, forget warts, flat chests and gold rings; I wouldn't go out with other men even if we simply had an understanding. You're safe on that score, honestly. But . . . but I'm like you, I want to be totally yours, totally committed.'

He had smiled, his face alight with eagerness. 'Then we'll marry, whatever your parents say? Unless they expressly forbid it of course, since you aren't going to be twenty-one for years. But if they do turn nasty we could always do the dirty on everyone and make a run for Gretna Green.'

But it had not been necessary. When she had explained, her voice breaking, that she and Philip had talked it over, thought it out, and come to the conclusion that marriage was the only thing that would satisfy them, her parents gave in. Gave in lavishly, as was their wont, turning in a moment from the niggardliness of disapproval to the generosity of giving, which was far more like them. They had masterminded all the wedding arrangements, spending as much as they could afford and possibly more, persuading relatives to lend this, give that. They had

146

invited Phil's parents and his elder brother, Jeremy, to stay for a few days and had been excellent hosts, and when at last his leave started and he had arrived at Rivington they had welcomed Philip like the son they had never had. Only Kay had spotted the coolness behind the warmth, the cautious look in eyes that dwelt on her beloved.

It had hurt, but even so she had understood. For more than eighteen years she had taken their word on everything, obeyed them, trusted their judgement. Now she had gone against their wishes, their advice, and they were neither angry nor offended, just terribly afraid for her.

'Philip is so good looking,' Kay's cousin Betty had said as she helped Kay with her headdress and checked her own appearance in the long cheval glass by the bedroom door. 'He's good fun, too, and awfully nice. I hope you know how lucky you are, Kay.'

'I know, Betty,' Kay had said, laughing. 'He's a dream come true, he's all I ever wanted, even though I didn't know I wanted anyone four months ago.'

'Well, I don't know why Auntie Sara and Uncle Ted were being so cautious about him,' Betty said frankly. 'They said they liked him, were happy for you . . . but I've known them all my life, I thought they sounded . . . well, unsure, somehow.'

'They'd be unsure about my marrying the Angel Gabriel,' Kay had said flatly. 'That's how parents are, Bet. But they'll come round – they've already made a start. They really do like him, even if they can't entirely approve of any daughter of theirs marrying before she's eighteen.'

'I'm glad, because your parents are great favourites with me and Ceddy. Anyway, I think Philip's a real catch; you're a lucky girl, Kay.'

147

'I know. And we're going to live happily ever after – if the war will let us, that is.'

Sitting in the railway carriage now, as the train began to slow at the first of the many smaller stations it visited before it reached Norwich Thorpe, Kay fished Philip's latest letter out of her respirator case. She kept it handy, knowing she would want to see it throughout her leave. She flattened the flimsy pages out and started to read.

'My dearest Kay,
Oh darling, I miss you so terribly . . .'

'Darling! What a miracle the train wasn't later, Daddy and I were in the buffet, having the most disgusting cup of tea and a rather dry sandwich, when it was announced over the loudspeaker system – we couldn't believe our ears, because the London train's always late! Gosh, I believe you've actually grown . . . oh, and you've got two stripes – so the course was a success? I always knew you'd do well in whatever you did, you were such a clever child at school, to say nothing of the debating society and amateur theatricals . . . Now where on earth has your father gone.'

Sara Duffield was a tall, vivacious red-head with deceptively sleepy-looking grey-green eyes and skin like milk. She was also a non-stop talker, a warm, giving woman who should have mothered half a dozen children at least; sometimes she almost swamped her only child but Kay never made the mistake of thinking her mother too forceful or too involved. Sara was a wonderful parent, a wonderful wife and the most popular auntie in the entire family. Cousins and sisters-in-law flocked to Sara for advice and comfort and Kay knew she was much blessed, even if her mother had not entirely agreed with her marriage.

'He got onto the train while we were having a cuddle and now he's heaving my case off,' Kay informed her mother, smiling at her. 'When I saw you on the platform all I thought of was of getting down off the wretched train and giving you a big hug – oh Mummy, I've missed you so terribly and I didn't even realise it until this minute.'

'Thank you kindly,' her mother said mockingly. 'Put that case down, Ted, and give the apple of your eye a peck.'

'That makes me sound like a blackbird . . . which reminds me, we've put some of those eating apples from the old tree at the end of the lawn aside for you to take back . . . well, Miss? Haven't you got a hug for . . .'

Kay swooped on him, knocking his check cap off, hugging him throttlingly. He wheezed a protest, hugged her back, kissed her forehead, then held her away from him as her mother had done.

'You've grown,' he said in a surprised voice. 'Or did I imagine you as daintier, somehow, less like your clodhopping mother? Darling, you look wonderful, very fit . . . aha, you're a corporal! Well, I wouldn't think much of an Air Force which didn't promote the daughter of two such remarkable parents, I tell you straight!'

'Thank God they promoted me, then; we wouldn't want your disapproval, Daddy,' Kay said. 'Did you drive here? How on earth did you manage that? What about petrol rationing?'

'Essential user,' her father informed her. He pushed his cap to the back of his head and crossed his eyes. 'I'm a varmer, now, my woman, an' don't you forget it,' he said in a thick Norfolk accent. 'I keep pigs an' geese an' hens . . . besides working in the Min. of Ag. five days a week, of course.'

149

'Which means I do most of the work,' Sara said, cuddling Kay's arm close to her side. 'I had hard work to persuade your father not to bring the tractor – he thought it would show you how agriculturally minded he's become.'

'I thought you were a Queen Bee amongst the WVS ladies?' Kay said, returning her mother's squeeze. 'Where does Daddy have all these animals, anyway? Our lawn isn't that huge!'

'Old Mr Langham who had land down by Harford Bridges died, and his smallholding was so – well, so small that no one else wanted it. So we clubbed together with the Mintons, the Ellises and the Pickmans and bought it and we're all farmers in our spare time. The others work hard too, and we're doing rather well. It's a sort of co-operative, which means we all share the work, the expenses, and the profits.'

They had reached the car by this time and Kay was climbing in when she stopped and stared, then began to laugh.

'Daddy, there's straw on the back seat! I can't believe it, and you've always been such a fuss-pot over your car! Or did you put a bit in to make me see you really were a farmer, now?'

'Rather not . . . I'll have that out of there, young lady,' Ted Duffield said, scooping the offending straw up in one large hand. 'We take it in turns to cart bales of hay and sacks of feed. Hop in then, your number one uniform is safe.'

'Oh, bliss,' Kay said, getting in and sinking onto the worn leather seat. 'I'm becoming resigned to all sorts of things, but walking everywhere isn't one of them! Now I'm settled, you can tell me all about home whilst I sit here in perfect luxury and enjoy myself.'

'There's nothing to tell, really,' Sara said, turning in her seat to beam fondly at her daughter. And proceeded, for the next ten minutes, to tell Kay exactly what had happened over the past six months. She had a beautiful voice, low and musical, and a delightful purr of laughter and Kay closed her eyes the better to appreciate and take in what had been happening in her absence and promptly fell asleep, waking only when they were drawing up before the white front door of Rivington.

'Mummy, how rude! I'm awfully sorry, I fell asleep, now you'll have to start telling me all over again. Am I the only one home, though? What about Sandy Mac and Lizzie Elf?'

'Alexandra is very busy being a WRN up in Scotland and Elizabeth is an RT operator, whatever that may be, in Sussex. But Steve Minton's back for a few days and Gubby Taylor, too. You know Gubby quite well, don't you? Only Steve suggested you might like to make up a foursome.'

'Does he know I'm married?' Kay said, bristling slightly as she got out of the car and followed her parent across to the front door. 'I'm not sure married women are supposed to make up foursomes, are they?'

'Anyone for tennis?' Ted Duffield said brightly, as they entered the rather imposing hall. 'That's what I call a foursome. Or bridge, of course, or possibly badminton.'

'Don't be silly, Ted. And don't you be silly either, Kay darling. No one suggested anything other than a friendly outing. But still, if you'd rather be at home with us, I'm sure they'll find someone else.'

'They?' Kay found herself bristling all over again, only this time at the thought of being left out, and by Steve Minton, one of her oldest friends! 'Who's they, Mummy?'

151

'Why, Steve, Gubby and Steve's girlfriend. He brought her round last time he came home, you probably know her, Hattie Featherstone.'

'Steve's girlfriend? Good heavens, I thought . . . did you say Hattie Featherstone? What a peculiar name. No, I've never heard of her; where does she live?'

'Darling, I've only met her once and though dear Steve introduced us, he didn't tell me her life history. She's not in the forces, though, she's something with the Food Ministry, I think he said.'

'Perhaps she gets him tinned peaches without points,' Kay said vaguely. She followed her mother across the hall, along a short corridor and into the kitchen. 'What's for supper?'

'Pork chops, mashed potato, carrots and apple sauce,' Sara Duffield said at once. 'It used to be your favourite when you were at school. Do you still like pork chops, darling? Only Mr Peters happened to kill a pig a week or so back and we have this friendly arrangement . . .'

'Don't let her tell you or you'll never eat your supper,' Ted Duffield said, coming into the kitchen and sitting down at the table. 'Your mother has so many swaps and deals and pay-backs going that I call her Queen of the Spivs. You'd be surprised, Kay, if you knew what she can get in exchange for a big cabbage or a dozen fresh eggs.'

'Are you starving, darling? Daddy's taken your case up to your room and I've planned supper for six-thirty, which is when we usually have it. But I've made some of those little potato pancakes you used to like and I've still got some honey left, so if you would like some.'

'Oh Mummy, you spoil me, and how I'm going to enjoy it,' Kay said happily. 'But actually, balloon ops are awfully well fed, because of the heavy nature of the work.

I gained a stone at Balloon School and then lost it as soon as we got going on the site, so they obviously fed us right.' She examined herself anxiously. 'I'm not fat, am I?'

'You're perfect, darling,' Sara said at once. 'Come and sit down now; it's your turn to tell us all about your balloon site No 12, and all about your friends . . . oh darling, I am awful – how's your Philip?'

'He's keeping well, though he's browned off with being abroad and so far away from me,' Kay said cautiously. 'He writes twice a week at least, lovely letters. He's hoping for a home posting in a year, but there's no telling, really. He says it's largely luck.'

'That's marvellous. Well, tell us everything!'

Kay woke early next morning and lay for a moment, luxuriating in the fact that she did not have to get up or do anything. She was enjoying the early sunshine pouring through the half-open window when there was a tap on the door.

'Come in,' she called, and her mother entered.

'Good morning, darling,' Sara said gaily. 'Haven't you brought us lovely weather? The sun's quite hot and there's scarcely any breeze. Now where can I put this?' She was carrying a tray which she placed carefully on the covers above Kay's knees. 'There you are, breakfast in bed! Does that appeal?'

'Oh Mummy,' Kay said gratefully, feeling a smile spread across her face. 'Oh, why did I ever leave home and join up? That tray looks absolutely wonderful.'

'You're impressed by the grape hyacinths in the green glass vase? That's my artistic soul showing, my darling, but it's nothing to the taste of an egg taken from the nest this very morning, and boiled for exactly three minutes.

153

We've got some poultry under the fruit trees at the end of the lawn. And the butter is butter, not margarine, and the marmalade's homemade.'

'But no one can get oranges,' Kay pointed out, eating the porridge without playing Marsh-Arabs, the way she had done as a child. Though that had altered from the time she had contracted measles and Steve, who had been responsible for giving her the dread disease, had been allowed to sit on her bed and talk whilst she ate breakfast.

'Why are you eating your porridge like that?' he had asked curiously, and Kay had been glad to explain that the milk was the river and the porridge was the marsh, so the Arabs made milky paths through the marsh in order to rescue the princess, who was the big blob of brown sugar.

'You're mad,' Steve had said. 'It's Hereward the Wake who makes paths through the marsh, not some silly old Arab. Hereward's hiding from the king's men in the marsh because they've wrongly accused him of trying to kill the king and he makes false paths . . . like this, and this . . . to draw the king's men away from his secret hideaway. See?'

Steve was two years older than she and bossy with it; it had seemed politic to agree with him and for many years Kay and Hereward the Wake had shared their breakfast porridge together.

'Who said it was made with oranges?' her mother said smugly, bringing Kay abruptly back to the present. 'It's amazing what you can do with carrots and honey . . . oh darling, how awful of me to boast, now you won't eat it. Daddy said not to say a word until you'd scrunched the toast down. He thinks you need feeding up, he says your cheeks aren't as pink as they were.'

'My cheeks were never pink,' Kay said, revolted at the

154

thought of herself looking like a marshmallow. 'That porridge was delicious – now tell me, Mummy, what have you got planned for today?'

'Darling, I hate to do it to you, but can you amuse yourself this morning? I've got a meeting at the city hall, I couldn't possibly miss it, and knowing how these meetings last, I can't guarantee to be home much before five o'clock. But your bike's still in the old stable and I know you'll want to look up old friends, snoop round your old haunts, so you won't be lonely, will you?'

'Lonely? Here, in my own home? Mummy, I'll be happy as a sandboy, honestly. In fact, if you tell me what to cook I'll get supper for you and Daddy when you come home. Bops have to take their turn at cooking, so I'm quite a dab hand at it. Well, at least I can do simple things, and actually, I thought whilst I'm home, I'd get you to give me a few lessons.'

'Lovely, darling, be glad to,' her mother said absently, leaning over the bed and giving her a scented hug. 'I must be off or I'll miss the bus. Take care, darling. Oh, and it's Chrissie's day for the floors, so don't get in her way, will you? She'll make you a nice lunch. See you this evening, love.'

'Bye, Mummy,' Kay said, dipping her bread-and-butter soldier-boy into the rich orange egg yolk. 'See you this evening.'

Eating breakfast in bed with a sunny day outside is wonderful, but Kay soon realised that it lacked a certain something. She wondered about snuggling down again and having an hour or so of extra shut-eye, but she could hear Chrissie crashing about downstairs, singing hymns and shouting at the dogs, and knew that sleep would not come under the circumstances. And besides, it would be a wicked waste of a day's leave – she only had a week.

So as soon as breakfast was eaten she got out of bed and padded through to the bathroom. She dabbled a hand under the hot water tap and thanked God for arranging that the Aga was going full bore, because the water was very hot indeed, so she ran herself a bath and climbed gingerly into it. She did feel a pang of guilt when she realised that she had drawn considerably more than the regulation four inches, but what the hell? She was on leave and it was a treat for a change.

She mucked about in the bath, too. After ten minutes she reached over the side for her bath bag. It was made of bright yellow string and contained an assortment of toys. Very soon two celluloid ducks bobbed around her knees, and the rubber goldfish with a hole in its mouth was held under water and filled, then squeezed so that it squirted like a water pistol. Kay held her toes to ransom – 'stick 'em up!' – and then shot them dead – 'take that . . . and that!' – and then found her diver and his submarine, only neither of them worked as well as she remembered so she repatriated them to the string bag just as she began to realise the water was going cold.

Shall I run some more hot water and muck about a bit longer? she asked herself, but her toes and fingers were going all crepey and crinkly and through the frosted glass of the window she could see that the sun still shone and the sky was still blue. Don't waste it, she urged herself, climbing out of the bath and dripping all over the bathmat which was shaped like a big green foot. Make the most of every day of this leave, you may not get another for months!

Chrissie was polishing the hall floor when Kay came down the stairs.

'Cooee,' she called, and Chrissie promptly dropped her mop, gave a strangled shriek, and pounded over to the foot of the stairs, holding out her enormous arms, a beam splitting her face almost in two. Kay, who had been carrying her tray with the empty dishes on it, hastily stood it on the newel post; she could see what was coming.

'Kay, my woman! Well, in't that marvellous to see you home after all this time! Ha' you seen the boy Stevie? He're been home a day or so, I said to your mum I said, let your daughter set foot in this here city an' the boy Stevie'll be round like a shot outer a bloomin' gun!'

Kay fell into the older woman's arms and they hugged fiercely and with mutual pleasure. Ever since Kay could remember she had tagged round after Chrissie, helping, hindering, talking. All her childish ailments, all her teen-age worries, had been confided at such times, and Chrissie had never broken a confidence, always supported her.

How lucky I am, Kay thought now, to have two such women as Mummy and Chrissie to bring me up. And Daddy always there, always supportive . . . how very lucky I am! But she said nothing of the sort aloud, because that would have embarrassed her friend. Instead she detached herself from Chrissie's tight embrace and said reproachfully, 'I'm a married woman now, you know, Chrissie. And Stevie's got a girlfriend, he won't come rushing round to see me like he used to.'

Chrissie cocked a belligerent eye. 'And why not, my woman? He've allus been your pal, you've allus been his pal; why should that change, eh, just 'cos one's wed and t'other's got a girlfriend?'

Twice in one day I've been put in my place for undervaluing friendship, Kay thought ruefully, agreeing with Chrissie that she was just being over-sensitive. I

157

really must stop thinking that people are matchmaking because no one's likely to forget I'm married, me least of all. And it would be fun to see Steve again, I don't think we've ever been apart for as long as six months before.

'Well, you've had your breakfast, your mum said you'd ate, so you'd best be off if you're goin' out,' Chrissie said. 'Give us that tray, I'll wash up after you this once, for a treat, like.'

They both laughed; Chrissie was always doing things 'just once, for a treat, like.' It was an old theme.

'I'll be back for lunch,' Kay called, going through to the kitchen to hook her old dufflecoat off the pegs by the back door. 'I'll just walk down the road, see who's out and about.'

'Oh ah,' Chrissie said, disbelief so strong in her voice that Kay could have screamed. 'See you later, then.'

Once outside, Kay strolled down the short drive with her dufflecoat unbuttoned, taking deep breaths of the fresh air, admiring a forsythia bush in full golden bloom, the pinkish scarlet of a flowering currant, the fresh and brilliant green of an ancient hawthorn. Later she would go round the big back garden, rich with memories of her childhood, memories which included Steve, but not yet. They had been so close, such good pals – why had he not come to her wedding? He had not written, either . . . but he was no longer a boy but a man, flying aeroplanes. Probably he scarcely thought of her now, his childhood playmate, yesterday's girl.

She walked down to the wrought iron gates, opened them, and stepped onto the sunny pavement, still thinking of Steve. He was the adored only son of parents who had not thought they were going to have a child. They had tried to shelter him, but even as a very small boy Steve would have none of it. He had gone his own way, played rugger and cricket, excelled at most sports. She had taught him rounders in self-defence when she was about ten, and they had co-opted other children and enjoyed many a game on Rivington's huge back lawn. In the winter he had wanted her to play rugger, but her father had rebelled. His lawn was a lawn, not a games pitch, he had told them, and paid for the pair of them to join a badminton club so that they could get rid of their energy less destructively.

She had had a marvellous childhood, Kay thought now, trying to peer through the Mintons' flowering hedge without being seen. What a time they had had! In Earlham Park they had taken flour bags on split canes and dipped tiddlers out of the river. They swam in that river too, sometimes from the bank at the park, at other times officially, at the Eagle Baths, which were just a section of river fenced off for bathers. They went to the Saturday morning cinema shows and leaned over the balcony, sending spit-balls spinning down onto the heads of the kids below. Yes, she had been lucky. For an only child she had seldom known loneliness.

Because of Steve, of course. She had followed him around like a little dog until they were old enough to enjoy one another's company, and then he had taken it for granted that whatever they did, they would do together. But that was yesterday, she reminded herself. Today was golden Philip, her marriage, her future. Steve was her past, as she was his, for before she had so much as left school he had begun to bring girls home, rather as a young pup brings in his first rabbit; part shy, part proud. She knew he was home, wondered if he, too, had been wandering around the garden, thinking of the past.

The Mintons' hedge was thick, though – too thick for

seeing through. It was an escallonia hedge, at this time of the year brilliant with pale pink blossom which smelled deliciously of almonds, sunshine, honey. Bees buzzed on it, and the scent made Kay feel quite lightheaded. But she couldn't wait around out here as she had once done, she had best make her way down to the shops and see if anyone had anything interesting to sell. Her sweet coupons had gone long since, but she might get chewing gum or liquorice wood, anything would do to keep her outside in this glorious sunshine.

'Kay! I thought it was you!'

She knew his voice instantly and turned on the words, a smile spreading from ear to ear. She jumped at him just as he held out his arms and they clung for a moment, Steve patting her back with a strong, competent hand, the way he had patted it when she fell over, skinned her knees, cried. Nothing has changed really, Kay told herself exultantly. We're like brother and sister – no, Steve's better than a brother, he's my best friend, the one person I trust completely, with my life if necessary. Oh, dear old Steve!

'Kay! My dear girl, you've grown a foot!'

'No I haven't,' Kay said, looking down at herself. 'I've still only got two!'

He knew what she meant at once, and gave her a friendly shake. 'Idiot, I mean you've grown twelve inches taller, as you very well know. You weren't even up to my shoulder when I joined up, now the top of your head is above my chin! How dare you change whilst I've been away!'

'I've been away too,' Kay reminded him indignantly. 'I've been flying balloons in London for months. I can't show you my stripes right now since I'm not wearing

160

uniform – and shan't, whilst I'm home – but I'm a corporal, really I am.'

He laughed, his eyes narrowing, his mouth curving deliciously, his expression at once mocking and delighted. He hugged her again, then held her away from him once more.

'I don't believe it: little Kay, a corporal!' Suddenly his smile faded, his eyes darkened. 'You're flying balloons in London, with all the bombing? Kay, why don't you remuster? It's hard, dangerous work, I've heard chaps talking about it. It's not for you, kid!'

'It is for me; I'm fully trained, we don't take risks,' Kay said. She remembered a night when she and Sergeant Potter had heard the balloon hissing gently as hydrogen escaped. He had heaved her up in his arms and she had stitched a patch over the hole whilst Potter told her that his legs were about to give way and to hurry before they were all blown sky high. 'Well, not many risks,' she amended.

Steve shrugged, then sighed. 'I can't talk,' he said. 'Second pilots on Wellingtons probably get pranged more often than balloon ops. I say, let's go down to Earlham Park and see if the minnows are still running. It's a lovely day, and we can talk as we go. I wonder if there'll be an ice-cream kiosk open? If so I'll treat you, and you can eat ice cream and tell me what's been happening to you. I might even tell you what's been happening to me, if you behave yourself.'

'All right, but we'll have to be home for lunch. Chrissie's doing something special, I think – you'll come?'

'Sure,' Steve said, falling into step with her as she turned towards the road which would lead them, eventually, to Earlham Park. 'My mother's in the city,

161

shopping, so she won't be home until Father comes in much later. We'll step out, shall we? Only it's a good walk . . . or we could catch a bus.'

'You've got no stamina, you Brylcreem boys,' Kay said mockingly. 'Oh look, here comes one!'

They ran, jumping on just as the rather bad-tempered conductor had rung the bell. He told them in no uncertain terms that it was 'agin the law' to jump onto a moving bus, then relented and took their fares, shaking his head at them as they collapsed onto a seat.

The journey was not a long one and soon enough they were getting down and walking past the tall gates, heading for the river bank.

'My hands are getting awfully tough,' Kay said idly as they made their way along the sandy paths. 'At first you get blisters all the time but then your hands get tougher and seem to grow accustomed. See? Hardly a blister in sight!'

She held out a hand. He took it, held it lightly, did not offer to give it back. Very gently his thumb caressed her inner wrist, almost absently. It meant nothing save friendship. Hand in hand, they sat on the gate, not saying anything, just enjoying this quiet moment.

But it couldn't last. Not now. Not ever again. Kay heaved a sigh and took her hand back, lay it in her lap.

'Why didn't you come to my wedding, Steve? I wanted you to meet Philip.'

'I couldn't. I was on standby. But I did write – didn't you get my letter?'

'Oh sure, yes. I thought . . . I thought maybe you didn't want to come, that you could have done it if you'd really wanted to come.'

'Not want to?' He stared at her, his eyes suddenly hard,

almost angry. 'My God, I wanted to come more than I've ever wanted anything. But I couldn't, and I wasn't about to let the chaps down by going AWOL when they needed me. And we all need each other, I can tell you.' He had been speaking softly, with a sort of controlled violence which Kay did not attempt to interpret, but suddenly he relaxed, turned and smiled at her. 'Sorry . . . was it a wonderful wedding? I expect it went off like clockwork with Auntie Sara at the helm.'

He had called her mother Auntie Sara since, at the age of five, he had come sobbing into their house with a split kneecap. Her mother had rushed him to hospital, comforted him, told him how brave he was, insisted that he call her Auntie Sara.

'Yes, it went well. Marvellously, in fact. Everything went well. We had our honeymoon in Devon and . . .'

'Don't.'

One little word, but with a world of meaning in it. She stopped speaking, sat very still, looking down at her hands. Wasn't it odd that they had never even held hands until a moment earlier, had teased and boasted and fought, made up . . . never considered the other anything but an old friend. Finally she sighed and spoke.

'All right, I won't. But Mummy said you brought a girl home on your last leave – Hattie something or other. Isn't she . . .?'

'No, she isn't,' Steve said. 'She's very pretty and rather fun, but I scarcely know her. Well, there have been quite a few girls, if I'm honest, and you went around with a bloke or two. Only marriage . . .'

He stopped speaking and stared out across the park with veiled eyes.

'Marriage what?' Kay said when it looked as though he

163

had said all he intended to say. 'Don't you approve?'

He looked at her then, curiously, as though he could not believe what she had just said. 'Approve? I suppose you're thinking it's none of my business, are you? And in a way you'd be right, only it – it just seems kind of – kind of sudden, kid. One minute you were tearing up the drive with pigtails flying, the next . . .' he shrugged helplessly, his mouth turning down at the corners, '. . . the next minute you're a married woman,' he finished, dropping his voice so that Kay had to strain to hear the words. 'I couldn't believe you'd go through with it, to tell you the truth.'

'Well, I did, and we're very happy,' Kay said, keeping her voice light. 'He's abroad right now but when he comes home you must meet; you'll like him.'

He did not look at her. But his head shook from right to left, from left to right. Then he jumped down off the gate, shoved his hands in his pockets, and set off across the park.

'Steve . . . wait!' Kay said, jumping up. 'It's awfully rude to simply walk away from someone without a word!' She ran after him, tugged his arm. 'Steve?'

He turned and looked down at her, smiling now, but she could still see the bleakness in his eyes. 'Sorry, it was rude. And I'm sure your bloke is grand. Now what'll we do today? Do you fancy catching a bus into the city, having a snoop round the shops?'

Much later, after they had eaten the delicious lunch which Chrissie had prepared, they walked down to the local for a pint, revisited old haunts, then against her better judgement they went dancing.

'Why not?' Steve had asked her plaintively, when she

said she thought it would be unwise. 'Don't you go dancing in London, then, with your crew?'

She had done so many times, and could not deny it. 'Well, just in a friendly sort of way, then,' she had said, and they had caught the bus and gone to the Arlington Rooms, where an Air Force band was playing. They were both good dancers, both enjoying the physical exercise as much as anything, and Steve bought them drinks, they won a spot-prize, they laughed a lot. And when they played 'You are my Sunshine', Steve held her very close, as she had known he would, and whispered into her ear that it was still their song no matter what, and every time he heard it he saw a mental picture of her, at that other dance, with her hair tied back high on her head, and the swirly grey chiffon dress which had been a leaving-school present from her parents, and the look in her eyes when they rested on him.

'I'm sure I just looked friendly,' Kay objected. 'It was all I felt, anyhow.'

But Steve shook his head at her and then held her tighter than ever, and sung quietly with the band until Kay had felt tears pricking her eyes.

> *You are my sunshine, my only sunshine,*
> *You make me happy, when skies are grey,*
> *You'll never know, dear,*
> *How much I love you,*
> *Please don't take, my sunshine, away.*

The dance had ended and they had returned to their table and presently the band played the last waltz and they swayed round the floor, closely clasped, and then came down to earth with a bump when they had to run for their bus and got separated, and Steve stood all the way back to Unthank Road.

They got off the bus and walked back to Kay's gate, where they parted and she walked slowly up the drive by the light of a crescent moon. I'm a selfish person, she thought sombrely as she let herself in through the side door and hung her dufflecoat up in the small cloakroom. I want everything – Philip, who is the most wonderful lover and husband, and Steve, who is my oldest and dearest friend. And I still don't see why I can't have it both ways, keep both my lover and my friend.

But in her heart of hearts, she acknowledged that it was going to be far more difficult than she had imagined.

Jo's leave was not the eagerly awaited treat which Kay clearly considered her own leave to be; Jo acknowledged it ruefully to herself as she walked up City Road, pausing to look down on the River Dee as she crossed the road bridge. Of course Kay had a lovely home in a leafy suburb of Norwich and Jo lived in the heart of the city of Chester, but that wasn't it.

You never should have left, a whining, treacherous little voice inside Jo's head remarked as she came to the junction between City Road and The Bars. You know very well that leaving home was a mean thing, so of course you can't look forward to going back, seeing what your selfishness has done.

That's nonsense, another voice in Jo's head said firmly, as Jo paused on Foregate Street to swop her suitcase from one hand to the other whilst examining a window full of willowy wax models wearing utility clothing. It was your duty to your country to join up, and that meant leaving home. No mother wants her daughter to leave home, but

166

you did it, all of you, Emily, Kay, Biddy . . . why should Jo Stewart have been any different?

Jo liked the second voice much better than the first, but she knew she was different, knew the voice had slipped up there. Her duty, ever since her birth, had been clear-cut, a narrow and stony path which should have carried her from cradle to grave had not the war intervened, allowing her a temporary escape.

And now you've escaped you don't want to go back, the first little voice whined. Well, you've got to face up to things, Josie Stewart, look truth in the face. You ran away; now you've got to see for yourself just how much damage you've done.

'Well, if it isn't the little Stewart girl! And in uniform – and a corporal! Thomas, do you remember this young lady?'

A tall middle-aged woman with windswept grey hair and weatherbeaten red cheeks caught hold of Jo's hand and pumped it up and down whilst Jo's mind raced fruitlessly around. Customer? Teacher? Parents' friend? The grey flannel suit looked like a teacher, the accent was more like a customer . . . not even the echo of a name flickered across Jo's infuriatingly blank memory though the face beaming down into her own was familiar.

'Sailing, dear,' the lady said, obviously recognising the despair behind Jo's polite smile. 'You were friendly with the little Tanner girl when she was crewing for Tommy – you both came to tea once or twice. I recognised you at once!'

'So did I, Mater,' drawled a deeper voice. Jo turned and looked into a tanned and handsome face whose narrow blue eyes were roving with decided appreciation over her neatly uniformed figure. Immediately her stomach did a double somersault and then kicked her in the ribs so hard that she almost gasped. Tommy Lucas, the King's School boy half her class at the Convent had dreamed of being seduced by! But Jo was no longer a simpering schoolgirl. She smiled as coolly as she could and drew her hand gently from Mrs Lucas's grasp.

'I'm so sorry, Mrs Lucas, I'm afraid I was in a dream,' she said politely. 'This is my first leave and I was just – just seeing Chester as a stranger might, I suppose.'

'Your first leave! My dear, how awful of me to keep you . . . just you run along, your parents will be anxious.'

Once, Jo would have used some excuse to linger, to exchange a few words with Tom Lucas, but not now, that was not how the new, worldly Jo Stewart behaved.

'Yes, I'd better be moving along,' she glanced with seeming casualness at Tom. 'If you need a crew during this next week,' she said offhandedly. 'You know where to find me.'

It should have been a good exit line, a real throwaway, except that Tom Lucas spoiled it.

'At the club, next Sunday?' he said. 'You'll have to be early mind . . . the starting gun's at nine.'

Jo's feet scarcely touched the ground for the rest of her walk up Eastgate Street. She did not suppose that she would be able to go to the sailing club, but just to have been asked was triumph enough. Indeed, her mood had been considerably lightened by the small encounter and as she made her way through the bustling crowds, eyeing the buses hurrying down the centre of the road, the bicycle riders tinkling their bells and the clean, though sparsely-filled shop windows, it occurred to her that Chester had, so far, been lucky. London was bombed out and boarded up, it was grimy, weary and battered. But this small, ancient city where she had been born and bred had somehow managed to escape most of the consequences of war. Indeed, it looked beautiful as ever to Jo's eyes, and optimism began to creep into her mind. Perhaps it would not be so bad after all, her leave. Perhaps she might even enjoy it.

But this lighthearted hope withered and died as soon as she opened the door beside the shop and began to climb the stairs. It was a dirty, narrow little staircase which led up from street level to an equally dirty and narrow door which led into the flat and somehow it brought all sorts of memories, few of them pleasant, flooding back. The stairwell, never large, began to shrink; Jo felt sure the ceiling was about to press down on the top of her head, the stairs themselves to squeeze closer like a concertina closing up.

For a long moment she stood there, halfway up the stairs, and wondered how she was going to make herself complete the climb. She would be blamed – and rightly, rightly! – as soon as she entered the flat for leaving, and all that conscience business would start again. She had been blissfully free of it ever since she joined the WAAF, where she was told what to do and left alone to get on with it. Here, it was very different.

But it was only for a week. And in her heart, Jo suspected that she might never live here again, not in a full-time capacity that was. Anyone can stand anything if it's only for a week, she told herself. So she gritted her teeth and stomped up the rest of the stairs, her kitbag over her right shoulder and her suitcase in her left hand. There was a bell booth outside the door and at the bottom of the stairs, but Jo had her own key. She fished it out of her

169

pocket, inserted it in the lock and pushed the door open. Then she paused for a moment; it wouldn't do to give her mother a fright.

'Mum? It's only me, Jo. I'm home.'

She heard the faint, answering hail from the direction of the sitting room and, having dropped kitbag and case on the faded hall carpet and slung her overcoat onto the hallstand, she made her way through to the front room. She pushed open the door and put her head round it.

'Hello, Mum . . . the train was a bit late, but here I am at last.'

Her mother had the wheelchair pulled up to the window so that she could look down on the busy street below. It was the only good thing about the flat, that window, because it was a big, square bay and when her mother had the wheelchair in the right position she could, by a mere turn of the head, see just about the whole of Chester's main street. If she looked left she could see the clock, suspended on the bridge which spanned Eastgate Street, with the people hurrying over the bridge and under it, too. If she looked right, up towards the cross, there was the imposing bulk of the red sandstone church and a tiny section of the cakeshop window. And if she looked straight in front of her she could see the black and white Elizabethan buildings, the façade of Brown's Departmental Store and the 'rows', for which Chester was justly famous.

'Josie! Well, well, well!' The wheelchair swivelled, its back to the window. Her mother's thin, pain-creased face was lit up by her welcoming smile. Her teeth, which always seemed too numerous for her mouth, smiled too, as though with relief at having escaped, for a moment, from their prison. 'Oh Josie, how I've missed you! Things

170

have been difficult . . . but you don't want to hear that, not now. I'll put the kettle on, make you a nice cuppa, and then we can have a lovely talk . . . only would you like to have a wash and brush up first? Journeys are dirty things, from what I recall, and your dad's doing one of his fire-watching turns tonight, so when he comes in he'll bolt his supper and rush straight out again. Though he'll be that pleased to see you . . . why don't you sit down, Josie dear, instead of hovering there? I may not be much use but I can make a cup of tea, you know that!'

There it went again, that horrible feeling, as though the room was actually getting smaller, closing in on her. Jo glanced quickly up at the ceiling, but it was still way above her head, then smiled rather stiffly at her mother.

'You don't want to be making tea . . . I'll do it. You stay there, I won't be a tick.'

'Josie Stewart, don't be so daft, I've had to learn to do things for myself lately, what with your dad out so much and you not here. So I'll make the tea, I insist, I won't take no for an answer. And you haven't even given me a kiss yet, so just you come over here a minute!'

Jo went obediently over to the wheelchair and bent over the small figure. Her mother's arms, thin as string but the strongest part of her, looped round Jo's neck and pulled her down. Her lips brushed Jo's cheek and Jo, feeling self-conscious and mean, kissed her mother grudgingly, then stood back. The Stewarts had never been a demonstrative family, so why this sudden urge to kiss? She could remember her mother waving her off on Chester Station, still grumbling, right up to the last minute, that Jo was selfish to go, never thought of anyone but herself, never considered the miseries of being tied to a wheelchair . . . and didn't Dad deserve some consideration, too? He'd

171

worked hard for them all these years, he was too old –
thank God – for any of the armed services, but how would
he manage with his wife crippled and a nuisance to
everyone, if their daughter walked out on them?

'I have to go, Mum,' Jo had told them when her papers
had come through. 'I've signed on, I can't get out of it.
And anyway, they would have conscripted me if I hadn't
signed because working in your father's ironmongery
isn't essential war work.'

It had not washed, of course, not with her mother.

'You've always gone your own way, Josie,' she had
grumbled. 'Maybe there's something in what you say,
maybe not, but I can tell you're longing to go off and leave
us, it's in every line of your face!'

The fact that her mother was right had not made it any
easier, either. She would not have gone but for the war, Jo
had told herself defensively; why did her mother always
make her feel so guilty, even if she only had an afternoon
out with a schoolfriend? But Dad had been decent about
it, had told her to go, said he understood. Not in front of
Mum, of course, that would have been asking too much,
but when they were alone in the shop downstairs,
weighing out nails, patching the bottom of a tin kettle,
waiting for the sound of Mum's bell, tinkling to say she
needed them, had fallen, wanted the toilet, needed a word.

But right now Mum was smiling at her, had just kissed
her, had seemed really glad to see her; so be thankful, Jo
told herself, and try to see things from Mum's point of
view. Stuck here in the heart of the city with only the view
from the window to look at, only her father's return from
work to anticipate, what else should her mother do but
think about her daughter and look forward to her first
leave?

'Of course, if you want to come and chat to me while I brew up . . .' Her mother threw the words over her shoulder, wheeling herself towards the kitchenette, '. . . I wouldn't mind a bit o' company, Josie! And I've got such a lot to tell you!'

Her mother always called her Josie, never Jo. Never Josephine, for that matter. Just Josie. But there are worse names, Jo told herself now, following her mother into the kitchen. I shouldn't feel hurt, though Mum knows very well I prefer Jo. If Dad can remember . . . but then perhaps there's more to it than that. Dad wanted a boy and he calls me Jo. Mum wanted a girl so she calls me Josie. Perhaps it isn't too bad, being all things to all men . . . and anyway, I'm the lucky one, I'm the one that got away. I'm only here for a week, after all!

'Well, old girl? Goin' to tell me what it's really like? Your mother's been marvellous, you know . . . did she tell you? She's been knitting for the forces, socks, balaclavas, gloves . . . and three times a week I carry her down to the shop and she sits with me and weighs out nails and sorts the screws and prices things. A different woman, that's what she's been – a different woman!'

Jo and her father were sitting comfortably by a log fire, with the curtains drawn across the big bay window and Eastgate Street wearing its ten o'clock hush. Jo kept glancing at the curtains, unable to believe that the noise really had stopped, for there seemed to be none of the tense, listening silence which fell on London with the advent of the dark. There was a blackout of course, but people walked, talked and laughed long after the evening had fled.

'Well, love? Did Enid say anything about her war work?'

173

'Mum told me she'd been helping,' Jo said slowly. 'It wasn't that I didn't believe her, I just didn't see what she could do. I mean you've tried to get her downstairs for years . . .'

'Aye, and she'd never go, except if one of us was goin' to push her chair to the market, or up to the shops. But she got lonely I reckon, without either of us up here, and eventually it occurred to her that, sitting in the shop, she'd be able to chat to customers, have a gossip with old friends . . . and help me out, too. Staff's been impossible; too much money about for anyone to want to work for the sort of wages I can offer. Still, your mother's been a tower of strength – a tower.'

'That's wonderful,' Jo said, finding, to her surprise, that she meant it. 'And she's been doing the ironing and mending your shirts . . . she's actually knitted you a sleeveless pullover, she was telling me.'

'Aye, that's right,' Mr Stewart said. He was gripping an unlit pipe between his teeth, and now he fished his tobacco pouch out of his trouser pocket and began to fill it. 'I've wondered lately, love, if I've reaped what I sowed in that quarter.'

'You mean now that you're too busy to do everything for her . . .?'

'Aye, summat like that. There's you gone, and me fire-watching, my ARP work, collecting scrap metal to help build a Spitfire, and forms galore to fill in if someone wants to buy so much as a pot of paint or a couple o' six inch nails. I tell you straight, love, that if it hadn't been for your mother's change of style I'd have gone under. I'd not have managed the way I have.'

'So . . . me going wasn't such a bad thing?'

'It were the making of her,' Mr Stewart said reverently.

174

'It took her right out of herself, made her see that if she wanted summat, she must up an' get it. And once she started, she realised she could. Oh, she misses you love, we both do, but it were the best thing you could have done an' that's the truth. Now then, tell us a bit about these here balloon things you're flyin'.'

'It's hard work,' Jo said. 'But I love it. I love being with the other girls, Dad, and doing things well and being told I do them well. Mum didn't mean to upset me, but when I was a little kid . . .'

'She never learned how to praise, bless her,' Mr Stewart said, smiling round his pipe. 'But she's learning, Jo. She's really learning at long last.'

In bed that night, lying in her tiny room with the blackout curtains drawn back so she could see the stars, Jo reflected on life. For as long as she could remember she had been at her mother's beck and call. She had carried her downstairs for the first time, appalled at her lightness, when she was only just past her fourteenth birthday and had been doing it ever since. She had pushed her mother's chair, manoeuvred her from chair to toilet, from chair to bath, from chair to bed. And Mum had complained that Jo was rough, careless, thoughtless. She had told Jo not to sing around the house because she had one of her headaches, demanded that Jo give up being a Girl Guide, attending live-saving classes at the local baths, going out with her friends on a Saturday.

Dad and I both made a rod for our backs, she thought drowsily, as her eyelids began to droop. I'd even begun to hate her for making me feel guilty all the while. Well, I'll never do it again – and next time I do something for her I'll make her thank me; I will!

The thought amused her so much that she was still smiling when she fell asleep.

'Janet, isn't this a break? I never ever thought, when I went into the market hall, that the first words your dad would say were, "Well if it isn't our Jo, home on leave at the very same time as our Janet!" I can tell you, my heart did a great big bound . . . oh Jan, I've missed you!'

'Yeah, and having joined up together, what happens? You get slung down one end of England and I get slung up the other – that is to say, if you can count Scotland as England, which the Scots wouldn't like at all!'

'I know what you mean, though thousands wouldn't,' Jo said, laughing. The two girls were sitting by the River Dee, waiting for the Bore as they had waited for it a thousand times before and watching a couple of servicemen, rods poised, fishing where the water ran deep under some willows. 'Well, Jan, are you happy in your work?'

'Oh aye, it's grand. I was lucky that I went in able to drive, and they nabbed me straight off. I drive the big lorries in convoy from one place to another, or I chauffeur officers in staff cars, and in between I service the vehicles, do my paperwork and fool around with any fellers who happen to be about. Oh aye, I enjoy myself all right. What about you, Jo? Do you like your new life?'

'It's tough,' Jo said cautiously. 'You have to be very strong and I am, of course. Why, ever since I was small I've been lugging Mum and her wheelchair all over the place, so I've had to be pretty muscular. It's interesting work, you couldn't ever get bored on balloons.'

'What do you do exactly?' Janet asked curiously. She was a pretty girl with soft brown hair which waved across her forehead and large blue-grey eyes. Now, in civvies for

176

the first time since they joined up, the girls lolled on the spring grass and lazily watched the blue-reflecting waters of the river as it rolled on by them.

'In a nutshell we get the balloons up when the instructions come through and then bring them down again,' Jo said. 'We're becoming a fast crew; they time us at HQ and let us know who gets their balloon up in the shortest time. But I can't tell you all the details because I had to sign the official secrets act; I expect you did too, didn't you?'

'Can't remember. I signed so many things that now it's all blurred,' Janet grumbled. 'Jo, have you met anyone . . . you know?'

'A feller, d'you mean?' Jo shook her head. 'Not really. That's to say I've met a few, but none of them's particularly special. It's hard luck when you're on a balloon site because it's nearly all girls, and you don't get to go to dances or into the cookhouse because there isn't one. So we're very cut off from the sort of life you regular WAAFs lead. I tell you one thing, though. I'm glad I'm not married. My best friend in the WAAF is married and it – well, it makes her quite different from the rest of us. It must be uncomfortable for her a lot of the time, because most of the balloon ops talk about blokes non-stop . . . and all Kay wants to talk about is her Philip, and he's abroad.'

'Perhaps that's why you've not met anyone,' Janet said suddenly. 'I bet that's the reason. WAAFs always go around in pairs and if your pal is married . . . tell you what, Jo, why don't you and I go dancing tonight? I know your mum doesn't like that sort of thing, but surely, now you're in the WAAF, she won't stop you, will she?'

'She'd better not try,' Jo said grimly. 'Yes, I'll come dancing with you, Jan. Actually, I'd love to. I just wish we could meet a couple of really nice chaps who were on leave like us, wouldn't that be something?'

Later that night, lying in her bed once more and trying to get to sleep, Jo wondered why she had not told Janet about meeting the gorgeous Tom Lucas and his invitation to the yacht club. Perhaps, she thought now, it was because boasting about a boy you'd both known at school seemed somehow juvenile, giggly. She supposed that Tom must be in the forces but she didn't actually know, and anyway, the time to talk about it was if she decided to go out with him . . . if she decided to go to the yacht club on Sunday, just for a start.

6

It was strange to go back to another balloon site, particularly as a corporal and not just a balloon op. The best thing about it, Kay decided almost at once, was Sergeant Jonty Smith, because he greeted his new corporal with open arms and told her, frankly, that he was relying on her to get made up to sergeant as quickly as possible, so that he might go back to his first love, which was aero-engines.

'But I haven't been a corporal two minutes,' Kay said, rather dismayed. 'I'm not at all sure I'm sergeant material.'

'Nonsense,' Jonty said briskly. 'You're a girl born to command, take my word for it. You'll be an officer next, you'll probably be running the WAAF singlehanded by the time the war's over.'

'Oh, you think it's going to last a hundred years too, do you?' Kay said gloomily. Her leave had been such bliss that the loveliest of balloon sites would be a let-down after it, and this site, with so many factory chimneys in such close proximity to the blimp made her heart quail. It was not an ideal starting place for a corporal who had only just attained her stripes. 'I can't say it's nice to know we share the same opinion, but at least it means we're neither of us optimists.'

'You're daft, girl! The war's simply waiting to be won and we're going to do it. In two years, or maybe three, we'll be clanging the church bells and hanging the bunting. But we were discussing the likelihood of you rising to the lofty height of sergeant, and you've been more or less in charge of the other girls ever since you arrived at your last site; your sergeant said you had what it takes and he's a stout feller, Sergeant Potter. Anyway, under my expert guidance,' he grinned evilly at her, 'you'll soon find you were born to command. And then I can go back to being a flight mech.'

'What stopped you staying there?' Kay asked curiously. They were in the small wooden hut which housed the tiny office, the telephone and a rather threadbare mess. They were both in the office though it was only Sergeant Smith who was sitting down, and he was perched sideways on the worn and creaky desk. 'I can't imagine why they should put you on balloons if you're so set on aero-engines.'

He waved an arm at her, and and for the first time Kay realised the hand had only two fingers on the end. She winced, but the sergeant had obviously come to terms with his loss. 'This is what done it, Corporal. Never go after a spanner when you drop it in the works and some young idiot decides he's finished and goes and turns the engine over. So when I came out of hospital they put me on balloons, but now I've proved I haven't lost much manual dexterity – and they need flight mechs terribly badly – they've said I can go back. See?'

'Right, I see. But they wouldn't make me up to sergeant and keep me on the same flight, would they? I thought they never did that sort of thing.'

'Well they will this time,' the sergeant assured her. 'Want to take your traps over to your hut? Whilst you do that I'll unbend from my powerful position as boss-man and make you a cup of tea. Or perhaps I'll get ACW Perkins to make it,' he added thoughtfully. 'She's the prettiest.'

180

'What's that got to do with her tea-making abilities?' Kay asked, turning back. She had been halfway across the office when his words had caused her to stop. 'I thought all WAAFs could make tea by instinct, anyhow.'

'The kitchen is small, and if I've got to be cheek to cheek with anyone in there, it might as well be ACW Perkins,' the sergeant said. He grinned as Kay snorted. 'Well, honesty's the best policy, I always say, and once I'm back on an airfield competing with aircrews I shan't see a great deal of the prettier WAAFs. So I'm making the best of it, see?'

'You ought to be ashamed,' Kay told him. 'Where is this kitchen, anyhow?'

'Oh sorry, didn't I say? Next hut along. Your sleeping quarters come after that. And if you find a repellent little mongrel lying on your biscuits just turf him off, will you? His name is Grouser and he does.'

Kay gave the sergeant to understand that any mongrel lying on her bed would most certainly be turned out, but she thought he was joking until she opened the door of the long hut. There, sprawled on the bed nearest the door, traditionally kept for the NCO, was a small black mongrel dog with very shaggy eyebrows and a tiny, pointed beard.

'Off!' Kay ordered him. 'And out!'

The small dog grinned at her and wagged a sweep's brush tail. It remained in the bed however.

'Come on, laddie,' Kay said and when the dog showed no desire to shift, she set down her suitcase and kitbag and pulled the blankets out from under him. 'Just you go and sleep somewhere else, my boy!'

The little dog bounced onto the floor and got slowly to its feet; Kay wondered rather apprehensively if she'd done it any permanent damage, especially when it approached her at a slow hobble, the smile much in evidence but accompanied this time by a definite cringe.

'Good boy,' Kay said encouragingly therefore. 'Are you all right? No bones broken? Only you aren't allowed to sleep on my bed, or anyone else's for that matter. Indeed, you shouldn't be in here at all.' She opened the door she had just entered by and held it invitingly open. 'Run along, fellow – I mean Grouser.'

The dog yawned, stretched and wandered out through the doorway. Kay realised she had been holding her breath and giggled at herself. She had been treating a slight battle of wills between herself and the dog as though it was a test of her abilities as a corporal – but at least she had won!

Jo's new site was a very short distance from Site 12, so she went straight to the familiar playing field first, to have a word with Biddy and Emily. They were on cooking duties so she found them in the kitchen, peeling a million potatoes – or so Biddy said – and sweating freely in the heat from the bottle-gas cookers going full bore.

'Jo! Oh, it's great to see you! Let's look at them stripes . . . hey, handsome!' Biddy flung down her knife and held out a wet hand. 'Congratulations, our Jo, you done bleedin' well, I can see that.'

'I haven't done anything yet,' Jo growled. 'I'm scared stiff, what's more. Suppose they won't do as I say?'

'Crack them over the head, like you used to threaten,' Emily said, smiling enormously. 'Ooh Jo, we've missed you, haven't we, Bid? And Kay, of course. Where is Kay, by the way?'

'Still in London, but on the inner ring instead of the outer. She'll get it hotter there, poor old girl, but she's nearer the action – the West End I mean.'

'And what about your leave?' Biddy asked, turning back to the sink. 'You don't mind if we get on? Only we're supposed to be servin' up in less than two hours.'

'Carry on,' Jo said grandly. 'I'd give a hand, only I'm a corporal now, you appreciate; we don't do menial tasks.'

The other two crowed and blew raspberries as Jo settled herself on the kitchen table, one leg swinging, and proceeded to cut the peeled potatoes into pieces and to remove the eyes for her friends.

'Your leave, Jo,' Emily prompted after a moment. 'What happened? Anything much?'

Jo giggled. 'A bloke I used to know asked me to crew on his yacht for him. So I did and he ended up in the 'oggin. But apart from that I had a good, quiet sort of time.'

'Tell about the bloke,' Biddy said at once. 'Nice, is he? What's his moniker? Good-lookin' feller, eh?'

'His name's Tom and he thought I was a pushover, once the racing had finished,' Jo said. 'He got very annoyed because we weren't placed in any of our three races. So after they were over he moored the boat under some willows with the intention, apparently, of first giving me an almighty dressing down because we'd lost and then when I was reduced to tears of apology, kissing and making up. Only it didn't quite work out that way.'

She smiled, remembering the scene. Frail March sunshine coming through the leafless branches, Tom's face as he harangued her, getting crosser and crosser when she refused to do anything but laugh and remind him that this was supposed to be a pleasure, not a penance.

'But the pleasure's in winning, you stupid little prat,' he had said angrily at last. 'Come here, let me show you something.'

183

She had moved along the seat, never guessing that he would suddenly grab her and begin to maul her fiercely and to kiss her so hard that her jaw felt dislocated. She tried a polite protest and when her mouth opened he very rudely pushed his tongue into it – what could she do but bite? And when he squealed and pulled back, she put both hands squarely against his chest, and the muscles which were in such excellent trim from fighting with recalcitrant barrage balloons thought nothing of exerting their strength, with the result that Tom Lucas suddenly found himself first airborne and then waterlogged, rising from the river with duckweed in his hair and murder in his heart. And Jo had laughed, which, apparently, had been the final straw.

'Bitch, bitch, unnatural bitch,' he had screamed at her, struggling out onto the bank. 'You wouldn't know what to do with a man even if you could find yourself one, which you never bloody will!'

'I know what to do with men, and I know what to do with spoilt little boys,' Jo had said, removing herself from the yacht with some speed, for she could see revenge in her erstwhile captain's bloodshot eyes and did not relish being tipped into the water in her turn. 'So don't try to get physical with me, sonny boy!'

Sonny boy was sobbing with rage, squeezing water from his shirt, still screaming obscene remarks, so Jo had just turned and left him to it. She had caught the first bus back into the city, and hoped she might never set eyes on Tom Lucas again.

'Why didn't it work out?' Emily asked curiously. 'And you never said if he was good looking, either.'

'It didn't work out because I bit him and chucked him in the water and he used horrible language and threatened

184

me,' Jo said, grinning. 'And yes, he was good looking in a smarmy sort of way.'

'If I could bag a good looking feller I wouldn't throw him in the 'oggin,' Biddy said wistfully. 'I'd take great care of him so I would! Still, I know what you mean, Jo. He didn't treat you with respect, did he?'

'He certainly didn't,' Jo agreed. 'And now tell me what's been happening here whilst we've been gone. Any sign of ACW Price becoming a human being, for instance?'

'Norra hope,' Biddy said at once. 'She's gorrit in for the new corporal, Jane Morgan, an' all, hasn't she, Em? At the height of the work last night she just calmly moved off the port guy round to the tail; said she didn't fancy pullin' next to me! Corpy's not as tough as old Withers, but the sarge gave Price a mouthful when he heard, threatened her with jankers for a week if she was ever insubordinate again. Dunno what difference it'll make, though. You know ACW Price!'

'I do, worse luck. And how's Moll?'

Emily turned from the sink and threw a peeled potato into the bowl before Jo. 'She's fine, doing very well, the leg's all but healed. Now that the lighter evenings are here we take her for a proper walk when we're not on duty and she's getting really good. She walks to heel, sits at the kerb . . . she'll not disgrace Site 12.'

'That's good. What about leave, then, you two? Any chance?'

'We're going next month,' Emily said. 'We're looking forward to it, aren't we, Bid?'

Biddy finished the last potato and brought it over to the table where she cut it into four pieces and added it to the bowl. 'Course we are,' she said shortly. 'Come on, Em, we'd better put these on to boil and then start prickin' the sausages.'

'Kit inspection this morning, Flight Officer Sue Sullivan does it, and laundry collection immediately afterwards,' Sergeant Smith told Kay next morning as they ate the porridge which the girls on cooking duty had made for them. 'Sue's one of the old school though, so look out.'

'Look out? Why?' In Kay's experience, senior officers had been helpful and sensible so what could the sergeant mean? She gazed enquiringly at him and he chuckled.

'She's in her late forties and a real martinet. She'll not enjoy a kit inspection unless she chucks at least one bed all over the hut and tramples a couple of clean shirts. I'm told she also likes to make at least a couple of WAAFs cry; she's that sort of officer.'

'It's a pity I'm not more into the job,' Kay said uneasily, scraping the last of the porridge off her dish. 'If the girls knew me better they could tell me any problems they might have about showing a full set of kit, but as it is I'll be very little use to them. Oh, and Sarge, any bods who need watching?'

'Isn't there always? Keep an eye on Shirley Bliss – was ever a girl so ill-named? – and her pal, ACW Ozmund, they call her Ozzie. A nastier couple you'll never meet and bully? Gawd, you have to watch 'em.'

'Right,' Kay said. Oddly enough, the information made her feel stronger and more capable of tackling whatever situation arose, because it was just like school. No matter how much those in authority tried, there were always the bullies and the bullied, the girls who could and those who could not get along with their work and keep on good terms with their colleagues. And now, Kay reminded herself, it's your job to sheepdog them all – guard them, keep them in line, bark at them when they stray. So start off by being pleasant but firm to this Flight Officer Sullivan.

When the mild days of April gave way to the warmer ones of May, Biddy and Emily had their first precious seven days leave.

'Why did it have to be May?' Biddy grumbled as they were packing their kitbags, for neither had enough personal possessions to fill a case. 'I hate May; always shall.'

'Because of the Liverpool blitz, you mean,' Emily said, folding her striped pyjamas and putting them carefully into her kitbag. 'Yes, of course, it must have been terrible. But you were lucky – you and your family survived.'

'Oh aye; but over a thousand died, y'know. An' the damage was like nothin' I've seen nor imagined. We had a whole bleedin' week of it, a week of sittin' there whilst the bombs crashed an' the fires burned. A week of cryin' an' prayin' an' countin' the dead.'

'Want to talk about it?' Emily asked.

Biddy thought, then shook her head decidedly. 'No, there's no point. Havin' nightmares is bad enough. Talking about it would make it worse. Talkin' never brought no one back.'

'True. I hadn't realised that this was the – well, the anniversary of that week, I suppose. But if you don't want to go back now, it isn't too late to change our leave around. If we went and talked to Sergeant Potter and the SO . . .'

'Don't marrer none,' Biddy muttered. She was always at her most Liverpudlian, Emily noticed, when discussing her home town. 'Tomorrer's as good as any other day – or as bad, likely. Let's go and see if our rail warrants've arrived.'

They had. Both girls took the warrants and tucked them into their respirator cases, Emily beaming with satisfaction.

'There we are! As good as home,' she said cheerfully. 'Come on, Biddy, let's go through for supper, then we can get to bed and it'll be tomorrow before we know it!'

It felt strange, Emily thought, to be sitting in a railway carriage with Biddy, both heading for their homes. It was strange chiefly because there was no sense of urgency, no feeling that she should be hurrying back to the site in case she was needed. Emily had not realised before how service life had changed her, so that she was always waiting for a command, a terse voice shouting at her to get out of bed, or out of the cookhouse, or out of the mess, to do this, fetch that, carry the other.

Now, sitting in the carriage and looking out of the window at the soft greens of an English May, she could appreciate, in a way she had never been able to do before, what an immense amount of pleasure she could get from simply deciding for herself what she should do. Choosing a seat in the train, deciding which odds and ends of food to take as her packed lunch, planning the journey, all these things had been done to please only herself. And Biddy, of course. Emily glanced at her friend, silent on the seat beside her. It was odd, because Biddy was a real chatterer, but it seemed that the sheer anticipation of seeing her family once again, to say nothing of her friends, was so great that it had rendered her speechless.

'Not long to Crewe now, Bid,' Emily said as the train

chuntered to a stop at a smallish station. 'There's a fellow selling tea and wads; want some?'

'No, I won't bother.' Biddy said, her voice small. 'I'm not 'ungry.'

Emily stared; miracles would never cease! But she was not all that hungry herself, so she would not get out of the train and chase across the platform after tea which was probably stewed black and a wad which would consist of National loaf, margarine and a smear of improbable fish paste.

The train did not stop long at the small station and presently Emily decided the time had come to fold up her newspaper and push it into her kitbag, which meant getting it off the rack and fumbling around in it. She managed to knock the hat off a motherly woman's head and bump the shoulder of a naval rating, but at least it gave her something to do other than to long to get out and give the slow old train a push. Emily settled herself in her seat once more, sighed and addressed Biddy again.

'Now don't forget, Bid, when we reach Crewe I change trains but you stay on this one. Now did you let your folks know when you were coming so they could meet you?'

'Oh Em, you know I didn't – there's no point, chuck. There's dozens of trains in an' out of Lime Street, an' I only live a stone's throw away from there anyroad. Your dad's meetin' you, isn't he?'

'Yes, because I'm getting the Chester train when we reach Crewe, and Dad says he'll fetch some cattle-cake from the Feed Merchants an' pick me up at the same time. He's an essential user, being a farmer, so he has a petrol ration.'

'Yeah, well, there you are, then,' Biddy said rather confusedly. 'Is this Crewe comin' up?'

Emily peered through the window, then got to her feet and began to fish her kitbag down off the rack. 'You're right, it is Crewe. Now Biddy, have a really good time and come back refreshed, like the section officer said. And do try to catch the same train as me – it leaves Lime Street exactly a week today at eleven-ten and gets into Crewe an hour or so later, which is when I'll come aboard. Save me a seat!'

'I will, Em,' Biddy said. She looked lost and small, the only person remaining in the carriage by the look of things. Emily felt a qualm at leaving the younger girl, but reminded herself that they were WAAFs, not a couple of kids, and gave Biddy an encouraging smile which her friend did not appear to see. The train jerked, stopped, jerked again, then finally shuddered into total stillness. Emily, who had been so anxious to arrive, found herself at the back of the queue to get out, so she employed the time by telling Biddy what train to catch all over again, and exhorting her to have a good time and try to lie in, mornings. Finally she jumped off the train, leaving her kitbag behind, so that Biddy had to lean out of the window and pass it to her, looking more cheerful than she had done all day.

'You're a cloth-'ead, Emily Bevan,' she shouted as the engine began to get up steam preparatory to leaving the station. 'Don't go gerrin' on the wrong bloody train now girl, lettin' the side down!'

This was more like the old Biddy; she was clearly no longer overawed by the thought of going home, Emily told herself. She charged up the steps in order to get to the other side of the line for her train just as the 14.02 from London Euston gathered its breath, gave a shrill whistle, and began to chug out of the station.

Emily paused halfway up the stairs and waved vigorously, caught a glimpse of Biddy, now squeezed into the corner seat Emily had just vacated, watching and waving too, and then it was gone and another train was coming in on the platform towards which Emily was heading.

Help! To lose her connection would not be clever at all, not with Dad waiting for her! Emily thundered up the stairs, along the landing and down the other side. The charge of the Light Brigade, the Campbells were Coming, the Relief of Mafeking all rolled into one, she tore onto the platform and leapt aboard the barely stationary train.

It was not crowded and she found a seat without any trouble, then sank into it, kitbag on knee, and leaned back to indulge in some serious anticipation.

The train may well have stopped at Lime Street, but Biddy didn't get off there. She got off at Runcorn instead.

She had an aunt in Runcorn and some cousins. She hadn't seen them for years, but she had to go somewhere, so why not there? One thing she did know – she wasn't going home, not she! No point. Everyone from her street had moved away after the May blitz, chiefly because there wasn't much street left for them to live in, and she didn't fancy going back there.

She didn't know Runcorn at all well, but she had never been shy about asking for directions. The second person she asked pointed out Poyser Street quite cheerfully and Biddy, kitbag on shoulder, headed in that direction. She looked around her as she walked; the famous bridge which crossed the Mersey loomed large, of course, but folk grinned at her, slogging along in her best blues with the kitbag weighing down one shoulder.

She reached 12 Poyser Street and banged on the door. It wasn't a bright, smart house, it was run down and grubby looking; the net curtains were grey and coming off the runner in several places. Auntie Ethel never were much of a housekeeper, Biddy remembered her mother saying. Still an' all, she's gorra great laugh an' her family eats well. An' there's norra lorra folk can say that.

That was an accolade for Marie Bachelor; she set considerable store by a good laugh. Biddy, remembering, felt her throat tighten for a moment and metaphorically dug herself in the ribs. Wharrever's up wi' you, old Biddy, she demanded crossly. You ain't goin' to see your mam this time, but she's there for you if you need her, so don't you worry yourself over it. Just you enjoy yourself with Auntie Eth and Cousin Herbert, if he's home, of course.

The door opened abruptly inwards just as she was about to bang again. Auntie Ethel's round, rosy face, with a smear of flour across one cheek, crinkled into a big smile, and then the tears came, rolling down her cheeks, plopping onto the front of her stained flowered overall.

'Biddy! Eh, you said you'd come, but I dunno, I weren't sure . . . here, gi's a big 'ug, queen.'

The two women hugged convulsively for a moment, then Auntie Ethel took the kitbag and slung it in the general direction of a row of pegs to the left of the front door.

'We ain't got much, queen, but what we've got is yours,' she declared. 'Come to think of it, a good deal of it come from you, chuck. I've been ever so grateful for the money, an' the soap an' the chocolate an' all. Eh, Bid, it's a wicked old world, but we're goin' to mek the best of it, you an' me. I gorra letter from your Uncle Josh two days ago, he's off in some jungle somewhere I daresay –

somewhere 'ot, he says. Now come along in, I'll open a tin o' salmon I've been savin' for months . . .'

'It's good to see you, Auntie,' Biddy said, shedding her battledress and heaving her tie over her head so that she could undo her collar. 'I brought you some rice . . . they say you can't get it much . . . an' some dried fruit . . . just bits, but I daresay you can make use of 'em.'

Auntie Ethel, a most satisfactory receiver of gifts, cooed and gurgled and promised Biddy a rice pudding made to her own special recipe and a cake which would make them all forget rationing for a bit.

'They stopped us buyin' icin' sugar last summer, but I've a bag saved,' she said, giving Biddy her guileful child's smile. 'Herby's at sea, but he's due back any time . . . he could take you to a hop at the church 'all, flower. You're a big girl now, and anyroad, your mam wouldn't mind, she'd know our Herby 'ud tek good care of you.'

'That 'ud be good,' Biddy said. 'You're right, Mam wouldn't mind. No word about me da, I daresay.'

Ethel snorted and patted a faded easy chair which stood by the hearth. 'Sit down, lovie, whiles I mek you a nice cup o' char. We never did gerralong, your da an' me. Some things don't change. He don't write, I take it?'

'Not to me,' Biddy said, grinning. 'Auntie Eth, are you sure it's all right for me to stay wi' you for the week?'

'All right? It couldn't be better,' her aunt declared. 'Eh, we'll 'ave a grand ole time, you an' me. An' Herby, too, if 'is ship comes back while you're still around. I put you in Herby's room for now, 'e can always kip on the sofa.'

'So could I,' Biddy said. She followed her aunt into the small kitchen and leaned against the rickety table, watching whilst the tea was made and brewed. 'I can sleep on a bloomin' clothes line – I've kipped in worse places than your sofa, Auntie.'

'Oh aye, but our Herby wouldn't 'ear of it I tell you straight, chuck. And if there's raids we've gorra cellar – real posh!'

'Oh, raids. We've 'ad a few o' them in London,' Biddy said with real understatement. 'They don't worry me none.'

Her aunt looked at her face for a moment, then dropped the tea cosy which she was about to put over the pot and came across the kitchen to take Biddy in her arms once more.

'No, they wouldn't worry you,' she said softly. 'You poor little bugger, you've 'ad a bellyful o' raids, you 'ave. Now let's 'ave that cuppa.'

For three days Biddy followed her aunt round the house, helped with the chores and relaxed. On the fourth day, Herby came home. He bounded into the house, grinning from ear to ear and tugging a bashful friend behind him. He hugged his mam, cuffed Biddy playfully across the shoulder, then flopped into one of the two easy chairs in the front room.

'Phew, wharra voyage,' he said in his husky, heavily accented voice. 'Mam, Cousin Biddy, this is me mate, John Arthur, usually known as Jinky, Gawd knows why. Jinky ole feller, that's me mam an' that's me cousin Biddy,' he added rather unnecessarily. 'Me an' Jinks is goin' dancin' tonight – wanna come, kiddo?'

'Don't mind if I do,' Biddy said. 'Anyone else goin'?'

'Just our Sal,' Herby said. He flushed, the colour rising in his round, good-natured face. 'She lives next door but one. Her an' me . . . we've gorran understandin'.'

194

'That's nice,' Biddy said. She grinned at Jinky. 'You're goin' to get landed wi' me,' she informed him cheerfully. 'Oh well, it's only for the first dance, I reckon.'

'That's okay by me, Biddy,' John said immediately. He turned to Auntie Ethel. 'Can I do anythin' for you, Mrs Mack?'

'The kettle's a-boilin', lad,' Auntie Ethel said. 'I'll bring you both a cuppa in a trice, an' young Biddy there brung 'ome a yuge tin o' corned dicky, so we'll be 'avin' that, an' cabbage from the allotment, an' a pile of mashed spuds . . . will that suit?'

'Our mouths is waterin' just at the thought,' Herby said reverently. 'I'm round to see our Sal . . . why don't you two go for a walk?'

Biddy said she must help her aunt with the meal but Aunt Ethel would have none of it.

'Go on, off wi' you, show John around the place,' she ordered. 'Biddy's in your room, Herby, so I'm puttin' you an' your pal in the cellar. There's two camp beds down there, you'll be snug as bugs.'

'That's grand, Mam,' her son said, beaming. 'Take care of our Biddy, Jinky . . . no funny business, she's a good gal, so she is.'

'We might as well walk up to the park,' Biddy said as she left the small house beside the young naval rating. 'There ain't much in the shops, I'm tellin' you, an' me auntie won't be more'n half an hour gettin' the meal ready. How come you know me cousin? Same ship?'

'Aye, we're both ratings on HMS *Aconite*; she's a corvette, escortin' convoys to Russia,' John explained. 'I only been wi' your cousin a couple o' voyages, though. She's me third ship. What d'you do, Biddy?'

'I'm on barrage balloons; they call us bops, short for balloon operatives,' Biddy said. 'You've gorra be tough to be on balloons, but from what I've heard you've gorra be tougher for corvettes. An' since the *Aconite*'s your third ship, I s'pose they must remuster you, too?'

'Aye, corvettes aren't a bed o' roses,' he agreed. 'As for remusterin', it ain't exactly . . . but how long are you stayin' wi' the Macklens?'

'Oh, not long, just for me leave – it were a whole week but I've only got another three an'a bit days. How about you?'

'We're in for a refit, so it might be a couple of weeks. You goin' home at the end of the week, are you? Back to the 'Pool?'

'No, I'll be goin' back to London. I'm on a site on the outer ring; it's all right, I like it. It's a much freer life than on a RAF station, you see, we can please ourselves, pretty well.' She turned to look at him as they reached a stretch of grass on which half a dozen small boys were earnestly playing cricket, armed with an ancient tennis racket and a couple of coats as a wicket. John – Jinky – had a squarish, tanned face, a rather beaky nose, light brown hair cut painfully short, and heavily lidded, toffee-brown eyes. He saw her looking and turned to face her, smiling wryly.

'Know me again?'

'I reckon,' Biddy said. 'Why didn't you go home, Johnny? Why did you come back wi' me cousin Herby?'

'Oh, I had my reasons,' the young man said. 'And you?'

'I thought I'd like a change,' Biddy said. 'Besides, everyone's been evacuated out o' the city, except for me dad and I don't gerron wi' me dad. I'll go home next time, maybe.'

196

'Aye, I'm the same,' he said. 'Maybe next time.'

They walked over to a bench and sat down and watched the children for a moment in silence. It was a fine evening, the sky blue overhead but paling to a singing green with a line of brilliant gold where the sun had just sunk beneath the horizon. There were birds twittering and chasing in the branches of the tree overhead and a small dog ran across the grass and leapt on the ball with excited yaps. The cricketers yelled, laughed, chased. The smallest of the boys had tow-coloured hair which looked as though it had been cut with blunt shears and a pudding basin. His ears were like jug-handles and his voice was shrill. He reminded Biddy almost unbearably of her Sammy, which was probably the reason for the tears which suddenly rose to her eyes and, much against her will, trickled down her cheeks.

'Biddy?' An arm encircled her shoulders. John's face was only inches from her own and his concerned eyes looked deeply into hers. 'What's up, chuck?'

'Oh, nothing, I were just 'omesick for a moment – that little lad, he's ever so like our Sammy and . . .'

He squeezed her shoulders. 'I'm going to tell you something, Biddy. I'm going to tell you why they call me Jinky. It's because I've had two ships torpedoed under me and when I got back after my last lot my home had been bombed. So they say I'm a jinx . . . all rubbish, of course, but it doesn't make things any easier.'

Biddy turned so she could look at him properly in the sunset's glow. She thought he had the gentlest face she had ever seen and his eyes were understanding as though he knew, instinctively, that there was something which she longed – and needed – to tell.

'That's bad,' she said quietly. 'They ought to call me

Jinky too, then, because the last time I were home wi' me family me mam sent me down the road to get some milk for the baby. The warning had gone but we'd not heard the planes go over an' I was a way from home when the raid started. It weren't easy to buy or borrow milk during the bombing 'cos everyone were keepin' their heads down, see? So I were gone a while, an' a warden grabbed me when the stuff were flyin' an' pushed me into a shelter for a bit, milk an' all. An' when I got back to me 'ome, it'ud gone. Them an' all, the 'ouse, the kids, me mam. Just gone, as though they'd never been. It were a nightmare.'

'Poor kid.' His arm tightened on her shoulder for a moment, then he let her go.'What was it?'

'Direct hit,' Biddy said baldly. 'They'd all bought it – me mam, me aunts, the kids. It's odd, one moment you've got scores of family, the next you're on your own. So I just walked away from it, like. Joined the WAAF, lied about me age, pretended it hadn't happened. That they was all there, in the 'Pool, waitin' for me to come home. I write letters to 'em, send money . . . only it goes to Auntie Eth . . . so no one can tell I'm . . . I'm alone.'

'But your aunt must know, and your cousin.'

'Oh aye, they know. But they don't go on about it, in a way they may even understand.' She turned to him, suddenly needing to explain. 'You see while I don't go back, it hasn't happened; whilst I'm away, they're still there. Mam's sittin' by the fire, cobblin' socks. Me sisters are quarrelin', fightin', takin' it in turns to make the tea, nurse the cat. Me brothers are sprawled on the floor wi' bits o' chalk they've nicked from school, playin' noughts an' crosses. It's all goin' on just as though . . .' her voice dropped, thickened, '. . . just as though there weren't no such thing as bombs, or Hitler,' she finished.

'Maybe you've found the best way,' John said after a moment. 'I was never one of a big family, it's just me, my parents and my brother, Sid. Now it's just me and Sid. We write, try to tell each other that Mum and Dad were happy, didn't know a thing . . . but it's never far from your mind. Yes, maybe you've found the best way.'

'It's a cowardly way,' Biddy said. She sat up and pushed the hair off her forehead, combing it back with her fingers. 'But it's all I can come up with, at the moment. Later, when I'm stronger, maybe I won't mind people pitying me. And you know what? When I'm in London, with the girls, it's true, Mam and the kids are still up there in Liverpool, because I can talk about 'em, and joke about 'em, and no one questions it. If I can just keep away from the 'Pool for the rest of me life, they'll always be there.'

'You do what helps. You're a brave girl, Biddy; that's what counts, in the long run.'

'I'm not brave, that's the trouble. Sammy won't never be more'n six, little Kenny'll never learn to walk, Mam won't ever tell me she's proud I got me Leading Aircraft-woman . . . but while I can kid meself they're up there in the 'Pool, waitin' for the war to end so's we can be together again . . . well, it don't seem so final, some'ow.'

He took her hand and it seemed a natural gesture. They sat on the seat as the light faded, as the small cricketers departed, trailing their makeshift equipment, their 'wickets' round their shoulders now as the evening chill deepened.

'We'll miss that bloomin' dance,' Biddy said at length, stirring herself. She felt so relaxed, so at peace with the world, and all because she had told a total stranger the secret which she had kept so carefully hidden from her dearest friends. 'And Auntie Ethel's makin' a special tea 'cos you and Herby's home.'

He stood up and took both her hands, pulling her to her feet. He smiled at her, and somehow the smile brought the blood rushing to Biddy's cheeks. She thought, confusedly, that she would love to be pretty for Johnny, but he seemed to like her well enough just as she was.

'You're right, we must get a move on. We mustn't upset your Auntie Ethel. Did you know your cousin's always called Mack, on board ship? He's a nice bloke and a good sailor. So let's put our best foot forward – or our best feet, rather – because I'm really looking forward to dancing with you.'

'How can you be?' Biddy asked, falling into step beside him and getting a wonderful thrill when he took her hand. 'For all you know I might 'ave two left feet!'

He laughed and squeezed her fingers. 'I'll let you into a secret – I'm the world's worst dancer but I'm very good at standing and swaying in the middle of a dance floor, especially with a girl tall enough so that we can dance cheek to cheek. And anyway, sailors all have natural rhythm, so even if I can't dance, I can look as if I can.'

'It'll be fun, anyroad,' Biddy said, making up her mind. 'I've got a feeling that most things are fun with you, Johnny.'

She expected him to laugh and disclaim, but instead he turned her to face him and to her immense surprise, kissed her, very gently, on the tip of her nose.

'We'll have fun together for the next three days, Biddy,' he said softly. 'I can promise you that.'

'Well, Biddy, you really did save me a seat! D'you know, it's lovely to see you again . . . didn't the week fly? I did all sorts, a lot of it just bits and pieces around the farm, but

200

I feel marvellous, kind of calm inside. Living in London doesn't half make you appreciate the hills.' Emily sank into the seat beside Biddy and looked a little apprehensively at her friend. Biddy had been strangely silent on the way up; how would she be now? 'Tell me, Bid, what did you do? Did you 'ave a good time?'

'Yeah, it were all right,' Biddy said, beaming at Emily. 'Went to the flicks every night, very near, chewed the fat wi' Mam an' the littl'uns, spent some time wi' me Auntie Ethel in Runcorn . . . an' I met a feller, Em! Honest to God, he liked me, we gorron grand. Aye, as leaves go it weren't bad.'

'It sounds lovely,' Emily said sincerely. 'I've often wished I had brothers and sisters, but it wasn't to be, and I'm awful fond of my mam and dad. I've aunts and uncles and cousins too, just like you, but they all live a way off. Still, we saw most of 'em in the course of the week.' She leaned back in her seat with a little purr of satisfaction. 'And now you can tell me about your feller; are you going to see him again?'

'He's a naval rating on a corvette, so it'll be touch and go with leaves an' that,' Biddy said. 'But we're goin' to do our best to meet up whenever we can, and we'll write, of course. I wonder what shift we'll be on, Em? I hope they don't throw us straight in the deep end, after our leave.'

'Bet they will,' Emily said. Close observation had told her that the Air Force did not waste much time in getting you back onto active service once your leave was over. 'Still, you never know. At least the sarge will have given out today's jobs, so we aren't likely to fall for cooking or guard duty.'

'True. Tell you what, Em, why don't we walk round to

201

the school when we get back? The fellers'll tell us what's been happening.'

'Wouldn't it look a bit . . . well, a bit pushy? As though we were more interested in Alec and them than in our site?'

'I am,' Biddy said baldly. 'C'mon, Em, be a sport!'

'All right, if we're early enough,' Emily said. She liked Alec very much but suspected he still had a soft spot for Jo. But Jo was no longer around; despite her promise to keep in touch she had only been over to Site 12 once. 'The fellers might make us a cuppa. But we mustn't be too late. I want to see Moll before bedtime.'

'Oh you and that bleedin' dawg! What's Moll been doin' whilst you were on leave, then? Pinin' and whinin', I suppose.'

'Maybe. Sarge said he'd have her with him though, so she'll have been all right, I expect.' Emily bounced once in her seat. 'I'm really quite looking forward to getting back and seeing everyone again!'

'Your wretched dog has been driving everyone mad,' were the first words which greeted Emily as she and Biddy walked into the school. 'Sergeant Potter brought her round to visit Sunny Jim because she'd been searching for you all over the site, and then she didn't want to be parted from him, so we had the pair of them here for a couple of nights.'

'Why didn't she stay for longer?' Biddy asked curiously whilst Emily, red-faced, tried to apologise for the dog.

'Because she and Sunny decided to fall out and had a rip-roaring fight all round our quarters – and as it happens it was one of the few nights that the sirens didn't go off

202

and the phone didn't ring, so next day I marched her back to Site 12 and told Bill Potter that he'd have to cope somehow. Don't you leave her another time, Em, you'll have to get a dual travel warrant.'

'I don't mind,' Emily said. 'But she does keep petty pilferers at bay, the sarge often says so, which was why I never suggested taking her. If I had, Mam and Dad wouldn't have minded, they're used to dogs.'

'Well next time, don't hesitate; take her along,' Alec said severely, but with a twinkle lurking in his eyes. 'Poor Em, what a homecoming, nothing but grumbles about your dog.'

'But she isn't my dog,' Emily said crossly. 'She wished herself on me, I never wanted her. And this isn't a home-coming, either.'

'Oh, I don't know,' Biddy said. 'It is a sorta second home you know, Em. I'm happy here, in me way.'

Alec shot an incredulous look at Biddy, met Emily's eye and immediately changed the subject.

'Your new corporal, Jane Morgan, came and wept on my shoulder one evening – she's a nice little thing but not up to the job, I don't think. Some girl called Rice or something had been giving her a hard time. She said she dared not tell Sarge again or he'd think her a right ninny – which she is, of course, poor kid.'

'And what advice did kind old Uncle Alec give?' Emily said, and was immediately ashamed by the caustic note in her voice. Alec was kind, no wonder the poor little corporal had gone running to him. And if he heard the nasty note, he did not comment or appear to notice.

'I told her to pick the girl out for all the dirty jobs, but only when Sergeant Potter was near enough to back her up,' Alec said with a reminiscent chuckle. 'I did that myself back in the early days when I had a bolshie gunner with a chip on his shoulder. Soon cured him.'

'Except I bet you didn't wait for the sergeant to be near at hand,' Emily said shrewdly. 'I sometimes think it's easier for men.'

'It's not easy for anyone to be in command, unless they're very experienced,' Alec admitted. 'We were all young and unsure once – anyway, you'd better be getting back to the site. You'll want to get Moll out I daresay.'

'Moll? Out? What do you mean?'

But Alec would only advise them to go and find out. 'She's been a handful,' he said mildly. 'She's a big dog. Come round tomorrow, and tell me all about it.'

'She's been shut up again in that earth closet? Oh Sarge, how could you?' Emily said, appalled at the way Moll flew out of her prison, almost off her head with excitement at seeing her dear Emily once more. 'We haven't out her in there since the night of that first bad raid.'

'She's perfectly all right: she didn't like it, but she wouldn't behave herself so she had to be jankered,' Sergeant Potter explained. 'She'll be all right now you're back, Bevan. And I've put you two on guard duty tonight, so if you want to grab some shut-eye now . . .'

'Oh come on, Moll, the man's got no heart,' Emily groaned, grabbing the dog by the ruff round her neck and giving her an affectionate shake. 'At least you love guard duty, you old glutton for punishment!'

Jo had expected to enjoy being a corporal but to her surprise it was a lonely and thankless job. Some of it was fun: she liked drilling her crew and they soon had their balloon craft off to a fine art so that HQ were often on the telephone to tell them that their site had got the balloon flying in the shortest time and brought it down to close-haul fastest, too. But for much of the time she was very conscious of being lonely and left out by the rest of the crew. The girls in her charge were a nice enough crowd. There had been a certain amount of bullying from a couple of big, masculine girls who had tried to use their strength to cow other, less able operators, but Jo had soon put a stop to that. Bullies, she knew, simply hate and dread a taste of their own medicine, so first she picked on them and then, if they did not reform, she made sure she was near them when they were hauling in a gale or oiling the perimeter cable in steady rain. She could trip a girl up, deliver a well-timed shove, hack an ankle, all under the guise of an accident, and bullies soon got the message: desist or be-done-by-as-you-did, as the old woman in *The Water Babies* would have said.

It might not have been so horribly lonely if she had had a woman sergeant, but as yet Sergeant Jim Abel reigned supreme and though he and she were good friends, she missed the companionship of other girls, the whispers and giggles in the hut at night. She was in the hut of course, but in a little room at the end so she still held back a little and did not encourage too much friendship. She did not, as yet, have enough confidence in her own ability as a leader to risk unbending. So though the girls occasionally made overtures, Jo did not respond.

Which was why, on a warm day towards the end of May, Jo was setting off once more to bicycle over to Site 12. She needed to talk to someone and though she was meeting Kay later that evening, she always felt shy about admitting to Kay that she was rather lonely. Kay would have opened those wonderfully blue eyes very wide and said, 'Lonely? With sixteen girls and a man on site with you? But Jo, there must be someone you can talk to amongst that little lot!' and Jo would have to either explain how she felt about making friends with other ranks, or let Kay think she was so unsuccessful as a person that no one wanted to be friends with her. But Emily and Biddy, on the other hand, never seemed to need explanations; they were friends, both towards each other and towards Jo, and they accepted her presence and her problems as naturally as though they had known one another all their lives.

And, of course, there was Alec. He was so nice, and extremely easy going, and Jo thought sometimes that he rather liked her. Of course it might have been wishful thinking, but he had taken her to the flicks one wet evening and had actually held her hand as they walked home afterwards. Jo had been almost paralysed with shyness and a desire to do – and say – the right thing, so it had not been a tremendously successful date, but it had been her first so far. Her only date, in fact, now that she thought about it, since you could scarcely count the hateful Tom Lucas's fumbling attempt to cuddle her as a date.

The bicycle was an elderly one and shared between the whole crew, in theory at least, but in practice the NCOs used it most often. The crew went around in twos, threes and fours, so one bicycle was not much use to them, but Jo often cycled off alone and so did Jim, when he wasn't on duty, and they were never off duty at the same time, of course.

So now Jo wheeled the bicycle out of its shed and across the site. This particular site was in the middle of factory and warehouse land and flying their balloon was a very fraught business. The site had been a football pitch

206

and Jim told Jo once that when there was a high wind and they brought the blimp down safely, he was sure he could hear sepulchral roars from the rows of empty and collapsing stands to the right of their sleeping quarters.

'Ghosties they is, girl,' he said impressively. 'Haunted this yur football pitch is; mark my words.'

Sergeant Abel was a Welshman from the valleys. He was in his late twenties, not very tall, only an inch or so taller than Jo, but he was wiry and incredibly strong. It was his boast that he had once flown the balloon unaided and Jo believed it. He told her he had been a miner until he had joined the RAF on his twenty-first birthday, and Jo had seen him stripped and washing when she had gone into the office early one morning. His broad, muscular chest and back had been covered with little blue scars and when she asked him what had happened to him he had grinned at her, showing a broken front tooth, and said happily, 'Dear God, girl, it's the coal – haven't you never seen a miner in 'is skin afore? We is all kissed by the coal-chips as we work. And we all work stripped, because of the 'eat down below.'

Some of the men on balloons fretted to go back into the main body of the Air Force, but not Jim Abel.

'It's not everyone can get on wi' balloons like what I can,' he declared. 'Found me niche I 'ave and glad of it. Yes, reckon I'll stick to ballooning yur until I've served me time.'

'It's because you hate spit and polish, Sarge,' Jo teased him. 'You like sloping around in battledress trousers and boots on a hot day, knowing there's no bloomin' officers around to take your name and put you on a charge. And where else but on a balloon site could you use your umbrella?'

Jim was frequently to be seen, when it was raining heavily, sheltering under a vast, brilliantly coloured golfing umbrella which he had bought from a neighbouring pawn shop. With the umbrella held aloft he would leap for ropes, arm the cable, dash across from one side of the perimeter wire to the other, and lead a parade of WAAFs to the public baths which, on this site, were a mere mile away.

Jim had grinned until his coal-black eyes were just shining slits in his narrow brown face. 'Maybe you're right and maybe you ain't; but so far as I is concerned, Corporal, you isn't steppin' into dead man's shoes – not unless I ups and dies on you, o' course. If you want to take your sergeants' exams good luck to you, but you won't work on Site 22.'

Since Jo had no desire whatsoever to take her sergeant's exams this suited her fine, and the two of them were a good team. Sergeant Abel said that the easy way to do something was always the best way because a lazy man always takes a short cut, and Jo was keen for Site 22 to be acknowledged as a crack flight, so at least they had the same end in view, even if they approached it from different directions.

So now Jo cycled slowly down the road and tried not to think about her sergeant or the crew or indeed anything to do with balloons. She really ought to be able to dismiss work from her mind on the few occasions when she wasn't in it up to her neck . . . if only I had a boyfriend, she thought longingly, it wouldn't take any effort at all to take my mind off balloons, it would happen naturally. I'll have a word with Em about Alec, see what she thinks.

Jo reached Site 12 when she calculated the girls should just have finished their evening tea and waltzed up the pavilion steps, to find Andy Andrews clearing away a meal whilst in the small kitchen Betty, up to her elbows in hot water, was washing the dishes.

'Wotcha, Jo,' Andy said brightly, putting down her loaded tray for a moment and dashing away the sweat which ran down the sides of her face. 'Come over for a natter? We were just saying how nice it was to have long, light evenings . . . even if we do get a raid later on, at least we get a bit of time to ourselves first.'

'Yes, I suppose we all like the light evenings,' Jo said. She perched herself on the arm of one of the easy chairs. 'Andy, do you know where Emily and Biddy are? I'd like a word.'

'We cut the cards and they won,' Betty called out from the kitchen. 'That Biddy's always lucky – likely they've gone dancin', or to the flicks.'

'Or round to the school,' Andy chipped in. 'They're friendly with two of the gunners, you know. I reckon they sit around in the playground and jaw and then if there's a raid the blokes get called out and Emily and Biddy come charging back here.'

'Yes, but they won't do that tonight because they're officially off-duty,' Betty shouted. 'Sarge said two could go and they won, so you won't see them till midnight or later. Hard luck, Corp.'

'Damn,' Jo said feelingly. 'I really did want . . . and what's even more annoying, it's my evening off and I could have biked round to Kay's site, only it's further off than this one and it seemed ages since I'd had a good session with Biddy and Em. And it's too late now to go waltzing off to Site 40.'

'Is Kay on Site 40? They were first up the other night – first down, too,' Andy remarked. 'I was on guard duty and

209

I really thought we'd made it, but there was a strong wind when we brought her down and Matthews, on the port guy, got her finger caught in the rope and gave such a shriek . . . anyway, she let it go and Bessie yawed . . . but we got her down pretty well undamaged in the end, though later than we should have by almost a whole minute.'

'You try the school, Jo,' Betty recommended, putting her head round the door and waving a wet hand vaguely in the direction of the wire fence. 'Even if they aren't there, the fellers will know where they've gone. Or they might, anyway.'

'Yes, all right, why not?' Jo said. She got to her feet, brushed both hands automatically across the seat of her serge trousers, and headed for the door. 'Thanks, girls.'

As she wheeled her bicycle back across the site, calling greetings to those girls who were within earshot, she reflected that since her main reason for coming over to Site 12 tonight had been to meet up with Alec again, going over to the school ostensibly to see if Biddy and Em were there was no very bad thing. Alec might ask her out, or give her some other indication of his feelings, or failing that, she could have a chat to some of the other blokes who might very easily talk about Alec if encouraged to do so.

She reached the school playground and saw several of the gunners kicking a ball around whilst Mollie's son Sunny, grown leggy and large, chased around after whoever was in possession, barking on a shrill, excited note and occasionally lunging after the ball.

'Well, if it isn't Jo Stewart – hello, stranger! What a surprise – do you like being a corporal, lass?' It was Bozo, extracting himself from the scrum, coming over and holding a hand out, grinning all over his face. His thin brown hair was plastered to his scalp and his glasses were on crooked but his pleasure was genuine. Does he like me? Jo wondered, confused. Well, of course he likes me, but that doesn't mean . . .

'Hello, Bo; nice to see you, too. I came over to visit Biddy and Em but they're out . . . I don't suppose you know where they've gone?'

It wasn't exactly what she had meant to say but it would have to do. If I start asking about Alec first they'll guess I like him, Jo reminded herself, and that would never do.

'Now there you have me; it's usually dancing or the flicks, and there are still dances held in the West End . . . I don't suppose you checked to see whether Moll was hanging around somewhere, did you? Because they won't let her into the flicks or the dances, so if they've gone on the town they leave her with someone, usually. Often it's us, actually, because she and Sunny play around together, but Moll isn't here this evening; I'd definitely have noticed if she'd been playing football.' Bozo grinned engagingly. 'She tackles much more roughly than Sunny does,' he finished.

Jo giggled. 'I can imagine she would, she's awfully hefty,' she said. 'But now that you mention it I didn't see her on the site so perhaps they've got her with them.'

'If so, they may have gone round to the Wilshers' place,' Bozo said. 'They've made friends with a family who live a few streets away, they go round there sometimes for an evening. I gather they play cards and kids' games and listen to the wireless and have cocoa and homemade biscuits . . . stuff like that. Biddy likes being with kids . . . she misses her brothers and sisters quite badly, I think.'

'What's the address?' Jo said, instantly practical. 'I could go round . . .' she stopped short. You are mad, Jo Stewart, she scolded herself. You're supposed to be here to see Alec, remember? But Bozo did not seem to have noticed her sudden silence. He was shaking his head and tapping his brow with his fingers.

'What street is it? Oh curses, and what was the wretched number? I do know it, Biddy's mentioned it more than once . . .'

'Well, is Alec about?' Jo asked, suddenly throwing caution to the winds. There was no harm in asking, surely? 'If he's here, perhaps we could walk round together and – and perhaps he'd recognise the house, if he saw it.'

'He's playing footer . . . no he's not, he left us a while back to go and clean his shoes or something similar. He'll be in the dorm . . . that's the second classroom on your right. Want me to winkle him out for you?'

'Oh, I don't . . .' Jo was beginning when a familiar figure ambled out of the porch and stood there surveying the players. 'Isn't that Alec now, Bozo?'

'That's him,' Bozo said. 'Hey, Alec, we've got a visitor!'

To do him justice, Alec came over at once, smiling broadly. A lock of gingery-fair hair fell over his brow and Jo's heart gave a small but hopeful leap. I'm pleased to see him, she noted, trying for clinical detachment and not succeeding awfully well. I'm excited to see him, too. Does that mean I'm beginning to fall in love at last?

'Hello, Jo; nice to see you. How's tricks?' Alec said, and not even to herself could Jo pretend that his tone was lover-like. 'We've missed you and Kay – it's been odd seeing two musketeers instead of all four of you.

Incidentally, I never could understand why they called them the three musketeers when there were really four – D'Artagnan was a musketeer as well as Artos, Porthos and Aramis, wouldn't you say?'

'Yes, I suppose I would,' Jo said. 'I've always loved the musketeers, how nice to be thought of as one of such a band of brothers!'

Alec laughed. 'That's it, only you're sisters, of course. And somehow that doesn't sound quite so dashing, does it? Four sisters makes me think of nuns for some reason; or chorus lines. How's Kay, incidentally?'

Jo bit back the frosty retort, 'She's married, just as she was before,' and smiled only a little stiffly. Why on earth did all the blokes fall for Kay when she was totally unattainable, wedded in thought, word and deed to Philip Markham without the slightest interest in any other male person? Kay was pretty and she was nice, but she was also spoken for, so Alec could just take that light out of his eyes and take notice of Jo for a change!

'How's Kay? I don't really know, I've not seen her for several weeks. But I'm sure she's well – Andy was just telling me that Kay's site were first up and first down the other night, which means she's on good form.'

'Glad to hear it. Lovely girl, Kay. And how about Biddy and Emily? Where are they lurking? I've not seen them this evening, so since Biddy came over earlier to crow over having won the card-cutting, I take it they've zoomed off to the West End to a dance or a flick.'

Well, he doesn't sound at all as though he cares where Biddy and Em are, Jo thought thankfully, so presumably he's still only friendly with them. How difficult all this was, though. She wanted to say, 'Alec, why don't you and I go to the flicks sometime, or we might go to a dance?'

213

but it was pushy, thoroughly cheeky, she could not bring herself to do it. And anyway, she thought gloomily, with neither of them ever sure when they would be able to get an evening off they could scarcely make a date like normal people. But Alec was looking at her; she had better do her best to answer sensibly.

'I suppose they might have gone up West but Bozo thinks they've probably got Mollie with them and she isn't allowed in cinemas or dance halls. So Bozo suggested they might have gone to visit friends, I can't remember the name . . .'

Boz was back in the football game, waving his arms and trying to scare Sunny off the pitch, but he turned his head long enough to roar, 'The Wilshers, Alec,' before plunging back into the game once more.

'Yes, that's it, the Wilshers,' Jo said thankfully. 'Only Bozo couldn't remember the name of their street or the number or anything. I thought I'd go round, you see, because I don't often get enough time off to come and see the girls and . . .'

'I can't remember the address but I'll walk you round, if you like,' Alec volunteered at once. I wonder how I got him to do that? Jo found herself thinking. Because it was just what I hoped he'd say. I really am managing this conversation rather well!

'Oh Alec, would you? That would be awfully kind.'

'Of course I will. We'll take Sunny, shall we? It will keep him off the football pitch for a bit at any rate, and then when you meet up with your pals I'll walk Sunny home again.'

'Grand,' Jo said feebly. A tête à tête shared with a lively Alsatian pup was not her idea of a romantic occasion, and she had hoped that Alec would spend the remainder of the evening with her, but beggars could not be choosers. 'Well, lead on, Macduff!'

'It was nice of Jo to come and see us; the Wilshers thought she was great fun,' Emily said later that evening, as she and Biddy were walking back across the site. They had bought four pennorth of chips between them and now their fingers were digging down at the very bottom of the newspaper cone to convey the last of the greasy, vinegary morsels to their mouths. 'I never thought Jo would hit it off with kiddies, but she did, didn't she?'

'Ye-es, but it were Alec they really liked,' Biddy pointed out. 'When he got down on all fours to be the elephant's baby or whatever it was, I near on died laughin'.'

They had played charades and Alec had proved to be very good at it, though Emily had suggested that Sunny, if bribed, would probably be happy to play the part of the Elephant's Child from the banks of the great, grey-green, greasy Limpopo River.

'Not with me playing the crocodile he wouldn't,' Jo had said. She had lowered her voice to a gravelly growl. 'Today I shall begin with Elephant's Child!'

'Yes, she was funny; it was nice having her back with us, wasn't it? Wish we were all together again really, though Corpy's beginning to get the right idea and Sarge has got us all taped. He thinks we'll both make up to corporal once they can spare us for the course.'

'I can remember a time when you'd ha' fainted sooner than give a command,' Biddy said. 'We do change, don't we? I wonder what Kay's doing? She's only been back once . . . but Jo's goin' to arrange a meeting for all of us. That'll be all right, eh?'

'It'll be great,' Emily said. 'Come on, Sarge is always happier if we're in before midnight and the time's creeping on. Shall we hustle?'

Mollie, ambling along beside them with her head turned chipwards – she was always given a share – promptly broke into a trot.

Emily giggled. 'Speaks English like a native, old Moll. Come on then, if we run we can be back before the guards change.'

Jo cycled slowly along the road, sticking close to the kerb because although the June night was very warm and starlit, it was almost impossible for her tiny slit of a front light to penetrate the darkness. She had not meant to be this late, but it had been fun at the Wilshers' house and although she had meant to keep an eye on Alec the games had been so fast and furious that she had not had much of a chance to do so. There were four Wilsher children, their ages ranging from four to fourteen, and so far as Jo could see Alec's attention had been divided between the kids with very little to spare for the three WAAFs or for the children's mother, Elaine Wilsher. But she was worried about Elaine's sparklingly pretty young sister, Rosa, who shared the house with her, because Jo could not imagine any man not falling for a girl so ingenuously charming – and Rosa was on the stage which must mean she knew quite a lot about men.

Jo was beginning to be increasingly conscious of her own lack of even the most basic experience of the opposite sex. She could talk to men and enjoy their company, but she had never flirted with a man in her life, had attended the all-girl Convent school in Chester, was the only child of two only children, so had no cousins of either sex and had, so far, been singularly unsuccessful in the boyfriend stakes.

The others, she concluded as she pedalled slowly along, were luckier. Emily's uncle, the one who kept cows, had three sons with whom the small Emily had played. 'Like brothers, they were, I suppose,' Emily had told Jo once. 'One's in the Navy, one's in the Army in India, the other, the youngest, is in his last year at school.'

Biddy, of course, had brothers, and Kay had cousins and had always, Jo suspected shrewdly, mixed with young men. I'm the only one who's starting from scratch, she thought miserably. It never occurred to me that you ought to treat men any differently from the way you treat girls until I began to notice all the eyelash flutterings. Though that isn't altogether true, because none of my friends flutter eyelashes . . . it isn't as simple as that, even.

So I've got to be more – more soft and feminine, I suppose. Well, I meant to try with Tom, but he was hateful and I didn't like all that grabbing, and besides, I was afraid of doing it wrong, whatever it is. But with Alec, I'm sure I could learn to do it all properly, I'm sure he wouldn't expect me to know things, he'd understand that I'm a learner. Oh, I do hope he isn't planning to get off with that Rosa, I really do!

When they finally left the Wilsher house Jo would have liked to suggest to Alec that he might walk some of the way home with her, but you just couldn't do that in wartime, particularly when one of you had a bike and the other had not. So she had seen Alec walking off between her two friends with rather mixed feelings – she felt he was safe enough with them, but that he would have been even safer with her. Or perhaps safer was not quite the right word – happier? Luckier?

217

But Jo was a realist. Alec's so nice he could have any girl he wanted, she concluded, as she turned into Site 22. At the moment, he may not realise he wants me – well, he may not want me – but if I'm sensible and good, surely he'll get round to seeing that I'm willing? And isn't that half the battle?

Jo cycled across the grass and parked the bicycle in the tumbledown little shed which leaned drunkenly against the large concrete slabs of what had, in peacetime, been garages for a block of flats. It was the warmest night they had had so far, she reflected, walking across the grass towards the draughty hut which housed their mess, the kitchen and what the sergeant called the admin buildings, though really that just meant a rackety little office and a section with a stove where, in theory, wet clothes could be dried during inclement weather. She crossed the tiny hallway, opened the office door, went through and closed it behind her. It had been warm outside but it was downright stuffy in the small office. The sergeant was sitting in the old office chair, feet up on the desk, eyes closed, whilst tiny snores bubbled from his lips. Jo cleared her throat and said 'Ahem!' and Jim gave a strangled snort and somehow managed to come to his feet and to attention at the same time, eyes wrenching themselves open, right hand flying into a salute. When he saw who had entered the room he groaned and sagged, then sank back into his chair again, eyeing Jo reproachfully.

'What are you tryin' to do, young Jo? Gi' me a heart attack?' he asked. 'Almost asleep I was then.'

'Almost asleep? Jim, you were snoring,' Jo pointed out righteously. 'Anyway, I only cleared my throat, ever so gently, too.'

218

'Ah well, there you are; awake I was, see? Oh my eyes might ha' been closed a bit . . .'

'Oh, pull the other one, it's got bells on, Sarge,' Jo said. 'You were asleep on duty, I daresay you could be court-martialled for that.' She wriggled her foot out of one shoe and rubbed her toes. 'My feet are killing me, they don't like shoes after boots. I'm off to bed, I shall leave you to stew in your own juice, Sarge.'

Jim snorted. 'Oh aye, and who's goin' to split on me, eh? What lion-hearted little WAAF's goin' to put her head on the line to make me suffer, eh? Put the kettle on, young Jo, and we'll 'ave a cuppa.' He glanced up at the clock ticking away steadily on the wall above their heads. 'The guard'll be round to take over from me in a few minutes, they do like a cuppa. And then you and I can make for our . . .'

The shrilling of the telephone brought his feet crashing off the desk again as he leaned forward to grab the receiver from its rest.

'Site 22, Sergeant Abel speakin'.' There was a rattle of speech from the telephone which Jim answered with a laconic, 'Right away,' and then the receiver was replaced and Jim turned to Jo, who was still standing there with one shoe off and one on.

'Awright, no more messin'. Get the girls up, we're flying at seven thousand feet. Heavy bombers comin' in over the east coast. Move, Jo.'

Jo wasted no time but sprinted across the grass, dot and go one, with a shoe in her hand and the other still on her foot.

'It's always the same, I never get a proper night off or a proper night's rest,' she muttered beneath her breath as she hurled the hut door open. 'Come on girls,' she shouted as she slammed the door behind her and began snatching the blackout curtains across again so that she could turn on the light. 'Get a move on, show a leg there, the balloons are going up!'

They had not had a raid for weeks. The girls usually slept at least partially dressed but because it was such a warm night most of them were in proper nightclothes. Suzie Clitheroe had curlers in her hair – she jumped out of bed and dragged on her overalls, then clapped her steel helmet down over the pipecleaners, swearing as they were jammed into her skull.

'Gawd, Corp, what a bloody thing, I was fast orf – here's me boots but where's me bloody mittens?'

Suzie hadn't been on balloons long and she had bought herself some mittens to try to stop her blisters bursting when the rope rubbed against them.

'No time to search,' Jo snapped. She hurled her shoe in the rough direction of her bed, kicked off the other one and crammed her feet into her comfortable boots, then ran out with the rest, cursing her skirt and the stockings which were certain to be ruined as they worked with the blimp. As soon as they reached the balloon she jumped onto the winch lorry and Evadne appeared at her side, to read out the height on the cable drum. 'Everyone set?'

'Aye aye,' came the subdued murmur from around her. Sergeant Abel had the armaments and a quick glance round confirmed that all the ropes had someone on them, waiting for the orders to cast off.

'Switch on winch . . .' Jo obeyed at once, automatically checking, out of the corner of her eye, that the sergeant was in position behind her.

'Untie ripcord . . . untie guys . . .'

The girls to port and starboard worked with swift confidence on the knots despite the darkness and warmth, which was making Jo's palms sticky. They had tied those knots so they could untie them, and in less than a second, furthermore.

'Untie tail guy . . .'

The familiar routine went on, with everyone responding immediately. When the balloon reached a thousand feet Sadie called out to Jo and she stopped the winch for long enough for the sergeant to clamp on the armament and they repeated the exercise at two thousand feet, and even whilst she obeyed, Jo said a little prayer that no friendly aircraft would fly into the cable and cause the bombs Jim had just clamped to it to go off, starting the sawing motion which would sever a wing in less than a minute.

'Right, that's it, seven thousand feet. Stop winch!'

Jo obeyed, rubbed the perspiration off the sides of her face, then looked up. Dark against the stars the blimp bulked, lazily swaying to air currents which could not be felt down on earth. Around them, the activity continued as Jo climbed down from the winch. Sadie, who could run like a rabbit, tore off to ring HQ and see if they had beaten the other crews tonight with their speedy take-off and Jim came round and stood beside Jo, head tipped back, staring up at their colossal baby far above their heads.

'Not a bad night for it,' he murmured. 'Though it's hot – I'm sweatin' cobs. But I reckon we got her up in good time.' He turned to the crew. 'Go on, get some kip – if the raiders come this way it'll be a different story but sleep while you can.'

The girls went off back to their hut, accustomed to the constantly interrupted sleep, the tensions, the sudden awakenings. But Jo walked back to the office with the sergeant, needing the cup of tea for which she had been boiling the kettle, wanting to find out whether they were first up, tonight.

'Site 40 beat us by a second, would you believe?' Sadie said gloomily as the two of them entered the office. 'That mate o' yours must be made of bleedin' lightning.'

'Aw, she's not so wonderful, we beat 'em last time,' the sergeant said, slumping onto his chair once more. 'What's she like, Corp?'

'Oh, Kay's all right, you'd like her. Men do,' Jo said rather gloomily. 'I'll make the tea, shall I? Who's doing guard duty?'

'Sanderson and Clippem; don't you worry about them, they'll be here in a tick. Smell tea a mile off, them two.' He glanced disapprovingly at Jo's legs in their grey lisle stockings. 'What on earth are you doin' in your best blues? Wha's wrong wi' battledress?'

'I was visiting friends, there wasn't time to change,' Jo said with dignity. She went through into the kitchen, leaving the intervening doors ajar so she could shout through to the office. 'I laddered my stocking though – I just knew I would. Kettle's boiling, Sarge, so the tea won't be a tick.'

7

Kay was in the office when the call came through to fly her balloon at five thousand feet. She was out on the dark grass in a trice, yelling to the guards to get the girls up. The guards were good girls tonight, they would do their best – but Sergeant Smith was having a night off, which might well mean trouble from the likes of Bliss. If Jonty had been there, Kay would have been in bed, as most of the girls were, because Jonty would have told her to get some sleep, but because he was away she had felt the weight of responsibility heavy upon her and had elected to cat-nap in the office rather than go to her own bed.

'You take it too seriously,' Jonty would say with his disarming grin. 'But you'll learn, especially once you get your sergeant's stripes up. You can't be all things to all men in this game, Kay me love, you've got to learn that. Sleep while you can, eat when you can, relax if you can . . . and leave the rest to the Air Force.'

Easier said than done, though. Acting Sergeant was better, Kay supposed doubtfully, than actually being Sergeant, but she truly felt happier as a corporal with dear Jonty to lean on in times of trouble. Except when he wasn't there, of course, like now.

So Kay, in her serge trousers and shirt because it was too darned hot for her battledress top, came out of the hut and ran across to the site where the blimp lay, snugged down for the night. The first guard, big Deirdre, was still rousing the girls but the other one, Kath, was already clambering up onto the winch. Kay arrived and glanced uneasily around. One girl came running, heaving dungarees on over what looked suspiciously like a white cotton nightie. You couldn't blame the girl for taking a chance and getting into something cool, there hadn't been a raid for weeks and sleeping in your clothes on a night like this would have been hellishly hot.

'Where's everyone, Freda?' Kay asked as the girl panted to a halt beside her. 'There's only three of us . . . oh come on, we'd better start. I'll start the run-down. Switch on winch!'

'Some of 'em are comin',' Freda said uneasily. She ran over to the port guy. 'Shall I take this one? It's usually first.'

Another girl came lumbering over; it was Deirdre. She gave Kay an uncertain grin, Kay could see the flash of her big white teeth even in the dark. 'I dunno whether they're coming, Corp, but I yelled 'em, honest. It's bleedin' Bliss . . . Some of 'em are more scared of her than they are of . . . of . . .'

Her voice trailed away; Kay ground her teeth. So they were more scared of Bliss than they were of Kay Markham, were they? Well she would soon change all that . . . only now she had a balloon to fly!

'Right, I'll clamp the armaments, you take the starboard guy, Deirdre, then run round to the tail guy when you've untied it, would you? Freda, after the port guy you'd better take the spider . . . pay it out slowly . . . ready? Oh, I'll read the drum and arm the cable. Off we go!' She was lucky that the girls who had turned up all knew their jobs; everything went like clockwork. They released the guy ropes, paid out the cable, armed it, paid out more, and the blimp came off the ground like a duchess rising from a curtsey, with a portly grace which made Kay feel quite proud. The four of them raced around, passing and repassing, until at last she could give the command, 'Stop winch!' whereupon Kath threw herself off the winch lorry like a human cannon ball and hightailed it for the office.

'I'll ring in,' she shrieked over her shoulder. 'What if we got the blimp up first, eh?' She rang in, then returned, beaming, with the news that they had made it.

'Well I'm damned – four of us, just four, and we got the blimp up faster than I've ever known it done before,' Freda panted as Kath returned. 'Who'd have thought it, eh?'

'I'm drippin' sweat, though,' big Deirdre said, mopping her brow. 'I say, Corp, what'll they say back at HQ? Will you tell?'

Belatedly, girls were shambling across the grass now, staring up at the blimp sailing against the distant stars. It was difficult to see any faces but Kay could tell from their attitudes that they were ashamed, perplexed . . .

'I don't know,' Kay said, therefore. 'I'll talk to everyone in the morning. But I want . . .' she raised her voice, '. . . a full complement to bring her down or there really will be trouble.'

'She's not in much danger up there, they probably won't bring 'em down till daylight,' someone ventured. 'Sorry, Kay, we come as quick as we could, that bitch Bliss locked the hut door, said no one weren't gettin' out, it was only Kath and Freda whipped out afore she got to the door.'

'Bliss? Come to the office at once now, at the double,' Kay snapped.

There was a short silence, then someone said, shamefacedly, 'She ain't here, Corp. She went back to bed.'

225

'Right,' Kay said. Her voice sounded light and pleasant but she hoped they could all hear the hidden menace. 'I think I can deal with Bliss.'

But it worried her, because Bliss was almost six foot and broad with it. She did her best to look like a man, sported a short haircut, had a jocular way with pretty, shy WAAFs which made Kay shudder, and had never hidden her dislike for the new corporal.

Still. Face that problem when it happens, Kay told herself resolutely, heading back across the site towards the offices. Then she paused, thought, turned towards the hut. The worst had happened, the girl had defied her and refused to come out to fly the balloon and she had still managed to get the blimp in the air. There was absolutely no point in cat-napping in a chair all night and facing tomorrow already well under par. She would sleep in a real bed and the guards could wake her when the call to bring the balloon down came from HQ. She was about to go into the hut when something else occurred to her and she made her way, instead, to the lean-to on the side where they kept various tools and pieces of machinery. After rummaging round for a moment she made her way back to her hut, determined to do her best to sleep until she was called.

And what is more, Kay reminded herself as she climbed with real pleasure into her rather hard little bed, I'm right here on the spot now and if Bliss tries to stop anyone leaving this hut she's in for a big surprise. Under her pillow, comfortingly heavy, was the spanner she had brought from the lean-to. If Bliss tried any tricks she would find that Kay and a heavy-duty spanner would be more than a match for her!

*

The footsteps running across the strip of concrete which surrounded the hut woke Jo so that by the time the hut door burst open she was already sitting up on one elbow and swinging her legs out of bed. ACW Sanderson saw that she was awake and slammed the door closed behind her, then switched on the light, for the blackout curtains had not been drawn back after the last alarm call.

'Jo . . . girls, call from meteorological bods; there's an electric storm in the vicinity, close-haul winch in third gear. Come on, can't you hear the thunder?'

They could hear it now that it had been drawn to their attention, grumbling away, distant still, but full of menace. And even as the girls seized their boots, crammed their feet into them and headed for the door, swung open by ACW Sanderson, they saw the lightning, too. A long spear of brilliance, it arced across the sky and then arrowed viciously to earth, the crack of accompanying thunder suddenly sounding both loud and remarkably near.

As they ran out into the open, Sergeant Abel came down the steps from the office at a run, umbrella, Jo was pleased to notice, furled but at the charge. If it rained, and the sarge seemed to think it might, then the danger of the lightning setting fire to the balloons was very much less.

'Jo, get on the starboard guy, Mansell, Sandy, you as well. We'll want less weight on the port guy . . . you'll do, Sadie, and ACW Turner. Evadne, you're on the winch, the rest of you do the spider and the tail guy. Right, Evadne, start winch!'

There was not much wind but the lightning was beginning to worry Jo. It lit up the whole scene vividly and the thunder was right overhead now, crashing and echoing off the tall buildings, now lighting the blimp up so that she looked like a balloon made out of platinum, now casting her into shadow against the livid flash so that she seemed black as coal. Jo, watching as the blimp came steadily lower, suddenly saw her yaw off sideways and glanced back at Jim.

'Why did she do that?' she yelled above the thunder. 'There's no wind!'

'Not down yur there ain't, but it's breezy as hell up there,' Jim Abel shouted back. 'Get ready . . . the starboard guy's only feet above your heads!'

Jo looked up and saw it; she leaped and grabbed, swung off her feet for a moment, then the others grasped the rope too and their combined weight brought the blimp slowly, slowly towards them.

Just as the girls on the starboard bow caught their guy there was a flash of lightning so vivid that for a moment Jo saw everything as brightly as she saw it at midday. She also saw the lightning actually crackle and curl across the top of the balloon, a sizzling line of fire, then earth violently down the cable. Fortunately no one was touching the cable at that point though Evadne, on the winch, seemed to shudder as the lightning struck. But then, muscles cracking, Jo felt a touch on her shoulder and there was Lizzie, calm and self-assured, holding the sandbag up in the air, reaching for the rope, bringing the two together . . .

'We've . . . almost . . . got . . . her,' Jo panted, heaving with all her strength whilst the sweat ran down her face and stung her eyes. 'How's the port bow, Jim?' She shrieked the remark against the thunder but the sergeant's boom came back to her, reassuringly loud.

'Port bow's touching down. They've nearly got the tail guy under control . . . hang on in there, starboarders!'

They hung on, somehow got the rope through the loop,

228

tied it down, moved on to the next. It felt like hours later, though it was probably only a matter of minutes, with Jo uneasily aware that they were working within a foot or so of instant death should the hydrogen in the balloon catch fire, when the sergeant gave the order to stop winch. As they stood back, Sadie set off to phone HQ and the rain started.

It was like the Flood. Girls with nighties under overalls, no shoes, hair still in curlers, stood around staring at the blimp bobbing and swaying forty feet in the air, now and then lurching hopefully sideways as if this cunning move might win her her freedom, but tethered, fastened, safe.

'Dear old pig,' Jo heard Jim bellow into the rain. 'You won't set fire in this, old gel!' And just as they were turning away, just as though Jim's words had triggered it off, they saw one more jagged spear of lightning fork across the sky, followed by a great and terrible flare of blue and orange flames.

'What was that?' Jo asked. 'A bomb, exploding in mid-air?'

Sergeant Jim Abel was standing beside her. He put a hand on her shoulder, warningly. 'More lightning, I suppose,' he said. The girls, however, were dispersing, running through the rain as fast as they could back to the shelter of their huts, so he turned to Jo. 'That was a balloon on fire, gel,' he said quietly. 'Some poor bugger's bought it. I pray to God it lands on a warehouse or in a railway yard and not on some poor bloody WAAF crew, somewhere.'

'My God!' Jo said wildly. She grabbed the sergeant's arm, shook him hard. 'My God, that could be Kay's blimp – or Site 12's Bessie Bunter! Oh Jim, what'll I do?'

'Go back to the hut and get some kip,' the sergeant said. 'No use worryin', Jo, that ain't our job. We've got the blimp in line, that's all we can do. Whatever happened is over now. Get some kip.'

'Can't I phone HQ? They'd know, surely? Oh Jim, I'll never sleep until I know whose balloon that was.'

'HQ won't know, where they are they won't even have seen as much as we did. Jo, there's nothin' anyone can do – got it? Don't make a fool of yourself, gel. By breakfast the grapevine will know what's happened but for now there's no point in thrashin' around feelin' bad. Go on, bed – and that's an order.'

Jim wasn't the sort of sergeant who pulled rank or bullied, but Jo recognised the command in his voice as being the sort you instantly obeyed. She nodded glumly and began to trail back towards her hut.

'All right, Sarge. Sorry I– I fussed. You're right, of course, I couldn't do anything even if I did know. See you in the morning.'

She went to her bed. But it was a long time before she slept.

Biddy was on the winch when the balloon caught fire. She felt the shuddering shock as the lightning struck without understanding what was happening and then someone grabbed her unceremoniously round the waist and simply heaved her from her seat.

'She's struck!' Sergeant Potter bawled. 'She's afire . . . get back, girls, I'll handle the winch!'

'Let me help!' Biddy shrieked against the thunder. 'I'm awright, I'll grab for the guys when she's low enough . . . she's not . . .'

There was a tremendous woof, the whole sky lit up with

230

a brilliant orange light and then the flames began to descend, falling like a curtain of fire all over the site.

'Get away!' Sergeant Potter bawled. He tumbled off the winch lorry and crouched beside it. 'Go on, get away . . . all of you . . . that's an order!'

Biddy had been knocked off her feet by the great blast of escaping air, or gas, or whatever it was that had woofed, but now she crawled towards Sergeant Potter, seeing Emily doing the same from the other side of the lorry.

'Sarge? You awright?'

'I'm fine. Get back, or . . .'

An object like a flame-sheet floated down from the darkening sky and draped itself half across the winch lorry. It enveloped Sergeant Potter and from the brilliant depths of it both girls heard a banshee wail ending on a hiccuping cry. Biddy got up off her knees and hurled herself at the flames. Beside her, Emily was sobbing, struggling out of her gas-cape, throwing it over a flaming mound which Biddy suddenly realised was Sergeant Potter. She screamed, then began to beat frenziedly at the man's jacket, at the flapping, flaming square of canvas which all but covered him.

'Yank it off, Bid,' Emily shrieked. 'When I say pull . . .'

They grabbed, swore, screamed with the pain of it, but heaved the flaming fragment of poor Bessie Bunter off the sergeant and then fell on his recumbent form.

'Take a leg each,' Emily sobbed. 'Pull him – away – from – the – fire.'

'Aye, gerrim out o' it,' Biddy gasped. 'Oh Sarge, dear old Sarge, you mustn't die, please don't die!'

They had moved him nearly six feet when the rain came. Sizzling and hissing, it extinguished the flaming fragments in moments, it slicked Biddy's hair to her scalp

231

and runnelled down the sides of her face, her neck, even down the front of her blue uniform shirt. It soaked small Emily, the blackened form on the floor, the girls who came out of the hut to see what they could do.

'Let's gerrim into the office,' Biddy said. 'C'mon, girls, gi's a 'and. But go gentle, he may be hurt bad.'

In the office, clustered round him, they saw the sergeant's eyelids flicker. He had no eyelashes, very little hair, but he managed to give them a weak grin.

'Who done it?' he whispered through cracked lips. 'Who got me out o' that?'

'All of us, Sarge,' Biddy said stoutly. 'Nell's phonin' for the ambulance, we'll soon 'ave you in 'ospital an' right as rain. Mind, you're bald as a coot,' she added wickedly. 'Ooh Sarge, all your lovely red curls gone!'

He grinned again. It was still pretty feeble, but better than last time, Biddy thought.

'You leave me red curls alone,' he whispered. 'You've allus bin jealous o' me beautiful 'air, ACW! But no need for 'ospital, jest get me to me bed.'

The ambulance came after a long wait and Sergeant Potter was carried off to hospital. He had been very brave but they could all see the pain on his face, the terrible burns on his scalp and shoulders.

'He'll never come back,' Emily said heavily as the ambulance sped down the road. 'It'll be months before that lot heals. He were a good bloke, Sergeant Potter – wonder who they'll send us next? I can't see Morgan managing, can you?'

'Not for long,' agreed Biddy. 'Not unless she can get Pricey moved, any road, and that'll take some doing. Pricey's goin' steady wi' the feller that sells stuff on the black market, the one what lurks round the gates at HQ. She won't move from 'ere willingly.'

'Then it'll be a new sarge and a new corp, unless they make one of us up,' Emily said. 'Not me, mind you – Drew's sensible, though. I wouldn't mind being told what to do by her, would you, Bid?'

It was 'new balloon day', which happened whenever the purity of the hydrogen in the balloon, which was tested daily, failed to come up to scratch, and bringing Bessie down, getting her folded away neatly and inflating the new Bessie would mean a great deal of work, so Biddy and Emily, along with the rest of the crew, were stoking up.

Emily had an uneasy feeling, furthermore, that something was up, though she could not say what. There had been too many inspections lately, too many people stamping around the site, staring at their arrangements. What was more, they had had so many temporary NCOs that her head was beginning to spin, though the latest one, Sergeant Green, seemed a pleasant enough girl.

Still, there was no point in anticipating trouble. After the fire they had packed the draggled remains of their first Bessie off to Balloon Centre and started to work with Bessie Mark 2. They had managed very well with the balloon despite the fact that they had suffered under a considerable variety of poor to middling NCOs; Bessie had behaved well and by now the crew themselves had sufficient experience to work with or without an efficient corporal or sergeant. Which should mean, Emily concluded as she reached for the bread and marg, that HQ, who knew more than they let on, appreciated that Site 12 were a good and reliable team who knew what they were doing.

But balloon changeover days were always hectic so, because of the work which lay ahead, breakfast today was something special. They had started with huge plates of porridge, followed this with a great mound of dried eggs, scrambled and piled on toast, and were finishing with big mugs of tea and slices of cold spotted dick, since past experience told them that they might not get any more breaks until the light faded. Emily was acting corporal this morning and the new sergeant, Joy Green, was sitting with them, eating with as much concentrated ferocity as any of her crew.

'It'll be my first new balloon,' she had told Emily earlier. 'And I don't want us to mess up. Thank heaven Price is on leave!'

'She wouldn't muck us about, not with the new balloon coming; too many strange faces and too many officers liable to pop over for a look,' Emily said composedly, between mouthfuls. 'Besides, they always send a couple of men, because they don't think we can handle it alone.'

Biddy snorted and took a swig of tea. 'Much they'll do! Still, it's nice to 'ave a feller around for a change. And talkin' of fellers, I wrote to Johnny yesterday, he's comin' down for a day or two next time he's ashore for long enough.'

'Lovely,' Emily said. 'It 'ud be nice to meet this paragon. We've certainly heard enough about him!' She drank the last of her tea and picked up her irons. 'Better get moving, or we'll be last on the site, not that we can do a lot until the lorries arrive. Still, we can make a start.'

The three of them went over to the bowl of tepid water standing just outside the kitchen door, dunked their knives and forks, dried them on a scrap of towelling, and hurried out into the chilly morning. A brilliant October had been followed by a dour and cold November and at this hour, for it was scarcely eight o'clock, a sullen mist hung heavily over the site and water drip-dripped from everything, including the tackle. If the sun had been shining, Emily thought ruefully, no doubt the drops of water hanging on the cable, guys, pulleys and blocks would have glittered like diamonds, but under the darkly overcast sky they simply looked very wet and extremely cold.

As they reached the balloon, bedded down and sagging all over the place as she was emptied, other crew members came trotting up. Sergeant Green blushed and took a deep breath.

'Right: flatten her out and make sure she's empty, then we can put her away.'

The girls dropped to their knees and began to crawl across the canvas, flattening any pockets of gas out as they went.

'Mucky old job – but Rita's doin' a steak and kidney pud for us dinners,' Biddy muttered to Emily as they crawled, side by side, across the stiff and smelly canvas. 'Look at Millie, scowlin' away. She's thinkin' that if Pricey were here she might gerrout of workin', some'ow.'

'Good old Rita,' Emily remarked. She blew a dangling plume of hair away from her eyes, then knelt back on her heels to push it under her woolly cap. 'Isn't it wonderful that she doesn't mind cooking? And some of the stuff she makes – well, it's a miracle, given that she gets exactly the same supplies as the rest of us.'

'Right, that's flat enough; get into two teams now and fold her away,' Sergeant Green called. 'Then we can bring out the new balloon.'

She sounded excited, Emily thought, obediently taking

her place along the starboard side of the now flattened Bessie. When Sergeant Green gave the word she lifted her side, along with the rest, and staggered with it into the middle, continuing to fold until the deflated balloon would fit into the canvas valise out of which the new balloon would presently be produced.

'Bows to wind, girls,' Sergeant Green called as they struggled to bring the new balloon into position. 'Bevan, Cross, Andrews, come and connect up the gas, pronto.'

'Aye aye, Sarge,' Emily said, though like everyone else she hated handling the gas cylinders when a balloon was being inflated. As they emptied ice formed thickly on the outsides of the cylinders and it was all too easy to skin your hands if you forgot and touched the metal without first donning gloves.

'Gas connected, Sarge,' Emily said presently, when the gas was beginning to hiss softly into the new balloon.

'Very good. Stay at your post, Bevan, the rest of you – dismiss!'

Damn, now I'm here for hours, Emily thought gloomily, as the rest of the crew scattered to their various tasks. Still, at least you don't have to think to change gas cylinders – I'll be able to have a good dream about home, and the farm. I might even slip in a little dream about Alec whilst I'm about it.

Because over the past months, Alec's friendship had begun to be something more than that. In the summer they had played tennis together on the local courts, even though tennis balls were scarcer than gold dust and when a racquet string went it took weeks of pleading to get it mended. When it grew chilly and the nights dark, they went to the cinema or up West to dances. They caught a Green Line bus out into the country and had a picnic or they walked by the river, lay on the bank and made daisy chains . . . kissed.

Yet they were still only very good friends, nothing more. Alec seemed reluctant to take their friendship further, as though he was happy with the mildest of kisses, the gentlest of hugs. And if I'm truthful I feel the same, Emily admitted to herself now, rubbing her arms and shivering in the damp mist. I'm only eighteen, I don't really want a lot of passion. It's not something I'd be comfortable with, but everyone else says if you like a feller and he likes you, something tremendous happens. Why doesn't it happen with Alec and me, then? Is there something wrong with me – or him? Should I show him in some way that I'm ready for more than light kisses? Only how do you do that without being a little trollop, like that Price girl? The questions were, of course, unanswerable and presently Emily's thoughts wandered again, to Biddy this time.

Biddy had been much happier since her leave, last summer. She had had nightmares once or twice, but never of the same frightening intensity as those earlier ones. She didn't talk a lot about her family any more though, it was all Johnny, Johnny, Johnny. She had gone to the local library and borrowed an atlas, and with great and loving labour had traced and copied a map of the world, several times enlarged, on paper which she had cadged from a local printer. With a box of coloured chalks – Emily suspected that Biddy had nicked them from the school cupboards, though she could not be sure – Biddy now solemnly traced the *Aconite*'s journeyings so that she would be able to imagine where John was at any particular time.

Now that's the way I ought to feel, Emily told herself,

struggling to disengage the hose from the empty cylinders and to connect it once more to the full ones. I ought to accept that Alec and I are taking the same road as all the others, only more slowly, and there's no harm in that. She tightened the connection and heard the gas start to hiss. A glance sideways confirmed that the balloon's cheeks were puffed out and it was beginning to sway on its bed.

'Won't be long now, Airwoman,' one of the visiting airmen said, grinning at her. 'Soon 'ave your baby back to full strength.'

Emily nodded and smiled and made some reply, then her thoughts turned inward once again. Biddy was a good little girl, she really was. She worked hard, never griped because the short leaves meant that girls who lived some way off couldn't get home, put up with teasing, bad manners and downright rudeness, all with the same cheerful good nature. If anyone deserves a really nice boyfriend, it's Biddy, Emily told herself severely, and that's just what she's got by the sound of it. Biddy never talks about mad passion or fumbles behind the pavilion or having to fight Johnny off; she's just sweet and dreamy and gentle about him. I bet they're just like Alec and me, I bet Biddy and her Johnny don't go round tearing each other's clothes off or make horrible animal noises like Waters and Harding did outside our sleeping quarters the other night, so the rest of us were too embarrassed to sleep.

'There, that'll do. Disconnect after this cylinder empties, Airwoman,' a RAF corporal said briskly, having examined the balloon as it lay, swelling gently, on the spread ground sheets. 'Then go and recall the crew; we'll watch you try her out.'

'Right, Corp,' Emily said. 'The last one's almost discharged.'

The crew, she knew, would be having their mid-morning break, lounging around in the mess with cups of tea and jam sandwiches. They wouldn't want to come out in the cold to fly the balloon – who would? – but they would do it, and then everyone could have a break!

A week after the new balloon had taken its place on Site 12, the bombshell which Emily had been vaguely expecting exploded. She and Biddy were cleaning the winch when there was a yodel from the site entrance. An officer, small, neat, well-groomed, was heading across the grass towards them and behind her the guards were galloping across to the pavilion.

'It isn't an inspection, because we had one yesterday, but I bet she makes us do balloon drill again, and we've only just done it,' Emily groaned. 'Jane's going across to winkle the cooks and Pauline out of the kitchen, and Laura's already on her way over. Mark my words, it'll be full bloomin' drill again.'

'Oh well, no one could fault our drill, chuck,' Biddy said philosophically, getting to her feet. 'But I'm covered in bleedin' oil, an' so are you . . . we'll look right idiots doin' balloon drill like this.'

But the section officer was not interested in balloon drill for once. She assembled the whole crew, and then addressed them.

'You've got a crew-posting, girls,' she said briskly. 'You're going to Site 2104, which is some way from here and a country site. I don't know how long you'll be there, but it'll be a change from the city. You'll be given a group rail warrant and you leave here first thing tomorrow morning. Any questions?'

I can't leave Alec, Emily longed to cry. We're still

making such slow headway, but we like each other very much, I can't just up and leave him! But she said nothing, because the Air Force would not be interested in her feelings, would in fact be horrified by them. 'You are fighting a war, LACW Bevan,' she could imagine the section officer saying severely. 'And when you fight a war men should be the last thing on your mind!'

'Please, Miss . . . what about them as is on leave? ACW Price is me best mate, an' she's on leave,' Millie Waters said plaintively. 'What'll she do if she comes back 'ere an' there's no crew?'

'She'll be notified and will join you at the end of her leave,' the section officer said patiently. 'Likewise anyone who's off sick – is anyone off sick?'

'No, ma'am,' Emily said. 'But LACW Andrews is away on a corporal's course. And what about Sergeant Green, ma'am? Will she be coming with us?'

'No. Sergeant Green will stay here to take her new crew in hand. Andrews would be going to another site normally, now she's a corporal, and it's been decided that, since you are an experienced crew, you will do very well with a full corporal and an acting. For the present LACWs Bevan and Peck will be acting corporals and you'll be met at Euston tomorrow morning by Corporal Webb, who will accompany you to your new site.'

She looked as though she was about to salute them and turn away. Emily hastily stepped forward. 'Ma'am . . . where is the site? You didn't say.'

The section officer smiled. 'Didn't I? Well, it's in Cheshire.'

Emily stepped back and, as the officer prepared to salute, stood to attention and brought her right hand up smartly, then sighed deeply as the officer strode back

240

across the site. She found suddenly that the hardest thing of all would be if Alec just waved her off with a smile; when she would miss him so horribly, how would she bear it if he plainly considered her posting as an event of little importance?

As soon as she was free she would go round to the school and tell him, see what his reaction was. And if he took it well then so must she; life, Emily Bevan, is too short to waste by falling in love with the wrong man, she told herself severely, then did a double-take. In love? With Alec? She had never put it into words before, but was it love that she felt for him? No, of course not, it couldn't be, they didn't know each other well enough, you had to know each other for ages and ages before you fell in love – it was a well-known fact. She was moving back across the site towards the pavilion where, she hoped, a hot meal awaited them, when it occurred to her that Kay had known Philip only a matter of weeks before they married – and you had to be in love, very deeply in love, before you took a step like marriage!

The rest of the crew, chattering like magpies, were ahead of her, running towards their dinner. Only Biddy hung back.

'Em? You all right? What is it? Is it Alec?'

Dear, clever, thoughtful Biddy, trust her to see what was bothering you and go straight to the point!

'We don't know one another all that well, but I can't say I like the thought of leaving him, going to the other side of the country. Still, it happens in wartime, doesn't it?'

'It does; look at Kay and Philip,' Biddy said. 'But being apart doesn't stop you . . . well, it doesn't stop you meeting, for instance. Me an' Johnny's goin' to meet up

241

when he's ashore next. It makes it harder in a way, but letters is lovely – letters makes up for a lot.'

'Ye-es. But I'm used to seeing Alec most days . . . not that there's anything in it, really. At least I don't think there is. We just like each other. Only . . . only I'll miss him dreadfully,' Emily finished in a rush. 'I'll go over and see him later, when we've had our dinners. Oh, Bid, I wish I could stay here!'

'Well, I dunno,' Biddy said thoughtfully, as they tagged on the end of the dinner-queue. 'In a way, chuck, it may be better bein' apart. Look at it this way. You and Alec's been cheek be jowl for months, right?'

'Cheek by jowl? Scarcely! But I see what you mean. Go on.'

'Well, you've lived in each other's pockets, then. And you've not come to an understanding or nothin', because you haven't needed to. But now, with you being posted, mebbe Alec'll want to know where he stands. Get it?'

'Ye-es,' Emily said. She smiled at Biddy, sure suddenly that the younger girl was right, at least this might bring things to a head. 'Oh, Biddy, you really are clever.'

'I'm not, I'm a thicko,' Biddy said at once. 'Took me all me time at school just learnin' to read an' write, queen. And as for all this maths . . .'

'Go on, you can't fool me, you're better at bookwork than you let on. But I didn't mean clever in that sort of way, I meant clever with people. You understand feelings and that, really you do, ever so much better than most of us.'

'Oh ah?' They reached the kitchen door where the cook stood, doling food out onto plates. Biddy leaned forward, plate in hand, and addressed Rita earnestly. 'Gimme a lorra spuds, chuck, I'm bleeding starvin'!'

*

It was dark crossing the site after their evening meal and Emily's torch was fading. Usually she went with Biddy, but tonight it was just her and Mollie, Mollie padding along beside her, sticking close as if she knew Emily's night-sight didn't equal hers.

Emily did not know what to do about Mollie; the dog didn't like strangers, had never really taken to Joy Green, let alone the rag tag and bobtail who had come and gone after Sergeant Potter's departure. Then, they had made Andy Andrews acting corporal and she had done her best to keep the bolshie element – ACW Price, her sidekick, Millie Waters and Millie's friend, ACW Harding – under control, whilst the full corporals and sergeants kept their attention focussed on the balloon and what was vaguely called 'moral discipline'.

Not that moral discipline had always been upheld by the various temporary corporals and first-time sergeants who had been wished on them by HQ. Why did we always get the peculiar ones, she thought now, turning into the roadway and walking along the short stretch of pavement which separated the site from the school gates. There was Sergeant Flint, whose voice was so thin no one could hear her in a high wind, and Corporal Pinter, who decided to stay in bed and let them get the balloon up for themselves on every possible occasion, until she had been found out by Flight Lieutenant Randall, their rather dishy officer, who had sprung a surprise visit on them in the middle of a raid. Then there had been Corporal Bucknell, who brought a young man into her partitioned-off sleeping quarter, and expected the entire crew to slumber whilst her bedsprings creaked and her companion uttered very un-WAAFlike cries. Then they had suffered under . . .

'Emily, is that you? I was just taking Sunny for his

243

constitutional; do you and Moll want to come along?'

'Alec! Yes, we'll come,' Emily said at once. 'I wanted to talk to you anyway. We've had a crew posting to somewhere in Cheshire.'

Alec had turned and was walking beside her. In the dark it was difficult to see his face but he stopped walking for a moment, then bent to adjust Sunny's lead before walking on again.

'A crew posting? Does that mean all of you?'

'Yes, that's right. Not the sarge nor Andy, because she's got her corporal's stripes now and will come back to No 12. But me, Biddy, all the others, even Pricey.'

'I see. Are you pleased? It might be a bit more civilised up there in Cheshire – you shouldn't see so much action.'

Emily could have screamed. His quiet, even voice did not tell her anything, they could have been discussing the weather or the price of bread! But she could not say so, she must behave with as much calm indifference as he.

She opened her mouth to say, calmly and indifferently, that no doubt Cheshire would be a nice change from North London, only instead of words, a miserable little moan came out, closely followed by something which, even to Emily, sounded very like a sob.

'I don't want to go anywhere,' she heard herself wailing. 'I want to stay here with Mollie, and Sunny, and – and you!'

This time his silence was charged; she could feel his embarrassment in her own hot cheeks and could have died of shame. But then he stopped walking and pulled her round to face him. In the dark she could not see his features, but she felt sure, suddenly, that he was regarding her with affectionate concern. How dare he be so calm, she thought, when she was just a jelly of painful emotions!

244

How dare he tell her to make the best of it, enjoy the change – she was sure the words were hovering on his lips.

But whether they were or not he did not voice them. Instead he dropped Sunny's lead, put a foot on it, and took Emily, very gently and tenderly, in his arms.

'Poor Em . . . new things and new places are always frightening at first, but you'll make friends there, the same as you have here! And Em, it may actually be a good thing. You see . . .'

'A good thing!' She tried to jerk herself out of his arms, suddenly hating him for simply not loving her even a little bit, for being so calm when her world was crumbling around her. 'A good thing, Alec? For you, perhaps . . . but what about me? I'm – I'm going to miss your company most dreadfully.'

'D'you think I'll not miss you? Sweetheart, I'll be aware, with every breath I draw, that you aren't on the site just around the corner, that I shan't bump into you if I go out for an evening walk or round to the chip shop for two pennorth of chips! But there's a war on, we can't please ourselves, and I've known, for a couple of months now, that I – I'm getting fonder of you than I should.'

He had never used an endearment to her and for a moment she was suffused in a warm glow – sweetheart, he had called her sweetheart! But his last words rekindled all her fury, her hurt.

'Should? Than you should, Alec? For God's sake, when you . . . yes, dammit, when you love someone, there's no such thing as should!'

He sighed and pulled her closer, ignoring her struggles to get free, kissing her brow, her nose, then homing in on her lips. Not until she had stopped struggling did he speak again, and even then he did not let her go but continued to hold her close, or as close as their greatcoats would allow. Trust me to have my one romantic moment in a greatcoat and wellington boots, Emily thought wryly, trying to ignore the sweetness of his kisses, trying to rekindle the fury.

'Em, dearest, the only reason why I haven't told you how much I care for you is because it wouldn't be fair. You are eighteen years old, I'm twenty-eight. You didn't have a boyfriend before you joined the WAAF; I've had several very – very close relationships with girls. I know a lot of blokes marry very young girls, but I'm not the impulsive type. I wanted us to make haste very, very slowly, so you had a chance to choose, weren't rushed into anything by the war, loneliness, or any of the other emotions which make people take a jump in the dark and live to regret.'

Emily sighed. 'You mean I've had no experience and you've had lots; is that what you mean? Well, if it is, how am I ever going to get experience if you keep holding back? If you don't like me enough, then all you have to do is say so and I'll – I'll quite understand. If someone else means more to you, then I'll understand that, too. But what I can't and don't understand is you c-calling me sweetheart and c-cuddling me and then talking a lot of blether about me being too young and you not being impulsive. Why, you'll say I'm too innocent next!'

He laughed against her hair, then began to unbutton her greatcoat. She stiffened with a mixture of fear and anticipation and Mollie, standing close by her, felt the change in her and growled softly under her breath. Alec laughed but continued to unbutton.

'My God, what a place to choose – a pitch dark street,

246

a couple of Alsatians straining at the leash, and the coldest night of the year, so we're both dressed up like a couple of bundles of laundry! And I'm very happy to say you're innocent because it's not a dirty word despite your disgusted tone – innocence is a beautiful thing. But you'll still be innocent with your coat unbuttoned, and we'll be just that bit closer.'

Mollie growled again and pushed her way between them. Emily uttered a small sound between a laugh and a sob.

'Oh Alec, this is absurd! I love you! Do you – do you like me, just a little bit?'

'Like you? I love you, dear little Em, but I felt it wasn't right . . . wasn't fair. Can you tell me honestly that you don't mind that I'm ten years older than you, a lot more experienced, a lot less pretty? I'm a boring old local government officer in civvy street living in digs in a small town in Kent, and when the war's over, I expect I'll go back to form-filling and adding up columns of figures and trying to make a small salary go a long way. Unless we go to Australia, of course, and start a new life out there.'

The buttons had given in to Alec's tuggings and she could feel his hands creeping round her waist under her battledress, very warm when you considered how cold was the night. It was a lovely feeling, she told herself, trying to suppress a shiver of excitement; she would only give away her extreme innocence, or ignorance, if he guessed that this was the first time a man had touched her.

'We? Did you say unless *we* go to Australia?'

She felt him nod, felt his hands tighten on her, pulling her so close that she could feel his belt buckle against her ribs.

'That's it, sweetheart. I'm probably never going to

amount to much, but if we could get right away, to a new country . . .'

'You amount to a lot already, darling Alec,' Emily said dreamily. 'There's a lot of sheep in Australia, so you'll want to get used to them. Why not come home with me, first, see what you think of a sheep farm? My da would like you and you'd like him, we could . . . Oh, but we leave tomorrow . . . I can't leave you, Alec, I won't leave you! I'll run away, I'll . . .'

'There you see, already telling you I love you has made trouble,' Alec said. 'Darling Emily, thousands of other blokes and girls are in a much worse position than us – think of your friend Kay and her Philip! We're going to be a few miles apart for a few months, maybe even a few years, but we'll get leaves, forty-eights, all sorts. And we can write letters, telephone . . . keep in touch. But if you run away or do anything like that then you'll spoil everything for both of us.' He touched her lips with his forefinger. 'Promise me you'll be my brave girl, and go away tomorrow without any fuss?'

'All right,' Emily said. 'I don't suppose I would have done anything, anyway. I'm not very brave really. Then are – are we going steady, Alec? Are you my real boyfriend?'

'I'll show you how real I am – look, let's get rid of these bloody dogs, to say they're getting in the way is putting it mildly!'

'I don't know what we can do with them,' Emily said. 'I've never heard you swear before, Alec!'

'You've never known me so totally frustrated before,' Alec said. He bent and picked up Sunny's lead then caught hold of Mollie's collar. 'Come on, old girl, you and Sunny are going to spend some time with the chaps. Come

248

on, Emily, if we get a move on we might have a few minutes to ourselves for once.'

They ran across the schoolyard, tipped the dogs unceremoniously into Class 1, where various members of the ack-ack battery were roasting chestnuts over their tortoise stove, writing letters and darning socks, and then Alec took Emily's hand in his.

'The other chaps use the air raid shelter; I wish I could find somewhere better, but just to be alone is so hard right now. Come on, sweetheart . . . mind the steps.'

They crossed the playground and descended the flight of concrete steps which led into the air raid shelter. It was very cold and very dark in there and it smelt of damp builders' sand, toadstools and wet cement, but it was private and out of the wind. The narrow wooden benches had not been built for comfort, but Alec sat down and pulled Emily onto his knee and excitement, anticipation and a desperate desire to giggle made Emily forget her surroundings. She was alone with Alec, and he was going to show her that she was his real girlfriend!

Her coat was still unbuttoned and Alec slid his hands under it, holding her comfortingly close, and began to kiss her. But these kisses were very different from his previous caresses. Emily, who had heard all about this sort of kissing but had never experienced it before, was not at all sure, for the first few moments, that she liked it. And then, suddenly, an imp of desire she did not know she possessed seized her and she began to respond. Her arms crept round Alec's neck, she pressed her body as close to his as she could get it, and let her lips soften beneath his. Alec held her in his arms and murmured love-words and after a good deal of kissing, he let his mouth wander from hers to travel softly over the skin of her throat. Quickly and neatly he unbuttoned the front of her shirt in order to slip a hand inside, fondling her small breasts despite the restriction of her heavily boned issue brassiere.

Emily arched her back, then began to stroke the nape of Alec's neck, where the hair grew short and bristly. Just the feel of those bristles on the tips of her sensitive fingers was an arousal, making her want – oh, what was it she wanted? She groaned, turning in his arms.

'Alec, oh Alec, we shouldn't! Please, Alec!'

He laughed a little breathlessly but drew back from her for a moment, in order to gaze lovingly down at her, his face a pale blur in the darkness. 'Shouldn't we? But my darling, all we want is each other, and you're going away . . . don't you feel we ought to get to know one another a little better in the time we've got left? We've wasted so much time already!'

'Mind the bleedin' step, you silly cow! Aw come on, the fellers are all inside, gettin' ready for tomorrer . . . come on, let's just 'ave a quickie, shall us, Maur? Gi's your 'and . . .'

Stumbling footsteps, heavy breathing, two stocky silhouettes against the dark night sky. Emily and Alec shot apart, Emily frozen with fear and guilt, but Alec, putting a reassuring arm around her shoulders, seemed not at all worried.

'Gunner Gilroy, get out of it! Take your young woman somewhere else or you'll find yourself on a charge in the morning.'

There was a startled silence, then the two interlopers crashed out as suddenly as they had crashed in.

'Sorry, Sarge,' Gunner Gilroy muttered. 'I didn't know you was . . . sorry, Sarge, we've gone, Sarge.'

Emily and Alec sat very still until the sounds of Gunner

Gilroy and his inamorata had thundered off into the distance – moving quietly seemed to be unknown to them – and then Alec began, very softly, to laugh. 'Well I never did! He recognised my voice despite the fact that he was about to have his way with his young lady! What a bastard he must think me, to spoil his fun like that. Was he with one of your girls, Em?'

'I don't think so,' Emily muttered. She felt suddenly cold and rather silly. What a good thing it was that Gunner Gilroy had come down to the shelter; goodness knows what might have happened had he not done so. She tried to stifle the wistful feeling that she would never know, now, what they might have ended up doing, narrow little bench or no.

'We'd best get out of here,' Alec said. He buttoned up her greatcoat with swift efficiency, then tilted her face up towards his. He was smiling. 'Poor Em! But it was probably for the best since . . . ready? Then we'll emerge.'

And presently, dressed and respectable externally, though a seething cauldron of newly aroused desires internally, Emily climbed the steps and sat on the little wall at the top of the shelter, with Alec's arm once more warm around her shoulders. In the dim light she smiled at him.

'You pulled rank,' Emily said. She felt beautifully warm and well-loved. 'Poor Gunner Gilroy.'

'And poor Maureen,' Alec reminded her. 'But never mind them; what about us? We could easily have been in trouble, back there. Seriously, pet, I might have gone too far . . . we ought to be thanking Gilroy and his girl instead of cursing them to hell and back.'

'Are you, Alec? Cursing them to hell and back, I mean?' Emily asked curiously. 'I nearly died when they came stumbling down the steps, but then I felt – oh, cheated, I think. I most definitely cursed them.'

Alec laughed and squeezed her. 'I'm only human, Emily, of course I cursed them too. But all's well that ends well – and there will be a next time, I promise you that. I've got some leave owing – I'll come up to your new site and we'll go dancing, to the flicks, we'll do all the courting bit, shall we? And some cuddling, of course.'

'Anything you like,' Emily said dreamily. 'Dear Alec, I'd best be getting back. We've got an early start in the morning.'

'And you've got Moll to think of – are you taking her with you?' Alec asked, pulling her to her feet and then steering her across the school playground towards the front door. 'I think you should, she's extremely attached to you, she'll pine if you leave her.'

'I'd like to take her, but what about the train? She won't have a warrant,' Emily said rather nervously. 'Won't I get into trouble?'

They reached the school building and Alec turned to kiss the tip of her nose. 'No, not if you box clever and keep moving her around amongst the crew. Don't worry, mouse, you're so sweet and pretty that no SP is going to suspect you of dog-smuggling. Shall I come to the station and see you off?'

'Oh, yes . . . no, better not,' Emily said in one breath. 'The others might think it odd and I might howl. Let's say goodbye now.'

'Righty-ho.' Alec opened the front door, then the door to Class 1, and Mollie zoomed out like a shot from a gun, all wagging tail and flattened ears at the sight of her beloved Emily. 'I'll walk you back to the site though, love. We'll say our goodbyes there.'

It had been a miserably overcast day but now the sky had cleared. High in the blackness a thousand stars twinkled and shone and the moon rode high, a sliver of brilliance against the dark. The two young people walked across the site and just outside the hut they kissed for a long moment.

'Goodbye, sweetheart,' Alec whispered. 'Take care of yourself, and write as soon as you've got an address to send me.' He turned to Mollie, pressing herself against the door, eager to get in out of the cold moonlight. 'Cheerio, old girl, take care of Emily for me.'

'Goodbye, Alec,' Emily whispered back. 'Come and see us soon.'

She stood against the door and watched until Alec disappeared round the corner, then went reluctantly into the darkened hut. Mollie immediately squeezed herself under Emily's bed and Emily began to undress, tossing her clothes onto the end of her bed where they would be easy to find if there was a night alert and would serve the double purpose of keeping her feet warm.

Service pyjamas were thick and sensible but even so Emily kept her socks on and added a jumper. Then she climbed into bed – and nearly jumped out of her skin when a hoarse voice spoke almost in her ear.

'You're late, Em – where you been? You said you was takin' Moll for a walk, norra trek to John o' Groats.' Biddy sounded injured, but curious, too.

'I went to see Alec; we're going steady,' Emily said, the satisfaction clear in her voice even in a whisper. 'He's going to take some leave and come up and visit me when he can. We're going to write every day.'

'It's took him long enough,' Biddy said. 'Everyone else

knew he were serious 'cept him, seems to me. You're glad, ain't you, Em?'

Emily, sitting up in bed, hugged herself and turned to beam at her friend. 'You know how you feel about your John? Well, that's how I feel about Alec. It's lovely, isn't it, Biddy? Being in love, I mean. And knowing the other person's the same.'

'Oh aye, it ain't bad,' Biddy acknowledged smugly. 'Get down the bed though, queen, or it'll be reveille before you knows it. We've gorra good long journey tomorrer.'

Emily had not expected to enjoy the journey up to Cheshire despite the fact that it would mean she was nearer home, because of Mollie, but it all worked out just as Alec had said it would. The girls agreed that they could not possibly leave Moll behind, to the tender mercies of a brand-new, probably nervous crew, and the ten of them piled into a carriage with Moll somewhere in the middle and hoped for the best.

Fortunately the train was crowded with soldiers, sailors and airmen standing both in the corridors and in the carriages, so no ticket collector actually came along the train at all after one abortive attempt. The one or two civilians who were travelling huddled at one end of the train kept quiet – they probably thought Mollie was a RAF mascot of some description, and travelled free, Emily assumed.

And Mollie did well out of the journey, better than the girls. She was much admired by the other passengers and revelled in bits of sandwich, cake and even some crisps, showing off wildly by offering a paw and doing a trick which came much more naturally. 'Show your pearlies,' Emily would demand, and Mollie would curl back her lip, exhibiting a frighteningly white and efficient set of choppers.

They reached the very large station at Crewe in mid-afternoon and piled off the train, stiff, hungry and thirsty, for, despite promises, the smaller stations through which they had passed had not been able to provide such numbers with tea or even cold drinks.

'There's a lorry waiting,' Corporal Saunders said wearily, rounding up her crew and heading for the stairs which led out of the station. 'We'll be on site in time for tea, no doubt.'

'Who'll make it? Rita won't mind,' Biddy said as they were bundled into a lorry driven by a pretty blonde WAAF. 'Or will this be a site where they bring food round from HQ, I wonder?'

Corporal Saunders raised her eyebrows. 'Food brought round? What's all this about?'

'Don't you know, Corp?' Emily said. She had heard on the grapevine that Corporal Saunders had come straight from lecturing at a balloon centre and it was obviously true. 'Well, some sites have meals brought out from HQ in heated containers. In London, on the inner ring, for instance, most of the balloon sites have meals sent over, delivered by ACWs on bicycles with hayboxes balanced fore and aft. It means that you're saved the preparation time, but of course it also means lukewarm food, usually badly jumbled up, and no chance of a quick jam wad or a crafty cheese sandwich between meals. And on some sites they bring the hot food on a lorry in tin containers, but though we were offered, we said politely but firmly that we would stick to the old arrangements, thanks, and we always prepared our own food. We're supposed to take it in turns but Rita, bless her, loves cooking, so she's usually in charge of kitchen and catering.'

255

Rita was forty-one and a bit of a tartar but she grinned across the lorry at Emily's words.

'Eh, I do like to cook, love,' she said in a broad Lancashire accent. 'Does tha' know, Corp, whether it's a cookin' site?'

'I didn't know there were any others until the air-woman here told me so,' Corporal Saunders admitted. 'And I believe we're a long way from the nearest centre, so I think you're safe, you'll be doing the cooking again.'

'I just hope there'll be a bath nearer than seven miles off,' someone else grumbled. 'And some fellers . . . we're gonna miss the ack-ack battery, else.'

'We should have asked the driver, except I don't suppose she knows,' Emily said. 'Well, we'll find out soon enough; the site can't be far from the railway station if our balloon's going to keep aircraft off the lines.'

The site proved to be good from some points of view and bad from others. Billeting arrangements were unusual, for a start. The site was the parkland in front of a big old manor house and everyone was billeted in the house itself. The kitchens were to be used as a cookhouse, the huge dining room as a mess. Beds had been delivered and stood in serried ranks in three other large downstairs rooms and there were actually two bathrooms – one on the first floor by the master bedroom, where Corporal Saunders would sleep, the other presumably intended for guests. It was a great, old-fashioned tub with two steps up to it and a lavatory big enough, Biddy said, to allow at least two crew members to occupy it at the same time.

'The aristocracy must 'ave huge bums,' she said in awestruck tones, gazing at the enormous mahogany toilet seat. 'And do they always tek a bath wi' their butlers and footmen? Cos I can't think of any other reason for mekin' a bath so big.'

'It's going to be tricky flying the blimp from here, though,' Emily said, having taken a long and critical look at the parkland. 'The trees are going to be a real problem when the wind's in the wrong direction. And that wood over there, and the tower-thing, are real hazards. What's in the woods, anyway? I can see what looks like a very large building.'

'It's the hush-hush factory we're here to protect,' Corporal Saunders told her. 'They make tanks and things . . . aircraft parts, too, experimental stuff I'm told. Apparently the Powers That Be hoped the jerries wouldn't get wind of it at first, so they didn't fly any balloons hereabouts, but then they were targeted one night, so now they want protection from low-flying aircraft, which is why we're here.'

'It'll be a new balloon, then,' Biddy said, with relish. 'I hate all the kerfuffle over blowin' 'em up and so on, but they fly real good when they're first filled.' The girls were standing in the doorway of the manor house, looking out across the park. It was a typical November day, cold and overcast, with rain dripping from the trees and a gusty wind blowing. 'When's she arrivin', Corp?'

'Tomorrow. A lot of the gear's here already, as you can see, but the actual blimp comes in tomorrow, and the gas and so on.'

'What'll we call her?' Emily wondered aloud. 'Not Bessie, Bessie's a London blimp. We want something simpler, something suitable for a country girl.'

'You're a bloody fool, Bevan,' ACW Waters sneered, but was shouted down by the others, who agreed that the name must suit the site. Naturally, this led to a long disagreement and many suggestions until just about every name they knew had been put forward and decided against.

'Let's call her Tess, after *Tess of the D'Urbervilles*,' Edna Cross suggested at last. 'She was a country girl as I recall.'

'All those in favour . . .?' the corporal said quickly. 'I think it's a grand name, myself. Show of hands, please.'

'Unanimous,' Emily said with satisfaction. 'Well, when she arrives, she's Tess. Until then, let's settle in, shall us? Are there any supplies, Reet? Because if so, the Air Force really is beginning to look after us – remember last time, girls?'

'We won't never forget it,' Biddy said. 'Nor will Jo or Kay. The worst of us bein' here is not bein' able to nip over to their sites for a quick word. They were good mates, we oughter write, tell 'em we've been posted.'

'We'll write tonight,' Emily said. 'Of course I'll miss my – my friends too, very much, but apart from that, this is a good place. I like being in the country better than the city.'

'I think I'll like the country, too,' Biddy said cautiously. 'Only . . . ain't it quiet, Emily? Is it always this quiet?'

'When spring comes and the birds start shrieking as soon as dawn breaks, when cockerels start crowing and cows mooing, you probably won't think it's so quiet. But we'll certainly be spared the traffic noise, and the constant aircraft movements,' Emily agreed. 'Tell you what, Bid; they said we were out on a limb at Site 12 and a long way from the action. Well, I reckon out here, apart from a weekly inspection, we'll be able to do anything we jolly well please! How about that, eh?'

'There's a searchlight battery the other side of that

wood,' Jean Saunders remarked suddenly. 'We'll have to go visiting!'

'Good idea; but right now we'd best make up our beds,' Biddy said and as soon as she and Emily were in their room, she lowered her voice and addressed her friend. 'Em, have you noticed how the corporal's easing up wi' us? She'll be as friendly as anything here, you mark my words . . . you won't have all that rubbidge about no fraternising 'cos if she don't fraternise wi' us, what'll the poor cow do? Oh aye, this is goin' to be a good site, all right!'

Although it was winter when they arrived at the new site, Biddy was full of the wonder of it. A city-bred girl and the eldest in her family, she had never before been close to the living, growing life of field and meadow, with the Watsons' farm only just around the corner. She haunted that farm, willingly helping to clean out cow-sheds for the pleasure of being able to stroke the soft hide of a young heifer and to heft buckets of swill over to the pigsty and watch the two huge sows contentedly snortling their way through a full trough. Mr and Mrs Watson were glad of anyone's help, as were the three landgirls who did their best to take the place of the Watsons' two sons and the younger farm workers, and Biddy was an eager learner.

'Johnny's like me, he don't know much about all this country stuff,' she told Emily after a couple of weeks. 'But I'm tellin' him everything 'cos it'll interest him, I know it will. He's goin' to come up to the site when he's next on leave so's I can show him round, so I'm learnin' as much as I can. I say, Em, did you know that a field of hay ain't just grass? Mr Watson were tellin' me there's all sorts in it, wild flowers, an' weed what's

259

good for animals to eat . . . all sorts. An' Johnny likes to read about meadows an' animals an' that when he's miles from anywhere in that dirty ole *Aconite*.'

'Wait will spring comes,' Emily said, smiling at her. 'We'll go bird-nesting – to look, not to interfere – and we'll collect wild flowers, watch the baby animals come, feed an orphan lamb from a bottle . . .'

'*Could* we?' Biddy said with such a wealth of longing in her voice that suddenly Emily could have cried for her. 'Oh, Em, don't feedin' somethin' give you a – a *tender* sort o' feelin', somehow? When I feel Prince's big soft lips goin' over me palm to find a bit o' crusty bread me heart fills up, sort of.'

So Emily, whilst she missed Alec, told herself severely that this place was doing her friend a great deal of good and told Alec, when she wrote, that he would hardly recognise the two of them next time they met.

'Biddy's made me so aware of the country, and how lucky I was to be brought up there you wouldn't believe it,' she wrote. 'I'd like to take her home to our place, some time. If she thinks this is beautiful, just wait until she sees North Wales!'

8

'Why don't you take your leave any more, Sarge? You should, you know, you need a break the same as the rest of us.'

Kay was having her breakfast with her corporal, Julie Packet, whilst around them the rest of the crew ate, talked, laughed. Presently they would go out and start the day's work but now, as she ate, Kay was writing a letter which, for a miracle, was not to Philip. After considerable heart-searching she had decided that she would write to Steve Minton because he was her oldest and best friend and because he wanted her to do so. It was unfortunate that Steve had expected them to be more than friends, if that was what he had meant when they met on her last leave, but it was scarcely her fault. And since she wanted his friendship and did not intend to lose it without a fight she wrote to him every couple of weeks and received his letters with a guilty lift of the heart.

Now, finding herself addressed however, she put down her pen, sighed, and smiled across at Julie. 'Sorry, what did you say?'

'I said you ought to take your leave, Sarge. All work and no play isn't good for you.'

'My dear girl, all I've done is turn down a couple of seventy-twos. It really isn't long enough to get all the way back to Norwich, it means I have scarcely any time with my family, so I decided to postpone it. It would be different if Phil was home, but he's still abroad, so there's no chance of us meeting up. There just didn't seem much point in taking leave in the circumstances.'

'You've got friends, relatives, probably, that you could go and see,' Julie pointed out severely. 'What's the point of not taking leave when it's offered?'

'I'm saving it up,' Kay explained. 'The section officer told me ages ago that I could, if I wanted. Phil's due home in March, and I shall want all the leave I can get, then. So there really isn't much point in squandering it now.' She did not add, as she might more truthfully have done, that she was afraid of going home in case she and Steve Minton met up again. He was her dear friend still, but she could no longer be quite at ease in his company, or so she told herself whenever he crossed her mind, which he did rather frequently. Now, she picked up a piece of toast and spread jam on it, then took a large, semi-circular bite. 'I'm just telling a friend about our sledging trip,' she added through her mouthful. 'How is Joan?'

Joan was nursing a fractured right wrist as a direct result of the sledging trip. Julie chuckled.

'She's doing all right, but she won't be heaving on guy ropes for a bit. Still, we can manage without her – just. Wasn't it fun to get away from London for a bit, though? I really envy the girls on the out-of-town sites, all that glorious clean snow instead of the mucky stuff we have to put up with.'

Kay put down her pencil with a sigh; if Julie wanted to talk who was she to dissuade her? She glanced outside though and saw, with some dismay, that it was snowing again. The trouble was the huts were so cold in the snow, so extremely inhospitable! Everyone did their best to keep warm at nights with as many extra blankets as they could beg, borrow or knit out of old woollen scraps, and no one undressed for bed any more. Indeed, ACW Brett had declared only the previous day that she had never expected to actually add to her clothing in order to climb between the blankets. And during the day they faced the weather with additional clothing too – everyone either knitted or acquired balaclavas, thick woollen mittens and extra jumpers. Now that winter was upon them the sea-boot socks which the Air Force provided were jealously guarded, as were the long woollen drawers. At first the girls had despised the drawers for their extreme ugliness but as winter advanced everyone realised it was a case of warmth before beauty, and the long drawers certainly were warm; provided you kept moving, that was. If you had to sit or stand around, nothing would conquer the cold.

'We'd better go and get on, Julie,' Kay said, stowing her half-finished letter away in her respirator case. She struggled into her yellow oilskins and fastened her sou'wester securely under her chin. 'It's inspection day today. How I hate unnecessary drilling and bulling – but that's the Air Force for you. And Radford's much better than some wing officers – she's interested in us, for a start. When she says, "Any complaints?", you can tell she means it and wants a truthful answer.'

'Yes, but I wish they could skip the drill on a day like this,' Julie said, following Kay out of the comparative warmth of the mess and into the steadily falling snow. 'She'll hardly be able to see us, you know.'

'I know. Well, at least we'll get it over with early, then we can get back in the warm.'

'That 'ud be nice,' Julie said. 'I could get on with my Tony's thick jumper. To be honest, if I don't get some time to work on it soon, peace will have broken out before it's halfway down his arms. Oh-oh, just in time, here comes Radford.'

The flight officer was a sprightly young woman probably in her early thirties. She cycled across the grass with great difficulty and dismounted beside them, breathing hard and trying not to let it show. Kay beckoned one of the airwomen to take the bicycle then turned to the officer, coming stiffly to attention and throwing up her arm in her smartest salute.

The flight officer saluted back, then smiled at them. 'Good morning, Sergeant, Corporal. All ready, I see. Shall we start, then? If you can run quickly through the balloon drill then I'll do a kit inspection and take a look in your domestic quarters. It's too cold for much, but I think you'll be getting orders shortly to bring the balloon down to close-haul. There's a big wind brewing, I believe.'

'If it's a big wind it'll be brought down and bedded,' Kay observed. Balloon officers, though charming people, often knew nothing whatsoever about balloons and Radford was definitely one of this number. But as Kay had said, she was anxious to learn, which was one big advantage. Many of the officers who had been wished on them this past six months had been as reluctant to find out about balloons as they had been eager to rejoin what they thought of as a 'proper' RAF flight. 'Shall I give the order to bring her down then, ma'am?'

'Yes, all right, if you would.'

Kay took a deep breath and began. 'Fall in crew!'

The girls formed two ranks, with their backs to the balloon.

'Attention – both ranks, number!'

Quickly, she rapped out the orders – the front rank would take the port guys as the balloon came within reach, the rear the starboard – then by number she allocated specific tasks; who was on the guys, the ripline, the spider and the winch. The girls moved with easy confidence to their places and the real business of the morning began. Kay's voice rose so that it would carry, though with the snow on the ground and very little wind, as yet, you could have heard a pin drop.

'Start up winch!'

Behind her Deirdre started the winch and the girls stood to attention, waiting. The blimp began to answer to the tug of the winch, to curtsey and sway and gradually descend. She would need topping up when she did come down, Kay saw, but for the time being she was concentrating on bringing her in under the benign but critical eye of the flight officer. She was coming down nicely, the looped guys were swinging gently just above the crew's heads. The crew had her, the winch was switched off and she began to be eased down, wobbling and uncertain, but docile for once.

'Man central snatchblock, spider and rudder!' Kay shouted. 'Haul in on bollard – watch blocks!'

The balloon was no more than five feet off the ground now and the girls rushed for the straw-stuffed mattress which was the actual balloon bed. Without the mattress the blimp would soon have chafed herself into holes on the ropes and wires, to say nothing of the cold, icy ground. The bed was spread out, the girls ducking and watching the great beast above them all the while; it would be fatally easy to get crushed by the balloon's descending weight if you lingered over that particular task. With the ease borne of long practice the girls had tied the guy ropes to the blocks, coiling them first to bring the balloon right down onto the bed. She was down, safe from wind and

265

weather. Kay found that she was smiling and saw the wing officer was smiling too.

'Furl fins and rudder, disengage winch!'

The girls scurried round, aye-ayes ringing on the air in true nautical fashion. The balloon was a ship so far as the Air Force was concerned, and they treated her as such.

'Very well done, Sergeant,' Flight Officer Radford was saying heartily. 'Dismiss your crew to kit inspection, would you? My rain cape isn't anywhere near as efficient as your oilskins, I fear.'

'Thank you, ma'am,' Kay said. She dismissed the crew and watched them scamper off towards their sleeping quarters. They weren't a bad bunch, even Bliss and her cronies had come to heel over the past few months. She would be sorry to lose them, but the Air Force didn't believe in letting NCOs settle in for long. She expected a posting some time in the next three or four months, and possibly yet another suggestion of moving over to do officer training. She had already warded off one such suggestion and she knew her refusal had been accepted mainly because the Air Force needed all the trained and efficient balloon people it could get. If they ever decide they don't need us, then I'll have to consider officer training, she told herself sometimes. But she loved working on site and had no desire to change the daily battle with the elements, the freedom, the comradeship, for the stuffy, hidebound attitudes which prevailed, she believed, in most WAAF officers' messes.

The hut was spotless, the girls' beds neat beneath their burden of pressed and polished uniform. Only from Kay's cubicle – the door open so that the officer could see inside – came a well-remembered snuffling. The hair rose slowly on the nape of Kay's neck – that bloody dog! There, in the

266

very middle of her neatly laid out uniform, sat Growser, grinning at her whilst industriously scratching himself and visibly scattering hairs all over her sheets, shirts, and best blues.

But the flight officer was nothing if not tactful.

'All present and correct, Sergeant,' she said, moving out of the cubicle and casting an eye across Julie's neat array. 'All correct there too, Corporal. Ah, Aircraftwoman, what's happened to your steel helmet?'

'Sorry ma'am . . . I must ha' knocked it under me bed,' ACW Belmont said, hastily retrieving the missing object and blushing scarlet as she did so. Kay, who knew that steel helmets were frequently used for very odd purposes – this one had been a wastepaper basket the previous day – hid a grin and moved up the room slightly behind the officer. She would have to do something about Growser, who wasn't supposed to be on site at all, far less on the sergeant's bed. But Growser was a nice little dog, good company when you were on guard duty or ill in bed, fun to take for a walk when you were off-duty. And the officer had very sensibly turned a blind eye – it might be better to say nothing.

'Stand easy, girls. Congratulations to you all; a grand turn-out,' the flight officer was saying now. She turned to Kay. 'Shall we make our way to your mess now, Sergeant?'

Kay, agreeing, breathed a sigh of relief; outside the snow continued to fall, which meant that it was unlikely they would fly the balloon any more today. Inside, the girls were preparing to put their kit away, looking forward to whatever the girls on cooking duty had made them for dinner. Flight Officer Radford was talking comfortably of the war effort, of a drive by schoolchildren to collect silver paper to make a Spitfire. The thought of a Spitfire made of silver paper zooming through the air rather amused Kay and she smiled and saw her smile mirrored on Julie's small, intelligent face.

'There's a good smell in here, Airwoman,' the officer said briskly as they entered the kitchen. 'Grub nearly up, eh?'

'Yes, ma'am; it's liver and onions today, ma'am, with mashed potatoes and swede. Followed by rice pud, ma'am, with a bit of raspberry jam on top.'

'That sounds excellent,' the officer said. 'Good, healthy British grub, eh?'

'Yes, ma'am. We like to give 'em something to line their little ribses,' the cook said. She hesitated. 'Would you . . . I mean we're just goin' to dish up . . .'

'A plateful of liver and onions would be very welcome, if I wouldn't be depriving anyone,' Radford said at once. 'I'm moving straight on to Site 7 after this so I shan't have a chance to get back to HQ for a meal. I'll eat with the sergeant and the corporal here.'

She's really nice, Kay decided as the three of them sat at the nearest table, elbows out, and attacked liver and onions. Perhaps being an officer wouldn't be that bad, after all. Only not while I can fly balloons. But if they ever move me on, or try to turn me into admin, then probably I could bear being an officer, just about.

Jo cycled round to Site 12, only to find that the birds had flown. There was a strange crew sitting round in the mess, a different corporal and sergeant in the office, even a new dog, a despondent little mongrel called Flannel which was suffering from mange so that it scratched constantly, making its lean flanks bleed.

The snow which was falling steadily outside did not improve Jo's temper, either.

'Why the hell didn't they let me know?' she demanded, having ascertained that the entire crew had moved on a matter of days before. 'Why let me find out the hard way? I suppose you're going to tell me next that the ack-ack battery's gone, too?'

The nearest girl smiled.

'No, they're still very much with us,' she assured Jo. 'They're awfully nice, aren't they, and very helpful. One of them actually came over and lit our tortoise stove the first day we moved in. Not that it stayed lit,' she added gloomily. 'And it hasn't stayed lit for more than ten minutes since, either. We think it's been sabotaged.'

'No, it's just incredibly hateful and spiteful and needs a good kicking,' Jo told her. 'We tried everything, but we never could get a good blaze. In the end we decided it was just a waste of fuel and stopped even trying to light it. We got straight into bed in all our clothes and prayed we'd live till morning.'

'That's what we do,' the girl agreed. 'Well, sorry we can't help you, but no one told us where your lot had gone.'

'It's all right; I'll ask the chaps,' Jo said, visited by inspiration. She still liked Alec most awfully and made a point of seeing him whenever she came to see the girls. But usually all three of them were there, which made it difficult for Jo to suggest an outing with Alec and, naturally, made it just as difficult for Alec to ask her for a date should he feel so inclined. But now the girls had gone, and the ack-ack battery were still there. What better reason for popping over to have a word with Alec than to ask him if he knew where Emily and Biddy had gone? He was almost certain to know, too, since the whole crew had seen quite a lot of the ack-ack boys, though only in a casual, friendly sort of way, Jo reminded herself hastily. She knew that Mandy had been 'walking out' with Gunner Blakeney and Edna had been seeing a lot of Gerald Muslow, but she would not be treading on anyone's toes by going over to see Alec; everyone liked him but no one, she was sure, had designs on him. Well, no one but her, anyway.

She found Alec sitting as close to the fire as he could get, writing something on a pad of paper. He looked up and grinned, his face lightening.

'Hello, Jo,' he said, getting to his feet – Alec was always punctilious about things like that. 'You were told all about the changeover, then? Quite a shock, wasn't it?'

'You mean the whole crew leaving? They didn't let me know, I found out just now,' Jo said, sounding aggrieved. 'I cycled all the way over here when I might just as well have gone and visited Kay. Now I'm at a loose end for the next three hours.'

Alec had been writing a letter. Now he put a sheet of blotting paper down across the page, sat down and indicated that she should take the chair opposite him.

'Park yourself, Jo and don't worry, everyone's at a loose end when it snows. We've been and done all the necessary to the battery, now we're going to be off-duty until evening. And unless there's a raid we'll not be on again until tomorrow. Most of the lads have gone to the flicks, but I had some correspondence to catch up on so I stayed behind.' He indicated his letter. 'Want to tell Emily you came visiting?'

For a moment Jo was shocked speechless; he was writing to Emily? What on earth for? Oh, they were friends, that was true, but you didn't write to people you met in the RAF once you'd moved away, that was a well-known fact. You didn't want entanglements which could come to nothing . . . she would write to the girls, probably, but that was different, that wouldn't give anyone ideas.

But Alec was looking quizzically across at her, waiting for her reply. Jo cleared her throat.

'Oh . . . yes, tell her I came round by all means?' Another idea struck her. 'Alec, how do you know her address? The crew at Site 12 didn't have a clue where they'd gone. Is it far? Within cycling distance?'

She had no intention of cycling off into the snow, not when she'd had the good luck to get Alec alone for once, but she could scarcely tell him that.

'They're in Cheshire; Site 2104,' Alec said. 'Emily wrote – I got her letter this morning.'

There was something in the way he said it . . . Jo stared at him very hard, and then, though she didn't realise it at the time, she put her foot in it. Up to the knee, very nearly.

'She wrote to you, Alec? How very odd. I mean it's not as if you were close friends or anything . . . I should have thought she'd have written to me or Kay first. We've known her ever since training centre.'

'We are close friends,' Alec said mildly. 'Close enough to be talking about getting engaged, anyway.'

'Engaged? Do you mean engaged to be married? You and Emily Bevan? B-but Alec, she's only eighteen and you're twenty-eight, and she's just an LACW and you're a sergeant!'

Alec grinned, though the colour had risen in his cheeks. 'You mean I'm too old for her and too high-ranking? Get real, Josephine Stewart! I'm a man and she's a woman; that's all it takes – or didn't you know?'

Jo had never known Alec to be anything but kind but she was no fool and winced at the sting behind his last words. She felt a tide of heat rush up to her neck, no doubt dying her face scarlet; how could she have been so crass, so stupid? Had she given herself away completely? Did Alec now know how she felt about him?

But Alec was kind; he saw her confusion and quickly came to her rescue. 'Sorry, Jo, I didn't mean that. I'm a bit sensitive over the age difference myself, though I don't think ranks matter at all, do you? But age and experience do count, I suppose – do you really think we're mad, Em and I, to decide to be together? I've been trying to pluck up the courage for months, and then suddenly this move came up and I realised that if I didn't tell her we might just drift apart. I'm too fond of her to be able to see that happen with equanimity, so I asked her how she felt and we went on from there.'

'I'm sure you're doing the right thing, if that's how you feel,' Jo said. She could hear the stiffness and reserve in her own voice but was powerless to prevent it showing. She felt that Alec had dealt her a cruel blow, now all she wanted was to get away before he realised it. 'Well, since the girls aren't here and you're busy letter-writing, I think I will cycle over to see Kay after all. If she's free we might do a flick – Tyrone Power is in *A Yank in the RAF* at the Adelphi.'

'Right, have fun,' Alec said absently. He moved the blotting paper off his letter and began to write, not even waiting until I left the room, Jo told herself crossly as she stamped out. Well, if he's that keen on mousy, milk-and-water Emily Bevan then he never would have done for me, that's certain!

Kay had not expected to have a visitor, not with the snow still on the ground, but after tea the sky cleared for the first

272

time for days and by the time she saw Jo cycling across the site twilight was falling and she was actually thinking that she might take herself out somewhere for a change from routine.

'I wouldn't mind seeing a flick,' Kay said when Jo came into the office and suggested a trip out. 'What's more it's about time I got away from here for a bit – I usually let the others go because they've got boyfriends and so on and Philip's still away. And I like Tyrone Power . . . yes, all right, I'll come. We can go up West and have a meal at the cinema café first, see the show, and come back here afterwards. Only Brett and Carnadine are cooking this evening and they aren't awfully good, so I wouldn't mind missing it. Any news, Jo?'

She asked because she could see that Jo was ill at ease over something, and knew that her friend was longing to spill the beans, whatever they might be.

'Oh . . . yes, I suppose . . . Kay, our old crew from Site 12 have been posted. They've gone to a site near Nantwich, in Cheshire. They can't be that far from my home, in Chester,' Jo said in lugubrious tones. 'But no one told me. I cycled over there to have a word with Biddy and – and Emily, and one of the girls told me they'd left. Sergeant Green was somewhere about I believe, but I didn't see her, just the ACWs.'

'That is a surprise,' Kay said. 'A crew posting, eh? So who told you where they'd gone? The ACWs?'

'No, not exactly. Oh Kay, I nipped over to have a word with Alec – it was him told me where they'd gone. He'd had a letter from Em, and when I-I said how odd for her to write to him first, he said they were going to get engaged! Alec and Em, Kay – engaged to be married!'

'I hope you congratulated him,' Kay said. 'Emily's

273

such a dear, and not nearly as meek as she was. I've often thought she liked Alec, but he always played his cards so close to his chest you couldn't be sure how he felt. He was so nice to all of us,' she added, greatly daring. It was plain as the nose on Jo's face that Alec's defection was being taken very personally, and Kay remembered, now, that Jo had always hung round Alec in preference to anyone else in the ack-ack battery. 'He was a great favourite of mine was Alec.'

'And mine,' Jo said gloomily. 'That's the trouble, Kay – I really did think Alec liked me, I thought that with the girls gone . . . well, it was a real shock that he and Emily were going to get married. And I think he may have guessed that I was surprised.'

'Oh, anyone would have been surprised,' Kay said reassuringly. 'I'm surprised, myself. I shouldn't worry about it, Jo. You – you didn't say anything unkind about Emily, did you? Not that you would,' she added hastily, as Jo began to shake her head and colour up. 'But you aren't the most tactful of souls, dear Jo!'

'No, I wasn't rude about Em – but I did say she was only eighteen and only a LACW, and then Alec was a bit sharp, only he said he was sorry and I think we parted friends. And when I think about it, I'm only six months or so older than Em myself, so it was a pretty silly thing to say. Not that Alec would realise, of course, because it's plain he never thought of me in that sort of way.'

'I don't think you thought about him like that either, not in your heart,' Kay said reassuringly. 'You'll meet the right man for you one day, Jo, but it hasn't happened yet. Why, look at me and Philip – one moment we were fancy free, the next . . . wham!'

'I expect you're right. Only I really can't see what Alec

sees in Emily,' Jo said, suddenly frank. 'I like her, she's very nice, but I wouldn't call her pretty, or even attractive. And she's little, Kay, I shouldn't think her head comes up to Alec's shoulder!'

'Some men like small women, and as for looks, Emily's a Becky Sharp type; no obvious attraction but lots of hidden charm. And now let's stop talking about Emily and Alec, and we'll get a move on, see if we can catch the five o'clock bus.'

The film was enjoyable and the meal good, though in fact they watched the film first and then ate, since by the time they arrived at the cinema the main feature was about to start.

'I adore very dark men,' Jo said as they came out into a keen wind and more flurries of snow. 'I wish I could meet a Tyrone Power in our RAF – but I'm not fussy, any handsome, dark-haired man would do.'

'We'll find you someone,' Kay promised. 'Oh blow, that looks very like the bus disappearing round the corner, to me.'

'It finished late, and then we spent too much time guzzling,' Jo said, trying to peer at her wristwatch in the dark. 'I wonder if I ought to go straight back to my site, Kay, and leave my bike with you for the night? Only it could be several days before I'm able to get it back, and the rest of the crew use it from time to time, though me and my sarge are the main cyclists.'

'If your bus comes along, then catch it and I'll cycle the bike over to you some time tomorrow,' Kay suggested. 'It would do me good, especially if the snow eases off a bit. But if my bus comes first, then you'll be home well before midnight, anyway.'

275

'I don't worry about time in that way,' Jo admitted. 'We're very free and easy and the new sergeant – not that she's particularly new, since old Abel buggered off to a training centre ages ago – couldn't care less provided she's got enough crew to put the balloon up and bring it down again. No, if I get back before breakfast she'll be quite happy.'

'Yes, it's the same with us,' Kay agreed. 'I don't mind how late the girls stay out. Well, we'll just have to wait and see whose bus comes first.'

They waited, at first patiently and then rather crossly, for the best part of thirty minutes. No buses passed them and precious few cars, though a number of servicemen and women cycled past, their bicycle wheels hissing on the slushy road.

'I think we're both going to have to walk,' Kay said at last. 'What a bind! Still, it's a clear night.'

'True. Let's hope it's snowing like stink in Germany,' Jo said as the two of them set off, shoulder to shoulder, in the rough direction of Site 40. 'My sarge's brother is a bomber pilot and he came over this morning to have a word. He was telling us that they'd just come back from a big raid over Germany, the first since November 1941; he was very cockahoop, said they'd inflicted a lot of damage and only lost one aircraft. They were after some big engineering works apparently and pranged it good and proper. But you know what the jerries are – they hit back, and quickly, usually.'

'Reprisal raids, you mean. Yes, so let's hope . . .'

They both heard the siren start to wail at the same moment and glanced at each other grinning.

'False alarm I trust,' Kay said. 'Want to take shelter?'

'Where? I don't know anywhere round here,' Jo

pointed out. 'And I don't suppose you do, either. Doorways are all very well, but I think I feel better out in the open, well clear of buildings, or with a nice fat chunk of concrete between me and any dropping bombs. Anyway the siren is a bit like those things in the cinema – "coming shortly", not "now showing".'

'You're probably right,' Kay was beginning when they heard the drone. A familiar noise to any Londoner and rapidly becoming familiar through the length and breadth of Great Britain after the Baedeker raids of the previous summer, the sound of heavy aero-engines as they came out of the darkness was immediately identifiable.

'Bombing raid – lots of kites,' Kay said rapidly. 'The balloons will have gone up, so all we can do is find an air raid shelter. There must be one about here somewhere!'

The drone was right overhead now, and even as she ran towards a side street they could hear the whistle of the first bombs descending.

'Down!' Jo shouted, and the two of them dived for a wall and crouched beside it whilst the sounds of the night suddenly intensified before the bomb exploded, so near that they felt the shock wave, distantly, through the soles of their feet.

A dark figure, running, slowed by them. It was a middle-aged man in a dark mac with a tin hat on.

'Get off the streets,' he snapped. 'There's a shelter a hundred yards down the next turning – make for it.' He left, pounding off, carrying something that clanked as he moved.

'Firewatcher,' Kay said, getting to her feet. 'That was his sand-bucket making the din. Come on, Jo, we might as well find that shelter.'

'I don't see why . . .' Jo was beginning, when there

was another wailing whine seemingly even nearer than the first. Kay grabbed Jo's arm and simply ran down the side street the firewatcher had indicated. They found the shelter and tumbled down the steps, pushing the sacking curtain aside and joining the people within.

'Sorry,' Kay said breathlessly as she trod on someone's foot. 'We were returning to our balloon site when the raid started – the warden sent us down here.'

'Hey, Mum, it's one of them b'lloon gels,' a child's shrill voice exclaimed. 'We loves them b'lloons, don't we, Mum? There's one comes right over our 'ouse, we calls it Friendly Fred.'

'Move over, Jimmy love, and let the ladies sit down,' a woman's voice exclaimed. 'Shunt along up there, give the balloon ladies an inch!'

'Or they'll take a mile,' a masculine voice said quite near Kay's ear. She squeaked and looked around but could see very little in the stuffy dark until a match flared briefly. In its light she saw a tall young man in RAF blue who took advantage of the momentary brightness to grin at her and hold out a hand. 'How d'you do, Miss Balloon Lady? I'm Paul Finney and the shadow on my right is Lyall Robb. We're up here for an evening out and look what happens – the bloomin' jerries decide to bomb us for a change. We thought we'd leg it home but we got herded down here by a warden . . . may I ask your name?'

'I'm Kay Markham and this is my friend Jo Stewart,' Kay said promptly. 'We were up for an evening out, too, but we got caught by the raid so they've had to put the balloons up without us.' An enormous explosion very near indeed caused her to stop speaking for a moment and somewhere in the shelter a baby hiccupped and began to cry. 'Gosh, they really are letting us have it; I wonder how long it will be before we can start walking back to our sites?'

'We'll walk you home,' Paul Finney said promptly. 'Won't we, Lyall?'

'Sure will,' the other man drawled. 'Be a pleasure.'

'You sound American,' Jo said presently. Kay chuckled to herself, remembering Jo's remarks about wanting to catch a rich Yank. 'Only you're in RAF uniform, aren't you? The Yanks have a much lighter blue, and their tunics are made from different material.'

'I'm Canadian, honey,' Lyall said. 'I'm with Paul's mob, have been since 1940.' The baby wailed again and the Canadian raised his voice. 'How about a sing-song then, to pass the time? Anyone know "Bewitched"? It just happens I've got my mouth organ here . . .'

He began to play the haunting, catchy melody and after a very few moments voices began to join in, at first uncertainly, then more confidently. Jo, who had a very pretty voice, sang a couple of solos and Kay realised suddenly that her friend's misery of that afternoon was quite forgotten. *I wouldn't be surprised if Jo hasn't already got over her annoyance with Alec*, she found herself thinking as Jo giggled over something Lyall had said. *If I'm right, then it's a good thing – a very good thing.*

It was a nasty raid and a long one, yet Jo thought she would remember the night with a good deal of pleasure in the years ahead. Lyall Robb, despite his name, was tall and dark and he had a pleasant, easy way with him. True to their promise the men walked the girls back to Site 40 and Jo very soon found herself laughing at Lyall's jokes, singing along with him quite unselfconsciously when he

279

played his mouth organ and agreeing to meet him again, to write, to send him a photograph.

When they got back to the site, though it was strictly against the rules Kay asked the young men in and they sat in the empty mess and drank cocoa and ate cheese sandwiches with homemade pickled onions and talked. Lyall was navigator and bomb aimer in a Lancaster, Paul was second pilot, and both were without what Jo would have called 'side'.

'I always pick the married ones,' Paul grumbled, but when they laughed at him he laughed too and said at least it showed he had good taste and could he have another mug of cocoa, please?

It was two in the morning before they parted, and then Lyall insisted on walking beside Jo and wheeling her bicycle for her, all the way back to her site. Paul tactfully disappeared, though Jo had the feeling that he had not gone far. Probably he was just hanging back and would join up with Lyall on the way home.

Being kissed outside the Nissen hut was lovely, too. Jo had dreamed of being kissed by Alec, but her dreams had always been a trifle fuzzy, not having any reality to back them up. But now she knew what real, proper kissing was like – and she thought it was absolutely wizard! She stood on tiptoe and put her arms around Lyall's neck and they hugged and he unbuttoned his greatcoat so that she might cuddle closer. For the first time in her life Jo felt small and feminine and in need of protection – and she liked it. Alec, a mere five foot ten inches tall, with his sandy curls and light brown eyes, was suddenly no more than a friend. I've confused friendship with something quite different, Jo realised. I was searching for a lover, and now I've found one – oh,

Lyall, how shall I wait until we can meet – and kiss – again?

The crew of Site 2104 found Tess to be one of the most difficult balloons they had ever flown.

'That's unfair, though,' Emily reminded them. 'It isn't that Tess is difficult, it's that we've got the most difficult site in the world to fly her from. What with the trees, that bloody factory tucked away in the wood and the manor itself being so close, to say nothing of the railway, flying Tess is worse than taking up a Lancaster bomber when you've only ever driven a car, before.'

But though the position of the site made flying difficult, it had a thousand advantages. Its remoteness, the country setting, the fact that they were lucky if they saw an officer once a week – and best of all, to the undisguised glee of everyone there was a searchlight site only a stone's throw away, in the wood which hid the factory from prying eyes.

Furthermore, the boys who manned the searchlights had a games room with two ping-pong tables and some dart boards and once they had persuaded one or two girls to go over and give them a game, it was only a matter of time before they were in the manor, feet under the table as Biddy put it, and helping the girls in all sorts of ways. They even fitted up a shower over the big bath, because it was ruinously expensive on hot water to get your regulation four inches in such an immense tub and a shower was both quicker and more convenient.

Work was satisfactory, too. Biddy had always enjoyed driving the winch but on Site 2104 she became expert, playing the huge balloon like a gigantic fish so that it came in to land on its bed and not where it would have greatly preferred to be – on the railway lines, the factory roof or the nearest tree.

They were settled in and beginning to feel they could not be happier when the telephone rang one morning and Colleen Webb came away from it looking extremely harassed.

'It's the big one, girls,' she said to the crew who were having their mid-morning break. 'Tomorrow it's Air Commodore's Inspection and he'll want to see the balloon go up to a thousand feet and come down at least to close-haul. They're arriving at ten . . . I don't know whether to pray for rain or sunshine.'

'Pray for a gentle breeze, or none at all,' Emily suggested. 'You know what Tess can be like in a wind.'

Corporal Webb shuddered; because of the lie of the land and the obstacles, Tess had tested their skills to the utmost almost every time she was flown, and to fly her before a number of high-ranking officers would be no picnic, even if the weather was perfect. Just thinking of the conditions which might prevail turned every cheek pale.

'And naturally they decide to do their ruddy inspection in March, when the winds are always fitful and gusty,' moaned Biddy. As winch driver she had spent many hours simply tricking Tess into her bed, letting her think she was about to be given her head, whipping her down to within a hundred feet of the ground, waiting her moment, bringing her lower . . .

'I'm sure it's windier in Cheshire than anywhere else in Britain,' Polly Williams said as they planned their strategy for the next day. 'Oh, Corp, you'd best warn Cupid's Cavalry to give us a wide berth tomorrow.'

'Cupid's Cavalry' were the searchlight boys, so called

because of their shoulder flash which was an upward pointing bow and arrow. Corporal Webb nodded gloomily.

'Yes, someone had better do that – Polly, you know the blokes best, perhaps you could drop them a hint? And we'll have to clean all the rooms in use up at the manor . . . but they won't expect miracles. They know it's unusually short notice. Apparently it's because they're coming to the factory to see something hush-hush, so thought they'd take a look at the new balloon site at the same time.'

'What about Moll?' Emily said suddenly. Mollie was extremely happy at the manor, spending hours rooting round the empty rooms in search of mice or following enticing smells in the garden or chasing rabbits across the open parkland. 'It isn't as if we can hand her over to the ack-ack battery, as we used to do during inspections, or shut her up . . . she'd make a devil of a fuss if we tried.'

'Charlie will have her; he'll take her poaching,' Biddy suggested. She was good friends with the long, lanky Charlie and openly admired his ability to live off the land. She had gone hunting with him, and told Emily that Charlie was a crack shot who had no difficulty in potting rabbits and had no scruples over 'releasing' various vegetables from the fields to stew with his catch. 'Go on, Em, let Charlie have him. They get on great, Moll and Chaz.'

'I don't mind, so long as Charlie doesn't come galloping in with Moll in the middle of the inspection,' Emily said. 'You can take her over first thing in the morning, whilst I'm ringing the met bods for a forecast.'

'Good idea,' Colleen Webb said eagerly. 'If the forecast is really bad, they surely won't risk us putting Tess up, will they? I mean an idiot could see that what

283

with the trees and the manor, she's no joke to bring down safely in a wind.'

Polly, who was waiting to go away on a corporal's course, shook her head sadly at the older girl.

'Whatever makes you say that, Corp? Don't you remember when you first came, how you thought that balloon work was simple? They won't have a clue, they'll expect us to manage whatever the weather, pretty near. Just you pray for a fine day tomorrow – or storm conditions.'

The next day dawned bright and breezy – far too breezy for the crew's peace of mind. Emily was on the phone as soon as she decently could be, getting the weather forecast. She came back into the mess, where the crew was eating breakfast, and reported gloomily that there would be sunshine, a dappling of cloud – and high winds, gusting fitfully.

'They'll admire the daffodils, cluck over the bath and the shower attachment, poke around in the kitchen and then go,' Edna said hopefully. 'We can do the balloon drill without actually shifting her at all, we've done that before in bad conditions.'

'They won't wear it,' Betty said. 'They like to see us frail girls battling with a thing the size of a house which could squash us soon as look at us. It gives 'em a thrill, I swear it does. Well, I'd just like to see one of them on the tail guy in a gale.'

'I'd like to see all of them,' Biddy remarked. She had taken Moll over to the searchlight site and returned, breathless, to say that Charlie and Kipper were going to take Moll down to the river to see how the fish were running.

'I thought fish swam, I didn't know they ran,' someone said facetiously, but for the most part the girls were too nervous over the forthcoming inspection to joke.

'Another two hours and they'll be here,' Corporal Web moaned, having done her own lightning inspection of both the house and the site. 'I think we're ready – if only the silly buggers don't expect us to put Tess through her paces in a force eight – and the wind is getting up, isn't it? It isn't just my imagination?'

'No, it isn't, unfortunately,' Emily told her. 'The wind is rising and the way I see it, we're willing to break our backs for our country but not for top brass. Oh well, let's hope they don't put us to the test!'

Biddy was on the winch and she was worried. It hadn't been easy getting Tess to a thousand feet but they had managed it and managed it well. The visiting brass had been impressed and it had all gone like clockwork. Tess had strained at the leash, but when you were putting her up she wanted to go – it was when you brought her down that the trouble started. And now, seeing her floating apparently placidly high in the blue March sky, you could not believe how she would behave when she got within five hundred feet of the ground once more and realised she was about to lose her independence again.

Not that she knows, of course, Biddy told herself, obeying the command to 'Start winch!' She's just a bundle of canvas and hydrogen gas and air, but she behaves like a monster who knows very well what you want it to do and is determined to do just the opposite, and she's so incredibly strong!

'Man the spider!'

In front of her, the crew were scurrying into position.

They were wearing their boiler suits, hats and mittens because though it was neither wet nor freezing cold they looked efficient. Anyone who knew them as Biddy did, however, could also tell that they were worried. Bringing Tess down in any sort of wind was worrying, but in a gusty wind like this . . . well, all you could do was pray the balloon could be brought down without doing damage.

The drill was beginning and Biddy put the winch into third gear and began to juggle her down whilst behind her, Corporal Saunders told her to go steady, to haul her in slowly, to keep an eye on the oak trees.

It was a hard one, this time, there was no doubt about it. Tess came down to five hundred feet without too much trouble, then suddenly yawed to starboard. Biddy had to hastily let out some cable or she would have caught the manor chimneys. Then, in a brief lull, she hauled again and heard, with relief, the corporal's voice behind her saying, 'She's on a hundred feet, Bachelor . . . dare you bring her a bit lower?'

'Yes, I'll . . . oh damn, no, I'll leave her at that until the next lull.' Biddy could feel the balloon straining, bucking against the cable, and again she chose her moment. Tess was swaying slightly and holding her height when Biddy drew her inexorably in once more, missing the trees by a hairsbreadth. She heard the gasp from her audience and felt tempted to turn and bow gracefully left and right . . . then Tess bounded in the air and yawed again and all Biddy's concentration returned to the job in hand. Although she knew it would not be her fault if it happened, she still felt she would die of shame if the balloon hit an obstacle.

But she did not hit, instead she came down almost inch

by inch, until the guys were within reach and the girls could grab them and begin to bed her down.

It wasn't easy. She was playing up again, skittish as a colt, tugging first this way and then that, carrying the girls with her until the starboard crew managed to get their guy ropes into the metal rings in the top of the concrete blocks.

'Watch your toes!' someone shouted, because the balloon could lift a block and drop it on an unwary foot, and then the girls on the port side tied her down and ran round to help Laura and Pricey, bucking and clutching at the tail guy, whilst the starboard crew unfolded the straw bed with great speed. Above their heads Tess's enormous belly loomed threateningly, before gradually easing down into an almost prone position.

'Crew Attention!'

Biddy had stopped the winch; now she got down and joined the rest of the crew, backs to the balloon, eyes front. There were some complimentary murmurs before they were dismissed, and ran back to the manor kitchen for cocoa and sandwiches whilst the inspection party made their way much more slowly to the dining room where they would be regaled with tea and biscuits by Wing Officer Sutton and Section Officer Ramage.

'Thank God that's over,' Emily said devoutly as she and Corporal Webb queued for their mugs of cocoa. 'It went well though, don't you think?'

'Couldn't have been better,' the corporal said thankfully. 'Everyone did us proud, and the house was first-rate, even Ramage said so and she's hard to please, everyone knows it.'

'Good. Then this afternoon I shall write to Jo and Kay and have a gloat,' Emily said frankly. 'Though Kay won't mind me gloating a bit – her husband's coming back to

Blighty later in the month, so she's walking round in a permanent state of bliss. Dear Kay – I do miss her so much!'

Kay had thought and dreamed about Phil's homecoming for months, but when it happened, when she should have been glued to the telephone waiting for his call, she was miles away, in Norwich.

The previous morning she had received a telegram and had torn open the little yellow envelope with shaking hands. It would be bad news, of course, no one would send anyone else a telegram in wartime unless they had bad news to impart. And she was right, although it was the sort of bad news which she should have been prepared for, really, since Sara Duffield had told her daughter several times that in her opinion Kay's Uncle George was too old to start schoolmastering all over again and that it would be the death of him. So in a way the telegram only confirmed Kay's mother's fears.

'Uncle George had heart attack yesterday. Funeral Wednesday. Can you come? Mother'

As soon as the news had sunk in, Kay cycled off to HQ and reported to her section officer. As luck would have it Sally Manfield was on duty that day and she came from Norfolk herself and had known Uncle George too, since her brothers had all attended his school. So Kay showed her the telegram and was granted three days compassionate leave – it would take her all the first day to get home, probably, and all the last day to get back, so though fair it certainly was not generous.

'I'm awfully sorry, Kay,' Sally said, when the formalities had been completed. 'Your uncle was such a good man. How old was he? But he did love his work,

288

didn't he? I don't suppose anyone had to persuade him to return, exactly.'

'No, he went back gladly. He was seventy-six,' Kay said. 'But what on earth will happen to his daughter Betty, ma'am? She's been acting as house-mother to the boys, taking care of Uncle George . . . she'll be lost.'

'If they've got any sense they'll keep her on in some capacity or another,' Sally said bracingly. 'She's too good to lose, I'd guess. Or you might suggest she joins the WAAF, Kay – she wanted to do so at one time, I know, but her father was such a responsibility and she felt it wouldn't be fair to leave him to his own devices.'

'I'll talk to her,' Kay agreed. 'If I can jiggle my time off around a bit, would it be possible for me to leave as soon as it's light tomorrow? Only you know what the trains are like and I thought I'd hitch-hike.'

'That's fine – you've got a reliable corporal and acting, haven't you?' And on Kay making affirmative noises: 'Good. Then you go off first thing and report back if you can before six on Friday morning. If anything goes wrong, telegraph me direct and I'll do my best to see you aren't landed in trouble.'

Because of the change in her circumstances, the day was a hectic one. Her corporal and acting corporal were sensible, down-to-earth girls who could, at a pinch, run the site almost as well as Kay could, and by the time she had genned them up she felt sure that, barring some dreadful emergency, they would do very well. March had been a wild and windy month with its fair share of difficulties – ACW Thrupp had tripped over a moving guy rope one pitch dark night when the balloon had been at her most difficult and had broken her leg, another girl having failed to let go of the tail guy when ordered had severe

289

rope burns on the palms of both hands which had put her on the sick for weeks – so neither Corporal Packet nor Acting Corporal Landsing lacked experience in dealing with such matters. They should, Kay told herself, lying snugly in her bed with the reprehensible Growser illegally curled up at her feet, do very well without her.

And in fact, though she had asked Sally's permission to leave at daylight, Kay had every intention of getting on the road well before that. She could cadge a lift from one of the many lorries which rumbled past the site as day was breaking, and go on from there. Just pray there isn't a message from HQ to fly, she thought as she climbed into bed. Because that would really put a stop to my plans for an early departure!

And just before she fell asleep, when she heard the midnight to four a.m. guard-change start, she remembered that Philip would be coming home the following day, that he might well phone HQ and send her a message, that she would not be around to take the call.

She sat up in bed, dismayed, then slowly lay down again. She was just being silly, she had no idea where or when he would actually arrive and when he did he would probably be far too tired to start trying to get through to her on the official phone lines which simply went from the sites to HQ. He would undoubtedly send a telegram, but that would wait until she returned from Norwich – if only she knew where he would be arriving . . . but she did not, so it was pointless worrying.

On her feet, Growser muttered a curse against restless bedfellows, then began to snore. I'll never sleep now, Kay told herself querulously; I wish I'd asked Sally if I could leave last evening, if I had I'd have been on my way by now, if not actually home. But it wouldn't have been fair and she wouldn't want to put Sally in a difficult position, which was why she hadn't asked.

She was snoozing when a hand shook her shoulder.

'Sarge, it's five-thirty, you asked us to wake you.'

Kay sat up. She had slept jolly well, despite her fears. 'Thanks, Sanforth, I'll get up now. What sort of a morning is it?'

'Dark, but there's a moon. A bit windy still but nothing like yesterday.'

They were whispering but even so someone further down the room stirred. Kay hastily slid out of bed and groped for her clothes. 'Put the kettle on will you, Sanny? A cup of tea would be nice before I set out into the wide blue yonder.'

Kay's last lift was with a staff car driven by a pretty little WAAF called Rose Bradfield who was on her way from Thetford to Norwich to pick up someone important from Thorpe Railway Station.

'You tell me where you want dropping off and I'll do it,' she said cheerfully. 'I like a bit of company as I drive.'

And she did indeed. They talked all the way from Thetford to Unthank Road, where Kay was dropped off virtually right outside her front door.

'Come in for a bite of something,' she said hospitably, 'My mother will be delighted to feed you, really she will,' but Rose said she would be late if she didn't get on and shot off with a wave and a grin.

Even with several lucky lifts it had taken Kay five hours to reach home, so it was getting on for eleven o'clock. She hurried up the short drive fishing out her key as she went and let herself in through the front door. The hall was dim and quiet but she could hear voices in the back so she hurried through to the kitchen, opening the door with a flourish.

'Ma, I'm home!'

Her mother was sitting at the kitchen table, drinking coffee. Betty, very pale, sat opposite her and Mary Minton, Steve's mother, was just cutting a sponge cake into small slices. They all looked up and smiled as Kay came round the door.

'Darling! You're earlier than I thought – I meant to ask you what train you were catching but then Mary here pointed out that you might not even know yet, and you could easily get a taxi from the station, so there you are. What train did you catch?'

'I hitch-hiked,' Kay said. She went round the table and touched Betty's shoulder lightly. 'Bet, I'm most dreadfully sorry. If there's anything I can do to help . . .'

'Thanks, Kay.' Betty reached up and squeezed Kay's hand. 'But Daddy never knew anything, he died in his sleep you know, and he was most terribly happy. Our house had just won the rugby challenge cup for the thirteen to fifteens, he was on top of the world over that. It was a – a good moment to go, I tell myself.'

'Betty's being very sensible,' Sara said decidedly. 'The head has asked her to stay on, but she doesn't think she will. They'll have to get another Latin teacher you see, and he'll probably be married and will take over the house. She thought that when the funeral and all that sad business is over, she might join one of the services.' She turned to her niece. 'You've always wanted to, haven't you, Betty dear?'

'Yes, Auntie,' Betty said quietly. 'I'm going to miss Daddy so dreadfully, though. I'm not – not thinking very straight right now, but when I've got things sorted out, I

292

think I'll apply for the WAAF.' She smiled rather mistily up at Kay. 'I might even volunteer for balloons!'

'What nonsense; you should use your existing skills; you can drive, write shorthand, type, and you're an excellent manager,' Mary Minton said briskly. 'A balloon barrage is a lonely place from what I've heard, and the work's terribly hard. Isn't that so, Kay?'

Kay shrugged. 'We don't mix much with the rest of the Air Force, I suppose, but we tend to be an independent lot – we go our own way for the most part. But I don't know that they're recruiting balloon ops right now, anyway. And you're right, Mrs Minton, it's dreadfully hard, heavy work.' She smiled round at them. 'I can't think why I love it,' she ended.

'Well, well, never mind, dears,' Sara said vaguely, as though to end an argument between children. 'Take your bag up to your room, Kay darling, and tidy up. Then you can come back and have elevenses; did you know that Steve's coming over for the funeral?'

'Oh . . . no, I didn't, but he's stationed at Marham now, isn't he? I suppose it's quite handy for getting home.'

'That's right,' Mrs Minton said rather shortly, Kay thought. 'He's got a very nice girlfriend, you'll probably meet her this time, Kay. I expect they'll both come to the funeral.'

'I don't see why she should,' Betty said. 'She scarcely knew my father. In fact I don't know that they ever met.'

'Ah, but if Hattie's going to marry Steve, Betty, then naturally they want to be together . . . she'll want to support him, I suppose.'

'Yes, of course,' Kay put in quickly, scenting trouble. Betty, the most even tempered and goodnatured girl, was flushing an angry red and seemed about to make a sharp

293

retort. 'It'll be nice to see Steve again and nicer to meet his – his intended. Are you coming up with me, Bet? You can talk to me whilst I tidy up as Mummy put it, though personally I don't think I've done too badly – I'm sure I'd be even dirtier if I'd just got off a train!'

As they left the room another neighbour came in through the back door, Mrs Headley who lived a bit further up the road. She entered talking, as she usually did and Kay just caught the resigned glance which passed between her mother and Mary Minton before the door closed behind her. She turned to her cousin.

'Did you see that, Betty? Mummy isn't over-fond of poor Mrs H and now she'll be stuck with her because she's bound to ask her to stay for a coffee. Now come and tell me why you snapped at Mrs Minton when she was telling us how nice Hattie is.'

'Mrs Minton is a silly old woman,' Betty said crossly. 'She's been shoving Hattie down Steve's throat ever since you got married, and she's the only person, I believe, who can't see he doesn't even like Hattie much. Oh she's great fun, very striking, very loud . . . but she just isn't Steve's cup of tea.'

'Nor yours, by the sound of it,' Kay observed. They went into her small bedroom with the built-in cupboards and the two long glass mirrors which reflected the sunny garden outside. 'Go on then, tell me why you don't like her.'

'I don't dislike her, I just rather like Steve and I'm sick of hearing his mother trying to marry him off to . . . well, to a girl who goes out with every Yank in Norwich when Steve isn't around – and there are a good few. To be fair, she doesn't pretend to be serious with anyone, it's just Mrs Minton. If you want the truth, Kay, I think she was

294

mortally offended to find that you preferred Philip to her one and only.'

'Oh, but that's daft,' Kay said. She had taken off her coat and cap, now she hung them up and began to brush her long, light hair, then to coil it into a bun on the nape of her neck. 'Steve's a very old friend, Phil is . . . well, he's my husband. The way I feel about them is quite different. Betty, I didn't like to say anything downstairs but have you heard from Ceddy lately?'

'Not lately, precisely. But he's all right, I'm sure he is. I got a letter four months ago . . . it was awfully out of date, but at least I got it. Kay, I really shall volunteer for the WAAF; won't it be fun when we're both in uniform?'

Kay couldn't see it quite like that but she agreed anyway, then brushed the shoulders of her tunic and turned back towards the door.

'I'm ready, or as ready as I can be. Betty, I take it the funeral party will come here afterwards? Look, I'm very fond of Steve but I don't fancy making a threesome with him and Hattie, so – so stick close to me, would you? It would be such a kindness.'

'Of course I will,' Betty said at once. She thundered down the stairs close behind Kay, talking all the while. 'You're ever so lucky, cousin, to have two fellows like Philip and Steve crazy about you. I mean I wouldn't change Ceddy for anyone or anything, but Phil's marvellously handsome and nice and Steve is real beefcake!'

'Steve isn't crazy about me, we're just old friends,' Kay objected at once. She wanted no rumours starting, particularly now that Philip was as good as home. 'Do be careful what you say, Betty dear.'

'I didn't say you were crazy about him, I said he was crazy about you, and he is, honest. I know he was half seas over, the last time he danced with me, but that was what he said. "I'm crazy about your li'l cousin, Betty, an' she's gone an' married some other guy." That's what he said, Kay, honestly it was.'

'People say all sorts of things they don't mean when they're drunk,' Kay said wisely. 'Forget it, Betty, there's a dear. I value Steve's friendship but something like that could spoil my relationship with Phil and no one, Steve least of all I'm sure, would want that.'

'No, of course not. Sorry, Kay, I'll keep my big mouth shut for once.'

'Thanks, Bet,' Kay said sincerely. 'Now don't forget, stick with me tomorrow.'

The morning of Uncle George's funeral was a sweet, blossomy day with the sun streaming through the window of Kay's bedroom and waking her very pleasantly.

'Funerals are always sad,' Kay's father said as they sat round the table, having breakfast. 'But George was such a happy man and had such a happy and successful life that one can only be grateful one knew him. Remember him at your wedding, Kay? One of his charms was that he always threw himself into everything he did with enormous enthusiasm; at your wedding several people thought he was the official photographer, you know.'

'He certainly took some good pictures,' Kay said. 'Oh Daddy, Mum has taken Betty breakfast in bed, but I thought I'd better tell you, I'm going to stick close to her today. We've always been quite good friends and I can tell how dreadfully she's going to miss her father. And not having Ceddy here makes it worse, of course.'

'Good girl,' her father said. 'She'll be so busy for the next few weeks, though, that she won't have much time to grieve. And if she then joins the WAAF she'll have a whole new life in front of her. Best thing that could happen, in my opinion. That girl gave up too much for other people, though I'd never have let George hear me say that. Now he's gone she can start living her own life.'

Sara Duffield entered the room just as her husband finished talking and nodded vigorously, then leaned over and picked up the last slice of toast.

'Anyone mind if I have this? Darling, I agree with you completely that Betty gave up a lot for George, but he was such a lovely man that I doubt if she felt put-upon. I was his little half-sister and probably a great nuisance to him since he was almost thirty when I was born, but he never let me feel anything but much loved. And you're right, of course, that Betty must start living her own life, but George would never have wanted to stop that happening, you know. He would have done anything for Betty and I'm sure he honestly thought she'd be happier with him whilst she waited for Ceddy than . . .'

Abruptly, she began to cry. Ted Duffield got to his feet and put his arms round her and Sara put both hands over her face and continued to weep. Kay was surprised to see that tears were fairly sprouting from between her mother's fingers whilst her whole body shook with grief. Presently she, too, stood up and touched her mother's shoulder timidly.

'Mummy, of course Uncle George didn't take advantage of Betty, she did what she wanted to do – she would have gone on doing it without a murmur of complaint, too, if he were still here. But Mummy, he isn't, that's what Daddy meant, so Betty's got to do something different.'

'He w-was the l-least selfish man I've ever kn-known,'

297

her mother wailed. 'I'm g-going to miss him so d-dreadfully, and I've got no excuse, because Daddy's the best h-husband in the world and . . .'

The rest of the sentence was muffled by Ted's jacket. Kay sat down again. 'I'll just finish my coffee, then I'll go up to Betty.'

Her mother emerged from Ted's tweed jacket, red-eyed but obviously in control.

'Sorry, darling, it just all got too much for me; I shan't make a fool of myself again I promise you. The funeral's at eleven o'clock so we've prepared a cold luncheon for anyone who wants to come back here.'

'Right, Mummy. Is it all right if I go in uniform, though? I don't think any of my pre-war clothes would fit, and anyway I don't have anything dark at all.'

'Uniform will be fine; George was very proud of you, you know.' Sara scrubbed at her eyes with the backs of her hands, like a child of five.'I've got a navy hat and coat; that will have to do.'

'Isn't it silly the way your mind works? During the committal, all I could think of was how glad I was that Uncle was a member of Eaton Parish Church, with its own graveyard and everything. Christ Church doesn't have a graveyard, though our parishioners get buried here, beside yours. Now that's a nice thought – all the Duffields and the Clarkes and the Mintons and the Radfords comfortably here together, in the end. And the view's rather nice, too.'

Kay knew she was gabbling to take Betty's mind off her loss as the two of them walked down the long path between the graves, heading for the lych-gate and the cars lined up outside. But it was better to talk, she thought, than to walk along in gloomy silence. As she spoke, therefore, she gestured towards the meadows, river and misty blue distance to their left. She kept her eyes on the view though she was tinglingly conscious of Steve Minton, walking behind them with his mother but without, she was glad to note, the wretched Hattie Featherstone. As they came out of the church he had grinned at her and touched his cap – he was in uniform, like her – but then he had moved away without attempting to exchange a word. Which was as well, Kay supposed, since her thoughts were all with Philip – or they should be, anyhow. As it was, the funeral and her family were, not unnaturally, uppermost in her mind.

'Yes, it's a nice churchyard. And it was a lovely funeral, wasn't it?' Betty said. Her eyes were still red-rimmed but she seemed peaceful, no longer wracked with grief. 'Mr Richards said some awfully nice things about Daddy. He's coming back to the house for some luncheon, I think the Mintons are bringing him; they've got room in the car, they said.'

'Yes, it was a lovely funeral, and Uncle George was a lovely man and deserved all the nice things folk have been saying,' Kay assured her cousin. 'And aren't you glad it's sunny? It'll mean that people can spill out of the drawing room and take their drinks and sandwiches into the garden. I know some people might feel the sunshine was a bit – a bit heartless, though. Would you have preferred a dull day, Betty?'

'Oh, definitely not; sunshine's best, because Daddy was a happy person. I kept looking round at all the daffodils and the blue sky and the pussy willows at the far end of the churchyard, and I couldn't help thinking that Daddy would really have enjoyed it. He did love family get-togethers.'

'So he did,' Kay said as they reached the car. 'You're going with the Sayers, aren't you? See you back at the house then, Bet.'

When it was all over and the guests had gone, Kay wondered whether to go and ring HQ, but it seemed pretty silly really. She would be home next day, able to find any messages for herself. And anyway, she was tired, lethargic, even a little sad. Not for Uncle George, because he was an old man and had died happy. She was sad, she realised, for herself, and for Steve.

After they had helped to clear away and wash up after the funeral tea, she and her mother had made their way home whilst Ted Duffield returned to his office. Kay and Sara had a quick cup of tea and then Sara telephoned Betty to make sure her niece was all right and Kay went for a walk, to enjoy the last of the sunshine, she told her mother.

She had crunched down the drive and out of the gates, turning automatically towards the Mintons' house, as though she had known Steve would be about. And he was. He must have let himself out of his gate at the precise moment that she had left her own garden, and he hailed her immediately.

'Kay! Hello, love. You all right?'

His voice was just as it always was, light with an underlying tenderness. Kay turned to smile at him, reminding herself that he was a friend, that was all, and she must answer him as such.

'Me? I'm fine thanks, Steve, though it's been quite a trial, one way and another. I go back to my site tomorrow though, so I just thought I'd have a bit of a walk before it's too dark to see. Care to come?'

Daft to ask him, daft to feel warm and pleased when he

nodded. Just remember that you're in love with Philip and that no one, no one on this earth, can be in love with two people at the same time, Kay reminded herself severely. And remember, too, that whatever he may think, Steve isn't, and never has been, in love with you. You're just good friends, that's all.

'Where were you going?' Steve said. He took her hand as naturally as though they were both kids again. 'We could walk round to Eaton Park, watch the kids playing on the swings and roundabouts. Or we could stroll down into the city . . . I'll stand you three pennorth of chips from the stall on the market if you're still hungry after all the food you've eaten today.'

'I wasn't going anywhere. I just felt like being out of doors,' Kay said honestly. 'How about taking a really good walk, though? Right out to Harford Bridges. Being stuck in London I miss the countryside . . . why, we could even feed the horses . . . there are still some very old apples in our loft.'

'Grand idea,' Steve said. 'Remember that time when we got free rides for apples? I held the pony and fed it apples whilst you climbed on its back and had a ride, and then we swapped. Awful little blighters, weren't we?'

'Speak for yourself,' Kay said, holding the gate open for him. 'I was a delightful little girl; it was you who led me into wicked ways.'

'It was your idea to ride those ponies! Don't you remember . . .'

'It was not! But I'd love a ride tonight, only I'm too respectable now for carry-ons like that.'

'Me too,' Steve said, with a deep, artificial sigh. 'Ah youth, youth! Gone forever, I fear.'

'Fool! Would you like to go into the loft above the

301

stable for the apples? Only it's a bit spidery and despite tackling all the WAAF have to offer, I'm still not too keen on spiders. Oh go on, Steve, show me how big and brave you are.'

'Okay, I don't mind if I do as the actress said to the bishop. Better tell Auntie Sara we'll be back late, though. I might buy you those chips as well as letting you feed the ponies.'

Presently they wandered down the drive again, their pockets crammed with apples, their heads close as they talked and laughed. Friends, Kay thought contentedly. Real friends.

9

Kay sat in the train heading north and felt, she was sure, the very same butterflies-in-the-stomach, dithery excitement which she had felt on her wedding day.

It was raining, so it was difficult to see out of the carriage windows, and the train was crowded, but the June air was mild and Kay was sure that by the time she reached Lincoln the sun would be shining and the birds carolling their little heads off.

She was going to see Phil for the first time since his embarkation leave almost eighteen months earlier – he was, at long last, within reach. When he had first come back he had been all over the place, a month here and a month there, finally going up to Scotland for a lengthy period. But then only a matter of a couple of weeks ago, he had written exultantly to tell her that he was going to a bomber station just outside Lincoln and would do his best to either come down to London for a quick forty-eight, or possibly he might get to Norfolk when she was on leave there.

It had been a long and loving letter, closely followed by their only telephone call so far, a crackly, hissing, dot-and-go-one conversation from a public call box in Oxford Street to his mess at Scampton. One call – and she had almost spilt the beans, almost told him that she'd been saving up her leave, that she would be coming up to see him. But she hadn't done it, partly because the line was so appalling but mainly because she had dreamed of his astonished surprise for months now. And this wasn't just a treat for Phil, it was a treat for her, too. To make up to her for what she had been forced to say to Steve.

It had been when she had gone home for Uncle George's funeral. They had walked, talked and laughed, held hands, mocked at each other's war-jobs. She had lectured him on the intricacies of balloon flying and in return he had lectured her on the difficulties of flying a large, draughty, Wellington bomber. And then he had gone and spoilt it and she – ah, she had ruined their friendship once and for all because she could see no alternative.

In the friendly dark outside her gate, he had put both arms round her and given her a quick, almost embarrassed hug. 'Kay, my dear, people make mistakes, do things they regret. If – if you ever find yourself in that position – regretting something you've done, I mean – you would turn to me, wouldn't you? Because I'll always be here for you; you know that.'

Stupidly, she could see Mrs Minton's face, hear her voice as she had heard it earlier in the day as she told Mrs Headley what a fool young Kay Duffield had made of herself.

'Because it was always Steve for her and always will be,' Mrs Minton had said smugly. 'I'm sure she's already realised she's made a terrible mistake . . . but Steve is such a dear boy, so sought after. I'm afraid she's made her bed and may well find herself forced to lie on it.'

The words had echoed round and round, hollowly, in Kay's head. So instead of thanking Steve, or saying she didn't know what he meant, or passing it off lightly, she had rounded on him like a tigress.

'If you mean I might find myself regretting my marriage, forget it,' she had said harshly. 'Phil's the best thing that ever happened to me and even if he threw me

304

over tomorrow – which he won't, Steve – I wouldn't turn to you.'

He hadn't said anything at all. He had just stood there, totally still. And then he had patted her shoulder clumsily and turned away from her, to walk towards his own gate. And she had known he was crying.

The pain she had inflicted! She had felt the echo of that dreadful, tearing pain in her own breast and clutched herself as though the blow she had dealt Steve had been dealt to her also. But she knew that hurting him had been the only way to cut him loose and told herself that one day he would thank her for it. She was married to Phil, she loved him very much, she simply felt dreadfully sorry for Steve – and for her sake as well as his own he must stop pursuing her!

And until the phone call to Phil, it had been hard not to think about Steve too much, to regret her words a million times, to start towards the phone a dozen time a day, to write him letters which she immediately tore up . . . in short, she had been thinking about Steve almost non-stop ever since her cruel words. So now, seeing Phil would not simply be wonderful, it would save her sanity, show her that she had done the right thing.

As the train got nearer and nearer her destination her heart began to lift. Once she was in Phil's arms again everything would be all right. She remembered their honeymoon with quickened heartbeats and wondered whether Phil had changed very much in eighteen months – whether she had, for that matter. She glanced down at herself. She was physically stronger because of the work she had been doing and more self-confident because she was accustomed now, to command. Would he like this new confidence, or would he see it as a threat to their marriage? She gave a very small shudder suddenly – a goose walking over her grave her grandmother would have called it – a tiny shiver of apprehension. They hardly knew each other, he was her lover but had not known her long enough to be her friend, this was all wrong, all haywire . . . the bloody war!

The train got in late, but with double summer time in full swing the streets of Lincoln were still light. Kay walked to a taxi rank and told the man the name of her hotel. She had booked a double room, though she knew that Phil would be unlikely to share it with her for a night or two. She wondered, now, what the hotel staff would think of a girl on her own booking into a double room and being joined, after a day or so, by the golden-haired and handsome young pilot officer. Would they think she was in love with Phil and coming up for a dirty weekend? A curtain ring on the third finger of her left hand, a flimsy nightie in her kitbag? Or would they smile mistily at young love, offer Philip second helpings, suggest outings, bring them tea in bed?

It wasn't quite like either scenario, however. The hotel was very busy, so busy that she signed in and was taken up to her room by a girl in her late teens without more than the most perfunctory glance.

'My husband's probably joining me in a day or so,' she said, as the girl dumped her kitbag on the stool at the end of the bed. 'What time is dinner? Oh, and I'd like to make a telephone call!'

'Box under the stairs and another outside on the corner,' the girl said briskly. 'Dinner's at seven prompt so you missed it but there's always sandwiches in the bar for latecomers.'

'That sounds lovely . . .' Kay was beginning, but the

girl had given her a quick smile and left, slamming the door noisily behind her. Kay shrugged and sat down on the end of the bed. She was suddenly extremely tired and actually played with the idea of not ringing Philip tonight, of leaving it until the morning. After all, the RAF flew night raids, leaving daylight raids to the US Air Force. The chances were that Phil might be flying tonight . . . why not leave it, a cowardly little voice whispered inside her head. Why not go to bed now and get a good night's sleep and contact him in the morning when you're all bright and fresh?

But she must ring tonight! There was always the chance that he might be free tonight, might rush into town, take her in his arms, come to bed with her . . .

She washed, brushed out her hair and pinned it up, shook out her tunic and skirt, creased from travelling, then dressed again and went downstairs. There was a queue for the hotel telephone so she went into the road and down to the corner to the public box. There was another WAAF using the phone here but no queue, so Kay waited. Inside the box the WAAF pulled faces, banged the heel of her hand on the shelf, sighed loudly. Then she leaned forward and began to trace her eyebrows with a wetted forefinger, as though the call meant nothing to her, the person on the other end less.

Kay waited. The WAAF – she was a LACW1 – hung the receiver on its hook and proceeded to remove from her respirator case a small stub of lipstick which she began to smear on her lower lip. Losing patience, Kay rapped on the glass. The girl jumped, coloured, then came out of the box.

'Sorry, Sarge,' she mumbled. 'Din't see you waitin' out there.'

'That's all right, Airwoman,' Kay said pleasantly. She went into the stuffy little kiosk. It smelled of the WAAF's face powder and of sweat. She checked her change, put her purse on the shelf, then picked up the receiver. Her voice shook when she said the number and in the cracked piece of mirror she could see her pale skin colouring up, her eyes beginning to sparkle.

'Put two pennies in the box, caller. Do not press Button A until you are connected,' the bored voice said. 'You're through, caller.'

A man's voice: 'Scampton Officers' Mess.'

'Oh . . . could I speak to Philip Markham, please?'

Her voice shook a little, with excitement and a sort of dread. Would he have changed very much? Imagine, in a couple of minutes she might actually be speaking to him! But the man's voice was answering.

'Philip Markham speaking. Darling, it's been an age since we last spoke – why didn't you ring earlier? Last night seems a lifetime away, but it's all I can think of, all I want to think of.'

'Phil? Wh-what do you mean?' Excitement conquered puzzlement suddenly. 'I'm here, in Lincoln!'

'And where else should you be, my lovely one? Look, if you're free for the evening I could be with you in half an hour. I'll book a room if you like, somewhere smart. You'd like that, wouldn't you?'

He knew she had arrived, obviously. But how had he known? Who could have told him? Unless he had rung the site and someone had blown the gaff, quite without meaning to do so, of course.

'Phil, darling, I've already booked a room – can you really come right now? How long will it take you to get here?'

'Of course I can come, sweetheart – haven't I done just that two or three times a week ever since I came up here? We'll meet in the usual place, then, in half an hour.'

'The usual place? Phil, I don't understand, I . . .'

'Janet, honey, when I say the usual place . . .'

She held the receiver away from her, staring at it. Janet? The usual place? Two or three times a week? Very slowly and gently, she replaced the receiver on the hook, silencing the small, quacking voice. She saw her voice in the piece of mirror. White. Shocked. No pain, not yet, just total, complete surprise.

Someone outside rapped on the glass with a penny. It made her jump but she turned obediently, almost blindly, and came out of the kiosk.

'Sorry . . . I didn't realise anyone was waiting.'

'S'orlright, luv. Hey, you've left a fortune in change, ducks . . . wait on, you'd best . . .'

He was a small man with greasy, thinning hair, wearing a big white apron. A hotel worker, Kay supposed dully. She walked on. He ran after her, put a hand on her arm. She could actually feel it, which seemed strange to her, since her whole body was numb.

'You've 'ad a shock, luv, I can see that. Come back wi' me an' I'll give you your change, then you can sit dahn in the hotel foyer for a bit. Bad news, was it? On the tellyphone?'

'It's all right. I'm staying at the hotel tonight. And it doesn't matter about the change. I shan't be making any more telephone calls.'

She got back to her room somehow and sat down on the bed. She even glanced at her watch. The girl had said they were serving sandwiches in the bar for latecomers. She was a latecomer. She was hungry. She had not eaten since breakfast. She must go downstairs, find the bar, ask for the sandwiches.

She stayed sitting on the bed as the dusk in the room gradually deepened. At three in the morning she lay down on top of the covers but though she tried to close her eyes they would not remain shut, they kept popping open to stare, hotly and sightlessly, straight in front of her.

At seven she got off the bed, straightened the bedding and picked up her kitbag. It occurred to her, as she looked out of the window at the bright new day, that she had, in fact, no real reason for grief. She had never truly known Philip, except, of course, in the purely physical sense. So she felt hurt, indeed outraged, but her heart, she discovered with a stab of pure astonishment, though sore, was not broken. He had been her lover but never her friend – and friendship, oddly enough, was the more valued of the two emotions. So she would have to think very carefully what she should do next and then . . . and then . . .

Plans would not come. She could not stay here, in Lincoln, that much was obvious at least, but where to go? Returning to the site with her tail between her legs was unthinkable, and staying in a hotel, alone, not something she could consider with equanimity. She must keep away from the site until her leave was up, then there would be no need to say much – thank God there would be no explanations necessary at home since she'd not said she had planned to spend her leave with Philip. And that was the answer, of course – go home! Mummy and Father would be delighted, friends would be pleased. And she could make up with Steve, though she could not possibly explain what had happened. Her embarrassment and shame would not allow explanations – not yet, at any rate. She needed to keep her own counsel.

She went downstairs to reception but the staff were changing over, day staff replacing night staff, so they had little time for her.

'First train to London? I dunno, I'm sure, but then I'm not a bleedin' timetable, am I, so if you want . . . well, I like that! She's bleedin' gorn an' never a word an' here's me rushed off me bleedin' feet . . .'

'Darling, I simply don't understand, and I'm afraid she's awfully unhappy. You could have knocked me down with a feather when she turned up here – to be honest I wondered if she was AWOL so I rang her HQ and they said she had two weeks' leave and that her corporal and acting, whatever that may mean, are managing very well. I really would like to know what's been happening to her – can you have a word with her?'

Ted Duffield eyed his wife lovingly. 'If you're appealing to me, you must be desperate indeed! Darling, no one knows Kay better than you, or understands her better, either. Have you thought that it might be Phil? He's back in England, isn't he?'

'Yes, but he's up in Lincoln, I believe. I did mention him and she just said very coolly and politely, that she'd not seen him since he got home, had only spoken to him twice on the telephone. And then she went into her bedroom and shut the door, very firmly, whilst I was still gathering my courage to ask a few more pertinent questions.'

'You can have a grand row over the phone,' Ted Duffield said wisely. 'I expect that's all it is, darling. Anyhow, I'll go up and do my blunt father act. Wish me luck!'

*

Kay was lying on her bed when her father came into the room. She stared up at him, trying to think what she should say, how she should placate him, keep him from learning the truth. She could not bear the pity, the *I told you so* which would follow confession. Daddy darling, you were right and I was wrong, Philip doesn't love me, he's been unfaithful to me three times a week with some horrible tart called Janet.

She had arrived home the previous day telling herself that things could have been a whole lot worse. She had found out in time to prevent further heartache. She had not made a fool of herself with Philip. But despite making every attempt to blank Philip and his infidelities out of her mind, she found she was still involved with him in an odd sort of way.

The worst of it was not understanding. I know I'm stupid, Kay thought wildly, but this sort of thing just doesn't happen. We actually got married; I thought that marriage was binding, that when you loved someone enough to marry them you didn't simply take on someone else, ignoring your marriage vows. You gave the marriage a chance – you travelled down to London to see your wife, you didn't have leaves in Lincoln and spend them with a tart called Janet. To her it seemed that Philip hadn't behaved logically, so why had he bothered to marry her eighteen months ago? Had he simply wanted to take her to bed and realised that it was marriage or forget it? Did men behave like that – men without consciences?

And strangest of all, he'd been back in Blighty now for almost four months and hadn't once tried to see her in all that time. His excuses had seemed so genuine, too; pressure of work, new techniques to learn, constant bombing raids on Germany. She had never doubted the truth of his stories for one moment, perhaps because her desire to see him had not been strong enough? Could the fault have been on her side as much as his? Oh, she'd not been unfaithful, but she hadn't gone flying up to his station as soon as he got home, chiefly because he had been constantly on the move, even spending some weeks up in the Orkney Islands, though what he had been doing up there she had never discovered. But perhaps a loving wife would have got leave and rushed to where he was no matter what the circumstances? She did not know, could not tell, but was willing, at any rate, to shoulder a share of the blame.

What she could not forgive, however, was that by embroiling her in his affairs, by marrying her, Philip had hurt Steve. Of course she had been the one who inflicted the wound, but at the time she had truly thought marriage was binding, something made in heaven which lasted for life, not for a brief honeymoon. I hurt Steve because I knew marriage was serious, not something you could just cast aside, she told herself, lying on her bed and staring up at the whitewashed ceiling above her head. I cut him free of me and now I'm free myself. He said to turn to him – but I can't, because I sent him away.

I made him cry. Why can't I cry, then? Everyone cries when they find a bloke's unfaithful to them, even when he was just a casual date that you rather liked . . . I remember Mandy howling when Jackie from the ack-ack battery went out with Sue instead of her, and there wasn't anything in it really, not for either of them. So I should cry. I cried when I hurt Steve, I cried and hugged the pain and wanted to tell him I was sorry. Why can't I cry for Phil, when he's done what he's done? The stupid thing is I still can't quite believe it, in my heart I'm telling myself that I must have misunderstood, I can't have heard properly. Philip was my darling, my beloved, he wouldn't talk to me on the telephone and think I was someone else! He has to love me, he's said so a thousand times, written it in a hundred letters. No one stops loving, just because they've been a long while apart. Do they?

'Kay, darling? Are you all right? Mummy's most awfully worried, she says you're acting strangely. Can't you tell us what's happened? You never said anything about coming home . . . Mummy wants to get Dr Norman to take a look at you . . .'

Kay sat up. This foolishness had gone far enough, if Mummy was thinking of calling in Dr Norman, who had known Kay all her life, who had come to her wedding! He had been one of the many people there who had smiled at Philip only with their mouths whilst his eyes searched that blond and smiling face with a shrewdness which she now recognised, almost welcomed. But she could not talk to Dr Norman about what had happened to her, not when she had not said a word to her parents!

'It's all right, Daddy, honestly. I'm all right. I had a – a bit of a shock, it'll take me time to get over it, but I'm all right, now. I'm puzzled, but getting less so as I think things through.'

'It was Philip wasn't it, darling? You went to Lincoln, didn't you? What has he said to you? I'd like . . .'

She kept her voice light, amused. 'Daddy, don't, it wasn't like that, honestly. The truth is we've – we've had a bit of a quarrel. Nothing much, but I decided not to spend my leave with him after all. I'm sorry I've caused you both so much worry, but I'm all right now. I know what I'm going to do.'

'And what's that?'

It threw her, of course, because she had no idea what

314

she was going to do, save that she would never, as long as she lived, have anything to do with Phil Markham again. But she would flannel her way out of it somehow, satisfy them that everything was all right.

'I'll write to him, I think. Perhaps we can patch things up next time we've both got some leave – he suggested coming back here, or perhaps meeting up in the Lake District, something like that. Now, what's Mummy making for dinner?'

Perhaps she should have told them, but she still couldn't manage it. It was a confession of failure so complete, so total, that it made her cringe just to think of it. Unable to hold a husband who had vowed undying love – unable to keep even a flicker of interest alive! My letters must have lacked sparkle, she thought with grim humour. Or perhaps I was an awfully bad lover and he just couldn't bear the thought of having to go to bed with me again.

That hurt horribly, but she refused to give the thought credence, or allow it to linger. You'll have to forget him and stop beating yourself over the head about his infidelities, she told herself. It's absolutely pointless. He isn't the man you believed him to be, now you must concentrate on getting free of him legally. See a solicitor when you're in the city, get proper advice and act on it. And in the meantime, enjoy your leave, you've waited long enough for it!

Kay had thought about ringing Marham and asking to speak to Steve Minton, but found she simply didn't have the courage. It was all right planning to say 'sorry' when she saw Steve, but ringing him up in cold blood, after the way they had parted, the way she had behaved – well, it was more than she could bring herself to do.

315

So she did not set eyes on him until the fourth day of her leave, when she got down off the bus, having had a rather difficult interview with a solicitor on Castle Meadow. She had explained that she wanted to start divorce proceedings against her husband, who was currently being unfaithful to her and the solicitor, a small, grey-haired man in his late sixties, had listened, steepling his fingers and resting his chin on them whilst she talked, and had then said simply: 'Proof?'

'Oh, didn't you understand . . . he called me Janet, he talked of . . .'

'Proof, Mrs Markham, not reported speech. How long have you been married?'

'Eighteen months.'

'That phone call – could it have been someone else on the line? Someone else called Philip? Even Philip Markham, perhaps. Markham isn't an uncommon name.'

Annoyance brought heat flooding to Kay's cheeks. 'This may seem strange to you, Mr Blundell, but despite not having spoken to Philip on the phone for several weeks, I recognised his voice after his first few words, though he did not pay me the same compliment. I have no doubt whatsoever that it was my husband who spoke to me on the phone the other day, and no doubt, either, that he's having an affair with another woman. Isn't that proof enough?'

Mr Blundell shook his head. 'Not quite, Mrs Markham. In peacetime I'd advise you to get hold of a private detective, but in wartime . . . I think your best course is to wait it out. Indeed, you might even consider a reconciliation; after all, war brings many troubles in its train. If you and your husband were leading normal married lives this

316

might never have happened. Won't you give him another chance?'

Kay said that she did not think she could, not really, and the solicitor gave her more advice, possibly it was good advice, but none of it was what Kay wanted to hear. Stupidly, perhaps, she had expected sympathy, disgust over Phil's behaviour and a quick solution, not this small, weary looking man advising her to stick her head in the sand, for that was what it amounted to so far as she could see.

'So you go home and have a good think – talk to your parents, a friend,' the little man said at last. 'I've disappointed you, I know, but life's never as simple as it seems, Mrs Markham.'

'I'm sure you're right, and I'll do as you say,' she said, therefore. 'Thank you for your time.'

'It's a pleasure. Tell my clerk that there'll be no charge since I was unable to help you.'

So here she was, getting off the bus halfway up Unthank Road, deciding that she would pop into Yallops and see if they had anything nice she could take home for her mother. But though outwardly she was being sensible, inside she was a seething mass of discontent. What was the world coming to when a man could be unfaithful to his new wife and the wife must have the sort of proof which only a detective could provide before she could divorce him? No one realised, apparently, that when you found you'd made a mistake your one great urge was to unmake it as quickly as possible. She did not want to be Kay Markham any longer, it had been a farce, a silly game of let's pretend. She wanted to be Kay Duffield again. But it seemed that it would take more than wanting to reverse her marital status. If only she'd listened to her parents, her

317

friends . . . but that was trying to turn back the clock and vain regrets never helped anyone.

So she jumped off the bus and almost landed on top of Steve. He was walking down Unthank Road towards the city and touched his cap, giving her a quick, embarrassed glance, then went to pass, but Kay grabbed his arm.

'Steve – don't go! I need to talk to you.'

He stopped. He looked guarded, almost ill at ease.

'Oh . . . sorry, Kay. I'm in a bit of a rush – I'm having a meal with Hattie, I don't want to be late.'

She nodded, then spoke steadily though her heart had lurched into her boots at his words. 'All right, I won't keep you. I just wanted to tell you that I've been to see a solicitor.'

'Really? What's happened?'

'I'm going to divorce Phil.'

She watched his face. A tide of colour crept over it but his mouth kept its hard line and the grey-blue eyes looking down into hers didn't soften or smile.

'I'm sorry to hear that, Kay, but it's no business of mine, is it?'

Pride dictated that she should agree, apologise for keeping him, walk on. But there was something in her which was stronger than pride, and lonelier, something which needed Steve desperately right now.

'Steve, can I turn to you? Are you there for me, the way you said? If not, I'll go now and I won't ever bother you again, I promise. But if you're just angry with me, and you've every right to be, I've – I've had quite a lot of punishment lately. And I can't tell anyone else about Philip because it's such an ugly can of worms. But I could tell you; we could always tell each other things, couldn't we?'

318

He looked at her for a long time and then he nodded, then took her hand and turned her with him, away from the small row of shops and towards the city.

'We always could. So I'm not having lunch with Hattie, not today. Is it over, Kay? Have you found out that Philip isn't quite the great guy you thought him?'

Dumbly, she nodded. She would have to tell . . . and telling Steve would be like telling herself, not that hard a task.

'Well, I think you and I had better have lunch together; then you can get it all off your chest. Agreed?'

Her heart leaped. She clasped Steve's hand fervently, nodding, knowing she must take it easy, must not simply rebound onto her old friend because he was there, because he understood.

They went to the Red House, on Exchange Street. It was not a popular place. Little old ladies ate sticky buns and drank weak coffee, the odd couple had a snack. Kay and Steve sat at a dark corner table and had spaghetti on toast and fizzy lemonade, followed by stewed apple and custard. And Kay told Steve all that had happened and every now and then Steve reached across the tiny, round table and stroked her hand.

'So what did you say to him?' he asked at last, when the pitiful little tale had been told. 'Did you give him a piece of your mind?'

'I just put the phone down,' Kay said, sounding surprised. 'It – it was a shock, Steve. At first I couldn't take it in and then later, when I had, I found I didn't even want to think about him, I just wanted to get away. Away from Lincoln, away from Phil, away from my marriage. It was a real shock to discover that you can't, not just like that.'

'Oh? What does it take, then?'

'Proof. Hard proof, photographs, an independent detective finding Phil in bed with another woman . . . cooperation, he more or less said. And I don't want to cooperate with him, I don't want anything to do with him.'

'But you want a divorce, darling, so you've got to cooperate to an extent.' She drew in her breath sharply at the endearment and he smiled, then took her fist and began to unfasten her fingers one by one, moving his own fingers on the softness of her palm as it was revealed.

'I think you should go back to the solicitor and get him to write a letter to Phil for you. You don't have to explain how you know he's unfaithful, just that you do know. If he's as keen to end the marriage as you are, he might admit everything, save you a lot of time and trouble, as well as money.'

'Ye-es, but I don't want to start lots of trouble, and then find out I'm still married at the end of it,' Kay said. 'The solicitor said it would be difficult to do much with the war still on, and . . .'

'Go to another solicitor,' Steve said. 'I'd come with you if I could, but you must realise I can't. Phil mustn't be able to say that you were having a high old time on your own account, that would nullify any chance you had of divorce. Can you cope alone, darling?'

'Why do you keep calling me darling?' Kay said breathlessly. 'Steve, I'm not asking you to take me on, you know, I wouldn't do that, it wouldn't be fair.'

He smiled at her, his eyes dancing. 'It has nothing to do with fairness. It's what I've wanted all my life, I guess. But the war happened and you were so young and I was a fool, I thought you'd need to have a few boyfriends before I got serious. Why even my mother talked about letting

320

.you meet other men . . . Kay, darling, we're being given another chance, do you realise that? It isn't something many people can say.'

'And we'll take it? When we can do it safely, without mucking up my divorce? We'll be truly together? Oh, Steve!'

'When you look at me like that I tell you straight, I don't think I can wait until your divorce comes through,' Steve said, between his teeth. 'I'd like to punch Markham on the chin so hard . . . no I wouldn't, I'd like to give him a great big hug!'

'You fool! Oh Steve, how did I ever get myself in such a pickle, and just because he had a handsome face and charming ways? I told myself this morning that vain regrets were a waste of time, but I can't help wishing I'd listened to all that sound advice I was given, instead of just leaping in the dark.'

'Never mind; I'm here to catch you,' Steve said. 'Come on, let's go somewhere quiet and dark – like to see a film?'

'Yes . . . no, I wouldn't. I'd rather be with you alone, somewhere quiet . . . and dark.'

Steve looked at her seriously. 'Do you know what you're saying, darling? I get the oddest feeling that you do, and I'd love to suggest a quiet little hotel somewhere down on the coast – there are dozens in Great Yarmouth. But that isn't what I want with you, darling Kay. I want you wholeheartedly, not just on the rebound from a dismal marriage.'

'I want you on any terms, any way,' Kay said frankly. 'Isn't it odd, Steve, I think I've known Phil was a horrible mistake from that first leave, but I couldn't admit, even to myself, that I'd done absolutely the wrong thing. I kept telling myself that no one could be in love with two men at the same time, and of course I was right – I was in love with one, and tied to the other!'

Steve stood up, then held out his hands, hauling her to her feet. 'Come on then, let's get moving! And since it's after lunch and we shan't get back to Norwich until tomorrow morning sometime, what'll you tell your parents?'

Kay felt her stomach lurch with delighted anticipation, felt a tingling tide of desire flood all over her. If we go away together there will be no regrets, no glancing-back, she warned herself severely. It's either what you want with all of you, or you don't do it; understand?

'I'll tell them I've met a fellow WAAF from Yarmouth and we're going down there for a meal and may stay over; they probably won't believe me, but that's what I'll tell them. What about you?'

'Yes, that's a point. I think I'll say I'm taking a girl dancing and might not be back until the small hours. Mother sleeps like the dead; I'll ring her again in the morning, tell her I missed the last bus. She'll take it like a lamb; mothers have to, these days.'

'And when your mum and my mum meet . . . oh, what do I care?' Kay said joyously. 'It would be worth any-thing, anything at all, to have a whole glorious evening with you.'

'Evening and night,' he corrected, taking the bill over to the lady in black who sat behind the small desk and took the money. 'And I know very well which you'll enjoy most, you seductress, you!'

They caught a bus down to the coast and booked in at a small hotel. Mr and Mrs Minton, not Mr and Mrs Markham. 'Safer,' Steve said, signing the register.

'Besides, we're only anticipating the truth by a few months. We'll get you sorted out, young woman, see if we don't.'

They had dinner in the hotel, then walked on the white-sanded beach in the moonlight, sat down, they lay . . . clung, kissed.

'That's the first time I've kissed you properly,' Steve said breathlessly after a while, breaking the embrace. 'But it won't be the last . . . oh Kay, have I ever told you I adore you?'

'No,' Kay said with lazy contentment, cuddling close. 'But I like it; say it again!'

'I adore you. And now, my pretty, witty Kay, we'll go back to the hotel and I'll prove it in the best way I know.'

It was impossible not to remember her honeymoon as she undressed in the moonlight, for they had dispensed with the light and pulled back the curtains to let the soft summer air flood in. But she did not remember it for long, because Steve was everything she had ever wanted, as different from Philip as chalk and cheese. He wooed her, delighted her, carried her with him to the heights, wanting her pleasure more, she thought, than he wanted his own. When they lay still and quiet at last she put a tentative hand on his cheek.

'Steve? Was I – was I awfully bad at it? To tell you the truth I forgot to try, I just enjoyed myself which is dreadfully selfish, but . . .'

He put a hand over her mouth, gently silencing her.

'Hush. You were just right. Darling, it isn't something that people are good or bad at, I don't think, it's something between two people which can be beautiful and deeply satisfying, or not. Depending.'

'Depending on what?' Kay asked drowsily. 'You were frightfully good. Honestly, I feel as if I've been swimming in warm milk. All soft and relaxed and gentle and – and well-fed.'

Steve snorted on a laugh. 'Well-fed? That, my darling, was your fish and chip supper, not my – my attentions.'

'I didn't mean well-fed, then. Satisfied? Is that what I meant? Totally, completely satisfied.'

'Kay, you couldn't have said anything nicer than that, honestly. And when I'm with you, I'm the same. Totally, completely satisfied.'

'Then we'd better stay together, this time, and not muck up,' Kay said. She sighed deeply. 'I'm so happy, Steve! I never thought I'd be this happy again. Oh, how I wish we didn't have to go our separate ways when my leave ends!'

'We don't, not in the way you mean. We'll write letters, we'll talk on the phone, we'll meet whenever one or other of us gets the chance. I know we mustn't jeopardise your divorce, but we'll get round it somehow, I promise you. I couldn't bear not to be constantly in touch, darling.'

'Goody,' Kay said dreamily. 'Isn't it a horrid thought that if it hadn't been for Philip's letting himself down and thinking I was his nasty Janet, I might have been trapped in a miserable marriage for years and years?'

'It's terrifying,' Steve said soberly. 'When you think that I was on the verge of asking Hattie to marry me, just so I'd stop thinking of nothing but you, day and night.'

'You weren't!' Kay sat up, then squeaked and grabbed for the covers as Steve rolled over and looped an arm round her waist. 'Don't tell me you were going to marry just to upset me!'

'No, of course I wasn't, I was going to marry because

there didn't seem any future for you and me – well, there wasn't, you'd said so pretty frankly – and I thought if I burned my boats I might be like you, or like I thought you were, happy with someone else.'

'Gosh,' Kay said, awed. She sank back against the pillows. 'Aren't we terribly, terribly lucky, Steve?'

He kissed her soft shoulder.

'Very, very lucky,' he murmured against her flesh. 'Oh Kay, I wish tonight could last forever!'

Kay decided to make a clean breast of it to her mother the day before she went back to the site. Steve had left for Marham the previous day and so she waited until Sara was alone in the kitchen, podding peas for dinner, and broke the news briskly.

'Mummy, I don't know whether you and Daddy guessed, but Philip and I didn't simply have a row, we don't want to be married any more. I'm going to try to get a divorce quite soon; Philip's being unfaithful on a pretty regular basis, I believe. And . . . and I think when I'm free, Steve and I will probably marry. Almost certainly. Well, absolutely certainly, actually. He has asked me, only he said he can't do anything officially whilst I'm married to Phil, so . . . oh Mummy, haven't I made a dreadful mess of things, and aren't I lucky that Steve's giving me a second chance?'

'Divorce,' Sara said slowly. 'Oh darling, I'd give anything to have spared you that. But better divorce than a miserably unhappy marriage, which is what I'm sure you'd have had with Philip, because he really wasn't your type at all, darling. Still, you seem to have discovered that – when did you, by the way?'

'Oh, Mummy, that was where I went at the start of this

325

leave. He's in Lincoln, so I went and telephoned . . .'

'Well, I underestimated Philip,' Sara said with admirable restraint when her daughter told her the story. 'I didn't like him, but I never thought he would turn out to be a two-timing little swine! When he's married to the most gorgeous girl in the WAAF how can he sink to some little trollop who'll say yes to anything in trousers?'

'Mummy, can you be prejudiced? But anyway, it doesn't matter; I'm safe from him now, I'll never go within a mile of him again and as soon as we can manage it, I'll divorce him officially. I must say, it's a relief to have told you. I've always hated being deceitful but I wanted to get things sorted out with Steve, first.'

'Wonderful, darling. And what a shame it is that you're going back to your site tomorrow. We could have gone together to see Mr Elstrode; he'd have sorted you out in no time. Never mind, we'll do it on your next leave. Are you going to tell Daddy or shall I?'

'You,' Kay said at once. 'I'm sure he won't be cross, but he did tell me, over and over, that I shouldn't jump into anything. Still, at least he's always liked Steve.'

'True. Very well, I'll tell Daddy some time before you go. And now, young lady, you can give me a hand with these peas or dinner will never be ready for when your father gets home!'

Jo and Kay met in November for one of their nights out, and when they got back to Kay's site, having been to a dance at HQ, they were sitting in the empty mess drinking cocoa when, on impulse almost, Kay told Jo that she was divorcing Philip.

'Divorcing him? I can't believe you mean it – he's so handsome, so fond of you . . .'

326

'He's found someone else,' Kay explained. She began to smooth down the hem of her skirt, paying great attention to the movements of her fingers on the serge material. 'It's very awkward; he came down to see me last September when he got my solicitor's letter, all pretended puzzlement and rather manufactured charm, saying he didn't know what I was talking about, he'd never so much as looked at another woman and so on. Then I asked him why he'd called me Janet the previous June when I telephoned him and he said: "Oh, so that was you, was it?" which was a bit of a giveaway, I'd say. Oddly enough, though, he doesn't want a divorce. He keeps saying I'm unfair, he may have had the odd date – who doesn't, in wartime – but he can promise that once we get back together I'll never find him anything but attentive.'

'And you don't think he's speaking the truth? Or you just don't want someone who's been playing around?'

'I think he's lying in his teeth, because I'm sure he'd go on having affairs, he'd just do his best to make sure I never found out. No, the truth is I can't even bear the thought of having him in the same room, let alone the same bed, and I want everyone to know, now, that I'll be getting divorced.'

'Have you told the others? Biddy and Emily, I mean.'

Kay shook her head. 'Not yet. It's rather a difficult thing to say in a letter and I can't see much possibility of us meeting up again, not until the war's over, anyhow. I'll tell them when the divorce comes through, of course.'

'Or when you re-marry,' Jo said with surprising shrewdness, for Kay had always thought her friend too wrapped up in her own affairs to notice other people's. 'Because you will marry again won't you, Kay? Is it that sergeant who was on your site when you first got there?'

'Who, Jonty? He's a nice feller, but . . . no, it won't be him. It'll be a chap I've known all my life, just about. We telephone each other a couple of times a week, write endless letters, plan our leaves to coincide . . . to tell you the truth, Jo, I never should have married Phil. But there you are, we all make mistakes. How's Lyall?'

'I don't like the way you say, "How's Lyall" directly after "we all make mistakes",' Jo grumbled. She got up and poked the fire, which was almost out. 'Dare we sneak some more coal for this, or would you be court-martialled? Better not, I suppose, I'll just slip my great-coat back on.' She slipped the garment round her shoulders, then continued talking. 'Actually, I haven't seen Lyall lately. It's Brett Moisovitch at the moment. He's a dream, honestly. He comes over to the site regularly and watches us handling the balloon, he's really keen, always offering to take over from me or one of the other girls, just to see if he could manage. He's extremely strong but as I keep telling him it isn't just brute strength, an awful lot is down to experience, that certain knack . . . But we aren't going to let him fly the balloon, anyway, and I think he knows it, in his heart. It was just an excuse to get to know us, at first. Oh, and he filmed us the other evening, when we were getting the balloon down in bad weather. He's going to bring it round and we'll have a cinema show one night, when the film's developed – would you like to come round? You could meet Brett and watch the show at the same time.'

'I don't imagine he should have filmed you, though it will be fun to see yourselves at work. I'd love to come over and meet him, even if he is a spy, which he probably is, especially with a name like Moisovitch,' Kay observed. 'Russian, is he?'

'American. An all-American boy he says, though he called his grandmother Babushka. He's awfully nice, you'd approve, Kay, he's your type of bloke. He's not just awfully handsome, like Lyall, he's very sweet and thoughtful, as well. You must meet some time, I think you'd like him, I really do.'

'And heaven help me if I didn't,' Kay said, smiling. 'And just what is my type of bloke, may I ask? Don't forget who made the awful mistake of marrying Golden Boy!'

'Yes, now you mention it, it is odd that you married Philip, because I've always thought you'd go for steady, reliable types,' Jo mused. 'Brett's dependable, somehow. I'm never afraid I'll make a fool of myself when I'm with him – he wouldn't mind if I did, you know.'

'That's nice,' Kay said. 'Want any more cocoa?'

Jo considered, then shook her head. 'Better not, thanks all the same. My acting's a nice kid, but if the balloon does go up I'd rather be there. I'll get my bike now and toddle off.'

'Ride carefully,' Kay called presently as Jo cycled off across the site. 'My turn to call for you next – a week today, all being well.'

'That's grand,' Jo called back over her shoulder. 'See you a week today then, Kay.'

'There's a letter from Kay, addressed to us both, Biddy,' Emily called as she entered the mess where breakfast was being served. 'I opened it and had a read . . . wait till you hear what she's got to say!'

'Oh, great, I love letters,' Biddy said. She was standing in line, with her plate held out for sawdust sausages, dried egg and lovely wedges of mashed potato browned in the pan. 'If I get your grub, will you get my char?'

'Okey-dokey,' Emily carolled obligingly. She had been at first distressed by the contents of her friend's letter, then cheered by it. Kay was being so sensible and down to earth and it was clear that she was very happy, though why anyone about to divorce an erring husband should be happy was more than Emily could understand. If it was Alec, she thought, I'd try to come to terms with it, get him to see the error of his ways, I wouldn't jolly well divorce him!

However, she handed the letter to Biddy and joined the queue for tea. Rita had become more or less permanent cook at the manor house, as well as full-time housemother, but she had a skivvy or two to help her out and today it was Ethel. Ethel poured two mugs of tea, slopped in a tiny colouring of milk, and demanded to know what Emily was grinning about. 'Cos it's an 'orrible cold day an' we shan't none of us be gettin' any leave over Christmas an' I'm fed up wiv wet cordage an' greasy cable an' stinkin' whippin' an' ripcords an' riplinks an . . .'

'I'm not grinning, I'm smiling,' Emily said. 'And I'm smiling because Biddy and I got a letter from our friend Kay today. She's happy.'

'She's in London,' the grumbler said sourly. 'If I was in the smoke I'd be 'appy an' all. I'd go 'ome to me muvver an' get myself outside of a big panful o' jellied eels an' plum puddin'.'

'Oh Ethel, do shut up! We're none of us going to get home for Christmas but we aren't all making such a song and dance about it. Look at Biddy, with a big family only fifty miles or so away, but she won't get time off at Christmas, either.'

'She wouldn't go 'ome if she did get time off,' the disgruntled Ethel remarked. 'She don't go 'ome no more,

330

she goes chasin' after that young feller . . . Johnny, ain't it?'

'Well, she never moans,' Emily replied with spirit. 'You're always grumbling, Ethel. It's time you took stock and thanked providence that you've got your health and strength.'

'Yeah, an' 'ow much longer will I 'ave that, wiv two gels off wiv broken legs, eh?'

'Don't exaggerate. Pammy's got a broken leg, I grant you that, but Laura's only got pulled muscles. And Pammy's was self-inflicted.'

Ethel snorted. 'Oo was on the winch that night, eh? Pammy said it jerked 'er orf of 'er feet.'

Emily snatched the two mugs of tea and snorted in her turn. Ethel was a real grumbler and no mistake, but she did not intend to hear anyone trying to blame Biddy for Pammy's accident, if you could call it that.

'Pammy held on to the tail guy, having been told to release it, because she wanted a ride,' she said severely. 'We've all done it, though we all know it's bloody dangerous. She just held on too long, that's all.'

'Aye, an' fell ten foot because the winch was paid out too fast,' Ethel said obstinately. 'I was there, Em, same's you.'

'Then you must know it was nothing to do with the winch driver, it was Pammy . . . oh there's no point in arguing, I'm going to eat my breakfast.' Emily stomped over to the table where Biddy was already sitting and eating steadily and thumped the two mugs of tea down so hard that it splashed over onto the wood. 'That Ethel! She's always moaning about something.'

Biddy looked apprehensive. 'She's not going on about Pam again, is she? Honestly, Em, no one were more

331

'orrified than me when I seen 'er whizz past . . . weren't she an idiot, though? Fancy ridin' the tail in them conditions, eh? Asking for trouble.'

Emily, agreeing, sat down and began on her own breakfast. The trouble was, the girls worked so hard and were so brave and uncomplaining that you couldn't blame them for having a bit of fun with the tail guy. They weren't like WAAFs on a regular station, given the chance of a flip in a kite when the aircrew felt generous. The only flying they did was by holding on to the tail guy when the balloon was on the way up. Usually you just got whooshed into the air and at four or five feet you let go and landed safely on your feet. But Pammy had held on for too long, got panicky, then fallen badly. They had all known her leg was broken as soon as she hit the ground, because it was doubled under her at an impossible angle, but even Pammy had placed the blame unerringly upon herself.

'It's awright,' she had panted, her lips blue with pain and shock. 'I done it meself . . . tripped over the handling guys, didn't I? No one's fault.'

If the Powers That Be knew about tail-riding they never said, but everyone knew without a word spoken that it would be a punishable offence. So they scooped Pammy up off the deck and carried her very carefully into the mess, then phoned HQ.

They had acted quickly and with good sense, but even so, Emily privately doubted whether Pammy's leg would ever be the same again. She had nothing against RAF doctors and hospitals, but she had seen so many balloon ops with twisted knees, badly set shin-bones, bent wrists . . . no, it was best to take care, to get nimbly out of the way when the balloon was bucking and rearing and the guys

332

were lashing around like live things, and to let go of a rope when you were told, instead of hanging on for a free ride.

'So what do you think about Kay?' she asked presently, when Biddy laid the letter face down on the table and began, rather noisily, to drink her tea. 'Surprised, were you? I wonder if she's done the right thing?'

'Oh aye, Kay's got an 'ead on 'er shoulders,' Biddy said at once. 'She'll not put up wi' a feller what messes wi' other girls, though. I don't reckon I would, either. What about you, Em?'

'I dunno. I can't see myself sending Alec off with a flea in his ear no matter what he'd done,' Emily admitted. 'I'm so awfully fond of him, and I suppose a bloke can make a mistake, can't he?'

'Oh aye, who can't? But from what Kay says, it weren't just one mistake. It were two or three times a week. That sounds as though her Philip was a real bad 'un, to me.'

'I agree, actually,' Emily said. 'If he'd just dated some girl up in Lincoln it could be friendship or anything . . . well, you and I went to the flicks with Chaz and Flicker but it didn't mean anything, did it?'

'No; they're nice blokes, but all we wanted was an evenin' out,' Biddy agreed. 'I bet you didn't even kiss Flicker goodnight, did you?'

'No, of course not,' Emily said primly. 'We shook hands.' She giggled. 'Your face, Bid – did you kiss Chaz?'

'Aye; on the chin,' Biddy said exuberantly. 'I'm real fond of Johnny, but it's been a long time since I seen 'im. Judgin' by our Kay, though Em, I oughter think twice before settlin' down with anyone. And seamen are supposed to have a girl in every port – I wouldn't like that.'

333

'Do you reckon he does? Have a girl in every port, I mean?'

Biddy laughed but she looked thoughtful. 'That's the trouble, Em, I don't know 'im well enough to say, and that's the truth. Still, we're young and we've got plenty of time. What are you down for today?'

'Balloon inspection first thing, then patching if there is any, and maintaining the winch. You?'

'Greasin' cables and wires, painting the brickwork round the balloon bed, checkin' the sandbags and blocks,' Biddy said resignedly. 'When we're off duty though, I'm goin' to get a bus into Nantwich and see if I can find some Christmassy bits. Comin' wi' me?'

'Yes, I wouldn't mind,' Emily said at once. 'I've got a few bob saved – one of the best things about being a balloon op is the money and out here in the sticks we don't get much chance to spend anything! Who else will be off?'

'Dunno, only there's Pammy an' Laura on the sick . . .'

'So they are. Well, with two short it's only you, me, Polly and Nell off today,' Emily said, after some thought. 'And you and I are on guard duty from ten until midnight. Still, we might catch an early house at the cinema. I wonder what's on?'

'Dunno. But we could have pie an' chips in town and make a night of it, provided we caught the 9.20 bus back to the site,' Biddy suggested. 'Eh, Em, do you remember when Kay was on her honeymoon, how we wondered what they were doin' and talked about it? What if they didn't do anything at all, eh? Would that be grounds for divorce?'

'Grounds for thankfulness, I should think,' Emily said, then bit her lip. Her own timidity about matters sexual was not shared by most of her fellow WAAFs, but Biddy did not take her up on it, merely chortling and remarking coarsely that she, Biddy, would remind her, Emily, of that remark the day after her wedding to Alec.

'I bet it's wizard, having it wi' a feller if you're fond of him,' she said. 'I can't wait for Johnny's next leave, so we can find out!'

10

Christmas was as much of a non-event as the girls had feared, though they did their best to make it something a bit special. A group of them went into the woods a couple of days before and cut down quantities of holly and quite a handsome bush of mistletoe, though Biddy assured everyone severely that she, personally, would not be using any of it for the usual purpose.

'I know I climbed the trees an' cut the bunch down,' she agreed. 'But that don't mean I'm goin' to be messin' about wi' any o' the fellers from the searchlight battery, an' they're the only fellers we're likely to meet in this neck of the woods. I'm savin' me kisses for . . . for them as deserves 'em.'

'Don't be such an idiot, Biddy,' Millie Waters said, laughing. 'A kiss under the mistletoe's just like a friendly handshake, honest it is. Your John wouldn't mind you getting – or giving – that kind of kiss.'

'An' who'd wanna kiss you, any road?' Gillian Price said sneeringly. 'You're a bloody great beanpole wi' a hooter on you the size o' Battersea Power Station for all you aren't out o' nappies yet. You're safe as 'ouses, you could stand under that bloody mistletoe till the cows come 'ome an' you wouldn't get bovvered by no fellers.'

'You should know, queen,' Biddy said equably. 'There's me, an ugly beanpole wi' a feller of me own an' you, kind o' – kind o' *squat*, I think I'd call you, wi'out so much as a smell of a feller. The mistletoe's all yours,

Pricey. Who knows? There ain't many blind fellers in the RAF, but someone might come along.'

'That'll learn you, Pricey,' Millie said approvingly. 'You can't beat our Biddy so you'd best not try. Who's going to help make paper chains? The battery boys are coming over after dinner and bringing corn for popping and some honey to dip it in; we'd best be all smart before then.'

So it had been a jolly enough Christmas, with a few small presents, parcels from home, as much good food as the Air Force could provide and games of charades and pass the parcel in the mess, with a brew-up of cocoa laced with a half-bottle of rum someone on the searchlight battery had acquired to round off the day.

But now, with Christmas over and Easter looming, the future, as well as the weather, had suddenly brightened up considerably for Biddy and Emily. The *Aconite* had returned to port 'rather knocked about', as John phrased it, so he would be in England for at least two weeks, probably more, and had suggested, rather diffidently, that he and Biddy might meet in Runcorn since her Auntie Ethel had told him that he might have his leaves with her any time. Coincidentally, Alec had also got some leave and with equal diffidence, suggested that it might be an idea for him to meet his Em's parents at last.

'Or you could come down to Kent and I'd introduce you to my uncles and aunts, and those cousins who are still around, but we'd have to stay in lodgings, since my digs aren't suitable,' he had written. 'Or I could come up to you in Nantwich and we could spend time together. Whichever you like, sweetheart, so long as we meet.'

Emily promptly wrote to her mother saying that she was thinking of bringing her friend Alec home for a few days, and Mrs Bevan wrote back to say that both she and

Emily's father would be delighted to welcome her friend. Biddy wrote to Auntie Ethel out of politeness more than anything, announcing their imminent arrival, and Auntie Ethel wrote back, assuring Biddy of a warm welcome.

'So all we need now is the WO's permission, which most people would have got first,' Emily said as the two of them set off on the unit's bicycles. Several more had been acquired since arriving in Cheshire since buses were infrequent and there were no spare lorries to take the girls into town when they needed to shop. 'It's a lovely day for a ride to Command Centre; let's hope we're as cheerful coming back as we are going out.'

'I think she'll lerrus go, 'cos we haven't asked for much before,' Biddy said with a confidence she was far from feeling. Johnny was so important to her, she could not bear the thought of being refused permission to meet him. 'Why not, Em? We've had our noses to the flippin' grindstone since well before Christmas, an' we ain't had no enemy action for ages. Oh aye, she'll not stop us from leavin' the site.'

'What's more, people are actually talking about victory and what'll happen after the war, instead of saying if, if, if all the time,' Emily agreed. 'I know the chances are that we'll both be away together, but that leaves everyone else to cover for us. No, I can't see the WO trying to muck up our plans.'

And nor she did. 'You're both owed quite a bit of time,' she said, scanning their anxious faces with twinkling eyes. She must have known all too well how few were the diversions available to girls on a remote country site, Biddy told herself. Probably the officers didn't do all that well themselves. 'Besides, the jerries don't seem too keen to use aviation fuel coming right across the country – and right over a great many ack-ack batteries – to lay their eggs on us. Exactly when will your young men be home?'

'My feller's an able seaman on a corvette, an' he'll be comin' up from Portsmouth any day now, please ma'am,' Biddy said with extra special respect. The thought of spending a few days away from the site and with her dear Johnny was heady stuff to one who had scarcely been off it, save for brief shopping trips into Nantwich or Chester, since their posting. 'We're both from Liverpool, an' they've not been raided for a while . . .'

'Good. Very well then, I'll tell your sergeant that you'll be off on a ten-day leave in three days time. I'll see you get rail passes . . . I assume you're taking your boyfriend home, Bevan?'

'Yes, ma'am,' Emily said. 'He'll not be in Wales for a week, but I'd like to get there first if I can. I'll have to borrow him a bed from relatives, since we've only the one spare, and that's mine, and I don't think . . . I mean . . .' She broke down into a confusion of half-sentences, blushing crimson, much to Biddy's amusement. As if the WO would expect her to share a bed in her mam and dad's house, she thought, grinning to herself. But it must have crossed our Em's mind or she'd not have said what she did.

'I expect you'll wangle something,' the warrant officer said easily, however, ignoring Emily's pink-faced confusion. 'He's RAF, is he?'

'No, ma'am, he's a brown job – I mean he's a soldier on an ack-ack battery in outer London,' Emily said. 'Do we have to come back to Command Centre to get our travel passes?'

'No, I'll have someone send them over. And I'll see if I can get a gharry to pick you up fairly early in three days

339

time so at least you'll get to the station without any trouble.'

'She's norra bad old stick,' Biddy said appreciatively as they cycled off. 'We'll be grateful for that gharry, ole Emily. I don't fancy ridin' to the station wi' kitbags an' that, an' the buses might not be runnin' early enough for us.'

'We'd better go straight on to the station now, see what time the first train leaves for Crewe,' Emily said. 'We'll have a fair wait, we usually do.' She beamed across at Biddy. 'Ten whole days, Bid! I can't perishin' well wait!'

Due to the unforeseen awfulness of the trains, which seemed to be running completely at random, Emily finally got a train which should have left Chester almost three hours earlier. She waved out of the window at Biddy, standing grinning on the platform with a cup of tea in one hand and a station wad in the other. Emily could see her friend's mouth moving, knew she was being told to 'Be good, an' if you can't be good be careful,' and waved an acknowledgement, then settled back in her corner seat.

The train was full, but was nowhere near as crowded as the two earlier trains had been, so though she was tucked into her seat like a cork in a bottle, Emily was not uncomfortable and could look round her as the train chuff-chuffed slowly along, enjoying the fresh and various greens of the trees and meadows, recognising, with a jolt of the heart, the gradual advance of spring.

She had not had time to do more than gulp at a scalding hot cup of tea on Chester platform but she had bought herself what the vendor had called 'an 'am sangwidge', and bit into it now, telling herself philosophically that there was little chance of anything else to eat until she reached home. Corwen was a tiny station and at their present rate of progress all the shops would be shut by the time they got there. Furthermore, because her parents were not on the telephone she had been unable to warn them that she would be arriving three hours later than planned, so she might have quite a wait before her father, in his battered old Morris, turned up to rescue her.

Still. Da knew all about wartime difficulties, and Emily guessed that he would probably simply wait until she did reach Corwen. There would be no service buses running to Cerrig-y-drudion so late, and anyway their farm was a good five mile walk from Cerrig . . . Yes, Da would certainly wait.

The train jerked to a halt at a small country station and Emily saw that the station master was growing a good crop of winter cabbage and some leggy sprout plants in the beds which, in happier times, had been bright with daffodils and narcissus. She gazed out at them until the train began to move once more, then settled back in her seat and closed her eyes. It had been a tiring day, she might as well try to get a bit of a rest before they reached Corwen.

The back seat of the old car was full of feed sacks, but Emily, enthroned like a queen in the front passenger seat and jabbering away in Welsh for the first time in what felt like years, was brimming over with happiness. Her father had indeed come to the station and waited for her to arrive, had insisted on buying her a newspaper package of fish and chips to eat as the car slowly traversed the fifteen or so miles which lay between Corwen and the farm, and had regaled her with all the local news.

The cousins were all in the services, but their parents

341

would doubtless want to see what sort of feller 'young Emily' had found herself, which might be a bit of a trial for Alec, though Emily did not think so.

'I thought we'd be having them over for a high tea,' Eifion Bevan said in his deep, slow voice. 'Easier it would be than trying to trek Alec round all the farms. Your mam said she'd do a bake, and the aunts will all bring cakes and that.'

'It's awfully good of Mam,' Emily said gratefully. 'D'you know, Da, I think this track's even rougher than when I left!'

'More traffic we do be having,' Eifion said. 'The people from the Ministry, checking up, and the milk lorry now, calling for the churns every other day, since we've only four cows. And then there's the landgirls.'

'What do they come up here for?' Emily asked, genuinely surprised. Her mother had not mentioned that landgirls had been working on the farm and despite the four cows, she could not imagine that there would be sufficient work for them. 'Is it the shearing, Dad? Only we used to manage that between us, with old Eneurin to give a hand.'

'No, not enough work for extra normally, but we share four landgirls with the folk round about,' her father told her. 'They do be a help too – they're all trained, you know – so they help at lambing, at shearing, and when I take stock to market.'

'Where do they sleep?' Emily said considerably surprised to hear that her father had consented to have female help. She remembered him when the war started being very old-fashioned about landgirls, though he had expected her to work as hard as any man. But that was different; she was his daughter. 'I say, they don't use my bed, do they? And what about when Alec gets here?'

'Steady on, girl,' Eifion said, laughing, as they juddered slowly up the heavily rutted lane between hedges only just beginning to show the first green buds. 'Share I said and share I meant. They don't live with any of us, none of us have the room to spare, and it wouldn't be right, to my way of thinking. They have digs in Cerrig, and a lorry takes them round the farms each day and drops them off where they're needed. Which is why the lane's more rutted than usual, see? The lorry brings 'em right down to the house when they're working for us, which don't do the lane much good in wet weather.'

'I see,' Emily said. 'Oh, Da, there's Jill! D'you think she'll recognise me?'

Jill was the Bevans' thin, sly sheepdog who had been Emily's constant companion before the war. Eifion was saying that he was sure the dog could never forget her when he brought the car to a halt just short of the back door and got stiffly out. As Emily began to tug at the passenger doorhandle Jill advanced suspiciously upon the vehicle, her hackles up, her lip raised in a snarl. There was a moment's hesitation when Emily got right out of the car, and then suddenly the dog shot across the yard and leapt into her arms, barking hysterically, wagging her tail so fast that it became no more than a blur, and licking every part of her mistress's face that she could reach.

'There you are,' Eifion said placidly, reaching into the car and beginning to unload first Emily's kitbags, then her respirator case, and finally the first of the feed sacks. 'If you think she's forgot you you must be mad, girl! Ah, here's your mam.'

'I've not forgot you either, my dear,' Siriol Bevan said, giving Emily a hug. 'Well, well, I do believe you've grown!'

'Mam, I can't possibly have – unless you mean I'm fatter,' Emily protested, picking up her kitbags and making for the kitchen door. 'We eat an awful lot of stodge in the service, and I've got stronger, so perhaps it's that. You and my da don't look any different – nor does Jill, except that she seems thin after Mollie.'

'You look grand, love,' Siriol said heartily. 'I made a hot-pot; good job too, since you're goodness knows how late! I'll just warm the potatoes through . . .'

Emily got up late next day, had a leisurely breakfast, helped her mother to wash up and put the crockery and cutlery away, and then wandered out with a bag of old cooked potatoes, chicken meal and household scraps to feed the hens. The farm consisted of the small, stone-built house, the farm yard itself, roughly paved with stone slabs, which was surrounded on two sides by long stone buildings with ill-slated roofs and gaping doors, and what they had always known as the home pasture, a smallish, well-hedged meadow where sick sheep had been penned, away from the main flocks which grazed on the open moorland.

The four cows were in the right-hand stone building where Eifion kept his elderly tractor and bales of hay, sacks of feed and various farm implements; what farmers called 'dead stock'. Or at least they must have been there when her father had brought them in to be milked, earlier. Now, Emily guessed, they would be out, grazing on any pasture sufficiently well-grassed to feed them. Her mother had told her about the cows in one of her letters and complained that they were having to feed them supplements for nine months out of the twelve since the sort of grass on which sheep can thrive will not support four milch cows. But they had bought the cows cheap, and her mother thought they were paying their way all right.

The hens did not have a run as such, though they had a partitioned-off part of the left-hand building where they were shut away at night to keep them safe from foxes and other marauders. Her father would have let them out as soon as he got up, but Emily knew how to attract them for their food – that would not have changed.

Accordingly, she stood in the pale sunlight, with the wind lifting her fringe of light brown hair off her forehead, and beat the enamel bucket of mash with the heavy tin spoon. At the sound hens came hurrying, looking, Emily thought, like fat old washerwomen lifting up their heavy skirts and running with that wide-legged, awkward gait peculiar to a bird whose preferred mode of travel should have been flight – except that their wings had been clipped, of course. Even so, some of them held their wings out and flapped them now and then, achieving short bursts of speed and arriving at Emily's feet before their fellows.

Emily began to spoon the mash out and to throw it around, but this was never enough for some hens, who kept trying to flutter upwards in order, apparently, to make pigs of themselves in the bucket. Emily, well-used to this, knocked them down with the spoon and continued to scatter food, finally standing the bucket down on its side so that her attackers could see for themselves that it was empty.

The hens pecked busily, examined the empty bucket and wandered off, uttering little croodles of discontent – considering that they had miles of open countryside in which to scavenge, Emily thought them pretty ungrateful

345

– so she picked up the empty bucket and went back to the house for the pig swill.

The pigs were in the partition next to the hens, and were reached by a wooden door divided in two. They also had a run, alongside the home pasture, which they treated with piggish disrespect, rooting and burrowing until there wasn't a blade of grass to be seen.

Today, however, Emily tipped the swill into the trough and then noticed that the pigs, whilst fine, fat and as greedy as ever, had not been digging; the grass was short but green and attractively powdered with the white blossom of the blackthorn bushes which formed part of the hedge.

She was still leaning on the mossy wooden gate, wondering why the pigs were acting so out of character, when a voice in her ear said gloomily: 'Looks better, don't it? Ringed them we have.' It was old Eneurin Evans, who lived in a tumbledown shack two miles away and helped her da out at shearing time.

'You've ringed the pigs? And that stops them rooting? Crumbs, I wonder why we didn't do it before, then?' Emily said. 'How are you, Eneurin? It's good to see you.'

'I'm fair to middlin',' Eneurin said briefly. 'We din't 'ave no Ministry before, interferin' with everything we done, that's why.'

'The *Ministry* made my father ring the pigs?' Emily said, much amused. 'How could they know what we do up here? No one's ever bothered us before.'

'Well, they do now,' Eneurin confirmed. 'Have you seed the paperwork your dad has to fill in afore he can keep a pig, let alone kill 'un? Why, they even count the hens, an' the number of lambs, come April . . . they telled us to grow oilseed rape alongside the brook, an' the land

346

there so boggy we'd have had to sow it, reap it an' stack it by hand, since you'd not get a horse nor yet a tractor out of it alive.'

'You wouldn't have got much of a crop, either,' Emily said with a chuckle. She knew the land alongside the brook – the rock there was so near the surface that only moss and the thin and wiry moor grass grew there, except for the boggy patches, which were under water all winter and thick with reeds and water iris all summer. 'So what happened?'

'Oh, your da telled 'em to come an' crop it theirselves, if they could. We din't hear no more about it. But your mam don't get no egg ration . . . an' we aren't meant to kill a sheep unless we hand it over to the Ministry . . . eh, it's a hard life for them on the land.'

Having commiserated with the old man Emily went indoors again, and found her mother cheerfully cutting bread off a homemade loaf and carving a side of ham into thick and fat-rimmed slices.

'I saw Eneurin telling you the tale,' she said cheerfully. 'Told you we weren't allowed to slaughter a pig without giving half to the Ministry, and that we have to hand over most of our eggs as well, and the lambs are all counted and so on, I expect.'

'Yes, he did,' Emily said, eyeing the ham as her mother went to the larder and produced an extremely large bowl of curd cheese. 'It sounded really bad, Mam.'

'Yes. Only we're a long way out, and the folk from the Ministry don't know the lie of the land,' Siriol said serenely. 'Brew the tea, there's a good girl. Your da will be in for his elevenses presently.'

'Oh! But if they count the lambs, and the pigs . . .'

'They can't actually *count* them, love,' her mother said,

returning from a second trip to the larder with a big jar of pickled onions. 'Most folk round here have a sow and a few piglets in the sty close to the house and another, tucked away somewhere. Same with the lambs. No use declaring them all, because some of 'em will die come winter sure as sure. But you can't expect the Ministry chaps to understand that, so we – we cover ourselves, you might say. Aye, and we've not done too badly, one way and another.'

'Oh, good,' Emily said feebly. 'Mam, I'm going to take a look round so I'll mebbe not come in for my dinner. All right? Only once Alec gets here it will be – well, different.'

'Right, love,' her mother said. 'Take some bread and ham with you; you can eat it on the tops, if you're going that far.'

Emily, grinning, complied. 'You know me so well, Mam,' she said, packing the bread and ham and pickled onions into a brown paper bag and then stuffing the bag into her pocket. 'See you later, then.'

On the day that Alec was due to arrive, Emily went by bus into Corwen. The weather had changed abruptly on her second day at home and it had rained for almost three days, but today, though overcast and cool, was at least dry, and there was a little buzz of excitement inside her because Alec would soon be here.

In other ways, though, her heart was heavy. And this was because she had realised, quite definitely, that she would not be coming back here to live when the war was over. It was beautiful, the most beautiful place in the world she thought sometimes, with such a variety of scenery that only a person who was both blind and

348

insensitive could not have been overawed by it. But having been away from it, she knew she could no longer be satisfied with the life that had pleased her so well before.

Apart from the occasional visits of the landgirls – and they would not be coming, now, until lambing started – the small farmhouse and Eneurin's shack were the only occupied dwellings for miles. When she had been at school there had been other girls to talk to and laugh with, and she had scarcely missed them in holidaytimes, so busy with the farm had she been. She had never realised before how little her parents actually talked, either. Nor how narrow their outlook was compared with most people of their age. But now she knew what it was like to have the constant companionship of a couple of dozen girls of roughly her own age, and not only that, her mind and imagination and her lively sense of humour were engaged for at least sixteen hours out of the twenty-four. She simply could not imagine living here again, helping her mother about the house, her father about the farm, and in between, catching the twice weekly bus into Cerrig-y-drudion – which was not exactly a centre of commerce – to do a bit of shopping, to have a cup of coffee in the café frequented by farmers and their wives, and perhaps to meet an old school friend for a brief chat.

In her small bedroom at the farm there was a bed, a wardrobe, a chest of drawers and a bookcase beneath the window. In that bookcase were all the books she had ever managed to acquire – perhaps forty or fifty small volumes, mainly children's books, none of them new, all of them passed down from cousins or on from her parents, or bought, on rare trips into Corwen, from the secondhand bookshop there. Her parents had never understood why she loved books, nor why she had yearned for a wireless set. Admittedly, they had one now, but it was only turned on at newstime. 'Keeps us up to date,' her father had said on her first night home. 'Gives us news of the war and such. Why, there's music on sometimes, and Sundays there's good services, some of 'em from Wales.'

Emily, greatly daring, had pointed out that there were also comedy shows, variety shows and a great many interesting interviews. Her father had grunted, and reminded her that there was not much time, when you lived on a hill farm, for such stuff. The farm was too remote for a newspaper to be delivered, though Eifion picked up the local weekly when he went into town, but books, news-papers and magazines had become a part of Emily's new life, and she found she did not want to give them up. Even on the remote Cheshire site there had been a library within cycling distance, as well as a number of shops, and though there was a library in Cerrig her father would have thought it very strange had she asked him to take her in a couple of times a week to change her books.

She had never regretted not having a telephone when she had lived at home; indeed, when she first joined the WAAF she had been rather frightened of the instrument. Now, it seemed positively archaic not to be within reach of such a marvellous means of communication. She telephoned Kay and Jo sometimes, Alec regularly, but when she needed to get in touch with her parents she had to ring the milkman in Cerrig, who would get in touch with the man who drove the lorry for the Milk Marketing Board, who would, next time he was at the farm collecting their churns, pass on the message that they were to ring their daughter, on such and such a number, at such and such a time. No one could call that a simple means of

350

communication. Indeed, it was faster and surer to write a letter.

Nor, she realised now, could she be philosophical about doing without those other things to which she had grown accustomed, like running water, close friendships, and the sort of pride in oneself which comes with being part of a smart and efficient unit. Even her care over her appearance was a new thing, for the old Emily had washed and dressed herself without a thought for how she looked. Now, she never left the hut without checking, in the glass by the door, that everything was as it should be. If she was going into town her shoes and buttons shone with buffing, her hair was smooth, her cap placed upon it at just the right angle. If she was going out to fight the balloon down from six thousand feet to close-haul she would merely see that she was warmly dressed, that all her buttons were done up and all laces and ribbons tied tightly. But at the farm, one wore one's oldest and shabbiest clothes and rubber boots all the year round and never thought about appearance at all.

I'm a different person from the one who left Mam and Da nearly three years ago, she thought miserably as the bus drew into Corwen at last and she prepared to get down. The girl that loves Alec – and is loved by him – isn't the girl who left Corwen station with tears and fears, and suffered from such terrible homesickness at first. The person I am now is self-confident, at ease with her peers, proud of her ability to issue commands and see them obeyed. But thank God that's the girl Alec fell in love with; hopefully, he'll understand that I don't want to live here after the war, that I'll go wherever he goes.

It went without saying, however, that her parents would not understand. Oh, they would understand if she and

Alec married, but she just knew that her father would invite him to take over the farm when the war was over. Indeed, he had more or less told her so already. 'I've no son to come after me, mun, but as my girl's husband welcome you would be here,' she imagined Eifion saying to Alec. 'I could do with another man about the place to tell the truth. You'd take to the life like a duck to water, with our Emily by your side, and she couldn't be happy anywhere else but here. The language? Oh, you'd soon get into the way of it, mun. Why, there's a feller out by Pentre Foelas, runs the village shop, who didn't speak a word of it ten year back but now he's as fluent as myself.'

The countryside was beautiful, of course, and if the sun was shining when the offer was made, who could say that Alec would not want to take her father up on it, bury them both here? He would imagine that piped water and electricity would come soon enough, that they would make friends, buy a car, go into the local towns whenever they wanted to see some life. He would not see in her mother's grey hair and toil-worn hands, her father's bent back, that it was the farm which had made them, in their mid-forties, look sixty. What was more, after the bustle and liveliness of the forces, Emily thought that the slow pace and the quiet would drive them both mad . . . it would be strange enough learning to live in a world at peace without adding the worse strain of taking on an old and battered farmhouse surrounded by poor land which, if the truth were told, was only fit for the rearing of the tough little hill sheep.

She reached the station and sat down on one of the wooden seats, putting her respirator case down beside her and pulling out her knitting. She was making Alec a pair of khaki mittens with the fingers out; she might as well get on with her work as sit here making herself miserable by imagining what the future held. She glanced up at the station clock; another hour to go before the train was even due. Sighing, she began, slowly, to knit.

Biddy jumped down off the train and scanned the platform eagerly, in fact was still scanning it when a pair of arms went round her and she found herself lifted off her feet and squeezed so hard that she gasped, twisting in the strong arms and then impulsively kissing the side of John Arthur's curly mouth.

'Oh, Johnny! I've missed you so much! It's – it's been so *long*, but we're here at last an' it's so good to see you!'

John let her slide from his embrace onto the platform, then he turned her to face him and they kissed; properly, Biddy thought ecstatically, like they did in the films. It looked rather silly when you saw other people doing it, but when it was you, and the feller was the person you cared about most in the whole world . . . it was great, just great!

'Eh, Biddy, you looked straight through me just now – don't say I've got so bleedin' handsome you didn't recognise me!' John said when at last they drew apart. 'You're growin up, Bid, an' gettin' prettier every day. What've you done to your hair?'

'One o' the girls cut it for me, she said it were lovely thick, shiny hair if it were decently cut 'stead o' me hackin' at it wi' blunt scissors. And she said to give it a chance an' not to keep screwin' it up in curl-papers, but I weren't sure . . . what d'you think?'

Biddy's hair, which had seldom stayed in its roll and was apt to descend at the worst possible moments, getting in her eyes and tangling in anything nearby, had been cut

353

into a sort of Dutch bob with a full fringe. As ACW Waters had said, with constant brushing and no fiddling about with curl papers, it now shone like silk and the darkness of it was shot with reddish highlights.

'It's A one,' John said simply. 'Like you are, Bid. I say, you're gettin' quite . . . that's to say there's more of your . . . only it's in all the right places, I mean.'

'You mean I've gorra bust,' Biddy said proudly. 'It's tuggin' that bleedin' balloon down when it 'ud rather be up, that's what done it. Do you like that an' all, Johnny?'

He gave her a little shake, chuckling and putting an arm round her waist, then taking the heavier of her two kitbags. 'Well, what do *you* think? I've never yet met the feller who didn't like a gel's figure, queen. But we'd best get a move on, your aunt's waitin', and there's something I want to do tomorrer, as soon as we've got ourselves up.'

'What? But there's plenty of today left yet,' Biddy said, obediently following him out of the station and into the street. 'We might go dancin', don't you think? I love to dance, I do.'

'Well, Auntie Ethel – she told me to call her that – has gorra special high tea waitin' for us this evenin',' John said. 'When you've got outside o' that, queen, I doubt you'll feel much like dancin'. But if you do, I'm game. I got here yesterday, so I'm fresh enough.'

Biddy, who had been striding along with a kitbag slung over her shoulder and a paper carrier bag in her other hand, turned to look at her companion. He was pale and weary-looking for all his brave words, she thought with quick compassion. 'Oh, I ain't particular about dancin',' she said casually. 'I'd as soon have a quiet time, our first evenin'.'

'Well, we'll see,' John said, striding beside her. 'Eh,

Bid, it's so good to be wi' you again! We're goin' to paint the town red, this leave.'

Despite Biddy's determination to get as much out of their leave as possible, they both decided to stay at home that first evening, and went early to bed, furthermore. Auntie Ethel woke them late next morning and insisted that they eat a good, hot breakfast before taking themselves off for the day. Biddy gathered that John must have confided in her aunt, but she said nothing, wondering what he had planned but sure that she would enjoy anything they might do together. But when he revealed his plans she was not so sure.

'We're goin' to catch the train again today, and go into the city centre,' John said once breakfast was over and he and Biddy had strolled out into the sunny morning. 'We'll tek a look at the shops an' the museum an' the Pier Head, get ourselves some dinner somewhere, see a flick later, if there's anythin' good showin'. But it's no use shuttin' our eyes to it for ever, queen. Liverpool's there, bashed about but grinnin' still, I bet. My mam and dad's gone, like your mam an' your kids, but life goes on, Bid. We've both gorra face up to it sooner or later, an' I'd rather we did it together.'

'Ye-es, but not today,' Biddy said pleadingly. The sun still shone, but the spring had gone out of her step just at the thought of the great city and its river some fifteen miles further along the railway track. 'Let's go on – on the last day of our leave, hey, Johnny? We'll be – we'll be stronger by then.'

'No. Today.' John said shortly. He put his arm round her and gave her a squeeze. 'Courage, our kid! Ever visited a churchyard, looked at the graves? Seen the grave of someone you know, mebbe?'

355

'Aye, years ago. Me grandad,' Biddy said after some thought. 'He were a Welshman an' wanted to be buried in Wales. Mam was the youngest of her family but she fair loved her dad, an' when I were little we went off into Wales twice a year. We caught the ferry, and then a bus to a little village called Farndon – he were brought up there as a boy. An' comin' up to Christmas we put a holly wreath on his grave, an' in the summer, when his birthday was, we put any flowers Mam could afford an' anything we could pick.'

'An' was it frightening? Sad?'

'Well, no, because me grandad was an old feller, an' I hadn't known him all that well,' Biddy pointed out. 'Besides, goin' to a grave . . . oh Johnny, don't let's!'

'We won't go to the graves if you don't want to, because we don't know for sure where your family's buried, and I don't want to drag you all the way to Anfield, because I dunno whereabouts me mam and dad's grave is, anyway. One of these days, Sid an' me'll meet up an' go out to the grave, put some flowers on it maybe. I'm not goin' there yet, though. But I do think you an' me should . . . well, face up to where our homes were, like.'

'Right. If – if it's what you want,' Biddy said in a small voice. 'Oh Johnny, I'm that scared! It – it'll make it all seem *real*, an' I've worked hard not to let it.'

'I think you'll find that it is real, and that it's better dealt with once you've come to terms with it,' John said, keeping his arm comfortingly round her shoulders as they walked down to the station. 'You're my brave girl, you're true blue, you'll never stain!'

'Oh, Johnny, me grandad used to say that,' Biddy said, between a laugh and a sob. 'Only I ain't brave, an' I'd rather you went on thinkin' I was.'

356

'I'll know you're brave, even if you weep buckets,' John said cheerfully. 'It's brave to take all the responsibility for yourself the way you've done, let alone joinin' up when you should still ha' been in school . . .'

'In school! We leaves school at fourteen down our court,' Biddy said at once. 'I were workin' in the chocolate factory on Picton Road – that were bombed an' all. But I didn't go back there, not after . . . after Mam an' the kids. I just left.'

'Where did your dad go? Hasn't your aunt any idea?'

'Nah, she never did like me dad. For all I know he could've been killed an' all,' Biddy said indifferently. 'The docks took a pastin', an' he was workin' down the docks. Oh aye, he could've been a goner an' all.'

'Perhaps you might find out,' John said diffidently. 'No harm in *knowing*, is there?'

Biddy frowned. They were standing on the platform now, awaiting the arrival of their train and she scowled down at the patchy tarmac, kicking at some loose gravel with the toe of her uniform shoe. 'I dunno about no harm, there's no *good* in knowing,' she said sullenly. 'What's the use of knowing he's alive, when I know they're dead?'

'He is your father,' John said awkwardly. 'Isn't that a reason for . . . well, for simply askin' around?'

'No,' Biddy said, far more definitely this time. 'I tell you, Johnny, he weren't no good. He – he drank like a bleedin' fish an' when he were drunk he'd batter me mam, me little brothers . . . me, too, when I were smaller. If you want the truth I bleedin' *hope* he's dead, because a bugger like that don't deserve to live. 'Specially when decent folk, folk who worked hard to feed their kids an' bring 'em up right, folk like me mam, are dead.'

There was a long pause, then John took Biddy's face

357

between his hands and looked deep into her tear-filled eyes. 'I didn't know, didn't understand,' he said quietly. 'My mam an' dad were different, see. Sid's more'n a dozen years older than me, so Mam an' Dad were old when I were born, an' they both did all they could for me. They were proud to have a son servin' in the Navy, they'd have supported me whatever I done, I daresay – an' the same wi' Sid, of course. So when you said you didn't like your dad . . . well, I didn't realise you'd a damned good reason for the way you felt. I'm real sorry, Bid.'

'That's all right,' Biddy said. She scrubbed fiercely at her eyes with her knuckles, then grinned at him. 'I said a thing or two I shouldn't have. Me dad may be different, now he's lost his family. But I reckon leopards don't change their spots.'

'I believe you,' John said. 'Look, mebbe I were wrong to try to make you go back. Do you want to turn round and go somewhere else, somewhere different? If you feel it's all too much for you right now . . .'

'No, you were right and we'd best go now, while me courage lasts,' Biddy said, as the train drew in beside them. 'An' there's another thing. We had some good friends what lived around our court – they won't still be there, but they'll have been housed somewhere else, I reckon. I'd like to see some of 'em again.'

The train drew in and people began to climb down. John and Biddy stood back until the last passenger had got off, then they climbed into the nearest carriage. John sat Biddy down in the corner seat and took the one next to her. 'Lime Street next stop,' he said cheerfully. 'Well, so far as we're concerned, anyway. And once we've done it, it's over and we can move on to other things. What say we go to New Brighton one day, though? You'd enjoy that, our Bid!'

They stood where once the Bachelor home had stood. Above them, the sky was pale blue, streaked with sun-gilded cloudlets, but in the court it was dark. At least two of the houses had been totally destroyed by the bomb, reduced to blackened rubble, but the houses that still stood were as black as though they, too, had been set on fire and the tall warehouse which closed off the far end of the court was blackened as well. John stared around him, wide-eyed.

'It's terrible, Biddy,' he said in a low voice. 'What was it like . . . before?'

'Like this, only a bit darker, 'cos the houses shut out more of the sky before,' Biddy said steadily. 'It never were red-brick, like other houses, or at least it must ha' been once, but not since I've knowed it. It's odd, ain't it, Johnny? When I thought about it, I saw it as – as kind o' lighter an' airier, but now I'm here . . . well, ain't it just grim, though? Why, if it weren't for all the poor sods what died I should think folks like me Auntie Ethel oughter thank the jerries for destroyin' this little lot.'

'It is grim,' John admitted. He took Biddy's hand and, together, they walked right into the court. 'My God, there's curtains at that end window . . . it don't look very safe, either. The wall nearest us is leanin' – surely that house ain't occupied?'

'It always leaned,' Biddy said. She sounded almost cheerful now. 'The Donahues lived there . . . reckon they live there still. Shall us give a knock to the door?'

'I dunno; do you want to?' John asked. 'If so, of course we'll knock. Why, do you realise, queen, that the folk round here might not know you're alive? Yes, we'll go and wake someone up.'

But Biddy was pulling back on his arm, shaking her

359

head, her pale face looking almost ghostlike against the blackened walls. 'No, Johnny, I don't want to. Let's leave. There ain't nothin' of me mam or the little'uns here now, an' I don't want to be told where me dad is, nor who else died that night. Come on, let's go, *please*.'

'Right,' John said. He about-turned smartly, heading for the arched entrance once more, beyond which the street outside showed colourful by comparison. 'D'you mind comin' out to my street, now?'

'Course not,' Biddy said sturdily. 'I'll come wi' you out to the cemetery, too, because I reckon that's where Mam an' the kids'll have been put.' She heaved a deep sigh. 'I reckon it's nice out there – a deal nicer than it is in our court, any road. An' I'd like to take 'em some flowers . . . Your mam an' dad too,' she ended in a rush. 'Johnny – d'you reckon they'd ha' liked me awright?'

'I'm sure of it,' John said stoutly. 'What 'ud your mam think of me then, flower?'

'She'd have loved you,' Biddy assured him. 'Same as I do. Can we catch a tram out to Anfield? Or d'you want to walk?'

They went and saw John's street, which meant seeing his house, too, since it had not been destroyed in the May blitz.

'Mam and Dad were in the Anderson shelter with neighbours an' friends. It was like your place though, it took a direct hit,' John told Biddy as they stood outside the terraced house. There were curtains at the window, the front step was whitened and the place had a cared-for, lived-in look. 'I wonder who's livin' there now?' he finished, but not as though he cared at all.

'Why didn't you and Sid keep it on for after the war?' Biddy asked curiously. 'It's a real smart little house,

Johnny – not so little, either. Bet you had two bedrooms, an' a parlour as well as the livin' room.'

'That's right,' John told her. 'We had the furniture put in store, such as it is, but we let the house go. What's the use of hangin' on to something you can't use, when others need it? The landlord needed his rent, an' me an' Sid had other uses for our money. Besides, Mam would ha' said it were selfish to hang on to the house when we couldn't use it. And after the war . . .' John slid a sideways look at Biddy, '. . . I reckon Sid and me will be married, an' livin' somewhere else.'

'Funny way you Arthurs go on, marryin' each other,' Biddy said, having stared long and curiously at the house in which her dear Johnny had been born and brought up. 'I'd ha' thought you'd ha' preferred a gel!'

'Oh very funny! Sid's got a girl, she's a nurse at the Royal. They got engaged ages ago, but they'll marry when Sid gets home and I reckon they'll not want to live in central Liverpool. One thing the war's done for us city slickers, it's showed us there's other places to live, places where you can see green grass from your bedroom window, an' hear the birds sing.'

'And we're goin' to tie the knot too, aren't we, Johnny?' Biddy said, taking his hand and hugging it between her own. 'I wouldn't mind livin' in Nantwich, if we could find work thereabouts.'

'We're goin' to tie the knot,' John confirmed solemnly. 'We'll have a double weddin', shall us? You an' me, an' Sid an' Susie.'

'Can't. We'll need to share the dress,' Biddy said, entering into the spirit of the thing. 'Well, we would if we was both WAAFs, anyway. Not that I care about dresses, much. I'd only look a fool in it.'

361

'You'd look beautiful,' John said reproachfully, and just as Biddy was beginning to puff out her chest, added dampingly: 'All brides look beautiful on their wedding day; fact of life.'

'Thanks, Johnny,' Biddy said, aiming a blow at his head. 'Oh c'mon, let's get on a bus. Judging from what I remember of the Pier Head after the May blitz, the trams won't be running.'

They were, though, and the two of them caught a tram out to Anfield Cemetery, where they found the Arthurs' grave without too much difficulty. They had bought flowers, sweetly scented narcissus and some expensive early tulips, and left half the bunch in the vase they found at the head of the grave. It took longer to find the Bachelor graves and when they did, Biddy stopped short and turned an amazed face to John.

'Well, who's done that, d'you suppose? Just look at them flowers!'

Together, hand in hand, they looked. The grave which held Mrs Bachelor, her five sons and three daughters was completely covered by plants with shiny, dark green leaves and the occasional sky-blue flower, and, running the length and breadth of the grave in the form of a cross, daffodils, in full bloom now, had pushed up between the leaves of the ground-cover plant.

'It's periwinkle, that blue stuff,' Biddy said. 'Who done it, Johnny? Ain't it beautiful?'

'Might it be your dad?' John asked after a moment. 'Or an aunt, or cousins? It wouldn't be Auntie Ethel, because I asked her if she knew where the grave was, and she said she didn't, she'd never been over.'

'Me dad! He don't know the difference between a daffodil an' an onion,' Biddy said scornfully. 'I don't

362

think any of me aunts or cousins would – they've big families of their own. As for me dad, it's hard work, gettin' things to grow. He'd not have bothered. But I'd like to know who it was, so's I could thank 'em.'

'You could leave a note, wi' your address on, propped up against the vase,' John said after thinking hard. 'Oh . . . there's no vase here – well, I suppose it would be hard to get it to stand up straight, with all that periwinkle stuff, an' the daffs.'

'Yes, an' mebbe it's best left as a bit of a mystery, 'cos it might ha' been done by anyone, come to think,' Biddy said. She handed the cut flowers to her companion. 'These are lovely, but I reckon Mam an' the kids would rather have livin' plants. Let's go back to your people's plot, Johnny, an' leave these flowers there, with the others. The vase'll hold 'em, and I thought the others looked a bit thin on the ground, like.'

They did as Biddy had suggested, and shortly after putting the flowers in water they left the cemetery and made their way, without having to think about it or discuss their next move, back to Lime Street Station.

'We'll go home, have tea, an' tell Auntie what we been doin',' Biddy said as they climbed into an almost empty carriage, for it was mid-afternoon. A long, thin man in clerical grey with a dog-collar sat in one corner reading a newspaper and opposite him a sailor slept deeply. 'Today's made me think, Johnny. I – I shan't mind comin' back to Liverpool no more. Well, not just for the day, anyway,' she added.

'Nor me, darling,' John said. 'It were nice to see Mam's house that she were proud of being looked after an' – well, an' loved – by someone else. An' if Mam an' Dad are anywhere up there, lookin' down, I reckon they'd tell us

363

life must go on, an' we'd best make the most of ours, same as they did.'

'Darling!' Biddy said, awestruck. 'No one ain't never called me *darling* before! It's nice . . . Darling Johnny!'

John laughed and leaned over to kiss her on the cheek. The clergyman looked severely at them over the top of his paper for a moment, then sighed and ducked out of sight once more.

'What'll we do tomorrow?' John asked tactfully, as Biddy began to giggle. 'You choose, since today was my idea. How about New Brighton, then?'

'Yeah, that 'ud be prime. Johnny?'

'What now, queen?'

'Is – is it awful selfish not to be sad any more? Or not sad in the same kind o' tearing, paining sort o' way? I mean just because of some periwinkle an' a few daffs?'

'Course not, Bid. Besides, it weren't just that, were it? That court – it wasn't a good place to live.'

'Nor to die,' Biddy said, grave suddenly. 'But I'm gettin' out, an' – an' them others, they didn't never have the chance.'

'Oh, Biddy, your mam wouldn't grudge you that,' John said, so quietly that she had to lean nearer him to hear the words. 'And who knows? Where they've gone might be every bit as good as where we're goin' to go.'

'Yeah, maybe,' Biddy said on a sigh. 'Shall we go dancin' tonight, Johnny? There's a hop on at the church hall down the road.'

'Why not?' John said bracingly. 'Eh, Biddy, I do love you!'

Emily and Alec sat in the train holding hands and gazing out of the window as the train bustled busily across the open countryside. Every now and then Alec would squeeze Emily's hand and Emily would squeeze back, then smile, because she wanted Alec to know how happy she was.

The days spent at the farm had been pleasant enough, she supposed, but she had soon realised that it was impossible for either Alec or herself to relax with her parents' eyes upon them. Mam and Dad, she had explained to Alec, were a bit narrow, a bit old-fashioned, so it wouldn't do for him to show too much affection. They did not think a couple should hold hands or kiss until after an engagement had been announced, and it would only make for difficulties if they thought their daughter was being led into evil ways.

'Then why don't we announce our engagement?' Alec had asked, sounding rather aggrieved. 'I can't buy you much of a ring . . . well, love, to be honest right now it would be one from Woolworth's, but if it would ease matters . . . you know I mean to marry you when this little lot's over.'

'No, Alec. We said we'd wait until the war was over, and wait we shall,' Emily had said firmly. 'Anyway, what I said wasn't *literally* how they feel I don't suppose. For all I know they might think only marriage entitles a girl and a feller to – to kiss and that. I think they're a bit embarrassed at shows of affection and . . . well, I think they want to hear us say we'll come back here and help on the farm . . . Dad means well, but he's tired, Alec. He's already told me he's looking forward to getting help from someone younger.'

'My God,' Alec had said devoutly. 'Em, I know nothing about farming! I remember saying something once about going to Australia, and you said Australia was full of sheep and so on, but I was only kidding! I'd like to go there all right, but to do work I understand. Accounts and so on, not sheep-rearing! You – you haven't given your parents the wrong idea, have you?'

'No,' Emily had said, laughing. 'And I'm not going to do so, Alec, because to tell the truth I've already realised that after the war's over I shan't be coming back here. Not to live here permanently, anyway. I couldn't take it, not after having had a – a taste of what life can be like.'

'Aye. The forces teaches you more than they realise,' Alec had agreed. 'But Em, how are we going to bear it? A whole week together, unable to so much as hold hands! Why, we were a good deal better off with that old air raid shelter. We might have managed if it had been summer, but what with the rain and no buildings, except for those around the farm, we might as well be back on our respective sites.'

'Yes . . . well, I've told Mam and Dad that we've only got three days,' Emily had said. 'I love my home, it's beautiful, but – oh Alec, I just want to be – be with you! So I thought we could take off the day after tomorrow and go – oh, anywhere! Because people need time together without someone else watching all the time, and I've got a bit of money as it happens. Mam and Dad are doing all right financially right now, probably better than they did in the peace, so when Mam gave me back some of the money I'd sent . . . well, I took it. It's probably enough for a night or two in a cheap guest house . . . I mean single rooms, of course,' she had finished hurriedly.

'Waste of money,' Alec had said, grinning down at her. It had been a fine, sunny afternoon and two of them had taken themselves up into the hills and were sitting on a boulder beside a noisy little mountain stream, with outcrops of rock and thin, twisty birch trees all around.

366

The sun gleamed on the raindrops still hanging from every twig, and the moss and grass underfoot steamed as the sun warmed them. 'We could call ourselves Mr and Mrs and share a double and behave with great propriety, because . . . well, because then we shan't have to be parted at all. No, it's all right, love, only teasing. Where d'you want to go for our three wonderful free days? Oh Em, if only the grass wasn't so wet!'

Emily kissed him, then they simply sat there for a moment, entwined, whilst they thought about being together, until she said, finally: 'Well, we could go to Chester; that's a big city. It would be lovely to go to Nantwich, only we'd be bound to bump into someone we knew, and that could be terribly embarrassing. I wonder if Chester might be too expensive for us, though?'

'We'll find somewhere reasonable,' Alec said comfortably. 'You aren't the only one with money saved, my girl, and I'll say one thing for the wilds of North Wales, you can't spend much money here! I was going to treat you to theatres, meals out, dances . . . but I'd much rather blue the lot on a bit of togetherness.'

So it had been agreed. Emily's parents had told her that Alec seemed a nice feller, though an awful lot older than she. 'And not really the farming kind, though doubtless he's a good soldier and understands that gun of his,' her father had said comfortably on their last night at home. 'No need to fret, though; he's your first young man; there'll be others, no doubt.'

'No, I'm not looking out for anyone else, Da,' Emily had said quietly. 'We're right for each other, me and Alec. And – and farming isn't the only way of making a living, you know.'

But that had been last night. This morning, nothing

could have exceeded the cordiality with which they invited Alec to come and visit again, nor the loving warmth with which they kissed Emily goodbye. Emily had felt a little guilty – well, more than a little – when she thought of her parents, struggling with all the work of the farm alone, getting older, wearier . . . but she told herself bracingly that she had her own life to lead and that she would not be much use to the farm anyway, if her heart and mind were with Alec.

The train was slowing, pulling in to a familiar station. Emily gave Alec's hand one last squeeze and stood up.

'Nearly there,' she said, smiling at him as he, in his turn, got out of his seat and reached up for their kitbags on the hammock over their heads. 'Hand me down my stuff, Alec; you've got enough of your own to carry.'

They found a room without difficulty a short way from the station. The house was terraced, with glistening paintwork – it fronted straight on to the pavement – cheerful checked curtains and a whited front step. The handwritten notice in the window said, *Bed and Breakfast, 4/6d, Light supper available* and swung above a large blue pottery bowl full of papery narcissus and golden-trumpeted daffodils.

When Alec rang the bell a youngish woman in a flowered apron with dark hair parted in the middle and a bright smile asked them if they were looking for a room, because if so, she had two very pleasant ones still vacant. She did not ask their names but it seemed to Emily that she was assuming they were married and whilst she was wondering when she should point out her single status the woman, who told them that she was Mrs Annie Fleming, ushered them in and led them up a short flight of stairs into a pleasant, airy room whose pink-curtained window overlooked the quiet road which they had just walked along. It contained a large double bed with a rosy pink counterpane, an equally large wardrobe and dressing table, an easy chair and an upright one, two bedside cabinets and a washstand.

'We've no proper bathroom, and the WC's out the back,' Mrs Fleming said regretfully. 'But there's a – a utensil in the bedside cabinet and I brings hot water up at whatever hour you choose – better than an alarm clock, I am. And I'll do breakfast whenever you like.'

Alec was nodding and smiling so Emily gathered up her courage and spoke. 'Umm . . . can we see the other room, Mrs Fleming? Only . . .'

'Course you can, dear, if this one doesn't suit. Only this isn't a large house, I've only room for two couples, so I do me best to accommodate me guests regarding meals and such. Will you be wanting a light supper later? I do simple stuff – eggs on toast, when the hens is laying, and beans on toast when they're not. And stewed apple and custard for afters, 'cos me husband's got an allotment and he grows all sorts there. The other room overlooks the back, and it's not as large as this one, but if you'd like to take a look . . .'

'No, this one will be grand,' Alec said, giving Emily a comical look. 'And we'd like to take advantage of your supper offer this evening, anyway. Em, darling, put your traps down and we'll have a clean-up and then go out and have a look at the city, and find ourselves a cup of tea somewhere, perhaps – by the way, what time is the evening meal?'

'There's only you in so far,' Mrs Fleming said. 'So shall we say six o'clock? Then if you want to go dancing, or to the cinema, you can eat first. Does that suit?'

'Admirably, thanks,' Alec said. 'We'll just unpack, then we'll come down.'

'Fair enough. I hope you'll be comfortable here. Oh, I never asked you how long you would be staying? Is it just for the one night? Only . . .'

'No, we'll be here for three nights,' Alec said quickly. 'Possibly four. We are stationed at opposite ends of the country, unfortunately, and we've not checked the train times yet, but I'll do so and let you know definitely, probably tomorrow.'

'That'll be fine,' Mrs Fleming said comfortably. 'Then I'll leave you to get unpacked. And as for a cuppa, when you come downstairs just give a knock on the kitchen door and you can have a tray in the front room. If you've been travelling most of the day you'll be glad of a sit-down, I 'spect.'

'Thanks very much,' Alec said, whilst Emily stood by the window, pretending to look out whilst her hot cheeks cooled. How could Alec have let the woman assume they were married and would share a bed! He had said he was only joking over sharing a room with two single beds in it – she had been brought up properly, didn't he realise that . . . that . . .

She tried to put her thoughts into words when Mrs Fleming had clattered down the stairs once more but Alec pulled her into his arms and spoke soothingly, kissing her burning cheeks, her tear-filled eyes, and lastly, her trembling mouth.

'Darling Em, if you really don't want to share that lovely, cuddly big bed with me, then I'll kip down on the chairs. There are two of them, after all, and I've slept in worse places. But don't you think we might be all right, sharing? We're both tired and we've come away for three

370

days to get to know one another. What better way to do it than to be together all of those three days – and nights? Or if you really can't bear the thought, then we'll go downstairs and tell Mrs Fleming the truth and ask if we can take both rooms. Only she'll have to charge us nine shillings, of course. But I'd rather spend the money than have you upset, or thinking me a cad of a fellow who's brought you away for a few days to seduce you and have my wicked way with you!'

Emily gave a watery laugh. 'Oh, it's not that, Alec, I want to be with you, I told you I did, only – well, I don't want to go disgracing myself and – and having people think me no better than Pricey or her pals.'

'My dearest girl . . . look, all I can do is promise not to seduce you! Will that do?'

'Yes, of course. Only she'll call me Mrs Culdrain and – and I'm not!'

'Well, no, you aren't, not yet. Does that matter so terribly?'

'No-oo,' Emily said doubtfully. 'And if anyone sleeps on the chairs, it will be me. I'm small enough to fit, you aren't.'

'Right. It's a deal. If you feel threatened, out you'll hop and I promise I shan't leap on you like a tiger and drag you back to bed to have my wicked way with you. Now can we go down and have that cup of tea? I'm so thirsty you wouldn't believe!'

'I've not got a wedding ring,' Emily squeaked, as Alec headed for the door. 'Oh, Alec, I can't face her when I take my gloves off and there's no wedding ring!'

'I'm afraid I didn't think to supply myself with one,' Alec said, walking back across the room again and putting a comforting arm around her shoulders. 'Then I'll nip down right away and tell her we're going to skip the cup of tea. And we'll go straight to Woolworth's – there's bound to be one in a big place like this – and buy ourselves a nice gold curtain ring.'

Despite herself, Emily giggled. 'Before, it was a Woolworth's engagement ring, now you've descended to a curtain ring! You certainly know how to make a girl feel cherished.'

He laughed with her, but began to put on his forage cap once more. 'All right, all right, you shall have your Woolworth's engagement ring as well. Now come along, no more fussing! Ah, I hear voices; that'll be couple number two I've no doubt.'

It was, which meant that Mrs Fleming was busy and clearly glad to be able to wave them off – and not to have to make them a cup of tea. The other couple were young, both in uniform, with shiny eyes and kitbags slung over their shoulders. The girl was a WAAF, the young man a sailor, and the girl smiled shyly at Emily and then glanced down at her left hand, with a shiny wedding ring on the third finger and a small diamond engagement ring, too.

'Newly weds,' Emily whispered as the two of them walked down the road in the direction of the city centre. 'Weren't they sweet? I shouldn't think she was more than nineteen or so, would you?'

'Don't know, didn't really look at her,' Alec said. 'I was too busy looking at you. Oh, Em, this is going to be such fun!'

Emily decided that she liked Chester, which she had never visited, except to pass through the station on her way somewhere else. She liked the rows, which were a sort of second street above the first, and she liked the red sandstone cathedral, and she liked the little alleys with their tiny shops, and the big streets with their department stores and elegant coffee shops. But most of all, she liked being with Alec. Together, they walked past the canal, where it cut through the red sandstone cliffs on either side, and moved mysteriously under the bridge, all dark green and sinister-looking. They had a cup of tea in a café where they could see the clock on the bridge across Eastgate Street, and found Woolworth's after that. Alec bought her two rings, one a plain gold-coloured band, the other a tiny blue stone surrounded by a cluster of little white ones.

'There you are, sapphires and diamonds,' Alec said, slipping it on to her finger after he had put the gold-coloured band there first. 'Now do you feel more respectable?'

To her own astonishment, Emily found that she did. 'I feel really married,' she said, tucking her hand into his arm and smiling up at him. 'But don't let that give you ideas, Sarge!'

'As if it would!' He beamed proudly down at her, then steered her out of Woolworth's and back onto Eastgate Street. They were outside an ironmonger's shop and he nodded towards it. 'Isn't that Jo's parents' place, Em? I seem to remember her saying they had an ironmongery on Eastgate Street.'

'Yes,' Emily said, beginning to walk more quickly and ducking her head to one side as though even the shop-front had eyes. 'Do you know, I completely forgot Jo lived here. Oh dear, don't let her see me – us! She'd guess we were up to no good the moment she saw the rings . . . oh dear, shall I take them off?'

'Don't be daft, sweetheart,' Alec said bracingly. 'You know Jo: I doubt if she'd notice. She never was particularly interested in other people's affairs. Dear me, what an unfortunate choice of words – forget I said it.'

Emily laughed, but tugged at his arm. 'Let's go back to our lodgings,' she implored anxiously. 'I'm quite hungry despite that cake. Wasn't it a treat to have a cream one?'

'It was only mock,' Alec pointed out. 'I can scarcely remember what real cream tastes like. All right then, take the next turning on the left. That will take us back in more or less the right direction and once you're out of Eastgate, you'll stop expecting a righteous Jo to step out from every doorway and accuse you of God knows what misdemeanour.'

Back at Mrs Fleming's, they found the other couple sitting in the front room over a tray of cooling tea and before they had done more than exchange names and smiles, Mrs Fleming was inviting them into the dining room and sitting them round the table.

'It's scrambled eggs on toast and plenty of hot tea, with apple pie and custard to follow,' she said briskly, bringing in a laden tray. 'And as much bread and marg as you can eat, with either honey – hubby keeps bees – or my raspberry and apple jam.'

Her guests set to with a will and when the meal was over they listened to the wireless until ten o'clock when the other couple, Peter and Jane Rayner, said they were going for a stroll before bed. Feeling her face beginning to burn, Emily said hastily that she and Alec would probably do the same.

Jane was a typist at a command centre and envied Emily her work with the balloons. 'I would have liked to do something practical, like driving,' she had said, over scrambled eggs. 'But they don't ask you what you want to do, they tell you what they need. I started off in the cookhouse and boy, I hated that, but I got a transfer after I'd stuck it for six months and they put me in the offices because I was a trained shorthand typist before the war. I was posted to Blackpool, where there's a lot of admin done – that was where Peter and I met, actually. He was there for rest and recuperation and we both like dancing, so . . . well, we got along fine. And – and one thing led to another . . .'

But now the four of them left the house together, to find that the moon was shining from a cloudless sky so that a walk was perfectly possible, even in the blackout.

'But we'd best stick to the area we know,' Alec said. 'The blackout's the very devil when you're in strange surroundings, though the moonlight's nearly as bright as midday. Want to walk down to the canal? It's not too far and it's a pleasant stroll.'

'That'll be fine, won't it, Pete?' Jane said. 'How long are you here for? Ours is only a forty-eight, worst luck. We'll be leaving first thing tomorrow.'

'We're here for three days,' Emily said. 'It's a beautiful town, isn't it? I live in North Wales, which is quite close, but I've never been here before. Wrexham's nearer, you see, and it's a good shopping centre so if Mam and I wanted clothes, or something which wasn't available in Corwen or Cerrig, we went there. There's a cinema there, and a theatre . . . oh, all sorts.'

Companionably, the four of them walked down to the canal and leaned over the bridge, gazing down into the dark, moon-reflecting water. Then they walked back, accepted a cup of cocoa and some homemade biscuits from Mrs Fleming, then made their way upstairs.

'I think we bagged the best room,' Alec said, holding open the door for Emily. 'But it's first come first served here, I think. Goodnight, Jane, Peter. See you at breakfast.'

Emily went and sat on the chair by the window and stared, large-eyed, at Alec. Suddenly this whole adventure stopped seeming fun and became serious. She was in a bedroom, alone, with a man who was no relation, a man who wanted to marry her in time. But . . . she knew her parents would have been horrified if they had known, and she had told herself often that she was not that kind of girl. Was she now going to prove herself to be every bit as bad as Pricey and her gang? Oh, how she envied Peter and Jane, properly and legally getting into their double bed, whilst she and Alec . . .

'Come on, chick, get into your cosy pyjamas,' Alec said. He was undressing in the moonlight, Emily realised with horror, and turned to stare out of the window whilst her face, she was sure, began to resemble nothing so much as a beetroot. 'Otherwise you'll feel silly because I'll be in bed, staring at you, and you'll feel like someone on a stage!'

'I shan't, because I shall pull the curtains,' Emily said huffily, but she began stripping off her clothes with trembling fingers and when she was down to brassiere and pants, realised that she had not yet unpacked her pyjamas and would have to search for them under Alec's interested gaze. Her hands flew to her hot face just as Alec said comfortably: 'They're on your side of the bed; I got them out earlier.'

'Oh, thanks,' Emily said weakly, turning and picking up the garments in question. She was about to put them on over her underwear when Alec said, 'You'll be boiling hot, chick; this bed is well-provided with blankets. Look, I won't watch. I'll make shadow rabbits on the wall where the moonlight makes a screen.'

376

Even in her panic Emily knew he would not lie to her. Frantic with haste, she stripped off her undies and scrambled into the pyjamas, then positively vaulted into bed, with her heart thudding like a trip-hammer and her breath coming in little gasps.

'There! That wasn't too bad, was it?' Alec said comfortingly. 'Cuddle up, baby. You like a cuddle, don't you?'

'Ye-es, but . . .' squeaked Emily, then felt Alec's arms go round her with thankful familiarity. This was all right, this seemed to pose no threat. 'Alec, I said I'd sleep on the chairs; don't you think that would be – well, safer?'

'No. I think you'd be cold and cramped and uncomfortable, and no safer,' Alec said. 'Ooh, isn't it nice to be close and warm and under the same blankets! Have I ever told you that your hair is like silk?'

'No, I don't think so,' Emily mumbled. She lay her head cautiously on his shoulder, then shot upright. 'Alec . . . where are your pyjamas?'

'I never wear 'em,' Alec said calmly. 'Why, do you want to borrow an extra pair?'

Emily giggled. She didn't mean to do so but could not help herself. 'No, of course I don't,' she said as firmly as she could. 'Only . . . well, you *ought* to be wearing them.'

'Why?'

'Well, because we're – we're both in the same b-bed, and it isn't – isn't very nice to be in bed together when one of you hasn't got pyjamas on. Are you wearing your underpants, then?'

'Guess! Or you could feel around and tell me what I'm wearing.'

'I'm certainly not feeling around, as you call it,' Emily said hotly. 'You're very rude, Alec.'

'Oh. Sorry. All right then, I am not wearing my underpants. Does that make you feel better?'

Another giggle caught at Emily's throat but she suppressed it and said, as calmly as she could, 'I'd better move onto that chair I think. There's no telling what you're going to say next.'

'Or what I'm going to do,' Alec said softly after a moment, when she was still in the bed. 'Dear little Em, do try and relax and enjoy our nice cuddling. Once we get all warm and cosy I expect we'll both fall asleep; that will suit you, won't it?'

'I think we've done enough cuddling,' Emily said primly. 'Let's chat, instead.'

'But I can't chat and kiss, and I've got an irresistible urge to kiss you,' Alec said reasonably. 'We've been talking all evening, and probably we'll talk all tomorrow. Em, dearest, now isn't the time for talking, truly.'

'Talking's safer,' Emily mumbled. She mumbled because she had just turned her face into the warm hollow between neck and shoulder, and found that she did not much want to talk after all. She kissed Alec's soft neck, so different from the hard, tanned skin of his face and hands which were exposed to the weather all year round. Alec gasped, and Emily felt a wicked little thrill of self-congratulation. So she wasn't the only one who felt that kissing in bed was – oh, different, dangerous. She hoisted herself up on one elbow and kissed little kisses as far as his ear, then breathed into it. Alec groaned, then seized her and pulled her down on him and began kissing her, as she had kissed him but harder, more excitingly. Her hair fell forward between them and he pushed it aside with his face and his mouth took hers with an urgency and an importance which she had never known before.

'Alec! We shouldn't . . . we mustn't . . .'

'Should. Must,' came the muffled reply. 'Oh dear God, Em, you don't know how much I've longed for this.'

'Oh, darling Alec, I do love you! But – oh, oh, oh!'

'Was that nice, sweetheart? Did she enjoy that, my tough little balloon girl, who can send me high as a kite with one glance from those long, dark eyes? Do you like being in bed with me as much as I like being in bed with you?'

'Yes, oh yes,' Emily said breathlessly. 'Only it's wrong, I know it is – *you* know it is too, Alec! What if . . . what if . . .'

'Babies? It's all right, babies are for later. For peacetime, when this bloody awful invasion is over, when we're married and in . . .'

'Invasion? What d'you mean?' Emily's voice was no longer soft and breathless but hard, suspicious. 'What's the invasion got to do with us?'

'Oh, hell . . . I didn't mean invasion, pet, I meant war. When this bloody awful war is over, that's what I meant.'

But Emily pulled away from him and stared through the moonlight into his dark and dancing eyes. 'I know there's going to be an invasion, everyone knows it. But you – you won't be a part of it, will you, Alec? I thought they'd leave you here to – to defend the rest of us with your guns.'

'You make me sound like a cowboy! Anyway, we aren't supposed to talk about invasions or anything like that. Remember? Walls have ears!'

'Not these walls,' Emily said, but she lay down again. 'Is that why you decided to take your leave now, after telling me earlier that you were waiting until the summer?'

There was a short pause, then Alec said flatly, 'Yes.'

'I see.' Emily thought for a moment, then leaned over Alec once more and began, deliberately, to kiss him. After a moment she rolled herself against him and put both arms round his neck and nuzzled her face under his chin. 'I love you, Alec,' she muttered. 'I shan't sleep on that chair.'

'No? Oh, my darling, I don't want you to do anything just because – well, because of what's possibly going to happen in the summer.'

'I won't. Whatever I do I shall do because I love you, and because – oh, Alec, because I want you just as much as you want me! There, and if that makes me like Pricey to hell with it. I suppose it just proves that we're all the same, under the skin.'

Alec caught her pyjama top between his hands and pulled upwards. 'Skin a rabbit,' he said as the jacket came neatly off without buttons popping and sailed through the air, to land softly against the opposite wall. 'If you take off those silly trousers we'll both be wearing the same.'

'I'm not wearing my pants under these trousers . . .' Emily began, then chuckled. 'Oh. I see what you mean. All right then.'

Seconds later the pyjama trousers fell on top of the jacket. And Emily and Alec melted into each other's arms.

'Did you have a good time, Em? You look . . . I don't know, sort of different. So pleased and happy, but your leave's ending, so why should you look so – so glowing?'

Emily and Biddy had met, as arranged, on the train returning from Crewe and now Emily slung her kitbags onto the rack and plumped into the seat which Biddy had saved for her. She grinned at her friend, thinking that Biddy, too, looked extremely well and happy.

'It was marvellous, thanks,' she said rather breathlessly. 'Alec went off first, so I waved him away, and then I waited for my train to meet up with you, of course. We really did have a good time, though it was a bit slow at first. My parents, you know, and being a stranger, and then it rained . . .'

'It don't sound much fun,' Biddy said. 'Johnny an' me, we did all sorts. When it rained we went to museums, galleries, or the flicks, an' we took long tram rides. And when it were fine we went to the parks and once, to New Brighton – that's seaside. Still, down to earth again now, queen! Back to the grind. First thing I'll do when I get in is write to Johnny. He'll be in Portsmouth for a few days yet I reckon.'

'Yes, I'll write to Alec as well,' Emily said. 'Oh, I didn't tell you, but we met Jo when we were in Chester one day. She's got ever such a nice boyfriend; his name's Paul Standish and he's an American GI. Doughboys, they call them. She'd taken him home for a forty-eight, to meet her folks, she said.'

'Well, if that don't beat it all!' Biddy exclaimed. 'Fancy you meetin' up wi' our Jo! And a Yank, too – well, she always wanted one. Did she say anything about Kay?'

'Said she was going over to her site when she got back, so I said to give her our love, but let's write to Kay, one of our combined letters with us each doing a few lines. It was odd meeting Jo, wasn't it? But nice, you know. Very nice.'

11

'1944's been a funny sort of year, so far,' Biddy said thoughtfully to Emily as they sat on the grass in front of their smart brick sleeping quarters, enjoying the warmth of the late June sunshine. 'Everyone knows we're winnin' the war but no one knows rightly how we're doin' it, or when it'll end. I thought D-Day would be the finish meself, but was it? Not bleedin' likely, it's still goin' on and D-Day was almost two weeks ago.'

The D-Day landings were the reason the girls had been posted from Cheshire to Hampshire a month previously. The Powers That Be had decided to pack the south coast with balloon barrages to stop any interference with the troops leaving the shores of Britain, and so the girls had been in the thick of it as the men slowly embarked. Indeed, they had never been more involved. They saw the crowds of personnel gradually gathering, sleeping in tents which lay like mushrooms on the fields and meadows, and saw, too, the craft which were to take the men across to the Normandy beaches gradually assembling. It had been an exciting and nerve-wracking time, for the enemy must have been aware that something was up, and raids were not infrequent.

But that had been weeks ago and now Biddy and Emily were sitting in the sunshine indulging in the crew's latest craze, string-bag making. Whilst they were in Cheshire someone had noticed the mounds of string – only it was cordage to the Air Force – which was piled up in odd corners and had utilised some of it to make a shopping bag for her mother. Since then every balloon op spent every spare moment making bags of increasing complexity and beauty, and naturally, when Biddy and Emily moved south they had brought the craze with them. As someone on their new site said, they could tie and untie a thousand knots, so they might as well make use of their knowledge – and make some money into the bargain.

'I shan't forget my leave just before D-Day,' Emily said dreamily. She glanced down at the tiny diamond and opal ring on the third finger of her left hand, tilting it so that the diamonds caught the sun and shone with a rainbow of colours. 'Seeing Alec after so long was wonderful . . . didn't he look fit, Biddy? And getting engaged properly, with the ring and everything, was a wonderful surprise. But the best part was being with him again, talking about what we'd do in the peace . . . of course we only had a forty-eight, but that was more than I'd even dared hope for. And he was all right a week ago, because of the message.'

The message had come with a shipload of wounded; it simply said that Alec and the lads were well and taking their battery slowly inland. Alec had added that he would keep in touch when he was able to do so, but could make no promises since communication in wartime was usually bad and Emily was on no account to worry.

'Wish I could hear from John,' Biddy said. 'The *Aconite* is on Atlantic convoy duty, I think, which means a good long while at sea. Still, I reckon no news is good news, eh? Oh, and one of the girls had a note from Chaz of the searchlight battery in Cheshire. He says Moll's settled well, though she still misses you, I reckon. I bet they miss us an' all – the searchlight fellers, I mean. They must be lonely wi' no bop crew to fool around with.'

Emily missed Mollie, but hadn't liked to bring the dog south with her, having no idea what type of site they were bound for and knowing that Mollie, having grown accustomed to the country, would not take kindly to a city site. But the battery boys had taken her on willingly, and Emily had every intention of going back for her, after the war. So now she picked up her work again.

'They'll survive. Are you going to finish that bag off with a row of tassels? Mine's for my Auntie Bronwen, I think she'd like tassels; but bobbles are nice, too. Or those pointy things, like eastern turbans.'

'Mine's for me Auntie Ethel in Runcorn. She'll get tassels and like 'em,' Biddy said, knotting string like mad. 'And when I finish this 'un, I'm making a few more for Mr Standish. I can use the dough.'

Mr Standish was a local shopkeeper suffering, as were most of his kind, from the empty-shelves disease. He had spotted one of the crew with her neat string bag and had asked her where she had bought such an elaborate one; in moments a new trade for balloon ops had been born.

'Biddy, you're spending like a sailor all of a sudden, just because we're near a town with a bit of life! What is there to buy, anyway? Apart from string bags, of course.'

Biddy giggled. 'Norra lot, but I can go to the flicks twice a week instead of once, 'ave fish an' chips whenever Puddy Rowe's on cookin', an' buy meself as many strawberries as I can guzzle.'

'Back in Cheshire, they paid us to pick strawberries,' Emily reminded her friend. 'Wonder if they would down here? Not that we need the money, but it gets boring on the site when the balloon doesn't go up, day after day.'

'There'll be more raids, I'll bet me bottom dollar,' Biddy announced. 'You can't tell me old 'itler's finished

384

just because our fellers 'ave got their tootsies on the continong! No, them jerries will be poundin' us again before long, sure as eggs is eggs. Hey, is that an aero-engine I can 'ear?'

'You're wishing raids on us,' Emily groaned. She put down her string bag and looked up into the clear and cloudless blue sky. 'Oh lor', there is something – perhaps it's one of ours.'

'It isn't big enough for anything but a fighter, anyway,' Biddy said. She had put her bag down but now she picked it up again and began to knot, though her eyes were on the sky still. 'Wharris it, Em, d'you reckon?'

'I can't imagine. It sounds nasty, though, like a furious bumble bee. Oh my God . . . it's those things, you know, they were talking about them in the mess last night, they've had ever so many hit London, they're calling them . . .'

'Got it, they're them flyin' bombs – buzz bombs they call 'em because of the noise they make! Christ . . . it's comin' right over the top of us!'

The two girls sat on the grass, staring up above them, at the squat, somehow evil-looking object, open-mouthed, too startled even to move.

'They cut out,' Emily whispered. 'Oh Bid, their engines cut out and they dive on you . . . isn't that what they do? Should we give the alarm, get the balloon up?'

'Too late,' Biddy said as the droning horror continued on its way to its target, wherever that might be. She shuddered. 'Poor ole London, Em – poor Kay an' Jo, havin' to deal wi' that – that thing.'

'You're telling me,' Emily said. 'But someone was saying in the NAAFI last night that it won't just be London, not once they get their range worked out. They'll

385

cut out over here, too. Oh damn, damn, damn! As if we haven't got enough to worry about, with Alec and Johnny somewhere out there.'

'I wonder why we didn't get a warning?' Emily said presently, when the drone of the buzz bomb had faded into silence. 'And I wonder whether the balloon would have helped, if we could have stopped it? There hasn't been much about them in the papers yet, so I don't know whether stopping it in the air does more harm than good.'

'We'll find out, I daresay,' Biddy said gloomily. 'Flight HQ won't let us get away with sittin' and watchin' the buggers go over, they'll want action of some sort. And incidentally, why didn't we dive for cover when it came over? We're only a few feet away from our shelter.'

It was true. The underground shelter was ten feet, no more, from where they were sitting. Emily glanced across at it, then shrugged.

'Never gave it a thought. Besides, if it had cut out . . .'

'Oh well, it didn't,' Biddy said comfortably, continuing to knot. 'Where's the rest of the crew, anyroad? We're lucky wi' this lot, Em, they're a good crowd.'

'Some are in Southampton and the rest are gardening, I imagine,' Emily said. They had had a good vegetable garden in Cheshire, but in the milder south the vegetables and fruit on this site really thrived and the girls, though they had to pool quite a lot of their produce with the rest of the Air Force, always managed to keep a good supply for themselves.

'Because of D-Day we've been left pretty much to ourselves, but it won't last, you know. This site seems soft compared to Cheshire, but once everyone's organised again it'll probably be all spit and polish, being so much nearer Flight HQ.' She finished her last knot and threw the

386

bag down on the grass. 'Hooray, it's done! I'm going over to the mess to make a cuppa; want one?'

A few nights later Emily was on guard duty from midnight to two a.m. She wasn't with Biddy, either, she was with a girl called Celia Caples, a warm and friendly girl but almost a stranger, of course, compared with Biddy.

The girl who had been on the previous guard duty woke her. Quietly, a hand on the shoulder, a voice hissing in her ear.

'Em'ly, wake up, you're on in ten minutes.'

Emily woke and sat up all in one movement. She scooped up her clothes and stuck her feet into her boots. It was a warm night so she would dress over her pyjamas, then it would be easier to strip off her outer clothing and get back into bed at two a.m. She did not bother to put a light on, it would have woken others and would mean she must draw the blackout curtains, which she had no desire to do on such a mild night. Instead, she dressed quickly, by touch, and saw Celia, further down the hut, doing the same.

Presently, fully dressed, the two of them set off to tell the present guards that they were relieved. They found Smudge and Sheila waiting by the office, eager to get back to their own beds.

'All right? Can we go, now? Thanks, girls,' Smudge said fervently. 'It's a lovely night, you can see right across to Southampton Water when you get to the top of the rise. It's lying there in the moonlight so calm and beautiful . . . well, you'll see it presently for yourselves.'

They would, because the site sloped up at one end and the guards had to patrol the perimeter as well as listen for the telephone and keep an eye on the blimp as she floated lazily above them, on a tail guy mooring because it was, for once, a nice night.

'It's on guard duty that I really miss Mollie, my Alsatian bitch,' Emily told Celia when they met on their rounds with only another half hour to go and stopped to gossip for a moment. 'I wanted to bring her, but we didn't know what sort of site this was going to be and she was so happy in Cheshire. And after so long she knew all the chaps on the searchlight site next door, so I left her there. But after the war I'm going back for her, because she'll need a home, then.'

'After the war!' Celia leaned back and sighed, staring up at the stars in the dark sky above. 'When's it going to happen, I ask myself? And what's going to be left? My sister's in the WAAF in London – Adastral House – and she says the doodlebugs are coming over night and day and they're worn to a frazzle. Three of her pals were doing a course in the Air Ministry, on the third floor, when they heard that awful buzzing overhead. They leaned out of the windows to see where they were going to land and were sucked out by the blast and fell to their deaths. It just seems to go on and on.'

'I know. The government keeps saying it isn't too bad, but that's not what the papers say, let alone friends. I had a letter from a friend this morning, she's on a site in north London. They've had an awful time with several casualties, the weather's been dreadful but the balloons have to be put up almost every night and now they're being flown most of the day, too. She says they've been told they'll soon be posted away from the capital with their balloons so they can stage a really heavy barrage all around the coast to stop the buzz bombs getting through. Incidentally, Kay says the fellers on the searchlights are calling them the Farting Furies, because of the noise they make! That cheered me up for some reason. And of course when they send Kay and her crew down to the coast she might end up quite near us, which would be wizard.'

'Oh? Well, I don't see the balloons frightening off those pilotless bombs, or doodlebugs, or whatever they are, do you? Though I suppose they might deflect them – the fighter boys have been doing that, so I've heard.'

'Let's go and put the kettle on,' Emily said. 'If we use the gas stove it boils quite quickly and we didn't have a cup earlier. I can't believe we're actually having a calm, windless night for once – we might as well just check round the blimp once though, before we make the tea.'

'Oh, right,' Celia said, cheering up. 'Just look at her, dreaming away up there. I bet she's whistling a popular tune under her breath and hoping she'll get hydrogen for breakfast!'

Emily giggled. 'Daft, you are! It's odd how real they seem, though, don't you think? I used to hate "new balloon day" because it meant the poor old girl would be carted off to Balloon Centre to have all sorts of remedial work done on her – she might even be cut up for her canvas if she was really badly worn. But by the next day the new one was just as much a character as the old one had been.'

'Wicked old bitches, most of 'em,' Celia said. 'Tear your arms out of their sockets as soon as look at them, break your legs with their handling guys or chop your head off with a trailing winch cable. They only look sweet when you're on the ground and they're at five thousand feet!'

'Yes, they don't improve on closer acquaintance,' Emily agreed. 'You check the cable and the tail guy mooring, I'll do the perimeter wire and the bed itself.'

389

Everything seemed satisfactory, so the two girls went into the mess together, by-passing the office with its phone which so often brought everyone stumbling out of bed, and the dining room or cookhouse, depending on your rank, where they all ate filling, boring meals together. The crew had told Emily that their previous corporal had always eaten on a tray in the office, to avoid mixing with the erks as she called them, but the present one, Corporal Taylor, ate with everyone else, though she usually sat at a table with her acting corporals.

'Char, char, glorious char,' Emily sang softly, taking the smaller of the two kettles off the stove and carrying it over to the sink. They had running water in here which was a treat for Celia, who had had to pump to get water on her last site, and a stove which ran on bottled gas, as well as several coal-fired ones. Whilst Emily ran water Celia got out the matches, turned on the gas, lit the stove and got two mugs out of the cupboard.

'You shouldn't say "char", that's a horrible brown-job expression,' Celia said as the kettle started to sing. 'We in the junior-but-best service call it tea.'

'My fellow – I mean fiancé – is a brown job,' Emily explained. 'He's on an ack-ack battery somewhere in France at the moment. We all pick up expressions from our fellows, don't you think? My friend Kay is – well, she's going steady with a bomber pilot and she comes out with the most peculiar expressions.'

'I thought your friend's fellow was in the Navy,' Celia said. 'And isn't she called Biddy? Weren't you lucky to get posted down here, incidentally? And you and that skinny girl actually got to the same site, when most of us get sent all over the place without so much as a by your leave, let alone together.'

Emily shrugged. 'Yes, it was lucky, because the Air Force moves in peculiar ways its wonders to perform. But I do have more than one friend, you know! Biddy's bloke is in the Navy – he's on the *Aconite* – but in fact I told you about Kay earlier, she's the girl who was with us at the training centre and later on our first site in London. She and Jo – another friend – moved on before Biddy and me because they were promoted. Ah, kettle's boiling; let's make that tea. And it's nearly time to wake Naomi and Marion.'

Kay was off-duty so she was walking. She had covered several miles already, she supposed, looking round her at the tired and tatty suburban streets. Normally when she had time off she spent it in the cinema, or she and Jo met up and did something together, but now she had found that she wanted to be alone and undisturbed and the best way to be both, she had discovered, was to walk.

It was a pity it was raining, but it had rained a great deal this month and would probably continue to do so and anyway, Kay didn't really mind the rain. She was not looking at her surroundings, and she was concentrating on the act of walking, watching each foot as it met the pavement, seeing the puddles, the broken paving stones, the gap-toothed appearance of almost every street, where the bombing had simply reduced respectable houses to the rubble upon which ubiquitous willowherb and sprightly silverweed were already flourishing.

The reason Kay walked so determinedly was, however, not simple. The truth was that Kay had lived through well over three years of war without ever knowing the pain of perpetual, gnawing worry for someone else's wellbeing. She had thought herself in love with Philip but she

391

acknowledged sadly now that she could not possibly have loved because she had never really worried over him.

But Steve! He was, quite simply, never out of her thoughts. She flew the balloon, attended lectures, led marches, watched drills, and there he was, in the back of her mind. How was he, what was he doing, had he flown last night and if so, was he safely down yet? Worries which had never crystallised before seldom left her now. She had nearly lost him, and now they had found each other again she knew, with every fibre of her being, that Steve was the only person who truly mattered to her, he was her raison d'être, her guiding star, her one true love.

And his job was so horribly, hellishly dangerous! She got books on bombers and read everything she could get hold of which dealt with them and the more she read the more frightened for him she became. Loving him was marvellous, but worrying over him was not. Many a long night Kay lay in her bed hearing the guard-change taking place every two hours and positively longing for morning, so that the worries would at least have to move to the back of her consciousness instead of stalking right across her wakeful mind.

And she bargained with God; I'll give you five years of my life for his safety, dear God; I'll never tell another lie, not even a little white one, I'll do more than my share of duties and let the other girls off, I'll go to church every single Sunday . . . if only You'll see him home, hold him in Your hand, breathe Your strong breath into him, keep him safe for me!

She heard the heavy bombers drone out on their way to bomb Germany, heard them drone back, knew that none of the aircraft passing overhead contained Steve . . . yet found herself trying to remember how loud the sound had

392

been on the outward journey, how much lighter the engine notes were now. I'm sure they've lost two, she would think, clenching her teeth and gripping her hands into fists in a frenzy of fear for him. Dear God, let him be safe, let it not be my darling, struggling in the cold water of the Channel, frying in an engine-fire, smashing down out of the dark sky and tugging fruitlessly at a parachute cord!

Communications were better, now. On this site they had a telephone just past the gates, right on the corner by the bus stop. From that now loved and familiar kiosk she rang Steve's station at least once a day. So far they had either assured her he was down safely but sleeping, or debriefing, or he came to the phone himself, laughing at her, promising her that he would take good care, reminding her that he was sometimes only flying once a week now, and that they would have a forty-eight together very soon. 'I'll come up to London, take you out on the spree,' he said. 'You must stop all this needless worrying and think about that, instead.'

She tried, of course she did, and whilst she was working it wasn't too bad, she could cope, more or less. Especially in the daytime, when she knew he wasn't flying.

'Things are looking up, Kay,' Jo had said bracingly the last time they had met. 'Even the blackout's not so severe any more, it's a dimout, much easier to live with. And they're scaling down the bombing raids over Germany, old thing. Steve must have told you.'

'He has; it's just the worry of not knowing which night to worry,' Kay had said, and earned a shout of laughter from Jo, who reminded her in the next breath, however, that other people had blokes who were risking their lives every day of the week, and they didn't make themselves ill over it.

'I'm not making myself ill,' Kay said stoutly. 'I'm just so terribly aware of the danger. I almost lost Steve, you know. I couldn't bear to lose him again, because it would be for good, this time.'

So now she walked, covering miles of wet pavements and eventually returning to the site glowing with exercise and with a big appetite, which pleased everyone because her crew hated it when their sergeant wouldn't – or couldn't – eat her meals.

In three more days, Kay told herself, as the site came into view once more, in three more days Steve will be here, in London, and we'll lie in each other's arms in a nice, quiet little hotel room somewhere, and forget the bombing raids over Germany, the vagaries of barrage balloons and everything about the war. We'll talk about marrying, the peace, our future. And for several days afterwards I'll be gentle and relaxed and I won't worry over anything at all.

'I had absolutely no idea that London was like this!' Steve stood, holding Kay's hand, staring unbelievingly round him. For the first time, Kay saw central London through a stranger's eyes – the battered buildings, the boarded-up shops, the craters in roads and pavements, the gaps where houses had once stood. And the people, she realised, were grey from poor food, lack of sleep and general worry.

'We're used to it,' she said, however. 'And it's been worse, oddly enough, since D-Day because now everyone is all geared up for the end, and victory, and it hasn't come. You get more tired of waiting, I think, than anything else.'

'Used to it! But my God, it's far worse than I'd imagined. I suppose the doodlebugs must be the last straw – my poor darling. I wish I could spare you this – well, I could, if only your damned divorce would come through. Then we could marry and you could apply for a transfer – the Air Force are being quite reasonable now over married couples at least being in the same county! Oh Kay, I hate to think of you going through all this!'

The V1s had been bad, Kay knew it. The balloons weren't much use against them, but even if the girls weren't needed to haul down or fly, no one on the sites could sleep. The horrible noise and the explosions were bad enough, but night after night they were dragged from their beds by the siren's wail, to huddle in the smelly, damp little shelter until either the all clear went or they got fed up and took their lives in their hands and ran to the mess to make tea and wads.

'Well, I've got news for you,' she said now, turning to face Steve, smiling up into his grey-blue eyes. 'I shan't be here much longer; they're moving us, balloon and all, out into the country, or at least to the south coast. We're to form a sort of barricade between London and the coast to keep the wild-cat raids high and to bring down as many of the wretched doodlebugs as we can. Or that's the theory, anyway.'

'The country! Oh darling, that would be marvellous. I know I tell you off for worrying because I always do my best for the chaps, and that means I'm doing my best for me, too, but I worry about you dreadfully, and having seen this devastation I shall worry even more – or would, if you were staying up here. Where will it be, do you know? How I wish they'd send you to Norfolk!'

'It'll be somewhere in Kent or Hampshire I think,' Kay said. 'The Air Force hate telling you anything, in case you haven't noticed, but they'd had to unbutton their lips more than usual because we're taking the balloons with us and

395

all our gear. It'll be in the next two or three days, they've said. So I'm double-lucky – I'm moving away from London and yet we're having our leave together. It won't be so easy if I'm stuck down in Hampshire, will it?'

'Oh, we'll manage,' Steve said buoyantly. 'I've booked afternoon tea in the hotel but I thought, if you'd like it, we might go straight back there now and have a lie-down, then do the town this evening – if there's any town left to do, of course.'

'Oh sure, there are theatres, cinemas, dances . . . and the Windmill, of course, if you fancy pretty girls, high kicks and nudes,' Kay assured him. 'Afternoon tea – how tremendously civilised, darling Steve! I can't wait, let's go back immediately.'

'Afternoon tea will be good, but an afternoon cuddle beats it,' Steve said, as they mounted the stairs with the key to Room 210 in his right hand. 'Aren't hotel staff tactful now? Not a word about Mr and Mrs, just a polite query as to whether we're dining in tonight and what time we want to be called tomorrow. Ah, this looks like our room.'

He unlocked the door. Kay walked through the doorway and looked appraisingly around the room. Carpet, curtains, a wash-basin, pink shaded lights . . . a double bed with a rose-covered counterpane and crisp white sheets.

'It's very nice . . .' she was beginning when Steve's arms went round her. She turned in his embrace and hugged him, hard. Presently he released her.

'Take off that starchy uniform,' he said thickly. 'I've thought of nothing but being with you again all this past month. But I want you all soft and cuddly and warm, not in a tunic with buttons that dig into me and a collar and tie just like a feller's!'

396

He sounded so injured that Kay laughed, but nevertheless she began to toss her clothes onto the chair. She
saw, out of the corner of her eye, that Steve was doing
likewise. When she was down to nothing at all she sat
down on the bed and smiled at him.

'Well? It seems an awful shame to rumple these lovely
white sheets, don't you think? Perhaps we ought to wait
until tonight, the way respectable people do.'

Steve sat down beside her and rolled her over onto the
covers.

'Bugger the sheets,' he said. 'And bugger respectable.
I want to show my best, my only girl, what it's like to be
loved!'

'I had a wizard leave thanks, Jo,' Kay said airily next day
when her friend visited the site. 'But you know I'm not
supposed to talk about it, because of my divorce.
Apparently if the courts knew, they could turn me down,
or something. So none of the girls here know anything,
they think I go and visit my old nanny I expect, though of
course they know I keep phoning an airfield "somewhere
in England", as they used to say on the news. But this crew
are a nice lot and don't ask questions.'

'Lovely, then. But did you go anywhere nice? Do
anything much? Or was it just being together?'

'Good God, girl, go anywhere on a forty-eight? We
spent most of the time in our room, except when we went
out for meals. We listened to the wireless after we'd had
dinner and they played our tune – 'You are my Sunshine'
– which pleased Steve, so we danced to it, round and
round in our bedroom, and giggled every time we passed
the wardrobe mirror. And I suppose we relaxed, which is
what it's all about.'

'Well, I'm glad you had a good time, but listen, Kay, we've got our posting. We're going down to Hampshire, to put the balloon up in this big barrage they're making down there. I shan't be more than five or six miles from Site 122, where Biddy and Em are! What about you?'

'We were only told about half an hour ago. From what I could make out we're all going to be tripping over each other – we're quite near Site 122 as well. I say, Jo, it'll be like old times, won't it? We'll be able to go into Southampton, the four of us, and live it up a little. Any news of Alec or Biddy's John, do you know? You've been much better about keeping in touch than I have – you even visited them in Cheshire, didn't you?'

'Well, yes, because it was so near my home,' Jo said. 'I'm afraid I don't know about John or Alec, but I do have some good news of my own. I hadn't heard from Brett since the Normandy landings and an awful lot of Yanks were killed, but this morning I got a letter – he's been wounded and he's in a field hospital in France. They're sending him back to Blighty as soon as he's able to travel.'

'Is that good news?' Kay marvelled. 'How bad is he?'

'Not very, I think,' Jo said. 'And is it good news? Kay, don't you realise, for two weeks I thought he was dead! Just knowing he's alive is enough to make me want to shout for joy.'

'Of course; I'm sorry Jo, I can be extremely unimaginative,' Kay said humbly. 'When I think how I worry and fret over Steve – in the first war they all wanted "a Blighty one", didn't they? Now we can understand why.'

'It doesn't matter, just so long as you don't think I'm heartless to be glad he's wounded and not dead,' Jo said. 'Look, I just shot round to tell you the good news that we're probably all going to end up within shouting

398

distance of each other, now I'd better get back. We're deflating poor old Mrs Miniver in half an hour. Don't forget, I'm on Site 2771, so if you don't know your number yet you'd better get in touch with me. And of course we both know where Biddy and Em are – this is a lot more exciting than D-Day to me, I really feel things are moving at last!'

'Mrs Miniver! Trust Jo to think up something daft,' Kay muttered to herself as she made her way across to where the crew were bedding their balloon firmly to the ground. 'Oh well, we might as well all relax now, because tomorrow we'll be busy until we leave to catch our train!'

Rather to Kay's surprise, the new site was delightful. There was a wood at its back and the site sloped gently down to a little stream and a low, unkempt hedge. Beyond the hedge you could see another meadow, then flat marshes and finally the silvery line of the sea. The crew would sleep, eat and live in Nissen huts, hastily erected with their backs to the wood. However, toilet facilities, which had been the height of luxury on the inner ring – a proper brick-built ablutions block had been put up just before Kay joined the flight – were once more a tin basin on a chair by your bed and the most basic of lavatories.

'You say they're our new lavatories? What *are* they?' Julie Packet said unbelievingly, pointing to the row of earth closets ranged a short distance from the Nissen huts. She accompanied Kay to have a closer look, then turned to her friend, eyes rounding. 'I don't believe it, they can't expect us to use those things!'

'They don't just expect us to use them, they expect us to empty them,' Kay said calmly. 'On my first site whoever was on the two to four a.m. shift did that and the rest of us took turns to dig a nice, deep trench. But I'm sure we can arrange for a lorry to do the necessary.'

'A lorry?'

Kay giggled. 'Julie, you'll be saying, "A handbag?" next, like the woman in *Charlie's Aunt*! What I should have said was that nowadays a fellow driving a lorry comes round and empties the buckets – there's a bucket suspended beneath the wooden seats – instead of us having to do it ourselves. I'm pretty sure that's the drill now, so we'll only be bucket emptying until I've arranged things with the authorities. Be thankful for small mercies, girl! Emptying those buckets in the dark, and cleaning them out afterwards, was a job everyone tried to avoid. Poor old Lavender Jim, of course, gets no choice, it's take it or leave it for him.'

'Lavender Jim?' squeaked Julie, causing Kay to double up once again. When she had finished laughing she shook her head sadly at her corporal.

'Such innocence! The nightsoil chappies are all called Lavender Jim, didn't you know that? Oh, don't mind me, flower, I'm just so pleased to be here and away from London that everything seems amusing. And now you can go and draw up a rota for digging the trench and another for carting water. It'll be hard work, but I still think we'll be fitter, happier and altogether better here than being plagued by doodlebugs and wild-cat raids in London.'

'She's in Hampshire!' Steve was reading Kay's letter over a late breakfast in the mess with his friend Toddy chomping toast beside him. They had flown over Germany the previous night and would presently go to their billet, but right now they were having their breakfast and trying to relax before they slept.

'Is that Kay? Pity it isn't a bit nearer us though, old boy. She's further off, in fact – you'll have to meet in London, I suppose.'

Steve nodded, then laid the blue sheet of paper down beside his plate. 'That's true, but I still thank God she's away from that other site. You've no idea, Toddy old fellow, what they were going through in London on the inner ring. Kay's face was dead white, with big, dark circles under her eyes, and she'd gone awfully thin . . . they get hardly any sleep what with the doodlebugs and the raids, and balloons are incredibly heavy work for slips of girls. She'll be much better off in Hampshire, much happier, even though she's further from me. And she's near her friends – apparently Jo is only half a mile off and the other lot she's friendly with are only five miles away and they all centre on Southampton, though Kay says it's been terribly knocked about.'

'What's the site like?' Toddy asked curiously. 'I've never seen a balloon site. Do they have a proper mess and so on, or do they have to make do? But being females, I suppose they have quite palatial quarters.'

Steve snorted. 'Palatial? Kay says it's a basin by your bed for washing and the latrines are a line of earth closets which they have to empty themselves for now, though later she thinks they'll get included on a lorry round. They're in a big field right at the end of a tiny, muddy lane, that's the snag, with a farm cottage their only neighbour. But the people in the cottage are ever so friendly, the old boy is going to get a couple of pals and dig them out a vegetable garden, and until it's producing he's giving them masses of cabbages and beans and carrots. Kay was very touched because she says the old couple – the Newmans – don't have much money, only endless friendliness and goodwill.'

401

'Country people are always best,' Toddy confirmed. 'Have you had as much toast as you want? Because if so we really ought to try to get some shut-eye. If I don't nod off before the drill sergeant starts shouting I won't get to sleep until he's gone for his elevenses!'

'Kay, storm warning! The blimp's on tail guy mooring but we're going to need the entire crew to get her storm-bedded and so far as a warning goes they're way behind . . . can you hear that wind?'

LACW Huggett was a small, round girl, with a rosy, cheerful face but now, as Kay struggled out of bed and reached for her boiler suit, she could tell that Huggy was really worried. And she could also hear the wind, positively howling round the hut whilst rain was being constantly dashed against the window panes.

'Right, get everyone out,' Kay said briskly. 'Is Corporal Packet awake? She and I will do a recce whilst the rest get dressed – tell them it's oilskin weather.'

She was reaching for her own oilskins as she spoke, dragging the leggings on over her boiler suit, jamming her feet into her wonderful seaman's socks and then hauling on her boots. Because she had been so deeply asleep she realised she was still moving more or less in a dream, so she didn't bother with her so'wester but shoved it into the pocket of her oilskin 'frock', then went briskly out into the elements.

One glance was enough to confirm what Huggy had said. The storm was scarcely imminent, it was very much with them, and the balloon was thundering round on the end of the cable looking positively fearsome in the half light. Huggy was still in the hut waking the crew, but the other guard, LACW Emerson, was standing by the tail guy, looking worried. She smiled when she saw Kay.

'Oh, thank goodness you're here, Sarge,' she shouted above the howling wind. 'The met chaps ought to have seen this coming, but they didn't and I don't know how we're going to get her down. Of course, everyone's in the same boat . . . look at that!'

'That' was a nearby balloon, bounding free from its cable and taking off into the stormy sky. Kay chuckled. 'Glad it wasn't ours – we'd best have Huggy on the winch, she's awfully good and she's truly awake, having been on duty for an hour already. I'll stand by her . . . it's so noisy that no one's going to hear my voice if they're more than a foot or so distant.'

The girls were trickling out now, pale-faced after their abrupt wakening, some in the new black oilskins which had been issued, others in the older yellow ones. Whoever changed the colours over didn't think, Kay told herself disgustedly. The girls in black were very difficult to see in the semi-dark and it did help if you could see your crew and check up on who was doing what.

'Right,' she shrieked as soon as Huggy had climbed into the winch cab. 'Start winch . . . the rest of you, get ready!'

Huggy was good on the winch; she brought the balloon down very, very slowly, using the force of the wind and the gusts to ease the great, storm-tossed mass lower and lower in the sky. Because the balloon was on tail mooring she didn't have too far to come, either, but several times Kay thought they had lost her and held her breath in an agony of apprehension, sure that the cable would simply snap under the strain.

It did not, but when they got the balloon to within

eighty feet of the ground Kay realised they were in for trouble. Not only was she fighting every inch of the way, she was sweeping round in huge circles and at times actually diving for the ground so that Kay was in deathly fear that she would kill or maim a crew member as she got lower. And presently she realised that the balloon had also moved round and would have to be turned before she could be storm-bedded. Fortunately, the crew were all old hands and realised it at the same moment. Girls scurried about taking up their positions and Huggy gentled the balloon lower . . . lower . . . until LACW March, who was almost six foot tall, could touch the looped up guys swinging madly in the gusts.

'Get the groundsheets,' Kay bawled when the blimp was yawing and veering at around eight feet. 'Spread them out . . . starboard side heavy, port side light. When she's ready I'll take No. 1.'

'No, Kay!' Corporal Julie Packet swung round to stare through the windy dark. 'Send someone smaller in . . . we need you to tell us what to do next!'

Whoever was No. 1 had to go right in, under the belly of the thrashing monster, to take the piano wires and lie them down on the bed by the wires and flying cables, covering them with a straw cushion so that the balloon, once bedded, did not chafe against the wires.

'I'm tall, so I can reach the piano wires easier,' Kay shouted back. 'I'll have more headroom to get out in; it's all right, I'll take care.'

But it was going to take a few minutes, she judged, before the balloon was brought low enough, so she stood beside the winch lorry and watched as Huggy inched her down, let her up a couple of feet, inched her down again.

Any minute now! The girls on the starboard side had

hold of the guys, the girls on the port were about to grab and cling on. All she had to do was to time it right. Run in when the balloon was making a bid for freedom and the sky, and run out before she lashed round, rebounding almost onto the winch lorry. All it needed was a steady hand and calm nerves – what was it Steve had said to her on that magical leave? The words came back to her, in his voice, as though he were nearby, giving her comfort.

'I always do what's best for the chaps, and that means it's best for me, too.'

Well, there you were, then! The best thing she could do both for her crew and for herself, was to get that bloody lunatic of a balloon safely storm-bedded as soon as possible, and that meant taking No. 1. But right now it was all hands on deck to turn the blimp. Kay joined the port crew and they heaved and pulled until their arms burned with pain and their stomachs ached with it, but they turned her. She was round, yawing and fighting still, but round, so at least they could begin to try to thread the guys through the blocks and onto the spider, to hold her steady that way.

'Riplink switched off and ripline untied,' someone shouted against the wind.

'Grand. Haul in on bollard,' Kay shouted. She decided she would wait until the balloon was more or less stationery and then she would go in and out where there were no wires, either moving or immobile, to impede her. At the last moment, just before she went in, she grabbed the corporal's sleeve. 'Julie . . . show me out with your torch, would you? I'll probably have to crawl, she's wild tonight, and I don't want to run into wires in the dark. All right?'

'All right,' Julie quavered. 'I wish you'd send someone else, Kay!'

'No. As I said, if you do what's best for the chaps it's best for you, too. Don't forget, light me out!'

'I won't forget. Go very carefully, Kay.'

But her words were almost lost in the raging of the storm and the balloon, of course, was making enough noise to drown out other sounds. Kay went in quickly, cautiously, with the straw cushion under one arm, the other hand held out before her. A loose wire could cut your face open like a razor slash and she didn't want that.

She stood on tiptoe to reach for the wire, then had to bend quickly as the balloon's underbelly came abruptly lower as the wind caught her. But Kay had the piano wires firmly in her right hand and she could hear the blocks thumping as they were lifted temporarily off the ground by the balloon's bucking and rearing, so this should only take a minute.

Kay got the wires down and bent to cover them with the straw cushion, feeling a tremendous sense of achievement. She had done it! Now all she had to do was get out – and quickly, for the balloon was moving still, the blocks were thumping, and if, at this late stage, something went wrong and the balloon got away, there was a wire cable almost as thick as your wrist here somewhere, which could whip across like a deadly steel snake, killing or maiming anyone in its path.

She dropped to all fours, to keep well clear of the blimp. She could see a light and she had told Julie to shine her torch to show her the best path out, so she must crawl that way. She dare not stand, though it would have been quicker, but the balloon had come so low that she could feel it rubbing against her hair if she put her head up – crawling was best. She began to head towards the glimmer of light.

*

406

'Curse it, my bloody battery's gone . . . anyone got a torch which works? I'm lighting Kay out, or I was, only . . .'

It did not occur to Julie to say more; the word was passed around quickly and Annabel, hanging grimly to the port guy, got a torch out of her inner pocket, not without difficulty, and flashed it at Julie.

'Is this strong enough, Corp? I'll shine it under the bugger so the Sarge can see . . .'

'No . . . NO!'

It was too late. They all heard a scream, cut off short, then Julie was shouting, 'Avast hauling . . . let me get under . . . someone show a light, she's hurt!'

'That's blown it, she's got loose! Did anyone notice if the ripcord worked? If not she'll be over France by morning! Come on, we can't just watch her go, we'll have to chase her. If the ripcord worked then she'll run out of gas sooner rather than later and we can nab her as she comes down.'

Jo was rallying her troops in the worst storm she had ever known; other sites had lost balloons, she had seen them hurrying past, but she had been so sure that their's was safe. And then the last gust had been too much for the cable, where it joined the balloon; it had snapped like a piece of string and the balloon had disappeared into the inky dark sky. They had been very lucky to avoid a nasty accident. Jo, who was on the winch herself, had cause to be grateful to the cage which had caught the lashing cable as it sprang back and one girl, who had unwisely hung on to her block for a second longer than necessary, had most probably had her arm broken. It certainly hung at an odd angle, Jo thought, as the entire crew minus the broken-armed one, cantered for the field gate.

There was a searchlight battery just down the road. The men were out seeing to their equipment and gave the crew a cheer as they rushed past.

'We saw her, girls, she went thataway!' someone bellowed. 'Want any help?'

'No thanks, we're okay,' Jo shouted back. 'Was she getting any lower, do you think?'

'Nah, headin' for the Milky Way at a gallop,' one of the men called back. 'You'll not see her again unless you can fly.'

Some of the girls hung back at the words, but Jo urged them on. 'You don't want to lose Mrs Miniver, do you? The bloody Air Force will probably charge us, we'll be paying for the rest of our lives! Come on, she can't have got far.'

And in fact, she had not. They found her a couple of miles further on, draped unbecomingly over a haystack. The farmer, woken by the din when she had collided with his Dutch barn, knocking the roof off, was up and grumbling as he tried to hook her down with the reluctant help of two very cross and sleepy landgirls, but Jo managed to persuade him that a pitchfork would do more harm than good and with the help of a couple of ladders and a good deal of patience, the crew managed to reclaim their balloon and were on their way back to their site by the time the sky was greying with incipient dawn.

'What a night!' Jo said, taking off her sou'wester and chucking it onto the table as they went into the mess for tea. 'How's the arm, Sylvia?'

'It aches dreadfully,' Sylvia said, her voice reed-thin with pain and exhaustion. 'Have you seen Val's foot?'

'No. Why? She came with us, didn't she?'

'Oh, I came all right,' Val said wearily. 'But I turned

408

back half a mile down the road. Look!'

Valerie was a smiling, rosy-cheeked girl but now her face was deathly white and she was exhibiting a foot which looked strangely flattened and was black and blue all over. Jo whistled.

'That looks really bad. Did you ring HQ, Sylvia? Are they sending a blood waggon?'

'Not until morning,' Sylvia said. 'Apparently half the balloons in the area have blown away, there are quite a lot of injuries, and one girl's been killed.'

'Killed? Someone on a site near here? Poor little rabbit, I wonder what went wrong?' Jo shuddered briefly. 'It's awful, but something like that should make us all more careful.'

'They didn't say how it happened, just that someone in the area had been killed,' Sylvia said. 'My broken arm seemed rather small beer after that, so I said the morning would do.'

'I'd give you some aspirin out of the first aid thing, only I have a feeling I shouldn't,' Jo said rather doubtfully. 'I'm not sure whether you ought to have tea, either.'

'Try and stop us,' Valerie said stoutly. 'When I've drunk mine I'm going to lie down; don't suppose I shall sleep, but at least I'll be keeping it still. It's bleedin' agony, I tell you.'

'I'm going to get an ambulance now, I don't care how busy they are; that foot is badly crushed and Syl's arm needs setting,' Jo said angrily, getting to her feet. She turned to the rest of the crew. 'One of you lot can make the tea whilst I telephone. I shan't be long . . . oh, and you might make some jam sandwiches, I'm starving and it's hours until breakfast.'

*

409

The balloon on Site 122 was bedded with great difficulty, but bedded she was, and then, because the night was so wild and the balloon was still fighting with everything she'd got, Corporal Taylor made them stay with her, six at a time, whilst the other four had a brief spell in the mess and drank tea.

'I've never known a night like it,' Emily said at one stage, whilst she and Biddy were adding their weight to the starboard blocks and running from point to point, hooking back and repositioning as the wind-maddened balloon bounded and swayed. 'We were lucky the pickets saw the way the weather was looking and decided to get Corporal Taylor out of bed. If not we'd have been like everyone else, in a pickle already by the time HQ gave us the storm warning.'

'I wonder why the warning was so late?' Biddy said. She was sitting on the rain-soaked grass in her oilskins, taking a rest from the constant chasing. 'They aren't usually that far be'ind the times!'

'Freak weather conditions, someone said,' another crew member volunteered, overhearing Biddy's words. 'D'you know, some of the telephone lines were down before the message was given? No wonder so many balloons went AWOL.'

'Yes. We've been lucky because when she rang through to say the balloon was storm-bedded, HQ told little Glenda that there had been a ruck of injuries and accidents,' Emily put in. 'Glenda said a balloon op had been killed, but perhaps they just meant badly injured.'

'I dunno,' Biddy said doubtfully. 'Balloons can kill people; that's why they have the cage over the winch driver, so if anything goes wrong the cable won't chop her bloomin' head off.'

'Yes, I suppose . . . aren't you glad Johnny's out in the Pacific or wherever though, Bid? Ships in the Channel will be taking a real pasting.'

Biddy shivered. 'Don't! Do you know, I believe the weather's easing up? It might be safe to leave the old gel and get some shut-eye if the wind drops any further. I'm on guard duty from six to eight, so I wouldn't mind some sleep, first.'

'I'm on with you,' Emily reminded her. 'Oh, damn, the second guy this side is beginning to unravel; more splicing tomorrow!'

The storm travelled across the country, wreaking all the damage it could, leaving smashed chimney pots, broken tiles, people blown off bicycles, trees down, in its wake. By the time it reached Marham it was growing weary, however, and though Steve stirred and sat up to examine his wristwatch, the noise and fury did not keep him awake. He was glad he wasn't in the air though; bad storms could bring an aircraft down just as surely as flak or enemy action could.

When he went into the mess for breakfast everyone was talking about the storm which had raged through Hampshire, Kent and Sussex. It had done a lot of damage, the man on the wireless reading the eight o'clock news had been full of it. An Air Force officer had been killed and several injured, they told him.

Steve went and fetched his mail; there was a letter from Kay! He got his breakfast, then sat down to enjoy his letter. Round him the talk ebbed and flowed, gossip, news, tittle-tattle. Steve smiled at his love's turns of phrase, at her small, neat hand, and listened to none of it. She loved her new site, was delighted to be so near Jo and the other two once more, had planned a cinema trip into Southampton the following day. Steve put the letter down and sighed thankfully; he could almost see the roses which would bloom in his love's cheeks with country living, the way she would blossom now that she was far from the exhausting life she had led in the capital. And they would be together very soon – he was angling for a seventy-two hour pass – he would book into a quiet hotel somewhere, and they would meet, kiss . . . make love.

'Stop grinning into space, Steve, and help me to fill in this last clue,' Roger said. 'The clue is "and never home came she – a girl's name".'

'Oh, it's that thing . . . you know, the one about the Dee estuary, everyone learned it at school . . . oh Wotsit come and call the cattle home, across the sands of Dee . . .'

'That's a great help! Wotsit indeed . . . anyone else know it?'

'It's Mollie, or Pollie,' someone called. 'Isn't that right, Steve? Mollie or Pollie?'

Steve, folding his letter and rising from the table, shivered. 'What a subject,' he said mildly. 'Yes, it's Mollie, that's right. See you later, fellers.'

12

Three members of Kay's crew acted as pall bearers, with Jo, Emily and Biddy to make up the numbers. They were used to carrying weights, but Kay's coffin was so light it felt like a feather across their blue-clad shoulders.

'She doesn't look hurt, even,' Biddy had whispered to Emily when they had gone to see her, needing to see her in order to believe that it was indeed the Kay they knew and loved lying in the chapel of rest. 'And she looks so beautiful! I always thought of her as very pretty . . . but she's beautiful, isn't she, Em?'

'Yes. Very beautiful,' Emily said steadily. 'And she – she didn't suffer, Biddy. The wire must have broken her neck at once; she was dead before her corporal had even got under the balloon, let alone brought her out.'

'Yes. It's better that way, I guess.'

But now, helping to carry the coffin into the small church between the two roads, Emily couldn't help remembering and feeling, in full, that useless bitterness which she had told the others they must not feel. Here, less than three years before, Kay had got married to the wrong man. In this city, after she had discovered her mistake, she had found the right man. For all her time in the WAAF she had worked hard at her job, done her duty, shepherded her little flock. And now, because she always did her job well – for had she been a shirker, Emily knew, it would not have been Kay who had gone in under the balloon that night – she was lying here alone, whilst her friends wept and mourned her.

As the pall bearers slid the coffin into its place by the altar and turned back into the body of the church, Emily saw, in one of the front pews, a number of blue-uniformed bomber personnel; Steve had come to the funeral and brought his friends to support him because it was all he could do, now. He had loved her, planned to marry her, lost her. It sounded so simple, unless it was you who was involved, you who had looked into the open coffin and seen the pale, serene face, the swathe of white-gold hair, the white lilies with their dusting of gold pollen with which the coffin was filled so that their perfume, for ever after, would remind you of this unbearable moment.

Emily took a deep, steadying breath. If she was suffering, how much worse it was for the people in the pew opposite them. Sara and Ted Duffield stood side by side, hands tightly clasped; last night Emily had seen the pain, the loss and bewilderment on their faces, whilst they tried to accept what had happened to them, tried to listen to the officers and crew who had known – and loved – their daughter.

'It was Steve we worried about, in case something happened to him,' Sara had whispered, all the lovely charm and self-confidence which Kay had been so proud of gone, drowned in the sea of her grief. 'We never for one moment supposed that we'd lose our girl.'

'No one ever does,' Kay's commanding officer had said sadly. 'I know that nothing I can say to you will help much, Mrs Duffield, but Kay was someone I'll never forget and I had little enough to do with her. For you, the loss must be all-embracing. Does it help to know she took on the most dangerous job herself, instead of sending someone else in there? It's what happened, you see, and it's something you should remember, for Kay's own sake.

She was a true leader, she never asked anyone to do anything which she wouldn't have done herself, and I'm proud to have known her. The No. 1 that night, LACW Morris, knows how easily it could have been she who . . . But that's for later, when the pain's less raw.'

Now, Emily slid into the pew after Biddy, knowing Jo would follow her, though she did not move up close but kept a short distance between them. That was what Jo would do, Emily reminded herself. And Jo's grief over Kay's passing had been painful to see because her friend was not a demonstrative person.

'It isn't fair,' she had muttered passionately to Emily, as they stood side by side in the little chapel, looking down at the coffin. 'She had everything to live for, everything! And she was careful, thoughtful . . . it's me who rushes in, mucks things up, does it all wrong.'

'It's happened,' Emily said matter of factly. 'You should be sad, Jo, we're all sad, but you mustn't kick against the pricks. Vain regrets never did anyone any good, I've heard Kay say it a hundred times, and bitterness will end up hurting you and not helping anyone else.'

'I deserve to be hurt because I'm still here, still alive, and Kay isn't,' Jo said violently. 'But I'm glad I came to the chapel, Em. You were quite right, if I hadn't seen her with my own eyes I'd never have quite believed. Where's Biddy gone?'

'Out. She's a lot younger than us, Jo. She's hurting and she doesn't know where to turn, not yet. But later she will because she's strong, is Biddy. Much stronger than most people realise. She uses experience, it's all part of her growing up.'

Emily was remembering the way they had felt as they travelled up in the train. A deep and terrible melancholy had filled them – three of them, when there should have been four – Kay should have been doing the honours, introducing them to her country, her city . . . her loved ones. Travelling down to Norwich without her . . . it seemed terribly wrong. She glanced across the aisle again, and saw a short, round little cleric making his way out of the vestry. He had a jolly face, but sadness sat easily upon it now and when he spoke his voice was clear, natural, not the false and booming chant which, Emily realised, she had been dreading.

'I am the resurrection and the life, saith the Lord: he that believeth in me, though he were dead, yet shall he live; and whosoever liveth and believeth in me shall never die.'

The words brought Emily abruptly back to the present, to the fact of Kay's death, to the pain of her funeral. Twenty years old, familiar with pain and grief, used to command . . . dead. Dead is all that matters now, Emily found herself thinking. Dead is all that counts, nothing else matters for Kay, and there's nothing more we can do for her now. Except to say goodbye in the best way we can.

Halfway through the service Biddy glanced over her shoulder, then dug Emily in the ribs. 'That feller's here,' Biddy muttered. 'You know – Philip Markham. He's snivelling into a great big blue handkerchief.'

Her tone of deep disgust was the first thing in a long time, it seemed to Emily, that had made her want to laugh. But she only smiled and raised her brows.

'So? He did her a great wrong but he may not realise that everyone knows, and he's still officially her husband; no one can deny him his right to be here.'

'I could.' That was Jo, speaking through gritted teeth.

'For two pins I'd march down the aisle and knock his teeth down his . . .'

'No point. No one will speak to him or have anything to do with him, and I expect he realises that. Best just to leave him alone. Besides, Kay would hate that sort of scene, and Steve never met him, did he?'

'No, I don't think so . . . oh, we're moving. What'll happen now, Em?'

'It's the committal; the actual burial. We'll fetch the coffin and take it outside now, and . . .' her voice failed her; she blew her nose and turned towards the aisle, glad to hide her face from Biddy, to see before her only Jo's blue-clad back. With the other pall bearers she collected the coffin and walked slowly down the aisle with it, behind the vicar, the cross-bearer and the choir. Emily kept her eyes to the front; she did not want tears to fall, she felt she would be letting Kay down if she wept and besides, the sadness she felt was, in a way, too deep for tears.

Outside, wind and sunshine awaited them. Christ Church had no churchyard, so everyone lined up to get into the cars which had been ordered to take them to Eaton. Mrs Duffield held on to her small black hat and put a restraining hand on her flapping coat. She was standing very near Emily and she turned to her husband, a smile breaking out.

'Ted, it was windy like this on her wedding day – do you remember . . .' her voice trailed into silence but when Emily glanced quickly towards her she was not crying. She was looking at the coffin and at the lilies piled on either side of it but her hand, gripping her husband's, was white knuckled. She was bearing up, Emily thought suddenly, and being wonderfully brave, but when this was

417

all over, when friends and relatives had left, when she had to get back to her ordinary existence once again . . . then God help her, Emily prayed, for no one else can. Her beloved only child – how would she bear it?

Eaton Parish Church was a small country church set in a quiet country graveyard. The cars came to a halt outside the lych gate and the girls took their places on either side of that light little coffin once again and threaded their way along the grassy paths, glancing neither to right nor left, minding their feet, until they reached the bottom of the churchyard and the newly dug grave. The vicar waited until they had all assembled, then his sonorous voice rang out, easily heard above the birdsong, the boisterous wind.

'Man that is born of woman hath but a short time to live and is full of misery. He cometh up, and is cut down like a flower; he fleeth as it were a shadow, and never continueth in one stay. In the midst of life we are in death: of whom may we seek for succour, but of thee, O Lord . . .'

The round-faced clergyman was saying the words as though he meant them and the three girls listened intently, trying not to let their attention stray, but Jo glanced around and drew Emily's attention to Philip, skulking at the back of the crowd, for the little church had been packed and almost everyone had come to the committal.

'The cheek of the blighter, he's come right out here,' she muttered. 'Look, over by . . .' She stopped short. Even as she spoke Philip saw them looking at him. For a moment he stared at his feet, then he turned and made his way quickly out of the graveyard.

'Good thing,' Emily whispered as Ted and Sara Duffield stepped forward and began to cast handfuls of earth into the grave. 'Glad he's got some shame.'

She glanced at Steve, but she was sure he had noticed

nothing. He was standing quietly, looking down into the grave. Ted said something to him. Steve began to shake his head, then changed his mind. He took a handful of the earth and lobbed it gently onto the coffin and almost before the brief rattle had died away, he turned so that he was standing with his back to them, gazing out over the older graves.

From where she stood Emily could just see his profile, and what she saw almost broke her heart. That anyone could feel such pain, such longing, and know it was in vain! She realised, with aching pity, that when you love someone deeply, without reservation, you are giving your heart into uncertain keeping, because man that was born of woman hath but a short time to live . . . And at her own recollection of the words she had just heard Emily, who had been so determined not to cry, felt the hot tears begin to slide down her cheeks and was powerless to stop them.

The Duffields asked Steve and his crew to go back to the house, but he couldn't bring himself to do so. The house where he and Kay had played as kids was somewhere he could not bear to go, would not be able to go for some time. Mrs Duffield said she understood, smiled at him, pressed his hand and let him go, but his mother was not so easily satisfied.

'Later, Mum,' he said, when his mother told him he really ought. 'Give it a week or two. But not yet.'

She sighed. 'People may not understand, they may think it odd; there was nothing official between you, bar friendship I suppose. Don't you think it would be better if you came back? Just leaving could give rise to all sorts of gossip.'

Anger was a healing emotion; at least it temporarily conquered pain.

'I really don't mind what anyone says about me, and it would be a brave man who spoke a word against Kay,' he said, trying for lightness and hearing his own failure, seeing it in the flush that rose to his mother's round, rather bulging cheeks. 'Leave it, Mum. The blokes and I will be on our way.'

She did not argue further but simply gave a petulant shrug and moved away from him. He knew he ought to go after her, give her a hug, try for a more acceptable explanation, but he turned back to his crew. They understood in a way his mother, poor woman, could not.

'Thanks for coming, chaps,' he said. 'And now we'd better be getting back to the station. Who's going to drive?'

Emily, Biddy and Jo went back to the house. They had helped to get a scratch high tea ready earlier in the day and now they helped to serve it, hurried to and fro with kettles of hot water, plates of sandwiches, cakes and biscuits.

Now that the funeral was over the tensions seemed less, though they were probably just waiting to pounce, Jo thought. She stood in the beautiful kitchen of Kay's home, patiently washing up cups and saucers and thinking about the day which had just passed. Kay's parents were plainly suffering dreadfully already, but when evening came and the house was quiet and empty . . . oh shut up, you, Jo ordered herself fiercely, there's no point in thinking like that. Time heals they say, so tomorrow I'll be sad, the day after less so, the day after that I'll laugh and swear when I break a shoelace, the day after that . . .

Life goes on. Kay would want life to go on, Jo thought,

420

surprising herself and yet knowing it was true. She washed up a delicate, flower-covered teapot and stood it on the draining board. Kay would be the last person to want any of them to grieve endlessly, and anyway it wasn't in human nature to do so. But I shan't ever forget Kay or what she meant to me, Jo told herself, because whenever I remember today I'll know a taste of sadness, whenever I smell regale lilies I'll find my eyes are filling with tears . . . for a time, whenever I see a slender, straightbacked girl with primrose-coloured hair I'll want it to be Kay and I'll know it can't be . . . but that's natural and right, that's how I should feel. Poor Steve, it's far worse for him.

Mrs Duffield came into the kitchen and touched Jo's shoulder lightly. She was still very pale but she seemed quiet, almost resigned.

'You are a good girl to help me so! Tell me, dear, do you have a boyfriend?'

'Yes,' Jo said. 'I've had several, to tell you the truth, and I don't think I've met the only one for me yet, but this one's called Brett, he's an American GI. He was wounded on the Normandy beaches on D-Day but they're invaliding him back to Britain quite soon. I don't think he's badly hurt or anything, I've had a couple of really cheerful letters.'

Mrs Duffield nodded. 'That's good. And the little one? Emily, is it?'

'Emily's engaged; she's going to marry a bloke called Alec. You might ask to see her ring, it's – it's very pretty. Alec's somewhere on the continent, he's a gunner.' She glanced uneasily at her hostess. 'Kay . . . Kay was very fond of Alec. We all were.'

'Yes, I remember. Wasn't he the one who gave the Alsatian puppy a home on your first site?'

Jo laughed; it was a relief to laugh, to hear her own voice at normal pitch and not hushed, sad.

'Yes, that's Alec. And Biddy's going out with a sailor on the *Aconite*, which is a flower-class corvette; his name's John Arthur. We've not met him, but he's a Liverpudlian, like Biddy, so they have a lot in common.'

'The *Aconite*? I believe Ted knows someone aboard her; certainly I've heard the name recently, anyway. Biddy's the tall one, isn't she, the one Kay said was very young but learning fast?'

Jo laughed again, contentedly this time. Mentioning Kay's name had not done harm, then; perhaps it had even done good. 'Dear old Kay, she certainly had us all worked out, didn't she? Biddy's grand, a grand girl. She's eighteen now, and she's been in the service for about three years – well, as long a the rest of us!'

'Heavens! Jo dear, I've been meaning to ask you, do you have to go back to Hampshire this evening? I'd be – most grateful if you'd both stay, you and Biddy. I do have a reason, but I'd rather not talk about it quite yet.'

'We could stay,' Jo said rather reluctantly. She found she wanted to get back to the site, to come to terms with Kay's death in her own surroundings, so to speak. 'But it seems unfair on you and Mr Duffield; we'd agreed between ourselves that we'd catch the evening train from Thorpe Station and spend the night in London.'

'Don't do that. Stay, if you can.'

Jo could hear the pleading behind the quiet tone. She nodded. 'Of course, if you can put up with us for a second night. I'll go and tell the others.'

Biddy was glad Jo had said they would stay. She really liked Mrs Duffield. She was just as nice as Kay had said –

nicer. Like the others, she had felt that perhaps they ought to leave, but when Jo said they were staying she had felt a warm glow, almost a cosiness, as though this house was her house and these people her kin and no longer strangers.

So she did her share of clearing away the high tea and later, helped Mrs Duffield to make what she described as 'a light supper'. Then Mrs Minton, Steve's mother came round, started to talk, and suddenly burst into floods of tears.

'I've lost my boy,' she wailed. 'Just as surely as you've lost your girl, Sara. He's gone and he won't come back, he doesn't want to come back, not now there's no Kay for him here.'

It was an exhibition of total selfishness; Mrs Duffield went white and glanced imploringly at her three young guests. Mr Duffield had taken his great-aunt and uncle home to Lowestoft and would not be back for some time and Jo and Emily immediately stepped into the breach. They took Mrs Minton into the other room and soothed her, jollied her along, explained that she had not lost her son, no indeed, she had merely misunderstood the depth and extent of his suffering, his deep loneliness.

'Give him a week or two and he'll come back of his own accord,' Biddy heard Jo saying reassuringly. 'You mustn't worry, Mrs Minton, Steve would never just abandon his home and his parents. But it's early days yet.'

Why didn't I go with them? It's not like me to stay out of trouble, Biddy thought. And turned to her hostess. 'Mrs D, I've been wantin' to 'ave a word. I've been wishin' I'd talked to Kay . . . but if you wouldn't mind listenin' to me for a few minutes . . .'

Mrs Duffield sat down at the kitchen table. She poured

two cups of tea and pushed one across to Biddy, then indicated that Biddy should sit down opposite her. After the slightest of slight hesitations, Biddy did so.

'I'm all ears,' Mrs Duffield said. 'I hope I can be of some help, Biddy.'

'It'll help if you listen,' Biddy said frankly. 'I've never told no one this before, Mrs D – not unless you count Johnny, me feller – but I don't have no mam, nor no brothers an' sisters, not any more. Not since the May blitz.'

Mrs Duffield's long blue eyes widened, but she said nothing, just nodded.

'They was killed,' Biddy said bluntly. 'It were a long raid an' me mam sent me out for milk for the baby. We had a cellar, see – it were deep, we thought we was safe enough. I was ages findin' someone who had some milk to spare an' the bombs was whistlin' down . . . it were that noisy an' frightenin', you've no idea.'

'Well, I have, actually. But go on.'

'I got back eventually an' there weren't no house . . . nothin' much on our side of the street, really. It were a tiny cul-de-sac, what they calls a court in Liverpool, wi' only eight houses all told, four one side, four t'other. The bomb had landed right on No 2, which were our place – a direct hit – and done in the whole row so no one much can live there no more. The other side were more or less standin', but the blast had every window out, an' the fire had jumped, so there weren't much left. And there was me wi' nothin', no house, no neighbours . . . no family.'

'Oh, Biddy, you poor child,' Mrs Duffield murmured.

Biddy nodded but continued. 'Aye, I were pretty shattered. But I din't hang about, see? I left, went, scarpered. No reason for me to stay no more, though I

424

din't know whether me dad was alive or dead. Didn't care, either. He – he weren't a good sort o' man. An' I din't want no one to start fussin' over me or puttin' me in a council home or anything o' that sort. I'd got nothin', but I prigged some cash from . . . well, from a bombed-out house to tell you the truth . . . found me way to Lime Street and caught the train for London. I lied about me age, signed on for the WAAF, put in for balloons – an' bobs your bleedin' uncle!'

'And you never told anyone?'

'Only Johnny,' Biddy said cheerfully. 'You see, Mrs D, while I didn't tell no one, it weren't true, it hadn't happened. I were real fond of me mam an' the kids an' I like to talk about 'em . . . they're still there, like, so long as I don't go back or tell no one the truth. It's a deal easier to bear I can tell you.'

'Yes, I can see that,' Mrs Duffield said after a moment. 'Biddy, why did you tell me?'

'Cos when I first lost 'em, me mam an' the kids, I wished I'd died too. I cursed the bleedin' bomb for missin' me . . . daft, eh? But later, I knew that wouldn't help none and weren't no way out, either. And today I saw you an' Mr D bein' so brave an' I knew what you'd be feelin', and I thought it might help if I told you that as time passes it gets easier,' Biddy said with all her usual forthrightness. 'What's more, I've begun to see it ain't no good livin' a lie, like I been doin'. It finds you out in the end and hurts you worse 'n if you'd telled the truth to start off. I wish I'd told Kay the truth, 'cos you didn't oughter lie to your pals. An' though it's taken me a while I reckon I've come to terms wi' what happened. You see, I've worked it out, more or less. They ain't gone for ever, not while you remember 'em an' love 'em, so now I'm goin' to face it, an' tell people there ain't no . . .' she swallowed, then rallied, '. . . ain't no brothers an' sisters,' she finished.

Mrs Duffield leaned across the table and took both Biddy's hands in a strong and gentle clasp.

'You're the bravest girl I know, Biddy Bachelor,' she said quietly. 'You'll go a long way, you will. And now I want you to promise me something; next time you get leave, come here, to me and Ted. You aren't our daughter and never could be – would never want to be – but it would be a great comfort to have you here from time to time.'

Biddy grinned, though there were tears in her eyes. 'I will,' she said. 'Honest to God, I'd like to come here an' see you. Why, I might even bring Johnny – Johnny's me feller, he's a sailor, you know, on HMS *Aconite*.'

'And for the life of me I couldn't tell her that we heard on the news that the *Aconite* had been torpedoed a couple of days ago,' Sara said to her husband as they lay in bed much later that night. 'She's a lovely kid, Ted, and she's had grief enough. I couldn't add to it. But I did tell Jo, and she'll see to it that Biddy hears in the right sort of way. Maybe Emily could break it to her. She's a nice girl, too.'

'Let's pray he was rescued,' Ted said. His arm was round her, his stubbly chin rested against her soft cheek. 'You never know, sweetheart; this time, someone may be listening.'

It was a fine, breezy September day with the late afternoon sun sending long shafts of light through the trees which fringed the back of the site, turning distant Southampton Water to molten gold. Biddy had just returned from visiting her Johnny in hospital, full of the news that he

426

would be going to a convalescent home for two weeks very shortly, since he was so much better. He had been fished out of the water, more dead than alive, but was doing very well now, she assured her friends.

Jo had come visiting since she had some time off so she, Biddy and Emily had been blackberrying and were coming back across the fields, fingers and mouths purple from the juice, legs scratched, but tongues wagging as fast as ever.

'So of course I told them I didn't want to remuster, that I'd been made up to sergeant two months ago and I wanted to stay as I was. Only they said that's impossible because they're doing away with masses of balloon sites or handing them over to fellows,' Jo was saying as the three of them breasted the rise and climbed the gate into their own meadow. 'But I tell you both, I don't intend to lose my rank or my pay and if I were you I'd say the same! You know that since we all volunteered for the Balloon Service we can't be forced to transfer to a trade we dislike . . . I've said it's flight mechanic or MT or nothing, and I thought you could both do the same. What do you say?'

Biddy had reached the top of the rise and turned to look at the view; for a moment she just stared, then she turned to her companions, her face gilded by the sunset.

'Eh, Jo, stop clackin' for a moment an' look at that! Have you ever seen anything more beautiful?'

Emily, used as she was to the breathtaking mountain country in which she had been born and bred, nevertheless stopped and stared out across the golden water. 'It is lovely,' she agreed. 'When you think of the London sites this is just about paradise, and only a fool would want to leave. But I think Jo's right; if they're really going to kick us out then it's only fair that they kick us in the direction we want to go. Don't you agree?'

'Course I do,' Biddy said impatiently. 'If Jo's right, an' we can stick our heels in, then that's what we shall do. But I don't fancy bein' court-martialled for disobedience I tell you straight.'

'They can't court-martial us for sticking to their own rules,' Jo said impatiently. 'My new feller, Ramsay Jolyon, was a barrister before the war and he says . . .'

'It is true, actually,' Emily said whilst Biddy rolled around blowing raspberries and repeating 'Ramsay Jolyon!' in tones of total incredulity. 'An awfully nice officer told me the same thing the day we went up to RAF Titchfield for that intelligence test. He said if they couldn't fit us into the trade of our choice we'd be called "mis-employed balloon ops" and we'd get Group 2 pay even when we were remustered to the trades we wanted.'

'Which one was that? The feller wi' the dark curly hair who offered to teach you to drive in one easy lesson?' Biddy turned to Jo. 'You should have seen our Emily tryin' to fend him off – he was all right, an' all.'

'It wasn't him, he was only a corporal,' Emily said scornfully. 'It was the officer who gave us the practical on the engine parts. It's odd, isn't it, how if you're wearing an engagement ring half the men in sight suddenly find you interesting?'

'It ain't the engagement ring, it's the glow,' Biddy said loftily. 'You glow, Em, didn't you know? Ever since Alec plonked that ring on your finger you've gone round glowin'.'

'If you two would stop arguing for a minute and listen, then we might get somewhere,' Jo said energetically. 'For goodness sake, what does it matter who told you what, or why you glow – whatever that may mean. What matters is

428

remustering and how we go about it. Have you filled in the forms yet?'

'No, we've been biding our time,' Emily said. 'But you are right, Jo. We both wanted MT because it would mean spending time out of doors and being more independent, but flight mech would be just as good – better, in a way, more interesting. So we'll go along with that won't we, Bid? We'll fill our forms in this evening and tell Section Officer McQueen tomorrow that we'll be "mis-employed balloon operatives" if they can't get us into MT or flight mech training.'

'Good for you both,' Jo said heartily. 'You won't regret it – though the war's bound to be over soon. I must say, I'd like to learn to drive on the Air Force, so to speak. And now I suppose I'd better be getting back to my own site – you'll let me have a share of the blackberry jam, won't you? I do love it.'

'Course we will; see you soon, Jo.'

The two girls waved their friend off and then made their way into the kitchen to dump the blackberries and see what the cooks were preparing for supper.

'Cheese and bacon flan with mash and runner beans,' the cook said. 'Followed by blackberry and apple pie . . . if I can use some of these?'

They assured her she could, then made their way back to the billet to wash up before the meal.

The balloon had gone days before, reduced to a huge moribund mass which they had packed away into a canvas valise and waved sadly off when the lorry came for it. Now the rest of the paraphernalia was being dismantled and sent away . . . very soon, the girls knew, it would be their turn. There had been disappointment over the compulsory remustering, but everyone knew that the real

429

usefulness of the balloons was over. Raids were less and less frequent and the balloons were useless against the V2 rockets, Hitler's latest secret weapon. They came from the stratosphere and plunged straight to earth, giving the balloons no chance to intercept.

'No more night-calls, no more dodging the wires, fighting on the guys, wrestling with the tail mooring,' Emily had said ruefully as the balloon was carried off. 'No more joy-riding, no more blackened toes from the concrete blocks, and very soon no more envious glances from other WAAFs when we tell 'em we're bops.'

'When Johnny an' me get married I shan't have a Balloon Guard of Honour, an' I were lookin' forward to that,' Biddy remarked. 'Still, me hands were gettin' awful calloused.'

And now they had nothing to do but drill – for the look of the thing – and carry out normal domestic duties, and wait.

Jo was jubilant when they realised their strategy had worked. They were posted to retrain as MT drivers and would make their way, by train, to a centre in London, where they would hand over their balloon gear and get anything else that was necessary for their new lives. Then they would go on to Weeton, to their new careers. They all left together, a group of suddenly sad little figures tugging their two kitbags for the last time because only balloon ops were allowed two kitbags: they had, indeed, little choice because of the enormous variety of their clothing and equipment.

'Say goodbye to beauty,' Emily whispered to Biddy, knowing how her friend had loved the Southampton site. 'Never mind, Bid, when you and Johnny get married perhaps you can come and live down here. You'd like that, wouldn't you?'

'Yeah, but I dunno whether Johnny would,' Biddy said. Although he had improved a great deal, she knew that he was still shaky and weak from the ordeal of losing another ship and spending thirty hours in the water with only a half-inflated life-jacket to keep him afloat. 'I don't intend to spend me honeymoon at the seaside,' he had told Biddy, only half laughing. 'In fact I'm thinkin' seriously of givin' up baths, an' all.'

'Oh, he'll get over that quickly enough,' Jo put in. 'Brett was funny about gunfire after he was wounded on the beaches. Get marching, girls!'

'No, let's hang on a moment, our Jo, an' just take a last look, eh? We was happy here, wasn't we? All of us.'

'Yes; Kay too,' Emily said, guessing what Biddy was thinking. 'I wrote and told Steve Minton that the sites were being closed down you know, and he came over. I think he wanted to see where – where Kay had been so happy.'

'You never told me that before! How was he, Em?'

'Better,' Emily said after a moment's thought. 'Calm and sensible, just like Kay would have been had things been reversed. I went with him to the site and he stood and stared out at Southampton Water for a long time. Then he gave a great big sigh and thanked me for being with him and we went and had a drink at the Grapes before he caught the train back to town.'

She didn't mention the other thing, the way Steve had glanced towards where the balloon lay tethered and had suddenly dropped his head, unable to bear even the sight of it. 'They should never have let girls handle them,' he had said under his breath, and Emily knew she was not

431

meant to hear the words. 'Other trades, sure. But not those great monsters.'

Emily had put a hand out towards him, then let it drop to her side. She said slowly: 'I suppose it was pretty hard for all of us, Steve. But at least Kay's death, and the deaths of other WAAFs, did have some purpose – they're remustering the bops to other trades because of her death. They won't let the rest of us go on, taking such appalling risks.'

And I was speaking no more than the truth, Emily thought now as she and Biddy leaned on the mossy gate and glanced across at the liquid gold of the sea and the flaming horizon. The WAAF balloon ops had been remustered and one of the section officers had said the high-ups had decided to do this mostly because of the number of deaths and injuries which had happened to female bops.

'Come on, you two; we've got a flipping train to catch!'

Jo's resonant tones brought them reluctantly away from the gate, to set off once more along the lane.

Emily waved reassuringly. 'It's all right, Jo, we're on our way,' she called.

The three of them, still heavily burdened with their kitbags and various possessions, began to walk along the dusty lane. Presently they passed a farm where two landgirls were driving a herd of cows in for the afternoon milking. One of them, a slim, golden-haired creature, began to sing and the tune drifted across to the three girls walking along between the high autumn hedges.

> The other night dear, as I lay dreaming,
> I dreamt that you were by my side,
> When I awoke dear, came disillusion,
> You were gone, and so I cried.
> You are my sunshine, my only sunshine . . .

'That was Kay's song; Kay's and Steve's,' Biddy said huskily, as the haunting melody died away. 'Whenever I hear the bleedin' thing I see her sittin' in our hut, tryin' to teach Jo her silhouettes, or marchin' us all off to catch the train to our first site, or holdin' out her plate in the canteen for bangers an' mash. Oh, Em, will it ever stop hurtin'?'

'It will, Biddy,' Emily said. 'It's the same for all of us, but it'll get easier. Time heals, they say, and we've got a whole new career to take our minds off – off things.'

'That's it; we're startin' our new lives right now,' Biddy said soberly as they hurried up the lane. 'We're lucky, aren't we, Em?'

She did not need to say more. As they reached Jo, Emily turned and took one last look at the site, already beginning to cast off the shadow of war and becoming just another long, sunny meadow again. Biddy meant they were lucky because they had lives, the three of them, whereas Kay and Steve . . . but it didn't bear thinking about.

'Yes, we're very lucky,' she said quietly. 'Come on, best foot forward; we don't want to miss that train!'